EDENFIELD

George R. Justice

Legacy Book Press LLC
Camanche, Iowa

Copyright © 2024 Geroge Justice
Cover design by Kaitlea Toohey (kaitleatoohey.com)
Cover art by Elle Reid

This is a work of fiction. Names, characters, business, events and incidents are the products of the author's imagination. Any resemblance to actual persons, living or dead, or actual events is purely coincidental.

All rights reserved. No part of this book may be used or reproduced by any means, graphic, electronic, or mechanical, including photocopying, recording, taping or by any information storage retrieval system without the written permission of the publisher except in the case of brief quotations embodied in critical articles and reviews.

ISBN: 979-8-9874823-8-4
Library of Congress Case Number: 979-8-9874823-8-4

To my son, Rob: once our warrior...now our angel.

Train up a child in the ways of the Lord,
and when he is old he will not depart from it.

Proverbs 22:6

Table of Contents

PART I

PROLOGUE
Like Sackcloth on a Sunburn

I left home in the summer of 1962, two weeks before my eighteenth birthday and just after Mother's desperate last-minute maneuverings saved us from a troop-train goodbye. At the time, it never occurred to me that my leaving would be for good, but that's the way it turned out…circumstances and a stronger-than-expected need for independence being the occasions of my fate.

It was a Greyhound bus that Mom and Dad put me on, right there in the heart of Chicago, right after Mother cried hard and openly, and after Dad squeezed a twenty-dollar bill into the palm of my hand. Four hours and twenty minutes later, I stepped out of that bus into Edenfield, a reverent little town nestled in the miles-from-nowhere countryside of southern Minnesota.

The plan was for me to work at Edenfield's sawmill during the summer, then attend Edenfield College in the fall. It was a plan born out of good intention and heaped with possibility, but, in the end, one that wore like sackcloth on a sunburn.

I'd never had any intentions of college. The Army had been all I wanted, but the crafted and skilled manipulations of my mother and the very Reverend Burton Mayfield had etched a place for me on Edenfield's fall roster.

The town of Edenfield was intimate, devoutly Protestant, and straightaway paranoid about influences from the outside world. The college was its mirror image. "Perfect" was how Mother described it. But it was there, amidst an ultraconservative fundamentalism, that I came to learn about such things as friendship and love and betrayal, sex and death and God…things that just seemed to surface from my own directionless curiosity and the misgivings of carnal malfeasance.

Outside of a suitcase and a string-tied cardboard box, the only things I knowingly took with me were the incidentals of adolescent mischievousness and the compliance that comes from a childhood of perfect Sunday school attendance. What I was unaware of taking was my father's blue-collar work ethic and my mother's neurotic fear of those with religion stronger than it ought to be. What I left with, though, was a profound sense of my own naivety and that there is no natural rhythm or order for anything that happens, only an abiding sense that it all happens for a reason.

CHAPTER ONE
Under the Bleachers

We left home before dawn and drove south to Edenfield. My wife, Holly, slept in the front seat next to me with her face buried in a pillow and her breathing in perfect harmony with the drone of our aging Volvo. It was nothing new that she was so mollified. She had always been a model of quiescence, even from the beginning. It had been her strong suit, and the thing that had attracted me to her in the first place. We were quite the contrast. Then and now. Our son, Harris, despite his six-foot frame, lay in the backseat, silent as a babe-in-arms. Harris was our only child, and the excitement of his going off to college had given Holly and me reason to feel united despite our multitude of petty differences. Their combined slumber was a welcomed solitude, one that gave me a chance to further ponder my return. It had been thirty years since I last set foot in Edenfield, since I walked away in the middle of my sophomore year. Still, to this day, I've never quite been able to clear my mind of that time, to allow myself the peace that comes from forgetting. Time and again I'm drawn back there, to the events of my carnality and the things surrounding my betrayal. Returning is what remains of my hope to lay at least some of it to rest. The irony, though, is that I'm less and less sure of myself the closer Edenfield gets. There's a part of me that wants to stop the car and tell Holly she'll have to go on without me, be both parents today, but each time I somehow manage to talk myself out of it, my responsibility to Harris being stronger than any need of my own. Then, too, it was the hope of coming to grips with the past, or maybe just knowing that it was time to try, that kept me on course. Edenfield was, after all, a place I once called home.

I'd watched the sun climb in a slow steady arc all morning, first from the car, then from the bleachers bordering the soccer field. It wasn't typical for the sun to be so brutal above the forty-fourth parallel, to be so torrid. Still, it hadn't slowed the number of families from packing the blue plank bleachers thigh to thigh.

In the middle of the field a huge purple banner emblazoned with gold block letters was stretched banjo-tight across the front of the speaker's stand: WELCOME, PARENTS AND FRESHMAN CLASS OF 1993. Its satiny brilliance glistened in the sun. I wasn't much for ceremony, yet I waited patiently. The fact that I waited at all was uncharacteristic. I was never very good at it, but today seemed appropriate that I should at least make the effort. This was our son, after all, opening a new chapter on his life, and I was determined to be a part of it. The sun, though, seemed determined to challenge my resolve in much the same way Edenfield had three decades ago.

Every so often a stray cloud offered an umbrella of relief and allowed me to scan the crowd without shading my eyes. Despite an added thirty years, there were faces almost familiar; brief eye contact, but no names. Did they recognize me? I almost feared they would.

Between the un-breathability of my polyester suit and the bunching of my boxer shorts, I was uncertain how long I could feign a pretext of wellbeing. All around me, others seemed so collected, so unbothered, including Holly. She sat undaunted on my right, not bothering to notice my anguish.

"Aren't you HOT?" I asked. She turned her face toward mine and examined me as though I was some sad little thing in need of a hug. It was a look I had become familiar with over the years, one that she woke with most mornings and one she embraced as the antecedent of who she was.

As a last resort, I rose and excused myself with only a faint look of apology. I could think of little beyond the cool shade beneath the bleachers. Holly watched after me without the slightest change in expression. She had no idea where I was going, only that I had reached my limit.

The underbelly of the bleachers was far from an oasis, but it was the canopy I longed for. Apart from the girders interlocking in a geometric zigzag, it was uncluttered, and except for the four-foot cyclone fence surrounding the field, offered an unobstructed view. I wasted little time in loosening my tie and perching myself on a concrete block supporting one of the steel uprights. I had found the one vantage point that afforded me the medicine of solitude and the place where I could dispose myself, without the worry of heat stroke, to the fullness of the day.

The students had been herded to sit together in the middle of the field. I spotted Harris right off, his hair as long and straight as his stature. He looked eager, ready for the likes of Freud, Blake, and Pythagorean theorem. I tried to imagine the magnitude and complexity of his ancestral pool, and the centuries of peasants and paupers, princes and princesses, it took to get him here. He gave me every reason to want to sing his praises. The only way I could have felt prouder was to have been by his side. In concept, I was. It was as though we were, at that very moment, connected, one and the same. I couldn't help but wonder what thoughts were going through his mind, and if I, even remotely, was a part of them. I couldn't be sure how much of me he carried with him today, because in some unspecific way he was somebody brand new, like someone I was seeing for the first time. I tried to liken him to me and the path I had chosen, but I knew we were too diverse, two separate entities in search of two different worlds.

I watched as he searched the bleachers and a throng of waving arms, trying to find the faces most familiar. But we were too many. His searching reminded me of his years in Little League and the times he stood alone on the pitcher's mound searching for my face in the stands, for its assurance and approval.

Harris had never given me a satisfactory answer as to why he chose Edenfield. I never thought his choice had anything to do with my having once attended. I didn't think what I did thirty years ago would be of any consequence, and that my skewed campus legacy would amount to little more than a few laughs for him and his friends. I figured that the accounts of my life during those times would have, if anything, worked to deter him. But it wasn't until he said, "You know, Dad, I'm looking forward to finding you at Edenfield ... I mean that part you said you left behind," that I realized my influence, whether I intended it or not, had been substantive, and that his decision had more to do with me than I really wanted.

Above me, applause was sudden and thunderous, echoing through the bleachers with the potency of cannon-fire for someone bedecked in a floral sport coat and edging his way across the speaker's platform. He was Dr. R. D. Yoglir, Exalted Deacon from The Church's World

Conference and a magnate among God's chosen. Despite his strong Christian presence, the sun still made no concessions. Dr. Yoglir seemed oblivious to the quiet suffering of his audience and spread his papers with deliberate care on the podium before him. He then surveyed them with a scrunched look and gave the microphone an annoying little knock.

"As we find ourselves," he began, "at yet another crossroad ..."

The loudspeakers sent R. D.'s greeting well into the surrounding alfalfa fields, and I would guess as far south as Elwin Cotter's where his moon-eyed quarter horses lazed in the shade of sourwoods. Straight ahead, the crown of the field swelled before me, a formidable reminder of Carol and Cheryl and Bonitasue. The three of them cheerleading on the sidelines. Three gyroscopes: oscillating, pom-pomming, the hems of their skirts higher than their eyes. Only their images were dull now, faded like sepia photos left too long in the sun.

"... we need *pause* to reevaluate who we've become and the influences that have shaped our lives..."

R. D. droned on, decisive and full of purpose, reading word for word what he so painstakingly prepared in what I imagined to have been the cool comfort of an air-conditioned room. I listened, hoping for something new, but then after a time realized his message was like so many others offering the same tired traditions, those of hope and renewal, much like the ones I so often delivered. But I was elsewhere today, unfocused, and before long his message was reduced to only a word here and there, then faded altogether.

For the moment, I returned to Harris, studied him and his assurances of youth. Mine were behind me now, taken up in memories. It was as if time had passed me by without warning, then flooded me with remembrances. For the most part, they were innocent enough, just flashes and glimpses of things I thought were long forgotten. But then there were those that refused to be overlooked, coming like uninvited guests demanding attention. Such was the case today. Only today they were not bits and pieces, but total ensembles. Nothing for me to sift through or decipher. Nothing fragmented or incomplete. Only the purest of images anxious to wash me in recollections. There, beneath the bleachers, they were as clear as day:

June 1:

"Mom."

"Not now, please. I'm trying to juggle too many things at once here."

"I just want you to know that I've signed up for the Army."

"Fine. Now take out this trash and make sure the lid is on tight. I'm tired of the squirrels ripping open the bags."

June 14:

"Well, son, now that you're about to graduate, have you given any thought to what you'll be doing?" Dad was never heady or lofty with his speech, but he did like to think of himself as the consummate authority on anything having to do with making a living. This was not always without its irritability. The fact that we never knew from one minute to the next what posture he might assume or what tack he might take, kept us more than just a little off balance most of our lives. One simply had to stay focused in order to stay in the game.

"You mean after the Army?"

"You know you can't just lay around and dream."

"You don't have to worry about that."

"You gotta make some kind of move."

"I have. I've decided to join the Ar-"

"Trade school or college. Anything. You might try *junior* college like your Cousin A.J. You remember your cousin, A.J., don't you? Aunt Alice's son? Down there in Dayton? Hell, he owns his own furniture store now. Drives a Cadillac everywhere he goes. Peaked though. Sickly looking, like he never had a bite of greens. Jesus. Been like that his whole life. No telling what's wrong with him. No sense in worrying about it, though. Anybody who's too cheap to go to the doctor when he needs to deserves what he gets. Whole family's the same way. Got every dime they ever made. God knows we'll never see any of it."

"Dad!"

"Listen, maybe you could go to one of them *community* colleges. Live right here at home. Learn a trade on the side. Matter of fact, Charlie Bevins is looking for a couple of roofers right now. Can pick up some good money roofing. Look at your Uncle Leonard. Roofed all his life. Stronger than a horse. Why I've seen him take--"

"DAD!"

"What?"

"I'll give it some thought … college and all."

"Yeah, well, Okay. I'm going to bed. One thing for sure though: you can't just lay around and dream. You gotta make a move. Oh, and listen, before you turn out the lights, take out the trash. And make sure the lid is on tight. I'm tired of the squirrels ripping open the bags."

June 25:

Induction day. I was up at four thirty, convinced that this was a day I would want to remember. It was a chance to be alone for a while and prepare myself for what lay ahead, a chance to ponder life and what roles providence and destiny might play. But other than a light-to-medium nosebleed, the morning passed without incident or revelation.

Dawn was like an inevitable messenger. Its pale lemon light bathed everything in a soft patina, including my dad's sleeping face. I woke him with a nudge. He looked up at me in a stupor, checked the time, and asked in a half-whisper if this was really what I wanted. My heart softened to his words. I was elated that he cared enough to ask but was somehow unable to separate my joy from my sadness. Why had he waited so long to ask? Why, after I had been saying goodbye for nearly a month, had he only now seen fit to offer consolation? Yet I knew this was him and took comfort from his having asked at all.

After dressing slower than usual, and without saying a word, Dad led the way to the car. Once there, we sat in near-perfect silence, staring straight ahead and searching for impossible words before he finally backed us down the driveway and into the street. It was then that Mother, in a nightgown torn under one arm and bleached beyond color, came running at us from across the lawn. She was crying, but through her tears she somehow managed to tell me that Reverend Mayfield was on the phone and was wondering if I had a minute to say goodbye. A phone call from Reverend Mayfield at six o'clock in the morning was a little obvious, but it was so like Mother to know when to sic God on me. It wasn't her first time, nor was I under the illusion that it would be her last.

Mother had, from the beginning, fashioned me from the blueprints of Levitical law, even though she espoused a discipline quite the opposite for herself. But it never prevented her from calling on the good Reverend Mayfield for support no matter what her need. I think she saw him as necessary, but only in the sense of servitude: something obligatory to his calling. It was Mother's world and she forever tricked it into being whatever caused her the least amount of pain. Reverend Mayfield was simply someone she used to help arrange it into neat little packages, to give it order and viability, especially the things she knew to be controversial, things certain to affect us in uncommon ways.

For Mother, the idea of my going off to the Army had been an act hefty and indignant, a precursor to what she saw as her diminishing control. The whole idea had flown in the face of what she intended for me and left her with no way to reinstate her will except to call upon Reverend Mayfield who, in turn, would call upon Jesus. It was Jesus who held the deciding vote, and there was no one better at wrenching it free than Mother. It was intervention of the highest order, what one did to restore and stabilize right and fitting dominion.

I was forever amazed at Reverend Mayfield's obligatory posture toward Mother, his compliance to her every whim. He was no better at saying, "No," to her than the rest of us. But to hear Mother tell it, he was holder of the keys and gatekeeper to the kingdom of heaven; the unrivaled staple and definitive connection to what God was speaking to our hearts. It was in this vein that she inserted her will, blended it with his *religionism* as things sanctioned by God. And although Reverend Mayfield's intervention and instruction had brought me back into the fold time and again, back to where he insisted God wanted me to be, I was never quite able to surrender fully to it, knowing that it was most likely Mother, not God, doing the wanting.

Mother had her own ideas about the stuff of religion, nearly all of which was wrapped around the rudiments of salvation and what it took to lay claim to it: mostly the unquestioning acquiescence to the messages she claimed to receive from Almighty God Himself; messages numerous and many layered, and, over time, what she hung on me as armor, things not to be removed or even maneuvered without the threat of being sucked down a rat hole straight into the jaws of hell.

The irony to Mother's willfulness was that it became a tie that kept me anchored, but never one that afforded sanctuary from the things that hounded and tempted and brought me, time and again, to the edge of my own abyss: to things beyond God and His waters of veneration. And though she made me believe that there would one day be a reckoning for things done beyond God's moral code and the conventions of religious certainty, I was somehow wont to do otherwise, to bring opposites to the mix. Ballast to my compunction was all I ever sought, hope and a breath of air beyond the suffocating stigma of what she embraced as sin. And though I understood Mother as the ultimate manipulative process, I grew to where I felt a sense of obligation to the things she laid claim to, things she coaxed and wheedled out of God and the likes of Reverend Mayfield.

Dad sat motionless behind the wheel, a combination of confusion and sorrow. Neither he nor Mother was ready for this. It had all been too sudden. A month hadn't been long enough to accept that I was serious about leaving.

Mother wiped her nose with one hand and swabbed the tears from her eyes with the other. "You can't keep Reverend Mayfield waiting," she insisted. Dad's eyes were locked on me. There was something eternal in them, something that pleaded with me to at least talk with Reverend Mayfield. It was a look I couldn't fight.

The minute spent on the phone with Reverend Mayfield was all the time he needed to convey that leaving without first stopping by the parsonage for a word of prayer would be like placing myself in jeopardy of reprisal from the Holy Spirit. I wasn't sure if this was intended as a witticism, but since humor was not one of his strong suits, though it never deterred him from trying, I took it as a fundamental cautioning. I imagined being placed on the same sin-level as Freddie Heartland if I failed to comply. Freddie was my lifelong friend who lived in the huge two-story bungalow across the street before he moved across town. It was about the eighth grade when Freddie started dipping into the Sunday School collection plate each week. He called it "taking tithing." In with a quarter, out with a dollar. It wasn't long before Mrs. Forsythe, the Sunday school teacher, asked him, very Christian-like and in private, if he had taken money from the collection plate. He assured her that he had, but that he was only making change since his tithing came out of his allowance. She was both relieved and re-warded, certain that she had been blessed for having asked. She was openly inspired and told Freddie that she thought tithing from one's allowance was not only a consecrated act, but a marvelous example of Christian training. She concluded by apologizing and even asked that he forgive her for thinking so reprehensibly. It was a done deal.

From that point on Freddie could easily count on the collection plate to double and even triple his weekly allowance. The amazing thing was that his exchange no longer had to be done by sleight of hand. It was done in plain sight and always under Mrs. Forsythe's approving smile. Freddie never missed receiving an award for perfect attendance.

I let Reverend Mayfield know that I was pressed for time but could meet with him if I left before my next breath.

"You know, Weldon," he said, "we have to be forever on guard because there are still levels of sin we know nothing about. Take locusts for example."

"Locusts?" I said.

"Yes. And your leaving without stopping by for a word of prayer could just very well be the first stage of a path strewn with locusts. I'm sure I don't have to explain myself."

His talking in parables was a thing most irritating, and I told him how frightening I thought it was, locusts and all, and that I was on my way to see him that very minute.

"What you have to keep in mind," he began again, "is that the Army cares little, if anything, about your spiritual wellbeing." I told him I couldn't agree more, and that I was coming right over.

"And there's no reason whatsoever why they can't wait while we share a word of prayer."

"Right!" I said. "I'm on my way."

"After all," he pointed out, "I'm commissioned by a higher authority. I'm sure you wouldn't want to argue the point."

I remember handing the phone to Mother, who by then was sitting next to me at the kitchen counter and sniffling into a paper towel. I heard her tell him that I was already halfway out the door.

CHAPTER TWO
Carol and Cheryl and Bonitasue

The parsonage office was clean and neat but smelled like a burying ground for old hymnals. The musk of mildew met me head on. Reverend Mayfield sat opposite me behind a desk that appeared too small for his huge frame. His red and blue plaid bathrobe fit him like he didn't care how it fit.

"Well, Weldon," he boomed, smiling, filling the room with his huge teeth. "So, you're off to join the Army!"

I nodded and smiled, then settled into a long and suffocating rehash of one of his old sermons: something about growing into adulthood, about discarding old things for new.

As far back as I could remember, the reach and influence of Reverend Mayfield had always been the lamb's blood on our door. For Dad, though, his inclusion in our lives was something far more meddlesome than corrective, and with enough sting to send him sneaking out the back door and over our cyclone fence whenever he came calling. Dad was uncomplicated enough to understand this as survival, and, after a time, it became equally uncomplicated for me.

I sat undaunted at the game we played, the one we'd played many times before: he in his shell of consecration and me in a state of contrition. Though I could never quite surrender to all his guidelines, laws, and doctrines he insisted he'd received from God, they had, over time, led to sizeable amounts of blame-filled self-examination. It was God's way, according to Reverend Mayfield, of purging me and bringing me into a place where I could be worthy enough to inherit the Kingdom of Heaven. Often, though, I saw it as his way of adding fuel and even fire itself to the guilt he left in his wake.

"It is our final hope," he said, his words leaching through the imaginary curtain I'd drawn between us. "Don't you agree?"

Without the slightest idea what he'd been talking about, I nodded my compliance, but not before he continued. Then, somewhere in the midst of his reflections, right after his account of Jesus' warnings about the end times, my attention drifted to someplace deep within me. The picture of Reverend Mayfield's large mouth and thick lips droning the lessons of spiritual responsibility sent my mind careening toward a world far beyond the cramped confines of his office; to prurient images of Carol and Cheryl and Bonitasue cheerleading along the sidelines of the football field, jumping, yelling, pom-poms flaring.

ON-WARD VI-KINGS
ON-WARD VI-KINGS
CHARG-ING DOWN THE FIELD

…hands clapping, outstretched arms swaying, urging the crowd left, then right. Voices screaming. Legs jumping, pounding, dancing wild and free.

CHEER FOR BLUE AND GOLD FOR-EV-ER
NEV-ER SHALL WE YIELD
RAH! RAH! RAH!

…they flowed. Evenly. In step. In time. Measured. Precise. Their skin, alive and satiny, glistening under the flood of lights. Their hair, long and flowing, tossing in a blur. Voices, lips, and eyes. Breasts and hips and thighs. Strong and seventeen.

THOUGH THE THUN-DER
BANGS A-ROUND US
WE WILL WIN TO-DAAAAAAAAAAY

. . . and always there was the spandex and the adumbration of what it masked. Only a suggestion of it, a microsecond, during cartwheels.

OOOOOOOOOOOOOOOOOOOOUR TEAM WILL
FIGHT LIKE CHAMP-IONS,
VIIIIII-KINGS AAAAAAAAALL THE WAAAAAAAAAAY.

"Well, what do you think?" he thundered.

"Think?" I queried, the interlude with Carol and Cheryl and Bonitasue still swarming at a delicious pace.

"Yes. What do you think? Do you think you'd like to give it a try?"

I stared straight ahead, my mind a blank, oblivious to what he'd been talking about or what he wanted me to try.

"I don't think you'd ever be sorry," he said. "Think of it as an opportunity."

I felt the temperature in my neck and face begin to rise, flush, and swell.

"Edenfield has long been an institution we've been proud of."

Edenfield? Is he talking about college? I hope he doesn't think I'm considering college. I'm going Army! It's set. Guaranteed.

"And think of the associations you'll make. Why, that alone is worth the money."

My head began to spin. I had to get away. If it meant everlasting peace and global prosperity, I couldn't go to college. I couldn't even pass high school algebra. It was Mr. O'Hanian who had offered to let me pass Algebra I with a "D" if I promised not to take Algebra II. Freddie Heartland stood a better chance than me.

He droned on, unaffected by my lack of enthusiasm. I continued to stare straight ahead, mesmerized by his gargantuan features and his refusal to lick the spittle from his lips. "I'm not only talking about a distinguished education," he said, "but a *Christian* education. A place where you can develop a personal relationship with God, a place where you can witness His work firsthand."

I felt a sense of isolation. What would I do amid those *born again*? Hundreds of them. All day. Every day.

"...Christian ethics and values, theological concepts..." He was relentless. Selling. "Well, what do you say?" he finally said, his grin coaxing me toward an answer.

For a moment I imagined myself at Edenfield, a white-robed choir in the background, their voices blending the strains of the Alleluia Chorus and blocking out images of Carol and Cheryl and Bonita Sue.

"Well?" he asked. The room seemed to swirl from the sudden hush.

"I don't have any money," I managed to mumble, inspiration having abandoned me.

"Don't worry about the money," he countered. "We can provide you with whatever assistance you need."

Caution lights flashed inside my head. "I mean NO money!"

He leaned forward, resting his hands in prayer-like fashion on top of his desk. "I *know*," he whispered through a half smile.

At this point I didn't wonder. Nor did I much care. The only thing I wanted was a quick exit. This whole thing had already gone too far. A word of prayer had turned into the ultimate shell game. My mother and the preacher. Hoodwinkers. Manipulators of the American dream.

But it was too late. I was going Army. I knew what I wanted. It was caissons. Over hill, over dale. No college flummery for this American boy. It's goodbye and good luck to you preacher man. Thank you and good morrow!

I arrived in Edenfield on June 29th.

CHAPTER THREE
Your Sins Will Find You Out

There was no terminal. No sign of other buses coming or going. Only a wide spot in the road. On the gravel shoulder. Directly in front of the sign proclaiming Edenfield College.

"Where do I go from here?" I said.

"Beg pardon?"

"I mean, is there a station? Somewhere I can wait?"

"This is it."

"What's it?"

"The station. This is it!"

The bus driver was a man of few words, but professional to the end and unloaded my bags with lightning speed.

"What if it was raining?" I said.

"What's that?"

"I was just wondering what I'd do if it was raining."

"Do?"

"Yeah, you know, where would I go?"

He slid his hat to the back of his head and gave a quick suck to his front teeth. "Listen son." He paused. "Do you think every fork in the road has a station?" He stared at me with raised eyebrows then added, "You know what I mean?" I wasn't sure that I did but nodded anyway. I was half expecting a smile to creep into the corners of his mouth, but it didn't.

After wrestling and rearranging a dozen or so bags in the cargo hold, he gave a shirtsleeve swipe at the beads of perspiration dotting his upper lip. "Somebody supposed to meet you?" he asked.

"Yeah," I said, feeling a little unsure of my answer.

"Well, you needn't worry. They'll be here soon enough."

"How do you know?" I asked.

"Well, the bus stopping here ain't no little thing, that's all. Half the people in town already know you're here." His eyes directed me toward the faces staring from Pauline's Diner across the road. He smiled for the first time.

"It's a small town, kid. Get used to it." He paused long enough to wipe the sweatband in his cap, then added, "They're all the same for the most part. Got all the same stuff, just rearranged a little different. Got everything you'll need, though. You may have to look a little harder to find it, but it's here. Trust me." He returned his cap to his head, gave me a quick wink, then climbed back aboard.

He paused just before closing the big passenger doors and said, "If it rains--"

"WHAT?" I interrupted, holding my hand to my ear.

"I SAID IF IT RAINS, I GOT A FEELING YOU'LL KNOW WHAT TO DO!"

Before I could respond, he touched his fingers to the brim of his cap in a mock salute and inched the bus's hulking frame back onto the two-lane. In less than a minute it had melded into Edenfield's western horizon.

Edenfield College loomed to my right. Its huge lawn, thick and shaded with maples, spread a lush green welcoming. It left me with visions of young Reverend Mayfields everywhere, coming and going like monks, Bibles cradled in the crooks of their arms.

Despite the newness of everything around me, the image of my mother in her tattered nightgown kept coming to mind. Her running with such abandonment across the lawn was a vulnerability I had never seen in her. It was a display of love as frightening as it was powerful. She had, in her fashion, spawned my arrival in Edenfield, and had even arranged where I would stay. The only thing she hadn't manipulated is where I would work. She didn't have to. The mill was the only job in town. It was where everybody worked. There just weren't any other alternatives.

It was only a matter of minutes before a red and white Volkswagen bus eased its way onto the shoulder of the road and stopped a few feet in front of my bags. A bald head, fortyish and wearing thick, black-rimmed glasses, leaned out the driver's window.

"WELDON?"

———∾∾∾———

"You'll want to make a mental note. Everything closes at five thirty. Everyday. Except Sundays, of course. Nothing is open on Sundays." Harmon Little's lips were full and the color of raw liver. He spoke as he drove. "And over there is the church. Sunday School at nine-forty-five, Worship Service at eleven."

Harmon was altogether matter of fact. In a span of seven seconds, he had extended his full greeting. It was a welcome of succinctness and formality, and without a smile.

"Sunday night service is at seven thirty," he went on, "and Vespers is every Wednesday night from seven to whenever we let go of the Holy Spirit."

Harmon was the financial administrator at the college and sole overseer of its multiple accounts and funds. Anything to do with money—past, present, and future—was Harmon's to delineate. His take on himself was that he was an extraordinary investment strategist and tactician, but to students with outstanding tuition balances, he thought that he was seen more along the lines of an accountant with a black hat.

"Did Reverend Mayfield mention anything to you about tuition?" he asked, trying for nonchalance.

"No," I said. "Just that I'd be contributing by working."

"Yes, of course," he said, his lips taking on a contemplative pucker. "And that's the library. And over there is the Administration Building." Harmon droned on about the sights of Edenfield while my mind drifted back to Reverend Mayfield and how pleased he was with himself that he had been able to secure a job for me at Edenfield's Sawmill. It was his idea of financial assistance. Dad had been ecstatic. "Hot damn! Going to learn a trade on the side!" Dad was always at his best when preparing for the prospects of hard times.

"As you probably know," Harmon labored on, "we offer no summer program at Edenfield, and the fall semester doesn't begin for another nine weeks." He glanced at me and added, "And that, as I see it, puts you in a most enviable position." There was a long dead silence before he recognized the bewilderment behind my Sunday-school smile. "For RECREATIONAL READING," he thundered, as if I had overlooked the most obvious of truths.

"How about girls?" I asked before I could catch myself. The slouch came out of his shoulders like he'd backed into a hot stove.

"Pardon?" he asked as if daring me to repeat myself.

"And guys … *classmates.*" I added quickly.

A look of disillusionment deadened his eyes. "Yes, we have both," he said, a little nerved at my attempt to direct the conversation, "But then I suppose there is reason to tell you about Kellen Manly." His voice was all at once weighted. "Kellen is one of our students who elected to stay in Edenfield for the summer. Feeds logs on the big saw at the mill. As it turns out, the two of you will be roommates in a manner of speaking." He then stopped. Just brought the car to a dead stop in the middle of the road, then hunched his neck and back, making himself smaller as if what he was about to share could only be appreciated if we were hunkered down. Then there was a moment of silence, his face a study of lamentation. It wasn't his intention for me to misinterpret its pain. "I'm sure you'll appreciate me telling you this, Weldon," pausing just long enough to focus over the top of his bifocals. "Kellen is challenged spiritually." He pursed his lips and gave me a very slow but forceful nod to reaffirm his disclosure.

I sat expressionless, holding a look of bewilderment at bay. Harmon's face grew ever ashen and solemn in the ensuing silence. I tried striking what I thought was my most noncommittal pose, hoping somehow to send a message that I was not the least bit interested in Kellen Manly's spirituality and could we please move on to something less ethereal like coeds, like those in the image of Carol and Cheryl and Bonitasue.

In the next instant, Harmon un-hunched his back and drove off as if we hadn't stopped in the first place. "Kellen is from Texas," he continued, "and from what we can gather, his home life was rather disruptive. There's question if it was even Christian." On we went. In low gear. In the ninety-degree heat.

Whatever problem Harmon may have been having with Kellen Manly's lack of spirituality was soon laid to rest when a crimson Cadillac convertible cruised past us in the opposite direction. It was an older model, and its paint a little faded, but with a vision of Jean Harlow sitting behind the wheel. It was all I could do to keep from turning around in my seat. But from the corner of my eye, I noticed the special attention Harmon gave to adjusting his rear-view mirror. "You know, Weldon," he said, his gaze still fixed in the mirror, "we must always and forever be aware of the good we can do for others."

～

"Well, here we are," he announced. Harmon's house was only about half a mile from campus.

It was an oversized bungalow covered with gray asbestos siding, and the place where Mother and Reverend Mayfield had arranged for me to stay.

"Right this way," Harmon said, walking me around to the side where several old cellar doors lay splintered in a heap. They had been replaced with ones made of aluminum. It was right away evident that I would be living in the basement.

"We've tried to make it as comfortable as possible," he said, but then lost me. The dank odor and the unpainted plywood partitions were anything but welcoming. Still, he smiled and pointed out the fresh layer of gray marine paint covering the concrete floor, and how his wife had taken it on herself to cut out and affix the semitransparent contact paper over the basement windows. It had taken her two full rolls and was a specially ordered stained-glass pattern.

"As you can see, it has been pretty well thought out," he said, "Bedrooms on one side, kitchen on the other."

I wondered for the first time if this was what Reverend Mayfield had in mind when he proclaimed Edenfield as a place where I could witness God's work firsthand.

"…and behind this plastic curtain is the bathroom."

"…and I'll tell you the same thing I tell my children, 'You don't have to flush after each and every time.'"

"…and I've taken the liberty of posting the refrigerator door with what I think are the fifty most important statutes for your living here."

I leaned in close. The first one swelled with huge capital letters. "BE SURE YOUR SINS WILL FIND YOU OUT," it said. The look on Harmon's face told me he knew it as biblical certainty.

"…and I want you to know that you're welcome to join us each night at six for family devotions."

"…and you shouldn't ever have to worry about locking your door. This is Edenfield, after all."

" …and I hope you're not squeamish about mice."

Harmon left me without as much as a *Goodbye* or a *See-you-later,* without even a *Good luck* or *I'll be upstairs if you have any questions.* Nothing. He simply walked out the door and sprung himself up the cellar steps. For some time, he stood surveying the sky, his pasty face squinting up at the sun. After several minutes he cupped his hands around his mouth and droned down to me, "By any chance, do you play the cello?"

With a degree of reluctance, I went through the initial laying-in of supplies. It was a fate-sealing gesture on my part, something that said, "Yes, I'm staying," convinced that it would somehow be a growth experience. I was right. What I failed to consider, however, was that growth was not without sacrifice, and most never without pain. Harmon Little being a case in point, his basement being another. But with optimism, I would, for at least the next nine weeks, submit to its potentials. What I didn't know was that I would come to know the sullen and joyless Harmony, Harmon's fourteen-year-old daughter, and the unfamiliar sounds she scraped and scratched from the strings of a viola. And for hours on end, I would come to know Harmon's violin and its errant sharps and flats, the false stops and starts, the uneven staccatos, and, at times, even the crash of his music stand. And I would come to know their duets, their sour and misgiven treatments of Mendelssohn and Stravinsky, and I would come to realize that there wasn't enough time in Harmony's life for her to reach her expectations. For her, wanting was not enough. Harmon, on the other hand, had arrived; had, over time, reached his potential, though it was the purest form of mediocrity. There had been too much time spent buried in ledger books, too much time debiting and crediting. But the two of them together were an inseparable force, one that would not be denied regardless of their suffering audiences.

On the other hand, I would come to know the countless strains of Protestant hymns played in a multitude of arrangements by Mrs. Little on her dark mahogany piano, the one that sat upright against the inside wall of her living room and directly above my bed. There were resounding hymns inspired by an elevated spirit; hymns that reverberated through the subflooring, so undulating they disturbed the fine network of rafter dust and caused it to drift soot-like and settle on my pillow and in my eyes. But there were simpler hymns as well, played as clear as crystal and as sharp and celestial as a first frost. From *Just as I Am* to *Onward Christian Soldiers,* she brought the right elements of time and tone to each note and each one thereafter. She was the perfect living-room concertmaster and the church's principal pianist.

She was plain, Mrs. Little was. Trying to picture her as anything else would have taken a forgiving imagination. Her dresses were as drab as they were shapeless, and she never, but never, wore makeup of any kind. Her hair was straight and wispy, of a color somewhere between dust and wheat, and always held back off her face with clear plastic barrettes. And although her eyes were pale and her lips were turned down at the corners, there was a softness to her skin despite its somewhat bloodless color. On the surface, she was the source of Harmony's every trait.

I would also come to know many things about myself that summer, what stimulated and what tormented, what drove me and what gave me cause to stay. And I would come to know some of the similarities that ran like smooth dark rivers through us all. And, too, I would come to realize how significant, even momentous, it was for those around me to lay claim to Jesus. But just as important, I would come to know the likes of Kellen Manly.

CHAPTER FOUR
Never Forget Rule Number One

His hat was cocked jauntily to one side. It was one of those Sam Snead straws with a wide grosgrain band. He seemed tentative, entering the room as if he wasn't sure he had even entered the right house. He was naked from the waist up, tanned to a dark chestnut and with a torso that looked like the dream of every athlete who ever lived. A tropical shirt with large yellow and purple flowers was hooked with a single finger and draped lazily over one shoulder. I sat upright about the time he stepped between me and the room's overhead light, his shadow falling across me and a sizeable portion of the wall behind me.

"You Weldon Thatcher?" he asked in a voice a little higher than I expected.

"Yeah," I said, smiling from my bed. "You Kellen Manly?"

"Sounds like somebody's been talking about me." He grinned and proceeded to stuff his shirt into a laundry bag that hung from the corner post of his bed.

"Yeah, but it was all in the name of love," I said, reaching out one wiry, pasty-white hand.

"In the name of love, or under the guise of it?" He smiled with teeth as white as my mother's bleached cotton sheets. He moved closer, towering over me, his thick torso blocking the remaining light.

"Glad to know you," he said, clasping his hand around mine. His grip was rock-like, granite padded with flesh. All I could do was nod. I felt dwarfed and even weaker than usual.

"Got here this afternoon I hear," he said, hanging his hat on a nail protruding from the wall. His hair had the patina of Brylcreem, thick and wavy, about half a shade away from coal black and well beyond the need of a trim.

"Yeah, about noon," I said, glancing at my white pencil arms and struggling for a moment with the inequities of gene pools.

"I also heard how excited you are about being here," he said, a wry smile giving him away.

"Mr. Little tell you that?" I asked.

"Harmon?" He winced. "Well, indirectly maybe."

"How's that?" I asked.

"It's a small town," he said. "What Harmon tells one..." He leveled his eyes at me. "Well, you get the idea. Word travels fast. Even faster in the summer. There's so few of us here, half the time people make things up to keep from talking about themselves. For now, you're the news." I nodded, thinking I understood.

"Harmon give you the welcoming tour?" he asked.

"You mean the campus and the basement?" We both eyed each other for a moment then chuckled.

"Yeah," he said, glancing up at the ceiling as though he was able to see through the rafters, "that's our Harmon."

"Have you met Mrs. Little?" he asked, motioning toward the ceiling.

"No," I said. "I guess Mr. Little hadn't thought it necessary." He paused, then nodded, his face widening with a smirk.

"So, do you want to sleep or swap lies while I pack?"

"Pack?" I said, thinking I had misunderstood.

"Yeah," he said, "I'm off to Texas. Or didn't Harmon think to mention that?"

"I guess he hadn't thought it necessary," I said, amused by my unintended repetition.

Kellen eyed me with a raised eyebrow. "It's hard telling what he thinks," he said, "much less what he thinks is necessary. He's got his own agenda, that's for sure, though it's scary to think what it might be. Like a chameleon, that one. Even to himself."

Kellen's tone was ringed with as much mystery as curiosity, as much sarcasm as foreboding ... in much the way I perceived Harmon to be. "He seems harmless enough," I said, not wanting to run afoul in either direction, "but a mite more complicated than I'm used to."

Kellen continued to pack with a sideways look in my direction. "Just be cautious," he said. "Don't offer any more than you have to. He's already got his mind made up about you anyway. About all of us for that matter ... from God on down." His look was one of you-know-what-I-mean? I wasn't sure that I did, but the word cautious seemed to reverberate.

"So how you getting there? Texas, I mean."

"Got a friend who drives a big rig between Chicago and St. Paul. Hauls everything from tombstones to hay and lets me know when he's coming through in case I want to ride along. Happens he called earlier today."

"What's that got to do with Texas?" I said.

"Well, from Chicago I hook up with truckers who haul beef to Oklahoma City. From there, it's about four hours to our front gate, so I just hitch it."

"You make it sound like you've done it before."

"Nine times," he said. "Easier than burning what little money I have on a bus ticket."

I knew all too well about the lack of money. "So, when you coming back?" I asked.

"Couple weeks," he said. "That's about all my pocketbook can handle."

I was all at once feeling the need for more information. If I was going to be abandoned, I wanted at least a working knowledge of who and what I'd be left with. Edenfield was, after all, sort of a Brave New World, and Kellen was, up to this point, my only link to it.

I'm sure Harmon figured he had given me all the information I needed when he made a special trip downstairs and taped a complete schedule of the church's activities to the inside of the basement door. But there were other things I thought I needed to know. Guy things. Things that Harmon would never admit he knew, and things that Kellen most likely took for granted.

Kellen continued to move about under the harsh light, in and out of the shadows it cast, and talking with a profusion of energy. There was an air of fascination about him, an uncommon familiarity. It was as if I had known him from another place and time. Feelings of deja vu were always disconcerting to me: too supernatural, always seeming to dangle out there on the fringes of my belief system. But there was something credible about the things he said and the way he said them. And though he knew Edenfield only as a student, he was able to offer opposing views of it, sometimes as nightmare, sometimes as magic.

After a while, his conversational style pulled me in, and soon we were going from one subject to another like we had known each other most of our lives. We talked in a steady stream, back and forth without a pause, like it was a continuation of things we had discussed many times before, like we had breached the conventions of time and given dormant memories new life.

Kellen liked all the bantering, all the questioning, liked expounding on Edenfield as he knew it. He wasn't altogether eloquent, but he did have an open, straightforward manner that dispelled any notion of pretense.

I don't remember how, but somewhere in the tangle of conversation we exchanged sketches of our families. My account of having parents from the heart of Appalachia, Dad being the oldest of twelve, and Mother growing up in a family of midwives and faith healers, seemed to fascinate him. And how my father, after working in the coal mines, discovered that running moonshine across the Kentucky-Virginia line was not only much more his style, but many-times-over more profitable. And how, after WWII, the two of them drove to Chicago with me and everything they owned packed into a 1938 Ford Coupe. It was an account that I had never known how to appreciate until right then. For the first time, I felt unique.

Kellen's account was much graver. His father had been an Army NCO, and his family had moved five times by the time Kellen turned twelve. His older brother, Ray, had been in trouble with the law about the time he cut his first tooth, and his mother had died with tuberculosis just after Kellen turned fourteen.

Two weeks to the day after his mother died, his father went AWOL, ran away with a neighbor's wife. And that was the last Kellen ever saw or heard of him. A week later Kellen and Ray were shipped off to Texas to live with their father's only sister, Irene. Ray lasted a week and a day. They simply woke up one morning and he was gone. No goodbye. Not even a note.

"We both knew he'd never be back," Kellen said. "Anymore, it's like there isn't even enough of him to remember."

Kellen said he stayed on with his Aunt Irene until he was almost finished with high school, up until she got herself married for the third time. "Just up and ran off with some pathetic looking diesel mechanic named Vester," he said. "Trouble was they didn't stay run off. And it wasn't long after they came back that Irene just stopped right in the middle of drying the supper dishes and said she was sorry and all, but she just knew that Vester was her last chance for happiness, and she couldn't risk screwing it up. Said she needed to devote what energy she had to making him happy. I said I understood."

He said when he was getting ready to leave, Irene packed him a lunch just like he was going off to school, just like he'd be back for supper. A few minutes later he said he stood there in the scrub grass in her front yard with most everything he owned packed in an old Navy duffle bag he'd borrowed from a friend, waiting for her to say something. Anything. Instead, she held herself upright and czar-like, and extended her arm to its full length to shake his hand. She gave him her widest and most nervous smile and suggested that he call her sometime. Kellen said his last image of her was in the side view mirror of Vester's old truck as they pulled away, the hem of her dress wafting in a West Texas breeze.

"As soon as Vester pulled his truck to a stop," Kellen said, "I climbed out and slammed the door without ever looking back. And as soon as he pulled away, I flung Irene's lunch, her Limburger cheese sandwich and Moon Pie, as far as I could. I never saw either one of them again."

Vester left Kellen standing in front of Stone and Judi Remington's. It was a large two-story house framed with a huge wraparound porch, and the place where Kellen had been invited to stay until he graduated. Stone taught Phys-Ed and Hygiene. He was also Kellen's track coach. He said it was still early when he made his way across the front yard, past the assortment of toys and a well-climbed cottonwood tree with a big black tire dangling from the end of a rope, still quiet when he knocked on their door. "But within a week," he said, "I knew them as family."

I lay on my side, my arm propped up under my head, not knowing what to say. A silence lingered between us. I watched him as he continued shoving one thing after another into his duffel bag, the muscles in his chest and arms rippling with every movement.

I couldn't help but feel that he had allowed me a deeper-than-usual glimpse into his personal life, as if he had been compelled to reveal part of the mystery that surrounded him. And though I was certain I knew more than most, there was still a part of me that wanted to know more. But that would come with time I figured, after we had time to adjust to what we could believe and not believe about one another.

"So, who will you be visiting?" I said, my voice sounding like a gunshot against the silence.

He paused, a thin layer of sweat making him appear satiny under the overhead light. "Friends," he said. "Old high school chums." There was a smile mingled with the look of a bitter taste. "But mostly Stone and Judi and the kids – what's become my family." His eyes, almost too pretty under his thick dark brows, scanned the room for anything he might have missed. "They write me every week and send me all the news – what little there is – always wanting to know when I'm coming home." He laughed. "They've adopted me. Unofficially, of course, but they're all I've got now." He looked at me as if hoping I understood. I did. "And my brother," he added without looking up. "Maybe he'll show up there one day."

He finished tightening the straps on his duffle bag, then said, "That's it! Gotta go!"

"Go where?" I asked.

"Up to the highway. I gotta meet my ride."

"TONIGHT? You're leaving TONIGHT?"

"In about ten minutes to be exact."

"Well, I don't mean to sound helpless, but where do I go and what do I do come Monday?"

I watched him examine the quandary on my face. "Okay," he said, "there are a couple of things."

All right, I thought, feeling like I was about to be dealt some secret formula for the meaning of life.

"It's all very simple," he said. "Show up at the mill at seven. Let them know who you are, and with any kind of luck they'll take care of the rest." The look on my face said I was not satisfied.

"Trust me," he added. My look softened to trust.

"As for Edenfield," he said, "there are only two rules, only two things you need to remember." The moment of truth, I thought. "Rule number one: Don't do anything to bring attention to yourself." I stood tensed, primed, waiting for the rest. "And rule number two: Never forget rule number one." He turned to give his duffle bag a final cinch, but not before giving my shoulder a squeeze and letting the seriousness on his face turn to a grin.

"That's it?" I asked.

"That's all there ever is," he said. "Think of it as survival. It becomes fun after that." Without waiting for a reply, he asked, "What were you expecting anyway, the meaning of life?"

I stood there feeling a little washed out. I wanted more than common sense and reality. I wanted mystic handshakes and shaman buzzwords. Logic was way too dissatisfying, altogether too much like the collaborations of Mother and Reverend Mayfield.

For the next minute, Kellen moved with the speed of a silent movie, apologizing all the while for what seemed like his deserting me. The next thing I knew, he plunked his Sam Snead straw on my head and brought his hand down hard on my shoulder. "Well, Weldon, I guess I'll see you when I see you." With that, he moved gazelle-like up the steps and onto the footpath that angled across the backyard and through the field to the highway. But before being swallowed by the night, he stopped and waved with huge sweeping motions. I waved back but was certain he couldn't see me against the darkness of the house. I started to move out of the shadows and onto the lawn where I was certain he would be able to see me, when I noticed Mrs. Little waving from a dimly lit corner window. It was nearly midnight.

Chapter Five
The Mill

My first two hours at the mill were spent sitting in an office barely big enough for a desk and chair, listening to Sara Bennett ramble on about her roles at the mill, the church, and in the community. A slow-moving ceiling fan and an open window were the only things that saved me from claustrophobic meltdown.

Sara's long-windedness was as annoying as her plain, bordering-on-homely face and her reluctance to be anything but serious and mature. If it hadn't been for her outsized bosom, I would have been hard pressed to find any charm in her whatsoever.

Somewhere amid Sara's maundering, Fulton Highlander, owner and overseer of the mill, stepped through the door. He was mid-to-late sixties, tall and tanned, and with his own teeth. A wide ingratiating smile and finger waves of silver-white hair marked his way, yet he seemed determined, despite the heat, to look out-of-place in a double-breasted wool suit … brown on brown.

Straightaway, Fulton gave me a no-nonsense handshake followed by a look of concern and a chesty comment out of the side of his mouth about my being so skinny. But before I could laugh to show him that I was one of the boys and a real sport about insensitive ridicule, he turned his attention toward Sara. After an uncomfortable couple of minutes, he turned back to me and said in an advisory tone, "I think we're quite through here."

I nodded, acknowledging his Grand-Dragon status, his sixty-plus years, his life and all that was right and good about it. For a moment he seemed to search my face before he turned to leave, but not before giving Sara a gentle squeeze to her shoulder, right at the spot where her bra strap cut the deepest.

I never saw much of ole Fulton after that, just glimpses of him now and again getting in and out of his Cadillac, and, on occasion, walking vendors through the mill. Sunday's church services weren't much different. Fulton was still the image of stewardship, as stalwart as the sunrise, conspicuous and full of purpose, greeting everyone as if he were taking attendance. Fulton was the senior member of the church council, and beyond life's trivialities and things like the weather, we shared nothing except an understanding of Edenfield's social order.

Only seconds after Fulton left, a man about my size, but twice my age, came through the door out of breath and smiling through bad teeth. Without wasting a second, he focused in on Sara's most prized assets and the things that left her blouse looking like it was two sizes too small. His inability to have any effect on her whatsoever, except by way of disgust, left us all even more aware of the heat and the low-level muscle spasms beneath his right eye.

"Name's Buzz Dither," he said, shaking my hand like he was holding onto a wet cat. "I already know who you are, so let's see if we can find you some work." I followed him with what I faked as enthusiasm. Stepping outside that little office was like being set free, only stronger, like having escaped. For just a second, I turned back toward Sara. She sat limp; her shoulders slouched as if weighted by the magnitude of her gifts.

"Well, I guess I'll see you around, Sara," I said. She looked at me like she was fully aware of this type of empty promise and innuendo, like she had lived this preposterous lie too many times before.

Buzz Dither was the mill's only foreman. He talked with a machinegun rapidity, took very short and very rapid steps and went through toothpicks like they were snack food. He was obsessive about picking the eczema on his elbows and resetting his glasses high on his nose whether they had slipped down or not. About every fourth breath he would try to suction out his sinuses with an irascible inhalation. At times it would sound like a hog feeding from the bottom of a trough, at other times like a train that had jumped its tracks. Other than the perpetual hives that dotted his forehead and the large patch of blotchy skin that erupted from his tee-shirt and crept across the front of his neck, he had no particularly distinguishing features. He did, however, complain, after knowing me for only a few minutes, that he was troubled with bleeding gums and more recently with intermittent hemorrhaging from the rectum.

"So, how'd you like the bus ride from Chicago?" he asked. Without bothering to ask how he knew where I was from or how I got here,

I said it had been uneventful. I was beginning to suspect that I had been Edenfield's foremost topic of conversation since my arrival.

My tour of the mill was conducted in whirlwind fashion. Buzz moved in a blur from department to department. I was dazzled by machinery and noises I never knew existed. When the tour was over, I was standing out back in the sun, in fresh sawdust over the tops of my shoes, and remembering nothing. About that time, a whistle blew and things went deathly silent.

"C'mon," Buzz said, "you can buy me a coffee."

From the loading docks we could see clear to the tree line that marked the southern edge of the mill's twenty-five acres. The land in between had been cut and cleared. Only a few tree stumps and an occasional scrub pine remained, all dotting the surface like the few strands of hair that dotted Buzz's scalp.

"See that big redheaded fellow out there balancing that axe on his head?" Buzz asked, pointing with a locked elbow. My answer was an acid-drip in my stomach. "Well, first of all, he shouldn't be doing that." He was looking at me straight-on while still pointing at Big Red. "But just tell him I sent you and that you're his new helper. He'll see to everything else."

With reasonable certainty, Buzz wheeled and headed back toward the bowels of the mill. For the first time I realized that aside from how *not* to fan Sara's Bennett's flames, he hadn't prepared me for much of anything beyond where the coffee machine was. I stood there frozen with doubt, watching his bony frame duck-waddle away. I was certain he was well intended, but at the same time he was a consummate reminder of the uncertainties that lay deep within me. His last pronouncement, an over-the-shoulder yelp directing me not to worry, only added to the reasons why I thought I should.

"DAMNED NEAR MAKES YOU WANNA CRY, DON'T IT?" Big Red was yelling over the big steel circular saw ripping its way down the length of a twenty-foot pine log. I had been paired with Duncan Skinner, who was about the size of a small single-car garage and one of a handful of students who had elected to ride out the summer in Edenfield.

"SAY WHAT?" I yelled back.

"THE SMELL OF CUT WOOD! MAKES A MAN JUST WANT TO WELL UP AND KNOCK A HOLE THROUGH SOMETHING! DOES ME, ANYWAY!" He grinned big and John Wayne like, displaying strong teeth and a hint of tobacco juice at the gum line. I smiled my biggest smile and nodded with as much mustard as I had in me.

"NAME'S DUNCAN!" he shouted, not bothering to wait for the saw to finish its cut, "DUNCAN SKINNER." He was tall and ruddy, and had hair that was reminiscent of briars, each strand springing up in total disregard to the one next to it. It was blaze red and shined like a trouble-beacon in the sun.

"NAME'S WELDON. WELDON THATCHER," I shouted, trying for imitation.

"YEAH, I KNOW," he shouted, giving my hand a single pump that I felt all the way up in my shoulder and into the right side of my neck. His hand was as rough and hard as sunbaked leather. I imagined it incapable of gentleness, but more suited to busting and carrying rocks.

"Gotcha' staying over at Little's, eh?" he asked, the saw now reduced to only a whir.

"Yeah," I said, realizing that my anonymity had all but crumbled under the weight of the small-town telegraph. I should have been angry, but the dynamics of the town's communication system was all at once something deserving of respect, even fear.

For just an instant his eyes narrowed and the tip of his tongue fondled the little knot of tobacco wedged behind his lower lip. He looked at me like he was deciding if he could trust me, or even if he wanted to. I could still feel the aftermath of his grip running up my arm and rubbed my elbow and shoulder as often as I dared while he hitched his britches and squeezed some of the slimy brown runoff from between his lips. "Come on," he said, pounding my back with approval, "Let's shag ass!" It wasn't instant chemistry, but I got the feeling that at least it was an acquaintance with possibilities.

The rough-cut saw operation was an isolated patch of outback separated from the rest of the mill by some fifty yards. Its outpost status was due to the god-awful noise it caused and the overwhelming amount of sawdust it created. It was referred to as The Hinterlands. It consisted mainly of a hundred-foot, power-fed conveyor line big enough to handle logs up to fifty feet long and two feet across. Midway through the conveyor was a huge four-foot circular saw, and directly over the saw was a ten-by-twenty-foot overhang of corrugated steel encased in rich brown rust. The saw operator's station was on an elevated platform under the overhang and opposite the direction of flying chips and sawdust.

Surrounding the conveyor line were some ten to fifteen acres of wood chips and sawdust, which were spread out as evenly as possible each day with the use of a small dozer. It was a torrid and humid bog, which sent water seeping up around my shoes with almost every step. Summer months left it ripe and rank and playing host to insects of every kind: arthropods, mites, nits, gnats, ticks, things that slithered, crept, and crawled, swarmed, buzzed, and bit. This is where I had been relegated to sweat out the summer with Duncan Skinner, a stone-deaf saw operator by the name of Cleveland Yates, and the larger-than-life Kellen Manly.

Cleveland Yates was sixty-six, and though he never shaved, his beard was never any more than stubble length. And although we were quite certain he never used soap, he somehow managed to stay within the boundaries of acceptability – the essence of pine tar as his unqualified identity. He was short and wiry, and next to Duncan looked like a seedling that had never been afforded the benefit of sunlight. As far as any of us knew, he never ate anything except Bear Claws and Honey Buns, even when other things were offered, and never-but-never removed the gargantuan plug of Beechnut from between his cheek and gum, not even when he ate. His teeth were the color of oil-stained mahogany, and his old gray felt Fedora was a collection of sweat and sun and rain.

According to Duncan, Cleveland lived inside a cardboard box along the banks of the Sands River. He let me know that Cleveland was amenable to taking in boarders, but was insistent that they have references. Duncan was relentless as an agitator and the unspecified champion of the personal barb. No one was safe. Not even Cleveland.

Given Cleveland and the Hinterlands, Duncan had complete freedom for his irreverence. He would, with heightened theatrics and without provocation, brandish about with cheek and flair, prance and dance upon the sawdust piles as though he was some troubadour gone to pieces, all the while delivering one barb after another, each more devastating than the last, gesturing and embroiling himself in a frenzy of drama. Then, at long last and with crazed eyes, go into deep multiple bows, responding to imagined curtain calls and the ovations of an adoring audience. Cleveland, stone-deaf as he was, would clap his hands and slap his knees, bend at the waist, and brace himself as though he were at the very edge of laughter collapse.

Duncan's play was, more often than not, murderous and beleaguering, but there was no sacrifice too great to satisfy his thespian hungers. He was, far and away, a one-man farce. And though he was anything but self-effacing, and though his remarks were, for the most part, mettlesome and calloused, his theatrics were unparalleled. Duncan and Cleveland together, each rollicking in his own brand of madness, was the stuff that Vaudeville was made of and everything that circuses hoped to be.

I learned early on what Duncan thought of Cleveland, but I could only imagine what went on inside Cleveland's mind, within his cauldron of open smiles and silent laughter. I had to believe he thought Duncan was either the greatest sideshow clown who ever lived, or the most complex package of lunacy God ever favored with breath. There simply wasn't much room for anything in between.

CHAPTER SIX
An L.L.Bean Catalog Cover Come to Life

So it went. Each day melding into the next. Each with its challenges and each etched on the learning scale of my memory; each with its sacrificial elements and unique brand of loathing; each with its labors and absurdities, its abnormalities and demands, and each in support of the other. There wasn't a day I didn't long for home.

I tried to imagine what direction my longing would have taken had I gone to the Army. At least here there was an option: I could always leave. It was a viable alternative. The Army, on the other hand, had no immediate antidote for loneliness or discontentedness, least of all packing up and going home. And though I had for the time ruled it out, I nevertheless took comfort in knowing it was always an available option.

I soon discovered that during the times I doubted the soundness of my decision to stay in Edenfield, I could always find comfort in calling Mother. She was always assuring, as long as she lived and breathed, that I would never have to worry about something to eat or a place to lay my head. It was her way of loving: to shelter my insecurities and instill the dependence that she would always be that one safe harbor from indecisive and even bad decisions. She had her own notions about keeping me from harm's way.

I was well into my second week at the mill before Duncan convinced me that I ought to loosen up and go *shaggin' ass* with him. I can't say that his invitation was all that appealing. In fact, it had undertones of being not quite right. I had nothing to support these feelings except preconceived notions and about two weeks of informal observation. On one hand, I couldn't conceive of two different and otherwise incompatible individuals shagging ass together when there was the freedom of choice to prevent it. On the other hand, and despite my preconceptions, his invitation did, in some small way, make me feel like I was being accepted. Not like I had made the team necessarily, but like I had at least survived the first cut.

The term *shag ass* was very much a part of Duncan's personal identity. It flowed out of his mouth as natural and unrestricted as rain off a tarpaper roof. It was one of those expressions that could be corrupt without being blasphemous, yet vulgar enough to be satisfying. Given certain volumes and inflections, whether used with a soft voice and a smile, or out of the side of his mouth with a snarl, he could use it to motivate, intimidate, or create moods for either fun or anxiety. It was all encompassing. And it more than suited him; it fit him like new socks.

The directions to his place were hazy, and it was some time before I was able to pinpoint where he intended me to go. But once I arrived, I realized at first glance that there had been no mistake. His residence was pure Duncan, identifiable even in a sea of Edenfields.

He lived in a World War II Army Cook Tent set in a small birch grove alongside a two-hundred-acre alfalfa field. Though it was his uncle's land, the campsite was at the same time as preposterous as it was spectacular, a veritable menagerie of texture and color, and a testimony of his character. It was enigmatic of manhood and in the style of a twentieth century outdoorsman; an L. L. Bean catalog cover come to life.

I approached with caution and to the posted warnings of rabid wildlife. Despite the camp's visual assault, there was a kind of order to it—not the kind I would allow for myself, but certainly nothing I would dare disturb. On one side of the tent, there were clothes lines draped with an assortment of rags and towels, and a picnic table that carried the markings of a nearby state park. There was a tree stump with a single bladed axe sunk deep into its center and about a half cord of freshly split logs stacked building-block neat between two small scrub pines. An old black bicycle with two brand new tires leaned against the logs. On the other side, there was a drying rack hewn out of fresh saplings and hung with a number of pots and pans and a large red gingham oilcloth. There were several mismatched folding-chairs leaning up against one of the tent poles, a galvanized washtub turned upside down in the grass, a dirty canvas hammock strung loosely between two thin and leaning Birches, several rod and reel combinations wedged in the crook of a tree, and two scarred and muddy horseshoe pits. Out front, there was a fire pit walled with fieldstone and laden with several charred logs. A full bushel basket of apples, and what appeared to be about a ten-gallon tank of water, were stored under the tent's canopy. Off to my right, there was a tree stand about fifteen feet up into the largest birch on the site, and the place from which he chose to welcome me.

"I SAW YOU COMING A MILE AWAY," he shouted down to me, then slithered with Tarzan-like agility down a rope ladder that hung from his perch. I was startled by his sudden welcome and his expert discipline with camouflage.

He couldn't have been prouder that I decided to come and wasted no time in describing and explaining, in infinite detail, the makeup of his camp. He was going to be a thorough host whether I liked it or not. I was, dutifully, the obliging guest. Yet, at the same time, I never ruled out the possibility that this might be some sort of test.

The inside of the tent was as formidable and functional as it was complete. We toured at great length, leaving nothing to chance. There were stoves and lanterns to explain, and butcher blocks and knives to examine. There were the ventilation and drainage systems to understand, and the adjustments for high winds and rains to be demonstrated. There was also sterilization to account for, refuse disposal, and how to protect against varmints and marauding wildlife. There was not only the preparation of food, but its storage and preservation. It seemed endless, and by the time we got through it all, the horizon was nothing but a fading backdrop for our silhouettes. I toasted his eccentricity, even though I made a point of saying inventiveness and pioneering spirit, then followed it with a long pull from a freshly drawn cup of water. I don't know if it was my show of interest, or if he wanted to impress me further, but he favored me with a couple of apples, a campfire of enormous proportion, and an unsolicited account of how his paradise was conceived.

He began by fixing his face with a look that said he was going to experience a tender moment. Then proceeded to tell me how he had come across a World War II picture of an uncle standing outside a mess tent somewhere in the Fiji Islands. The picture had been taken only days before his uncle was killed. The rest was history. The camp, a tribute. A living monument. Dream conceived; dream born.

His account was as concise as I could have ever hoped for, and it was followed up by one of those well-what-do-you-think smiles. For the first time, I felt that he had, in his untillable fashion, identified us as friends.

"Well," I said, trying to head him off before he could launch us into another adventure, "that was fascinating, but I'd better be headin' back. It's getting late."

"C'mon," he said, jumping to his feet and kicking dirt on the fire, and ignoring what I just said, "LET'S SHAG ASS!"

My first instinct was to run. "Where?" I asked. He just looked at me and smiled.

Misguided compulsion can be unnerving when it's aimed at the pitch black of night, but his burst of energy convinced me that maybe it didn't matter where we would be going or even why … sometimes survival just meant going along.

It was important for Duncan not to be detected, so we spent the next half hour or so stumbling through woods and meandering along back trails, even though it was close to ten o'clock and everybody within a five-mile radius had been asleep for the past hour. To my surprise, he led us out of the woods and onto the soccer field at the extreme north end of the campus. I followed him with tennis-shoe silence to the main quadrangle where I stood guard while he climbed through an unlocked basement window in the girls' dorm. Two minutes later, he pushed a big box at me through the window. It was a case of toilet paper. He was so excited I thought he was going to go back for another. To him it was like discovering gold or recouping a substantial portion of his tuition costs.

We backtracked as far as I cared to and finally settled alongside one of the small duck ponds just northeast of the soccer field. Duncan was still excited and carried the big box high on his shoulders. It was his sacramental link to the spoils of war. When I mentioned again that I thought I'd better be heading home, he insisted that we had just begun and that he knew where we could get all the apples we wanted. But the only thing I wanted at this point was to put as much distance as I could between me and his ideas of *shag ass*. I headed for Little's despite his protests and with his whispered promises of "even better times to come" trailing after me.

By this time, it was nearly midnight, and except for the infinite number of crystal chips and diamonds masquerading as stars, I walked in total darkness and with an ear for anything beyond the cadent sounds of bullfrogs and crickets – their raspy, hypnotic concert adding to the restlessness of an otherwise draped and silent world.

CHAPTER SEVEN
Fishes and Loaves

The Fishes and Loaves grocery store sat unornamented and glistening with whitewash on the corner adjacent to the college's front concourse. It was the only grocery store in Edenfield and located in direct route from the mill to Harmon Little's. Within the first several weeks, I had made a number of stops on the way home and each time had been the sole customer.

"That'll be four sixty-five," she said, careful not to make eye contact. She had been cat fast, ringing up my six items as though there were an army of impatient customers stacked up behind me. She was Becky Summers, the bull-necked daughter of Basil and Clovis Summers, and sole heir to The Fishes and Loaves. Under her tightly fastened coarse blonde curls, her face glowed unpainted and doll-maker pretty. She came across as being bleached and scrubbed, so clean that she gave off the aroma of soap. With her white clerk's coat that contained as much starch as fabric, she was as wholesome looking as *Elsie the Cow* in a green pasture on the sunny side of a hill. From the whites of her eyes to the porcelain quality of her teeth, from the unblemished texture of her skin to the perfect pink in her unpainted nails, she exemplified the virtues of fresh dairy products and top-quality U. S. Government inspected meats.

"Out of five," she said with a terse business acumen. The exchange of money was intricate and cautious, eliminating any possibility that her hand might touch mine. It was far too risky to chance skin against skin, especially with that of a stranger.

Over my shoulder, Basil Summers worked with great effort and speed behind the meat counter. Dressed in a long white coat, he looked more like a doctor than someone in charge of sweetbreads and ribs. He had the same scrubbed appearance as Becky and exuded the kind of confidence that comes only after years of feeding a community. He never looked up, just kept chopping and cutting, weighing and sorting.

"That's thirty-five cents change," Becky said, dropping the coins into my hand as if she were dropping a mouse into the mouth of a snake. I started to ask if she attended Edenfield College but thought it would have been like asking if water runs downhill.

"Thank you and come again," she said just before stuffing the last item into my bag. Without a single wasted motion, she slid the bag to the end of the counter, turned and readied herself for the next customer.

I paused just long enough to give a quick glance over my shoulder, thinking I may have missed someone lurking in the aisles. But there was no one besides Basil squinting through his wire-rimmed glasses, tirelessly trimming and sorting loins and cutlets and briskets.

"Well, so long," I said. She gave me a little nod, quick and neat, without looking directly at me.

Outside, the bright sunlight greeted me with the same intensity as Becky had displayed at the checkout register. I crossed the street and walked two short blocks before taking the shortcut between the post office and Celestine Tucker's secondhand shop. Behind me, The Fishes and Loaves sat simple and forlorn, alone at the foot of its own long shadow. I could almost make out the camphor aroma of its wares, could almost hear the hollow slam of its big screen door and the creak in its hard oak floor beneath Becky's feet. And though no one came or went, I couldn't help but think how Becky was probably still standing there at the register, waiting with all her might for the next customer. From all appearances, she was a serious devotee, as efficient as she was competent. It was almost enough to help me overlook her rock-solid, five-foot, two-hundred-pound frame, and her being the only girl to pick up a two-hundred-and-ten-pound calf at the Minnesota State Fair, but not quite enough to get me past her being the sole love interest of Duncan Skinner.

Chapter Eight

La'Randa and Lo'Randa

The mill's gravel parking lot was alive with the crunch of trampling feet and spinning tires. It was quitting time. No time for the faint of heart or those without reserves. It was a time for renewal, a time cherished by the workingman, mill hands, and those who would be catapulted beyond the constraints of moderation. It was also Friday night. Payday. And amid exhaust trails and the late afternoon sun, I tried with the usual amount of nonchalance to position myself for Sara Bennett's promenade from the office to her car. Just as I was craning my neck for a more wakeful perspective, a coral-colored Lincoln Continental came to a sliding stop beside me. Almost before I could react, one of the rear doors flew open, and Duncan, braced on an angle between the dashboard and the front seat, shrieked some profane and garbled order for me to "SHAG ASS," which meant for me to get in. I could see straightaway that he was besieged with witlessness; his whole demeanor thick with glassy-eyed wildness, without form or sequence. In the next instant, and before I could understand why, I leapt headlong into the back seat, the Lincoln's tires cutting into the gravel even before I could close the door. By the time we hit the highway, the sound of squalling rubber sent us fishtailing past Pauline's Diner like banshees that had been released through a crack in the walls of hell. The veins in Duncan's neck were bulging with laughter and the rush of adrenaline. By the time the Lincoln shifted into high gear, Duncan's cries of SHAAAAAG AAAAAAS caterwauled from one alfalfa field to the next. It was then that I noticed the driver for the first time. It was Buzz Dither. The Buzzard. Between him and Duncan was a guy from the mill who everybody called Rooster. Everybody except Duncan. Duncan called him Hen. Rooster was tall, smooth and black, and responded only with soft laughter and meager objection to Duncan's antics. Next to me in the back seat was another guy from the mill who Duncan introduced as Marblehead, a moniker not sanctioned. He was small and thin, not quite as dark as Rooster, and responded with frantic bits of vulgarity each time Duncan called him Marblehead. Duncan was in ecstasy. On the other side of Marblehead was none other than Cleveland Yates, looking and smelling like only he could. He was ecstatic that I had been corralled and rocked back and forth in silent glee. Duncan taunted him at a steady clip and without the first signs of mercy, but not enough to penetrate Cleveland's silent world or detract him from his awkward attempts to open a warm bottle of Pepsi with one of the keys he kept strung on a huge silver ring. After a number of unsuccessful attempts, he finally worked it loose and added its warm sweetness to the fresh plug of Beechnut wedged in his cheek. About that time, Buzz pulled the big coral Lincoln off the highway and under the huge tin carport protruding from *Bacchus' Hair of The Dog.* It was a party store in the middle of nowhere, an oasis for the common man and about as far from the precepts of Edenfield as night was from day.

No one had to move. Curb service was Bacchus' specialty. Buzz shouted out his order for a case of long-necked Budweisers, then told them to throw in a banana snack cake for Cleveland. There was reason to celebrate. Buzz had quit the mill and was going back to Oklahoma. Said he was going to be managing a feed store for his cousin Dillard. "Going to be top-dog foreman," he said. "Back there in God's country."

It was only minutes before a very hairy woman in the fashion of a sumo wrestler came wheezing toward us with our order. She let the bulky case slide out of her hands and settle with a thud on the floor between Duncan's feet. Exclamations of satisfaction rose all around me. Duncan, in a fit of merriment, proceeded to open one bottle after another with his teeth. I hesitated when he handed one of them to me. At that moment I knew I was where I shouldn't be. BE SURE YOUR SINS WILL FIND YOU OUT loomed at me from Harmon's refrigerator door. I was trapped. Locked in. The thought of the small-town telegraph sent a shiver. Was I a goner before I even began? Right at that moment, I was pretty sure I could smell my own fright. It was as thick as the smell of pine tar coming off Cleveland. But time and place proved to be more powerful than my watered-down convictions, and I took Duncan's rough and rowdy laughter to be assurances that everything would be okay. I decided in that moment to trust him.

With everybody except Cleveland talking, and with the windows rolled down and the radio tuned in and blaring the sounds of Mo-town, we headed for Castle City and a birthday party for somebody named Alford.

The day had moved into long shadows before we were able to un-scramble the directions to Alford's. Duncan had scribbled them in a phone book, then left part of them behind when he tore out the page. By the time we managed to combine the elements of fate and luck, it was dusk, and the party was in full bloom.

It was a large clapboard house we stopped in front of, listing about three degrees north and thirsting for paint. But what paint was left gave off a semi-translucent glow in the twilight. Cars were parked bumper to bumper up and down the road and in total disarray across the huge lawn. People milled about everywhere: across the front porch and down its steps, onto the lawn, and all the way out to the road. Through the front windows, throngs of people congealed under colored lights and the rhythmic tempo of The Four Tops.

Rooster motioned for me to follow him. Though the rest of the crew had dispersed in different directions, I could make out Duncan's bright red hair bobbing above the crowd. I couldn't tell if he actually knew anybody he was talking to or if he was acting out some thespian fantasy, pretending to meet and greet a swarm of well-wishers and admirers. On the other hand, Rooster seemed to know everybody and was greeted with the ease of an evening breeze. My presence seemed to be of little, if any, consequence. Still, I craned and stretched to look for familiar faces. In particular, Edenfield faces. The ones that might have dared beyond their boundaries, or who were sent by God to ferret me out. After more than a few nervous moments, I realized I was a total stranger, but no one seemed uneasy about it except me.

The long-necked bottles of Budweiser were gone about the time the sun dipped beyond the horizon. They had served as dinner and as a base for the vodka and Kool-Aid highballs that fermented sweet and unchilled in a giant glass bowl at the far end of the porch. Directly above it hung a big red and white banner that read "Happy Birthday Alford." I hadn't the slightest idea who Alford was, only that he was wearing a pointed birthday hat and was lying across a chaise longue in what appeared to be an alcoholic coma. Even Rooster, with Budweiser fueling his veins, was helpless to revive him.

With his easy style, and with his cherry-flavored glass of vodka held as if lighting his way, Rooster guided me through a throng of limbs and faces and into a miniature clearing where he introduced me to a set of twins named La'Randa and Lo'Randa.

Almost before I could begin to feel uncomfortable, he and Lo'Randa locked themselves together from cheek to thigh, and in serpentine fashion, began writhing to the beckonings of Curtis Mayfield.

All around me bodies began locking together. Almost immediately, the miniature clearing began to disappear, forcing La'Randa and me even closer. I'd had enough Budweiser to make me feel like a buck in rut, and it was always those feel-good times that left me wondering what God had up His sleeve, what lesson He was about to have me learn … or suffer.

In the throng, I could see Rooster attending to Lo'Randa's gentle rhythms, lifting and guiding her to where she was more than obliged to go. Watching him flow so free and full of confidence made me all the more aware that there was an abyss between who I was and who I wanted to be.

I could feel La'Randa's stare, and finally returned it. It was only meant to be a glimpse, a flash, nothing more than a confirmation of her presence. Instead, it settled into a look not unlike the one she was giving me. It was a moment that gave way to an understanding. Without words, we leaned in, touched. Warmth and electricity mingled with the tempo of Smokey Robinson and the Miracles, and we let it work its own power, inching us even closer. At last, and in perfect time, we pressed ourselves together.

Flashes of color and light swirled around me. Somewhere far-off, Duncan's high-pitched laughter was reaching out, rising beyond the music. They were unmistakable bursts, hyena-like to my full-blown vertigo.

Somewhere in another dimension, with the siren sounds of Little Anthony and the Imperials, Teddy Pendergrass, and Percy Sledge, I glided and rolled together with La'Randa's lithe and delicate form, locked and frozen within the sea of her perfume. In and out of shadows, in a labyrinth of motion and color, we pressed in, hard and unashamed. But somewhere beyond the wantonness of it all, beyond the world of placating rhythms and the blended falsettos of Sam Cooke and Marvin Gaye, The Platters, and The Temptations, beyond the velvet haze of beer and vodka and the indulgences of the night, I stepped and swayed and finally slipped beyond the fringes of what was conscious.

The sun bounced off the windshield with blinding indifference. I felt dazed and pressed the palms of my hands against my eyes.

"Here, have one of these," Duncan said, sticking a fifteen-cent hamburger under my nose. The pungency of its mustard and fried onions had the intensity of a mulch bed under a July sun. "C'mon," he insisted, peeling back part of its grease-soaked wrapper. I took it only so that I could hold it away from me.

"Where are we?" I coughed, trying to cradle my head.

"Buster Burger's," he mumbled, his face plunging past the waxed paper and into the fifteen-cent world of double mustard, double onion.

"How'd we get here?" I managed to whisper, trying to contain a sudden brain-swell.

Duncan stared at me, his powerful jaws working, devouring. After swallowing hard and flushing with a long gulp of orange soda, he said, "You gonna eat that or what?"

I looked down at the hamburger in my hand. It looked like the heart of a flower, its wrapper unraveled like a huge paper petal. Except for the alternating pain and disorientation, I could feel little beyond the alcohol fermenting in my stomach. I slid the burger across the seat toward him and leaned back against the door, reaching for more air and a new wave of sleep.

"WELL," Duncan boomed, his voice cascading like it had descended from the rafters of a belfry, "IT'S THAT TIME AGAIN!" His voice had broken in unison with the tires leaving the highway and rolling onto a dirt road. I began to grope for some semblance of life. That's when I first noticed The Buzzard and Cleveland Yates asleep in the back seat. At first, I thought it must have been some adverse reaction to a second wakening, but Duncan said it was just the DT's. It was his way of comforting.

"Where's the rest of us?" I managed to say.

"Three words," Duncan said, "LA'Randa and LO'Randa."

"Oh," I said, remembering. Duncan surveyed me and let me know that I looked like something that needed fixing. "My stomach feels like it's been turned upside down and inside out," I said from my crumpled position. He looked back at me and smiled, then looked at The Buzzard and Cleveland asleep and breathing like fresh-fed hogs in the back seat.

"You're all so weak," he said.

I could feel the weight of my head, my neck almost powerless to support it. For a second, I squinted just enough to pan past Duncan into the humid sun-soaked morning. We were at his compound, clear to the back of the birches. Back where there was no road, and where the blue jays squawked at us in a frenzy. We had intruded on their sanctity, and they were riotous, excitable as inextinguishable fire. Duncan didn't seem to notice. Instead, he stepped from the car and inhaled deeply. A look of satisfaction washed over his face as he surveyed his holdings. He looked back at me then leaned in through the open window. "You look like you've been sleeping with the devil," he said. His smile was gone, and his tone had a familiar ring, like something I would have uttered into a mirror.

"I suppose I have," I said, imagining the truth of it.

"You'll toughen up soon enough," he said, "so long as you don't forget THEY wouldn't like it – you sleeping with the devil an' all." He nodded toward Edenfield's big church steeple in the distance, barely visible above the tops of the trees, to indicate who THEY were … then paused to spit and watch it ooze its way into the sand. "Fact is they don't like much of anything that doesn't remind them of glory land." His sarcasm was followed with a long uninterrupted stare, the Kool-Aid vodka still at work in his eyes. He straightened himself just long enough to tuck in the tail of his shirt. "And you know why?" he demanded with alarming seriousness, confident of his territory. I didn't feel like I had the energy to answer but did anyway.

"No. Why?" I wheezed.

"Cause they got a right handsome stake in it. Can't let the likes of you go messing about, muddying what's been bought and paid for by the grace and redemptive blood of His one and only son."

I stared at him trying to decide if he was suffering the same pain that was at that very moment rampaging through my temples and behind my eyes, or if he was just spewing a jaded kind of beer-and-vodka logic. "Well," I said, "what do you suppose THEY would do if they found me like this? Kill me and eat me?"

"Sort of," he said, inserting the tip of his little finger inside his cheek to pick at whatever was caught between his molars. "One thing for sure," he said, stopping just long enough to examine what he'd dislodged, "you need to keep in mind that this is *Edenfield.*" His eyes were the red of poppies. "Canaan land. The salve of righteousness right here in the middle of these alfalfa fields." Duncan's ramblings were nothing new, but even if he had something worthwhile to say, it was becoming lost in my inability to decipher it. "I'm talking about a centuries-old spiritual network of Bible-thumping good ol' boys ready to deal you to the devil and haunt you after you're gone if you give'm cause." With Duncan I could only guess what was real and what was theater. He never missed the chance to reinforce the fine line separating the two. Today, though, I chose theater. It was my way of not having to give serious thought to what he was saying. He leaned in through the window again, his head and neck extending like a turtle's from under its shell. "Then," he said, "they'd likely hold hands and dance around the flowers on your grave, rectitude in their every step." He was looking at me somewhat bug-eyed and with tiny balls of spittle in the corners of his mouth. I got the feeling he was waiting for a look of revelation to wash over me.

Duncan being awake for the last twenty-four hours was starting to take its toll. Being drunk on top of it added a bit of brittleness to his bliss. That's why I made a point of keeping my eyes focused on his. Though his lids struggled against the pull of gravity, he somehow seemed disappointed that I might not have grasped what he'd said. I didn't much care. I just figured somebody had done a thorough job of stuffing his brainpan with an abridged rendition of good and evil, and the further away from it I could get, the better off I'd be. I guess he figured I didn't care one way or the other, so he turned and eased his way to the back of the car. It was only seconds later that The Buzzard's chesty hacking joined the sound of Duncan's piss splashing in the dirt.

"THE WAGES OF SIN," shrieked Duncan. I felt my head throb as the fatigue and vertigo sent me slumping even deeper into my seat. I wanted more than ever to go home. Edenfield's thorny bag of rightness had proven a tad weedier than I was ready for … like I was in a freefall without a net.

The Buzzard drove away late that afternoon after a long goodbye. He swore he would drop us a line to let us know how he was doing. We believed him. But little did we know that when he waved to us through the Lincoln's curling cloud of going-away dust that we would never hear from him again. Cleveland left shortly afterwards – in a zigzag toward the mill where he'd left his truck, and with a fresh plug packed tight twixt his cheek and gum.

I stayed in camp with Duncan for the rest of the day, sleeping on a cot outside his tent. When I woke, it was still light, but just barely. I hadn't as much as turned over when I felt the finite and unmistakable trickle inside my nose. Nosebleeds had become just another inconvenience, nothing to be alarmed about. My dad had them as a boy, and to hear him tell it, much worse than any of mine. So I slumped off toward the deep shade of the birch grove and the stream than ran through it. By the time I got there, the trickle had turned into a gusher. It was pitch dark by the time I got it stopped and worked my way back to the campsite. My trouncing through the brush was enough to wake Duncan, and minutes later we sat huddled around a fire he felt compelled to make. "Gotta have a fire," he said, sending a short burst of tobacco juice hissing against one of the logs. "Helps maintain order. Lets critters know who's top of the chain." Duncan was full of reasons why he did what he did. Best I could make out, it didn't matter if any of them made sense, so long as they justified his going through the motions. He lived by his own code.

"You're looking a little peaked," he said.

"Feeling that way, too. Fact is, I'm feeling a whole lot like I don't like myself."

"That's called guilt, son," he said grinning around his chaw. "The one thing that'll cripple you quicker'n anything else. *The pang of conscience* my old man calls it. I was raised with it. Had it served up to me breakfast, lunch, and dinner … my old man being a preacher an' all. But I'm done with it now: with all that shoulda-woulda-coulda bull dung. Better off for it, too."

Duncan's words were stout and full of what he figured was relevant. "Maybe so," I said, "but I still got this far-away feeling. Mother would say I need to pray. Way I'm feeling, I'm thinking she might be right."

The look on Duncan's face became scrunched, as if he was trying to rid himself of some obnoxious taste. "Pray?" he said. "Why is it that everybody's all the time thinking they need to pray?" It was right away evident I had said the wrong thing. I hadn't even meant it. It was just a comment, words to fill a void. "You think you have to pray to feel good about yourself? —to score points with God or for His will to be done?" Duncan had launched a potent offense, one question after another and each strong enough to be its own answer. "You think God's just waiting around for you to pray so He can dispense His will? —that it won't be done unless you pray?" He was relentless, preacher's son that he was. "What you need to keep in mind is there's nothing that will prevent His will from being done. He's God! Infinite and forever, not just some mystic who keeps everything on hold just waiting for you to pray." He had found a cadence, a rhythm. "If we're all so sure that He has a purpose for our existence, then why can't we just be content to let Him do His job? What's all this praying about? Way I see it, it don't amount to much more than interfering." He stopped, slacked jawed, his cud loose in his cheek.

I tried to avoid his limpid stare, but found myself nodding, giving him the nonverbal permission to go on. "OR," he said, "could be people feel they know more'n He does, and just can't resist telling Him what He needs to do. Maybe giving Him advice or offering solutions why He ought to do things their way." I could only imagine the times he had delivered this sermon to himself. "You know what the trouble with all that is?" he asked, not really expecting an answer. "The trouble with all that is we actually think we can influence divine providence. When what we ought to be doing is gettin' the hell out of the way, recognize that He knows what and when, where and how much." He was bugged-eyed again and spit three or four times into the fire. It wasn't until he leaned back onto one elbow that I knew he was finished.

Neither of us said much after that. I didn't feel that I had the spiritual moxie to counter anything he had said, especially when there was the possibility he may have been right. The notion of prayer was confounding enough without any inclusions on my part; inclusions, I figured, that would be parboiled at best. I had to wonder if this was the Edenfield Reverend Mayfield had in mind when he talked about it being the place where I could develop a personal relationship with God. I reckoned that Duncan had already developed his, though I wasn't so sure it was the kind that would work for me.

I had reservations enough about this tangled web that stretched between God and man, it being so wraithlike, and my last two days with Duncan had only confounded it; only added to its mystery and the chance that I'd ever see it any different. It seemed to me that Freddie Heartland waxed more prophetic than anybody when he heard I was going to Edenfield. He said the best I could hope for was a miracle.

I waited until after dark before trudging back to my basement sanctuary. The night was warm and thick with clouds. From the field to the west, I could see nothing but a faint black-on-black outline of Little's house. Even the familiar faint glow that radiated from the kitchen's nightlight was off. I entered with the stealth of a thief, without the benefit of a light or even a chance whisper to myself, then wasted no time in pressing myself into my slightly soiled and familiar smelling sheets. My last thought was of Harmon Little and Fulton Highlander holding hands and dancing in wide circles around the flowers on my grave.

CHAPTER NINE
Harmon and Harmony

Kellen's three-week absence was steadily becoming an irritation. It was as if he had escaped to a land of freedom, and returning to Edenfield was the farthest thing from his mind. It was just one more thing that left me feeling like an orphan; just something else that reinforced the notion that I had less and less reason to stay. It wasn't any easier knowing that it was my choice that I remained here, fixed in Little's fruit cellar and bound by want of every kind. It was only my contrivances, my fantasies and illusions of bachelorhood, things like parties and coeds and the freedom of having no one to answer to that made it all tolerable. It was these prospects alone that made it possible to forgive myself for standing pat.

During the week I belonged to the mill, body and soul. Seven to four, Monday through Friday. Saturdays being mine, and Sundays belonging to the Lord without condition. It was Sunday school, then church, then church again Sunday night. Save for Church and things like reading and writing, Sunday was a day defined by the absence of any real activity. It was a quiet time, one for reflection and the denouncement of sins, for the rest and regeneration of the spirit and to grow one's personal relationship with the Almighty. It was a time at odds with the flesh and the world, a time given to the preparation of tomorrows. And my being here meant that I would forever be a disciple to it.

My evenings amounted to little more than shooting baskets through a netless rim at the end of Harmon's driveway. On occasion, Harmon would press his face close to the screen in his bedroom window and offer himself for a game of ping-pong. I always accepted because I didn't know how to refuse without him feeling rejected. Why I thought I needed to please him, I didn't know. The only thing for sure was that I did it at my own expense. I knew there was never a chance of beating him, much less liking him.

Suffocated was probably the most apt word to describe how I felt around Harmon Little. It was a feeling of my own making, nothing Harmon was responsible for except maybe his fervency toward those of us who lacked an open declaration of salvation. I was able to tolerate his outward sentencing, his heavy-hearted posturing and expressed joylessness only when I thought of them as the buttressed expressions of his soul – there to prod at my spiritless world. Beyond that, I was ripe for suffocation.

Harmon's method of advocating for the Holy Spirit was lavish admonishments of guilt. It was simply what worked, and there was nothing so *centuries reliable* as ample doses of it. Thus, the case with his repeated invitations to join the family for evening devotions. As often as I told myself I wouldn't, it was only a matter of time before my excuses took on a sodden tone. In the end, I proved to be no contest for my own remorse. Guilt was simply what evolved, what triumphed. I suppose it was due in part to a sensitive conscience, but it was enough to finally edge me into an evening with the family and their dedicated observances.

We sat in the living room on chairs brought in from the kitchen. There were four of them, and Harmon arranged them in what was supposed to be a circle. We sat facing inward, and just far enough apart so that our knees didn't touch. I sat facing Harmony.

We began with prayer ... always with prayer. Prayer was what brought us into focus, centered us and welcomed us into the presence of the Holy Ghost. Harmon was masterful in his offerings, lavishing thanks for our being together and asking for divine guidance and an ear to hear what the Spirit was saying. At the point where I realized his prayer was going to be one of duration, I opened my eyes ever so slightly, only to find Harmony staring back at me. She made no attempt to look away but smiled as if we had made some cosmic connection. Under the circumstances, I gave her what I thought was an acceptable-but-curt smile, and returned, before being discovered, to a prayerful state: head bowed, eyes closed.

Throughout Harmon's opening prayer and his litany that followed (a ten-minute discourse on things pertaining to forgiveness), Harmony kept me locked within the crosshairs of her open-faced gaze.

I felt myself being chipped away, but was unable, for some reason, to keep my eyes from drifting to her time and again. Each time, her gaze seemed to take on new intensity, each time more rock-clad than the time before. Yet, each time, I was compelled to give her a tight little smile before turning away. Mrs. Little sat stiff and upright. For the most part, her look was blank and emotionless, aimed only at the floor in front of her. Harmon seemed oblivious to their detachment and focused his attention on me alone.

When Harmon finished, he asked if there were any questions or if anybody had anything to add. The ensuing silence was deafening. Harmony sat smiling back at me, unnerved in the least. In a final attempt to engage us, Harmon asked Harmony if she had any comments. She ignored him, never once lifting her eyes from mine. Deep swells of warmth crept into my neck. "Well, okay, then," Harmon said, accepting that he had done all he could. "Weldon, would you like to close with prayer?"

POW! It was a direct hit, and I went immediately into a tailspin. Spiraling. Down and down. All was a blur. Air! I needed air!

"Weldon?" Harmon echoed. I rolled my head in his direction. Harmon had chosen me to close with prayer. It had been a question, a request, yet at the same time a command, one without the choice of refusal, because it was acknowledged as a privilege to be asked. There simply was no such thing as *No thank you,* nothing anywhere that allowed for anything but *Yes, thank you, I would be honored.* I needed air.

"Are you alright, Weldon?" Harmon asked. I nodded, then with my tongue nearly sticking to the roof of my mouth, managed to thank the Lord for our time together and that we would be reminded of what was said and be able to apply it to our lives. Amen jumped out almost ahead of the last word. When I opened my eyes, the first thing that greeted me was Harmony's all-consuming stare and the tip of her tongue tracking along her upper lip. I wasted no time in thanking everyone, returned my chair to the kitchen, then left for the safety of the cellar.

From start to finish, evening devotions had only taken twenty minutes. But it was Harmony's stare that had given it the illusion of hours. After only one session, I was all but filled up with Harmon's devoutness. To avoid having to decline any further invitations, I traipsed home with Duncan each night after work, staying until I was sure that family prayer-time had been laid to rest. At other times I would go off on my own, into the adjacent fields where the roads ended in circle turnarounds, and where the houses sprawled in the shadows of oaks and alongside weathered and listing barns; out where the ground rolled in giant swells, and the weeds and wildflowers erupted in endless profusions of colors and shapes for what seemed like miles; from one rise to the next and from one farm to another. I liked walking without the slightest idea of where I was or where I was going. It seemed to free me from the constraints of my ever-shrinking world. It never mattered that it was often after dark before I returned. Just being out there, out of earshot and away from the challenges of ping-pong, the invitations to prayer and the collaborative violining of Harmon and Harmony, was enough. I began to understand after several such excursions that I was capable of being alone and thinking about things that, until now, seemed reserved exclusively for people like my mother and her friends.

My escaping to the fields was a respite in many ways, but it didn't always save me from Harmon and Harmony's stringed malaise. I soon learned that destiny was not above dealing a crippling hand, in particular on nights when their sounds came vexing at nearly ten o'clock. I also learned that I was not alone in my wanting to escape. There was Mrs. Little. And despite the agony Harmon and Harmony unleashed into the air, she was always there before too long to remind them that they had done well, and how fortunate it was for everyone who enjoyed their music as much as she did that tomorrow was another day. There was only so much even a mother could endure.

Mrs. Little following them on the piano after she had chased them away was maybe too harsh, but she did it anyway and with redeeming passion. Maybe it was to make up for what they had failed to do. Maybe it was to stir a fire, or maybe to squelch it. I don't know which. But I listened, part captor, part intruder, as she slipped into worlds, I was certain, that were unlocked only by her composition: pleasure palaces of the mind where her notes, lingering and haunting, sought cause for their passion; a place where she could lose herself in a symphony of abandonment, oblivious to anyone or anything except maybe the presence of God. It was music with unending variation, brief and unmistakable journeys into whatever it was she kept locked inside. It was those very melodies spiraling in my head that would make me think again and again of leaving. They were reminders of the restlessness that made me want to be someplace other than where I was, and of the emptiness that went beyond being homesick. At other times, those same melodies worked as connectors to a world of unknowns within me, even held me to the fantasy that I might somehow fit in after all, even have that all-allusive personal relationship with God where I would come to know His voice and He mine. But it was in the aftermath of silence that the mysteries of God played their awful tunes, where I reeled deep in skepticism and lack of faith, and where I knew my only relationship with God lay lost in some vast unknown; an unknown that reached upward and outward and beyond anything I had heretofore known, beyond anything I could fathom, even beyond the expectations of hope.

I didn't know what it was that kept me from drawing closer to God, from knowing His presence … only that I would never be any closer to Him than I chose to be. And though I knew little of that vast unknown, I was certain of its pull and of its portion. And that was oftentimes enough.

Chapter Ten
To the Right of John Birch

Highway 31 was a two-lane blacktop and the main artery in and out of Edenfield. It ran east and west, dividing Edenfield equally into north and south. Neither, however, was distinguished socially or economically. It was simply Edenfield, as homogeneous as the Anglo-Saxon Protestants who settled it in the early 1800's.

The houses that lined the highway, the ones that were there when the highway was still a dirt road, were, in total, large two-story frames with nothing to distinguish them except huge porches and clapboard siding, and nothing to suggest that they were of any historical significance. Beyond the highway in both directions, houses sprawled with simple boredom. The roots of the community, however, ran at unfathomable depths within the scriptures according to King James, and within the doctrines of God's Church. God's Church was the all-encompassing name inscribed by its founding fathers. Since it was the only church in Edenfield, and for miles in all directions, it was simply known by the locals as The Church.

Most everyone in Edenfield was tied to The Church in one way or another. It couldn't be helped. The Church owned everything. It had built the college and the lumber mill, had even chartered its own bank, which meant that it held the lion's share of the town's liens and mortgages. All in all, it accounted, directly or indirectly, for a good eighty percent of Edenfield's paychecks.

The Church was, for all intents, Edenfield's governing body, a collective non-bargaining unit on the side of God and God on the side of it. It was the past, present, and future of Edenfield's existence; a closed loop system whereby each member catered to the causes and concerns of the next; an institution sanctioned of God and a source of all that was right and good, and where its members understood their vulnerability .. even with its blessing.

In light of its politics, Edenfield was anything but bipartisan and every bit as predictable as its religion. Its whole political structure was probably best depicted by Orlo Kirkum, town constable and official precinct guard on election days. This alone made him the primary target of reporters from the local television station in nearby Castle City who were interviewing locals during the Kennedy-Nixon elections.

"Well, Mister Kirkum, can you give us your opinion as to how the voting might go here in Edenfield?"

"Well," Orlo said, "let me put it to you this way. There's what you call your moderates, the ones who'd vote conservative most of the time. They're the ones who be out there just to the right of the elephant. Then you got your Barry Goldwaters'. They're the ones who are a good shoutin' distance to the right of the straight voters. Then you got your John Birchers who're about a good five iron to the right of the Goldwaters'. Then finally you got us folks here in Edenfield. I guess you might say we're about a day's drive to the right of the Birchers."

There was so much knee slapping and ballyhooing, and everybody milling about to slap Orlo on the back, that one of the voting booths got knocked against the precinct's fuse box and sent sparks flying like it was a fireworks celebration especially intended for the brief-but-artful fame Orlo Kirkum had brought to Edenfield's political landscape.

Even though Nixon lost the election, Orlo's interview had created such a stir that the college newspaper ran a story on it and even took a picture of him standing outside the precinct grinning like he was running for governor. In tribute, the Young Republicans enshrined the story along with Orlo's picture in a gold leaf frame and hung it on the wall of Samson's Barber Shop right between a set of elephant tusks and a picture of Abraham Lincoln. It was, in its own small way, a monument to the town's political makeup and a statement as precise as the hand tooling on Orlo's Colt 45.

CHAPTER ELEVEN
Rising Up Out of the Heat

With Harmon Little being the financial wizard for The Church Board, and Gretchen Little being the principal pianist for The Church choir, it was not at all uncommon that they be gone for hours at a time attending to their respective ministries. It was during these times away that Harmony began showing up in the basement with undeviating regularity, enough to rule out mere co-incidence. Most often she came with a basket of ironing or a load of wash, and each time wearing the tightest and shortest shorts – red and satiny – and the only pair of its kind, I was certain, in all of Edenfield. So short they looked to be a size too small and made her bony, sun-starved legs seem far too long for the rest of her. And there was rouge and lipstick the same color as her shorts, and dangling earrings, and a redolent trail of jasmine following after her ... the same sweet cloud that always seemed to waft with such sufficiency from my mother's purse and from the women who sat too close to me in church.

More was always the norm for Harmony, and she found it in a variety of ways. There were shirttails wrapped and tied around her waist in such a way that allowed her bellybutton the freedom of light and air. And her hair: swooped and gathered and tied up so high that her neck seemed to elongate, even swoon. And there was throat clearing and gum chewing and great expulsions of breath, and the sort of humming that comes from someone hard and fast at work. And always the faint and pining stream of songs: Johnny Mathis, Gene Pitney, The Lettermen cascading from her transistor radio. Still, none of it would ever do until she came around the corner to arrange herself, jack-legged and gangling in the doorway, like we were the most intimate of friends.

"I'm doing a load of wash," she said, her eyes liquid and lazy, "and was thinking I could put some of your things in with mine if you'd like." She was far shrewder than she was fourteen.

"Naw," I said, not bothering to look up from the magazine I was pretending to read, "I'll take care of it myself." I glanced up just long enough to give her a thanks-anyway smile. She looked lonely. In some primal way, I wanted to befriend her, to talk with her, but held back out of some profound sense of self-preservation.

We waited in heavy silence, she clearing her throat more than necessary and me flipping pages in rhythm with her agitation. "So," she said, "you like it here or not?" There was a bit of swagger in her jaw.

"It's alright," I said. Then more silence.

"So, when's Kellen coming back?" she asked.

"Soon," I said, wishing it could be at that very minute.

"Well, I know my mother will be glad about that," she said out of the side of her mouth and to no one in particular. Then, with a sudden gasp she turned and bolted up the stairs as if trying to outrun snakes. Harmon and Gretchen had returned sooner than expected, the headlights of their Volkswagen bus lighting up the driveway like a Labor Day parade.

Sunday afternoon and the sun was merciless, cooking in a cloudless, crystal blue sky. Other than grasshoppers sending out mesmerizing vibrations from the field behind the house, all sound lay muffled under the weight of the day's heat. I was sitting with my back pressed against the basement's cool cinder-block wall, trying as best as I could to fit into the sliver of shadow alongside the house. I was pretending to concentrate on a book Harmon had given me that cross-referenced The Church's doctrine with that of the Old Testament. It was nearly nine hundred pages – Volume One in a set of ten – and laden with extrapolations from a man named John Wesley and dusted with the views of someone called St. Francis of Assisi. I hadn't the slightest notion who either was and felt even less inclined to find out. Besides, I was much too involved with my own immediate misery – having just spent a good half-hour tending to a testy nosebleed – to give the book the attention it deserved, or any attention at all for that matter. After a short charade and fighting the glare bouncing off the white gravel driveway, I discovered that its nine hundred pages made a much better pillow than a book.

It was only minutes later, after the sun had inched its way behind the roof's overhang, that I saw him. He was like a vision rising up out of the heat. He was coming across the field, his gait steady and powerful, his bag riding high on his shoulder. Kellen Manly had returned.

Kellen could jump out of bed at six-thirty, piss, splash water on his face, dress, drink three raw eggs from his Roy Rogers tumbler, sprint the half mile to work, and be there a minute before seven. Always.

I never knew quite what it was that drove Kellen, only that he was obsessive about living every minute. Being around him was like celebrating the Fourth of July every day. I was never quite sure if his energy level had a limit, or if it was so high that it acted as its own stimulant.

Sleep for Kellen was only something to be tolerated, and for never any more than five or six hours a night. I suppose he was afraid of missing something while he slept, of being denied even the smallest morsel that life might cough up. I couldn't imagine what there was to miss in Edenfield at any time, much less during the middle of the night, but what I failed to consider was Kellen's instinct for unearthing most everything the night had to offer.

His first night back was as familiar as our first meeting. It was like we hadn't missed a beat, like he had never left. We talked for hours, reliving most of what each of us had been through these past weeks. We were bawdy and irreverent and without the least regard for Sunday Evening Services.

That night, Mrs. Little played thunderously and well past the family's bedtime. There were a number of marches and show tunes, some old Hit Parade numbers, and even some borderline boogie-woogie. It was a cascade of rhythms. One tune after another. Effortless. Camp. Full of the night. Lusty and lifted. Reckless and naughty. Harmon was silent through it all.

What Kellen and I did to amuse ourselves was limited only by our imaginations, but the after-sundown options were infinite. We would, in the course of a night, pull up shrubs and switch them with those of the neighbors; switch license plates on cars and build bramble-and-log blockades in the middle of streets. We would push cars out of their driveways and leave them in the middle of the road, raid orchards and help ourselves to apples by the armloads, and stand knee-deep in the back waters of Loon Lake and fish for hours in total darkness. On nights with a full moon, we'd ride Elwin Cotter's biscuit-eyed quarter horses, bareback and hanging on for dear life, through his three hundred acres of alfalfa. We were like Comanches, wild and free.

One night we hitchhiked to Castle City to the Empress Lilly Burlesque. It was more wondrous than anything I had ever seen or imagined for that matter. We walked the entire seven miles back to Edenfield and never once talked about anything except the enchantment of the main marquis attraction, Miss Bubbles Clitor, and the dazzle she brought to her profession.

Once, we played a game of Ping-Pong to five hundred, with time-outs only to eat and use the bathroom. I defaulted after eight hours, exhaustion and delirium wearing me down long before they did Kellen.

More than once we raided Floyd Hanna's chicken farm on the west end of town. Floyd was old and crafty and lived believing that there would always be chicken thieves, so he slept with a twelve-gauge shotgun within arm's reach, or at least that's what folks claimed. True or not, it made little difference. We stole Floyd's chickens anyway and stuffed them into mailboxes alongside the road. We suspected he got most of them back, but he and Orlo Kirkum gave us many a long cold stare in and out of The Church. Nobody, though, seemed more put out than the mailman. His constant whining about nearly having a heart attack every time he dropped the door to a mailbox never seemed to lose its appeal. His being forever unnerved somehow swelled us with accomplishment and made repeat performances all the more satisfying.

The night we decided to raid Duncan's camp started out as an idea with little more than the potential for a laugh; then soon became an idea that wouldn't leave us alone, like a scab that demanded picking despite the many reasons that warned about leaving it alone. Leaving it alone, though, seemed too much like cowardice. Then, all the reasons *why we shouldn't* became the very motivators for *why we should.* It became a question of courage, something that appealed to our baser selves and with the right elements of danger and intrigue: things that made the night worthwhile.

The approach was all-important, even more so after we had worked our way to within thirty feet of his tent. Some sort of light, barely discernible, cast an amber glow through its canvas, a glow so dim that it appeared to be for nothing more than effect, like a lightning bug in a jar.

"What do you think he's doing?" I whispered.

"Shhhh," Kellen hissed, convinced that silence was our greatest ally.

Twenty feet. Kellen was no longer confident to shush me. He simply put his finger to his lips. Uncompromising silence was now the only thing that stood between safe harbor and an all-out Duncan Skinner keelhauling. I followed with blind allegiance and all the stealth that remained from my Cherokee ancestry.

What little moonlight there was lay hidden by the woods around us. It was so dark that it took us ten minutes to move another ten feet. But at this point, we had moved close enough to detect voices: gruff and mournful and distressed. A mixture of timbres, high and low. A kind of guttural brutality and an underpinning of forcefulness that spoke of Cro-Magnon; something that needed nothing but itself as a source of strength, and so vivid that it brought to mind the smell of sweat.

"What the hell...?" I whispered. Again, Kellen's finger shot to his lips, only this time his face was only inches from mine and grimacing. It was a reprimand. He meant for there to be exacting silence, severe, grave. I assented.

When we were within arm's length, the tent seemed to shudder and the noise, now something similar to grunting and rooting, took on another octave, then fell to something softer, but no less expressive. In an instant, the reality of what we were hearing came clawing its way into my consciousness. I was right away too warm. Guilt and embarrassment hit me with a double load, and I was desperate to be gone. I wanted to run, but somehow Kellen sensed it and clamped onto my wrist like he meant to snap it if I dared. The next thing I knew, the noises became strained and violent, the kind that came so often with nightmares. I waited, listening to those voices crescendo, then cascade to cleansing breaths, and then to solitude.

We waited until we heard stirring and fumbling before we slipped into the clump of trees at the back of the clearing. It was only minutes before the flap of the tent was thrown open and a pale light spilled onto the ground in front of it. It was little more than a candle glow, but enough to see that Becky was the first one out and that Duncan was not wearing a shirt. She had taken no more than a few steps before Duncan grabbed her and pulled her tight to him. I cursed myself for being there, and even more for not turning away. But at long last, she left without the aid of a light or without him by her side. We watched her disappear into the blackness and Duncan return to the orange glow inside his tent.

Kellen and I came away with a sense of guilt for having made ourselves a part of their rendezvous. We knew beyond a doubt that if Duncan ever found out, he would, in all likelihood and without regard to consequences, murder and mutilate us and our families as well. From that point on, fear replaced any sense of responsibility to confess. Becky Summers walked home alone in the pitch black that night, never knowing what Kellen and I knew. It would remain our secret forever.

I saw very little of Harmony after Kellen returned. She had long since ceased having dress-up performances for my benefit. From the full-throttle discourse that had come resounding through the floorboards after her last visit, I knew she had been found out – red shorts and all – and that the basement had, without any misgivings, been declared off limits.

My intimate knowledge of the Littles' affairs came to me with regularity through the floorboards, and often left me feeling like I was eavesdropping. I don't believe they were ever aware that their voices were so penetrating, or that the floorboards were such excellent conductors of sound. I'm sure it was the reason they never felt much compunction about discreetness. In the end, I was happy that Harmony had been reined in. She was already years ahead of herself and me to boot. Somehow, though, I didn't think I'd heard the last of her.

On nights without a moon, Kellen and I would swim naked and without as much as a splash in the highly chlorinated, in-ground pool in Marsha Tidewater's backyard. Though I could never convince Kellen, and God knows I had no way of proving it, there were nights when I swore I saw Marsha's curtains being swept to the side and her image etched opaquely in the window. The last time I ever swam there was the night she proved me right by joining us. It was dark enough so that the only thing I could be certain of was that she was tall and wispy and every bit as naked as the two of us. The rest of her was like a silhouette of a silhouette, dark on dark, visible only through a wishful imagination.

Marsha Tidewater's sense of play was immediate, and her stealth every bit as rehearsed as our own. But the thought of her being The Church's soprano soloist was enough to keep me very low in the water. The idea of the three of us naked in the pool seemed to serve Kellen well, seemed to make him more alive to its eccentricity. But as much as it was an affair with the senses, there was a kind of spirituality attached to it, a kind of alliance with the seeds of abandonment. I suspected that hers was a world in close proximity to ours; a world not intimately tied, but not altogether separate either.

I tried to keep my distance from Marsha as we swam, tried as best I could to go east when she went west, and vice versa. Kellen, though, had no problem in joining her, stroke for stroke; lithe and silken, and gliding like otters. Synchronized, choreographed, as if they had re-hearsed time and again; to the point where I wasn't certain she even knew I was there. That sense of wanting to be more than I was crept through me like an ageless and tireless enemy. It made me want to run from the realities that mocked me: my pale skin, my bony physique, all the unkind particulars of my gene pool. But I'd run before only to find nothing had changed when I stopped. So I stayed.

After a few minutes, I slowed down and swam only to observe and listen to Kellen and Marsha's throaty breaths. I thought about Carol and Cheryl and Bonitasue, wanting all three of them alongside me, here and now. And I thought of La'Randa, and what it would be like to know the touch and feel of her pressed against me in the water… skin on skin.

After a time, Marsha began swimming closer to me as if she had somehow sensed my longing, heard my silent pleas. Finally, I stopped in the shallow end where I could feel the force of the water flow past me as she made her turns. I was amazed at how purposeful her turns were, how hard she pushed against the end of the pool, then glided away straight and long. After a few turns, I maneuvered myself so that when she made her turns, the soft underwater swells would waft with volume between my thighs. Then on her next lap, I'd drifted so close that when she turned, her foot pushed against the top of my thigh. But almost before I could comprehend its magnitude, almost before I could ready myself for her return lap, she stopped at the other end and climbed out. She toweled off just enough so as not to drip, then disappeared under the cover of night, back behind her opaque windows and the sweep of her curtains.

I waited for some time before I got out. I needed several minutes to quiet myself, to think about what just happened. Kellen and I slipped out together, dressed without drying and walked home barefoot. He swore he was as shocked as I was about what had happened but said the most important thing now was to never tell. Telling would mean the end of Marsha Tidewater, and the definitive end to the two of us. She had to know we would never utter a word.

The fact that Kellen never wanted to disrupt his nights with more than a few hours of sleep often left him alone after I had gone to bed. I never suspected him of taking advantage of our sworn secrecy, but on more nights than one, when he finally wound his way to bed, he brought with him the faint bleach smell of chlorine.

There was a closeness I felt with Kellen that I could never quite explain or understand. It was just there, had been there all along, from the very first time we met. But there was something deep within me that resented him for being what I knew I could never be, for having what I knew I could never have, in particular when I thought of what he might be sharing, and what I knew I would never share, with the likes of Marsha Tidewater.

Chapter Twelve
Finesse and Know-How

To watch Kellen at work was a marvel. He was possessed with the strength and coordination that made everything he did seem effortless. His motions were not only smooth but he made each of them count. He was a man's man and everyone's envy except maybe for Duncan. He was someone whom most of the guys wanted to be like and most of the girls wanted to be with. He was blessed with presence, or aura, or karma, or whatever it was that affected those around him: gifted with finesse and know-how, like an old soul who had been here many times before.

Duncan was another story. He was every bit as capable a worker as Kellen, but less sophisticated, wrestling and muscling everything into place with brute force. There simply wasn't the patience for things like finesse. The older ways were what he knew: an honest day's work for an honest day's pay, a work ethic that had worked for his father and his uncles alike. It was good enough for them and that, by itself, made it good enough for him. Given his size, it was a formula that worked. Finesse was for piccolo players and people with concentrations in papier-mâché – people with delicate little hands and fingers.

Despite their differences, Kellen and Duncan were a team, laboring together and each pretending to be unmindful of how the other performed. Their competition was fierce but subtle; neither of them acknowledging that it even existed. And so it went, day after day. Never a victor or a victory, never a declared champion. But there were breaking points to such rivalries, times when other-than-honorable tactics were brought to play.

"Surprised you were able to keep up today," Duncan said, "what with all that homework you got." Duncan winked at me, though he was talking to Kellen. I noticed a hitch and a slight pause in Kellen's step. He knew exactly what Duncan meant. It wasn't the first time he had made inference to Kellen and Mrs. Little. Inferences that I had begun to suspect but could never know with certainty. "Yeah, sometimes makes me wish I was staying over there with you." Duncan's voice was slightly above a whisper as if it was a secret known only to him and Kellen. "Well, see you boys later," he said, peeling off toward The Fishes and Loaves.

I stood there alongside Kellen and watched Duncan take his long strides across the highway. "DUNCAN!" Kellen yelled. It was a commanding summon, just enough to ugly the air. Duncan stopped and looked back just before opening The Fishes and Loaves' big screen door. Kellen stood like he was rooted to the earth – feet planted and shoulders square to the highway – much like I imagined a gunslinger would stand just before going for his six-shooter. A longer than usual pause lingered between them, a pause that caused Duncan to let go of the door handle and turn around to face Kellen. An understanding grew out of their silence, more ominous than the dead-calm that followed.

Kellen brushed his lips with the back of his hand and asked in a tone just loud enough for Duncan to hear, "Just out of curiosity, how big a tip does Becky get for a midnight delivery? Figured you'd be the one to ask." And for the first time Duncan knew that we knew. He stood without batting an eye, locked in a death stare with Kellen. Seconds later, he turned back toward the big screen door and flung it wide, cold-staring us until it banged shut behind him. "Touché, Jackass," was the only thing I heard Kellen mumble. After that we walked the rest of the way home with nothing but the sounds of our footsteps and the weeds along the path brushing against our jeans.

"So what's the story with Mrs. Little, anyway?" I asked. I was tired of the mystery, the secrecy. What did Duncan know that I didn't?

Kellen lay on his bunk facing the wall and thumbing through some old dogeared issue of *NEWSWEEK.* He was dressed and ready to move into the night without a moment's notice. He knew I was really asking "What's the story with *you* and Mrs. Little" but gave no indication that he heard me.

"I mean why is she so subdued?" I asked. "So quiet?" He continued thumbing only now with a slight exaggerated flip of the pages.

I took it as a signal. There would be no response. "So standoffish."
I was pushing.

"I think the word you're looking for is *reserved*," he said, his words
firm, measured.

"Oh, *reserved*," I said.

He licked his thumb before turning the pages, and he turned them
much slower.

"As in *gathered?* " I asked.

There was a telling silence before he said, "Yes. Becoming though.
Don't you think?"

"In an odd sort of way," I said, "but it doesn't explain much. I just
think she's not altogether happy."

"How insightful!" he said. "Why didn't I think of that?"

"Why do you think that is?" I said.

"LOOK," he snapped, turning with lightning speed to face me. He
started to point but stopped. I waited, more frightened than I wanted to be.

In a semi-submissive gesture, he lowered his voice but not his eyes,
and in a suggestive tone said, "Maybe she just doesn't have what she
needs in her life." He looked at me without blinking, the way my
father did when I failed to see obvious truths.

"Do you know anything about dreams?" he asked. He was focused, serious.

"Dreams?"

"Yeah, dreams. The things you hope will come true; things you
believe will alter your life for the better."

"My daddy says if you were to put your dreams in one hand and
shit in the other, it'd be hard to tell which was which."

He looked at me as if I wasn't deserving of anything he had to say.
"Maybe for you," he said, "but my dreams are my hope. Hope, for
better or worse, is what sustains me."

I wanted to ask what this had to do with anything, when he said,
"But I do know this: when the day comes and we realize our dreams
will never be anything but dreams, hope dies."

I struggled for a meaningful comment, but none came. "Are you
talking about Mrs. Little?" I asked. He closed his eyes and turned
again to face the wall.

"So …" I said, feeling my way, "you're telling me she's lost all
hope for things ever changing … ever being better." He lay quiet and

still like some unmovable Buddha. I waited while he waited. "Makes me wonder what she had hoped for in the first place," I said. "But I'm guessing it was something more than Harmon." I knew full well Kellen was not about to let me enter this sector of his world. It was his and his alone, and I would have to find another way if I were to ever be allowed beyond his locked and guarded gate. "Right?" I asked, trying to puncture his silence. But his gesture had been a final one.

I rolled over and faced my own wall, the one that Harmon had built with his own hands out of half-inch, second-grade plywood. I lay awake for a long while before reaching for the switch to the overhead light, then lay awake in the darkness listening to the bullfrogs and crickets, and long enough to hear Harmon's grandfather clock strike midnight. I waited for a sound from Kellen, something other than his drifting in and out of sleep, something other than the low indiscernible mumblings directed at his dreams. But none ever came.

There were times, though not often, when pensiveness would seem to overcome Kellen almost against his will. Without warnings or precursors, at least nondetectable to me, he would slip into silences that were more than just momentary preoccupations, but more like distant journeys. On the surface, he was dead still, chameleon-like, as if the very air around him had snuffed him out and sealed him off. But more than anything else, it was his eyes that were the abdicators: hollowed looking things, opaque marbles without dimension or focus, vacant and unblinking and locked in eerie luminescence.

The first time he slid into this netherworld, I was caught unawares. It was enough, though, to make me survey the room around me, to map out various escape routes should it become necessary to save myself. I was not above a quick exit if the situation called for it. His *episodes* as I called them, made me aware that I was not above running and hiding if it would negate personal pain and suffering. I reasoned it was not cowardice, but something well within the framework of an acutely tuned sense of self-preservation.

Even from the beginning, it was clear that Kellen would have to get through these episodes without me. There wasn't anything I could do to change that. His departures were far and away too unpredictable a thing for me to understand. I was never sure if they would, without warning, turn him into a homicidal maniac or leave him on some catatonic plane where he would remain forever. It wasn't even something I wanted to explore. But after a number of them, I found myself becoming more intrigued than frightened, considering how fast they came on … and at the oddest times. I didn't know if he was even aware of them, but try as I may, and did, I could never dismiss the air of sinisterness that surrounded it. And on more than one occasion, I found myself feeling as though we weren't the only ones in the room.

How fragile he appeared during these times, as if he had been temporarily excused from life; as if he were lingering, blank and faceless, in a calm and meditative place comfortable enough to stay forever. I never knew what it was that possessed him, only that it did, and with imposing ascendancy.

Chapter Thirteen
Muted in Amber Hues

Kellen was through the cellar door and had leapfrogged over me and the chair I was slouched in before I could react. The chair tumbled backwards, spilling me and a half glass of grape Kool-Aid across the basement floor.

I was blurred by his attack and shrieking laughter. Sneak attacks were part of our play, and I was at once caught up in a centrifuge of color and crashing furniture – survival being the precursor and possessor of my will. And though I was shocked with adrenaline, I was no match for Kellen's strength and speed. I tried in desperation to spring free, but he had me by an arm and a leg. I felt like a sparrow in the jaws of a lion. I pleaded, but it made no difference. They were like ululations in the wind. Mercy was not part of Kellen's repertoire today, yet I struggled for the sake of dignity, clutching onto table legs and door jambs, anything within my grasp that might help spring me free.

Within seconds, he had wrestled me onto the floor of the shower stall, and despite my continued struggle, held me there long enough for jets of cold water to souse me clear to my underwear. My only consolation was that he, too, was soaked in the process. Ten minutes later we were shooting free throws in the driveway.

The evening was warm and humid and without a breeze, the kind where sweat comes without effort. Kellen was in a good mood and kept alluding to having a surprise for me. Something he said he had been saving. It was right about the time my skin was taking on a heavy coat of lather that I noticed a red Cadillac convertible pulling into the driveway.

It was like a dream: the blonde in the red Cadillac convertible had appeared out of nowhere, as solemn and forbidding as she appeared on my first day in Edenfield. In an instant, Kellen was at her side, smiling down on her behind the wheel. She seemed to radiate in the twilight, like she was the only living thing in a still-life photo, like everything around her was suppressed and muted in amber hues. Apart from a spaghetti-thin strap across each shoulder, she appeared naked behind the wheel. I stood motionless and alone in the driveway, waiting with a pronounced sense of fear for an invitation to come say hello.

There's a genuine sense of helplessness that comes from being alone in the middle of a driveway. And it wasn't until I had nearly exhausted myself with the pretense of being calm and collected that Kellen finally called me over. It was only then that I realized I was still holding the basketball. With a spike of adrenalin, I wheeled and let loose a fifteen-foot jumper. It was off the mark and ricocheted off the steel rim with convincing momentum, enough to send it slamming into Harmon's galvanized garbage cans that went crashing and banging down the cellar steps. Kellen's laughter rode high up in the evening air as I stepped weak-kneed toward them.

Right about that time, Harmon appeared at the side window, squinting at us as though he were staring into a bright light, then retreated.

"This here is my roommate, Weldon," Kellen said. He was all of a sudden genteel. "Bea Ardor," he said evenly, his head and eyes directing me to her radiance.

"How are you, Weldon?" she said, extending her hand. I watched as it came toward me, slowly and frame by frame, reaching for some invisible mark. I took it almost apologetically, as if I were somehow undeserving. With art and wonder, she made sure the soft flesh of her palm pressed fully against mine. I wanted to tell her I was fine, and then thank her for asking, but a surge of anxiety had shunted the circuit between my brain and my voice box. I knew the odds-on chance of my voice cracking at a time like this was too great to chance it, so I did what I thought was the next best thing: I held her hand a little firmer, shook it a little faster, and nodded in like time.

"Fine," I finally managed with more air than voice, escaping like it had been held under pressure. That's when Harmon reappeared, only this time at the front door.

Harmon gave the appearance of someone who had been napping. Extraordinary long pieces of hair, usually combed up and over the top of his bald dome, were hanging over his left ear, almost touching his shoulder. "Hello Bea," he said through his screen door, trying to wave and tuck his shirttail in at the same time. Bea managed to smile and wave before easing the Caddy into reverse. But Harmon was onto the porch, down the steps, and across the lawn in his stocking feet before she could get very far.

"It seems like such a long time," he said, gathering his long strands of hair and swooping them up and across his head, pressing them against his sweaty scalp.

Bea hesitated while smiles passed back and forth between them, and while Kellen climbed into the passenger's seat beside her. She said something that was eaten up in giddiness and why she needed to be getting along, all the while easing the Caddy into the street. But Harmon paid little attention and followed her all the way, calling out how wonderful it was to see her again and pleading with her not to be such a stranger. Without another word, Bea gave us a big wave and rolled off into the night.

Harmon and I stood there like a couple of lampposts by the side of the road watching the Caddy's taillights fade into nothingness. He was distant and silent, indifferent to my presence. I felt that he was, at least for the moment, operating somewhere outside of The Church's tenets. Looking at him standing there in his stocking feet and with his shirttail dangling like a piece of dirty laundry down the front of his pants, with his hair cursed to an eternity of disarray and his pants rumpled and hanging on for dear life to his all-but-non-existent rear end, I couldn't help but wonder if he had ever given thought to how he might be perceived. My guess was he hadn't.

He stood that way for quite some time, his hands buried deep in his pants' pockets and studying the now-empty road. As far as I could tell, Bea's visit had been more than a wistful diversion for him. It had been more like a fantasy fulfilled, however brief. And as revealing as it had been to his character, I couldn't help but have a little compassion for his despair. And even though the whole thing belied a bit of the wretchedness in each of us, his was one underbelly I wish I hadn't seen.

Without attempting to defend him, I recognized that it wasn't every day that a man's most intense fantasy appeared in his very own driveway, half naked and looking like Bubbles Clitor on a fuchsia-lit runway. It almost bordered on being unfair, considering that a fantasy is all that it would ever be. In this light, I didn't see him as being any different than anybody else. There had to be at least one such fantasy in each of us, one that victimized and reduced us to raw emotion; at least one that never quite let go until it had had its way with us, until it had driven us to the brink of our own myopic, self-centered longings and left us to dry and wither like so many grapes on the vine; at least one that connected us all to the world of infatuation, one that even time couldn't heal.

As I turned back toward the house and with the garbage cans still askew in the stairwell, I noticed Mrs. Little standing at the front door. Her eyes, too, were reflecting on the faded lights and the road that led everywhere if one only dared to take it.

The summer was not the same after I met Bea—my days or my nights—her voice and the touch of her tied in some inextricable way to my every thought, something I was careful to keep to myself, much like I expected was true for Harmon Little.

"What do you think of Sara Bennett?" I asked Kellen one afternoon as we were leaving the mill, and as Sara was making her way across the parking lot.

"Do you mean *what do I think of her abundance*?"

"Well ... yes!"

"Well, all I can say is wait till you meet Lizzy!"

Chapter Fourteen
A Hothouse Flower in the Middle of the Desert

Summer had clicked along at a rapid pace, but I had been too busy living it to pay much attention to its passing. The idea that I had survived it as well as I had, and without the aid of my mother, had significant implications for me, something I freely credited to emerging autonomy. I was comfortable with the idea that I had begun to make my mark on the world, at least in my own mind, at least for the time being.

Despite the frightening aspects of having to assume responsibility for my life, I was, in the quieter recesses of my mind, still living with my own sense of illusion and contradiction. My biggest concern was that my newfound sense of independence might somehow become barnacled with compromise. I saw compromise as a denial of instincts in favor of socialization. I wanted no part of it. I wanted intrinsic freedom, the kind where I alone determined everything from *how much* to *how often.* But then this, too, seemed contradictory what with my being at Edenfield. Still, I entered the school year certain of only one thing: that I saw myself as a hothouse flower in the middle of the desert.

Three days of freshman orientation came and went with a fervor. It was a whirlwind of faces and presentations; long days full of information similar to what was attached to Harmon Little's refrigerator door, none of which went without a complete and thorough assessment. As much as anything, it had demonstrated what a stranger I was to the world of academia as well as to The Church's policy and doctrine.

Throughout orientation, oddities arose with amazing regularity. But, by far, the most notable were the odds and ends of womankind. More to the point, the scarcity of the well-favored. It was as if a profusion of ill-fated blooms had been culled just for Edenfield in order to restrain the satyr within us. Of course, there were the exceptions, those few who were combed and creamed and precisely crafted and leaving one short of breath even at first glance. But it was those far from the likes of Cheryl and Carol and Bonitasue that held the greatest sway and made selecting a subject for healthy fantasies seem like work.

A one-on-one session with someone from the finance department highlighted orientation's final day. I was assigned to Etta Pritchett. Etta was from Michigan's Upper Peninsula and spoke with a part Canadian, part Scandinavian accent. Etta also shaved. She shaved each morning and, because of a pronounced five-o'clock shadow, each evening before dinner. Her face was oval, but flat and with a very strong-set jaw. Her skin was pulpy and fish-belly white, and her eyes held a hopeless and distant look that projected what she knew inherently: that spinsterhood would likely be her only bedfellow. Her hair was a dull brown and without the lightest wave. She kept it combed back flat against her scalp and fastened in a bun at the crown of her head. Her habit was to tie it so severely that it looked like a wet knot. Her dress was restricted by her own conviction: nothing beyond plain white blouses; long, loose-fitting black skirts; and black orthopedic shoes…sensible shoes. It was her life's uniform. Things like makeup and jewelry were nonexistent artifacts, reserved for people in other places and lands, people she prayed for regularly. Although Etta shaved her face, she refused to give the same consideration to her legs and was known campus-wide for not trusting deodorant. And though not openly condescending, she was forever on guard and only tolerant-to-a-point of anyone who she suspected was not born again. Etta was Harmon Little's secretary.

"Name?"

"Weldon Thatcher." There were no signs of breasts under her starched cotton blouse.

"Oh, so you're Weldon Thatcher," she said with a slight chink of surprise, but without a smile, her eyes darting cat-like between my crotch and the top of my head.

"In the flesh," I said.

She looked at me as though I had blasphemed. "And I, for one, am thankful you took the time to cover it." I waited for a smile, but it never came. She was serious.

"WELL, HELLO THERE, WELDON!" Sara Bennett's voice came

resounding above all the rest.

"Well, Sara," I said.

"Surprised to see me?" she asked with a broad smile, her cotton blouse stretched to the point of letting go.

"Well, yes!"

"I work for President Cannon during the school year," she said. "I only work at the mill during the summer."

"Oh," I said, struggling to keep my focus above her neckline.

"I see you've met Etta."

"Sort of," I said, not really wanting to formalize the acquaintance.

"Well Etta and I work here in the office. So, if you have any questions, we're here to help." She gave my arm a quick squeeze, flashed me a sugar-coated smile and walked off as if she had just found Jesus. Etta and I both watched after her as she sashayed in the direction of President Cannon's office. My gaze lasted a little longer than it should have; something Etta could not help but notice.

"We are each given certain attributes, Mr. Thatcher," she said, attempting to refocus me.

"Pardon me?"

"Some of them are gifts, others are millstones we must constantly work to overcome." Her eyes, as pale and chilling as an upper peninsula winter, bore into me without blinking, held me captive until she was confident that a word to the wise had been sufficient. "Well then," she declared, "down to business."

It took little more than a minute for Etta to compute the sum of my worth. And though it was no surprise, except to Etta, that I was penniless, it still served as an awakening; a time when I had to sit square shouldered to the world and announce that I had no money beyond what Etta and the Good Lord paid witness to at that very moment. Not only was there very little up-front money, but no back-up money either. None beyond what could be sweated out at the mill. Beyond my junior high school experience of being the only guy in the locker room without pubic hair, it was the most embarrassing experience I could ever remember.

I walked out of Etta Pritchett's sector feeling almost as dejected as I was humiliated. I had signed papers guaranteeing repayment of loans and affixed my signature to documents that would obligate me, I was certain, long past the time I would start to shrink. Debt, as swift and indelicate as any guillotine, had claimed me as one of its own.

The final ceremony of orientation was a cookie-and-Kool-Aid, get-acquainted-with-the-faculty affair. That was the first time I met Dr. Mack Cannon, the college president. From our very first hand-shake, I had the feeling of being drawn into an omnipotent presence.

"Weldon Thatcher," he said, his smile matching the crystal clarity of his voice. "It has a sound of greatness to it." I returned his smile, drawing my parched lips across my teeth. "I trust that your transition to Edenfield has been satisfactory?"

"Yes," I said, nodding my assurances.

"Good," he said. "And your summer at the Littles'?"

"Oh…memorable," I said, not doubting that he knew something about each person in the room.

"Good," he repeated. "I'll take that as a compliment to the Little's and use it as a way of welcoming you."

"Thank you," I said, eager to turn away from his direct eye contact.

"It's good to have you with us, Weldon," he added. "I hope we can come to know each other as friends and that you'll see me as a brother in Christ." He then gave me a gentle nod and a pat on my arm before moving on to the next waiting freshman.

Mack Cannon was the consummate college president. From the service of office to the presence of mind, he was, for all the right reasons, the college's guiding light. He was the man selected by the board of directors, in conjunction with The Church Council, as the marquis for Christian living and learning. Dr. Cannon was by all rights a scholar: dignified, poised, with the wit and charm to influence at all levels, and he did. He was capable and willing to captain a finite ship, and he did. He led by example and did it with compassion. He was honored among scholars and clergymen alike, and respected by both the student body and the community at large. He was their champion. And though his life reflected a profound dedication to academics, he was first a man of God. It defined him as clearly as his slender frame and the wave in his dark and meticulously combed hair. He was a man truly at peace with himself and his God, and Edenfield College had him as their very own.

I watched Dr. Cannon throughout the evening, moving from one student to another, touching, healing. He appeared to be giving bless-ings more than making introductions, moving among the students as an apostle of righteousness, a holy man doing what he does best.

Like Fulton Highlander, Dr. Cannon was a prominent member of The Church Council and an integral factor when it came to directing the flock. Between the two of them, they left little doubt about whom the Lord had chosen to map The Church's course. They were the stewards and guardians of The Church and all that it embodied. Not only were they appointed by the membership, but the product of their prayers as well.

Just prior to Etta Pritchett closing the evening with prayer, Dr. Cannon announced with a tone of regret that Dr. Elizabeth Llewelyn DeForté, professor of American and English Literature, would not be on campus for the upcoming year. She had taken a one-year sabbatical to pursue a course of study on John Milton. She was to be part of an independent group from Bob Jones University bent on providing us with evidence that Paradise Was Not Lost. He made a point of saying that she regrets her absence but feels blessed by the opportunity to serve with such distinguished fellows whose strength is clearly defined by their objective. She feels that her absence is an answer to God's calling and respectfully asks for our prayers.

From all those who knew her, it was evident that Dr. DeForté saw much work to be done in support of the scriptures. There were simply too many in the world who laid no claim to Jesus. I came to understand that her real quandary, though, along with a clear majority of the student body, was trying to understand why.

Chapter Fifteen
So Far It's Worked Pretty Good

"Do you ever pray?" I asked.

Kellen had the front brim of his Sam Snead straw turned straight up, making him look a little like Bugsy of the Bowery Boys. "Why do you want to know?" he asked.

"Just wondering, that's all. Wondering what you rely on for inner strength."

"You're beginning to sound like Harmon. You been hanging around Harmon?"

"I'm too fanatical for Harmon. I just want to know what you depend on when you're down or maybe a little scared. You know … when you're feeling unsure about things."

"Pretty heavy stuff there, Weldon ole boy. You feeling a little unsure about something?"

"You never know. But how about it? Do you pray?"

"…I don't know if I'm in the mood for this."

"Okay, forget it."

"Look," he said, "you feel a little unsure sometimes. So what? You have a bad day. Who doesn't? You think if you say a little prayer, do this little spiritual mind dance, God's going to come and wipe up after you?"

"Isn't that the way it works?"

"For some it might. And I guess for some, He's done just that. But I'm not so sure it's a *guaranteed* thing. I mean if it were foolproof, He would have cleaned up Harmon Little a long time ago."

"Maybe Harmon's happy the way he is."

"Now I know you've been hanging around him. The two of you play Ping-Pong, right?"

"Is it your opinion that I'm benefiting from your sarcasm?" I tried not to sound edgy.

"Hey, look, all I'm saying is that you've got to keep perspective. You're not going to get everything you want, even if you pray. Life is not that way. It's not that painless."

"Are you saying I shouldn't pray?"

"I'm saying you shouldn't place your God in an obligatory position."

"What's that supposed to mean?"

"It means you shouldn't expect Him to bail you out without some effort on your part."

"You mean, like playing by all the rules?"

"Yeah. *His* rules. It's a contingency."

"Always?"

"No self-respecting God would have it any other way."

"So where does that leave me?"

"Well, for what it's worth, I believe there's a plan for each of us. And as best as I can tell, you just gotta play the hand you were dealt. That's about as close as I can come to making sense of it."

"That's it then? You're telling me you don't pray?"

"I didn't say that."

"So, you *do* pray?"

"I *have* prayed."

"Well thank you for half-answering the question."

"You're welcome."

"But when you prayed, where were your prayers directed?"

"What kind of question is that?"

"Humor me. Who did you pray to?"

"To God. But then Jesus is mixed in there too. I mean, Jesus is the only one, as far as I know, to ever come back from the dead, so I'm thinking that makes him omnipotent enough to be part of the prayer chain."

"So, you *do* pray."

"I *have* prayed," he said, annoyed that I would ask him again.

"But how about *these* days? Do you pray these days?"

"I think about it. But to tell you the truth, that last time seemed to do it for me. I prayed that it would cover me for all time."

"And ...?"

"So far it's worked pretty good."

CHAPTER SIXTEEN
War Was Always Imminent

Two days before classes began were given to registration and the mayhem of returning upperclassmen. What with all the moms and dads, trucks and cars, and the army of relatives and friends, the campus took on a look of three thousand rather than its standard enrollment of just over three hundred. Kellen and I carried my suitcase and my single cardboard box from Little's to my new home on the third floor of the dorm in one easy trip. I had accumulated little over the summer beyond a couple of *Crime and Punishment* magazines and a tattered copy of *Lady Chatterley's Lover,* all Duncan Skinner hand-me-downs. I was comfortable with having little. It was tidy.

My last night in Harmon's basement had been underscored by a note that Harmony left on my pillow. It said to meet her at midnight in the field behind the house. The word *urgent* was printed in big block letters below her name. Her defying the edict to stay out of the basement was an act of daring, something that made me want to be more like her, but the idea of a clandestine rendezvous with a fourteen-year-old in hotpants exceeded even my wildest notions of boldness. Just before midnight, I burned her note over the stove, then lay in my bunk thinking how she was most likely out there in the field at that very minute, waiting. At one point, I thought about going to her just to hear what she thought was so urgent, then thought that my not going would be a clearer message than anything I could say in person. I slept with a restlessness that night, half expecting to wake and find her standing over me, staring at me in my sleep. As far as I know, she didn't.

Kellen chose to stay at the Littles' rather than the dormitory. He insisted that living alone had become a necessity for him, that it made him an all-around better performer. Besides, the unusual hours he kept were less likely to be noticed, less likely to be challenged. He was among a handful living off campus, in housing similar to the Little's.

My roommate was a Roadrunner look alike. He was short and wiry with coarse auburn hair and had a medium-to-severe overbite and skin emblazoned with pimples. His speech was rapid and adenoidal, and he reveled in the fact that he was from North Carolina and had been raised, along with four older sisters, by his fully ordained and Pentecostal preaching grandmother. He had, very early on, been redeemed by The Holy Spirit and saved and sanctified at the very altar where his grandmother preached. For the most part, I found him courteous to a fault and humble to the point of embarrassment. He continually called me "Sir," and punctuated most everything said with "Praise the Lord," "Amen," or "Thank you, Jesus." His thanksgivings were endless, and he never left the room without his Bible, carrying it with him like a shield, even to the bathroom along with his toiletries. His name was Erlin Shadwell, and aside from his nightly and undeviating compulsion to masturbate, he was the benchmark for Christian young men everywhere.

Masturbation was simply part of Erlin's routine. An activity much like working out; something to help shed the anxiety and stress of academics and the complexities and ambiguities of transitioning into adulthood. To his credit, he would hold off until lights were out and his prayers no longer rended the air. The act itself, though, was aggressive and assaulting, done with force and determination, and sounding like someone sawing meat with a dull knife.

"Erlin, what's going on over there?" It was always my intention to be obvious.

"WHAT? Nothing!" He sounded winded. Like he had just made several fast breaks up and down the gym floor.

"Are you alright?"

"Yeah. Why?" I could hear him swallow hard, frustrated that darkness hadn't been an adequate shield against his trespass. "It sounds like you're beating yourself up or something."

"Oh. I'm just a little restless, that's all." His voice had tremor.

"Well try some deep breaths or counting sheep," I said. "You're keeping me awake." I wanted to suggest a cold shower but dismissed it in lieu of his sensitivity. But the fact remained that he needed direction, and the shower stalls seemed to be the perfect answer. They were private and clean. They also provided the perfect alibi if he got caught. He could always say he was simply washing his penis. And given that it was his, he could wash it anyway he saw fit. It made perfect sense.

Before too long, our room took on a heavy rancor of musk. It was on the level of a forgotten, sweat-soaked jockstrap that had smoldered in the bottom of a gym locker through the months of July and August. It only took one visit to my room to convince Harmon Little that my complaint was more than just my imagination.

Some days later, Harmon pulled me aside to let me know that he had *fellowshipped* with Erlin and that everything had been restored spiritually. For Harmon, trouble could always be traced to a tear in one's spiritual fabric. I interpreted what he said to mean Erlin had been given a sermonette of sorts, one filled with things like guilt and the moral responsibility of restraint, something Erlin would be eager to embrace and even find delight in its ensuing remorse. In the end, Harmon's resolution was that I should simply buy a wick air freshener for the room. He thought pine scent would be nice.

With a student body of just over three hundred, it was still possible, though barely, to retain the practice of serving meals family style. Sitting eight to a table, boy-girl-boy-girl, was part of the socialization process, which forced us to feel the presence of one another and mingle our auras, whether we liked it or not.

The staging area prior to meals was a huge common room outside the dining hall. As soon as the doors were opened, the girls would lead the way into the dining hall and occupy every other seat around each table. The boys would then follow and fill in between them. There were no alternatives. Without such an arrangement, many might never have known the wonder of opposites.

There was little that could depict the dauntlessness with which the girls filed past us at mealtimes except to say they did it in much the same easy way that heifers go to milking. In turn, some of the boys were driven to mimic the urgent and disquieting sounds of bulls: their expressions of what they saw as nature being *out of balance.*

Skirmishes between the floors—pranks of the most egregious kind —were a common practice. Though the third floor against the first floor was probably the most embattled. I was caught up in it from the outset and developed an almost patriarchal pride in the third floor's defense. There were only two things from my perspective that loomed as major concerns. One was that Erlin, and a disproportionate number like him, were my comrades in arms, which meant their combined offense and defense amounted to prayer and turning the other cheek. The word VICTIM oozed from their every pore. The other was that Duncan lived on the first floor.

Duncan and I continued to work at the mill as our schedules permitted. We were friends, through-and-through. But each night after the library and the snack bar closed, and when everyone had pretty much ambled back to their rooms, all bets were off. War was always imminent.

Chapel was every morning from nine to ten, complete with a boundless entourage of speakers from seminary students to retired clergy, from missionaries to members of the staff, from the president of the student council to the president of the college. The roster was inexhaustible, and each delivery as diverse as its deliverer. The speakers condoned and condemned, praised and cajoled. There was humor and reason, unction and revelation, apportionments of motivation and guilt, and even motivational guilt. There were prophecies, moments of hellfire and damnation, and most always testimony and song. To Edenfield, chapel was its all-inclusive vehicle to exaltation, and its messages the road maps to our destiny. They were, altogether, indisputable truths ... but only as The Church knew them. I went because they took attendance.

The dorm wars began in earnest during the third week of the semester when someone defecated squarely in the top-dead center of Erlin's pillow. It was an ominous looking thing, dead but very much alive. Even the pine scent air freshener was no match for its bite. Erlin and I stood flinched and reverent before it, almost as if we expected it to speak. It railed with density and size. It was a trophy.

Neither of us said anything. The shock was, by itself, a silencer. Finally, Erlin murmured, "Thank God none of it got on my grand-maw's bedspread."

Before disposing of it, Erlin thought the third-floor proctor ought to see it. The proctor was an upperclassman, seasoned in such matters, and immediately had the entire third floor file past so they could get a good look. Amidst the combined disgust and hilarity, the message echoed clear: this had been an open act of aggression and a declaration of war, and any one of us could be next. It was then and there that the most ill-conceived group of semi-intellectuals ever assembled declared a united front. As could be expected, though, there were a few dissenters who wanted to pray about it first. With or without them, war had begun.

After an exhausting time at the library listening to Duncan prattle on about how insignificant and unnecessary small men were (men like me), and that there was already strong evidence that natural selection was making fewer and fewer of them, I headed back to the dorm. I could only sit for so long in the cradle of such scholasticism.

As soon as I reached the top of the stairs, I couldn't help but notice a total lack of activity. There were, however, strange noises, intense and painful, filtering into the hallway. And the closer I got to my room, the more pronounced the sounds became. What I feared most was soon confirmed. The sounds were coming from my room.

My entrance was one of thundering bravado: nostrils flared, chest pumped, adrenaline at its peak. What I fully expected to find was Erlin working his way toward orgasm. Instead, what I found were twelve fully clothed Edenfieldians crouched and kneeling in every square inch of the room. They were huddled shoulder to shoulder, slumped over beds and desks, dressers and chairs; one was even inside the closet. Their hands were clasped, and their heads were bowed and bobbing. Their bodies heaved with the sorrow and joy of heavenly contact. They were praying, one after the other. The smell of perspiration stung the air.

I stood frozen, unsure of my place in the universe. It was like having stumbled into a great unknown, not knowing which way to turn, or whether to turn at all. They continued totally unaware of my presence. I was alone amid their frenzy, alone amidst the heavy traces of body heat and breath. I wanted to leave, but there was something keeping me from it. The whole scene, though mystifying, felt out of sync with my body rhythms, with my personal solstice. Yet, I stayed and watched in amazement while their voices continued to mingle and mount. They were expressive and unencumbered, hawkish and full of celestial fire. And when one finished, another would begin.

I soon discovered that prayer meetings were a nightly thing. Substantive. A chance to relax with the boys. A bona fide alternative to poker.

We were never able to gather any hard and fast evidence as to who fouled the gold floral pattern of Erlin's pillow, but the name most immediate on everyone's mind was Duncan Skinner. The act itself was almost a dead giveaway. Who else would have been so brazen as to mark the enemy's camp in such a fashion? And who else could have produced a thing of such proportion?

Without much difficulty, I was able to scrounge a stack of *Playboy* magazines from the boys at the mill and place them in the back of Duncan's closet. Their frayed and dog-eared condition was a clear sign that they had been pored over and studied at length. I then placed an anonymous and well-meaning phone call to the dorm director urging him to visit Duncan Skinner's room. I hinted that there were items in his closet that led me to believe he was in need of prayer.

The visit brought scandal. Duncan was caught in the crosshairs with nowhere to run. He was brought before the dorm council, reprimanded by President Cannon himself, assigned fifty hours of campus service and placed on behavioral probation. The final straw was his parents being informed that he might benefit from a run of spiritual counseling. War had now moved to a heightened level.

Each class began with prayer. It was in the spirit of learning that we were all asked to bow our heads while the instructor prayed that we be granted refinement, inviting such things as wisdom, insight, reasoning, and understanding. The more creative would pray for things such as perception, intuition, reflection, and inquiry. And those who thought we might actually be listening would ask that we be blessed with things such as augmentation, resolution, cognition, and even invention. It was just another tool.

For Edenfield, spiritual enhancement was the precursor to redemption, the school's life's blood and the irrefutable purpose for its being, not only its foundation for Christian learning, but the premise for a life of service to God and man alike. The meek shall inherit the earth; the first shall be last and the last shall be first were the cornerstones of its faith and the manifest priority for all who held tight to its teaching. Enhancing it was Edenfield's out-and-out charge. It was a trust that filled our days and nights, and one that worked to shore us against the debilitation that comes from idle hands and minds. It was intended as integral to our Edenfield experience and tied to the hope that it would become our avocation, if not our vocation. Participation, however, was dependent on one's conviction. If conviction was soft or lacking, then there was peer pressure and guilt to restore one's sense of discipleship. Peer pressure was a natural outcropping of campus life. Guilt was more of an administrative function.

From the faithful to those who tried to be; from the saved and sanctified to those who weren't so sure; and from prospective converts to those who had fallen away, there was a club or an organization. Their purpose: spiritual enhancement … of course. They were varied and far-reaching, accommodating enough to reach even the most sensitive and susceptible. For the idealists, there was *The Sound of God's Children.* For the extroverted, there was *The Crusaders.* For the opportunists, there was *Young Christian Republicans.* However, there was no *Young Christian Democrats* (it was not an oversight). For the beleaguered, there was *Christian Youth Services.* The needy found purpose in *The Church League* where they were allowed to usher, set up tables and chairs, and bake for faculty and community functions. For the servile, there was *Future Ministers, Future Missionaries,* and *Disciples for Christ.* For the idle, yet well-intentioned, there was *The Edenfield Society* and *The Christian Women's Auxiliary.* For the undefined, there was *The Yearbook Staff.* And for those who were just somehow unable to identify with any particular faction – those islands in a stream – there was always church on Sunday.

My connection to the mill was tied with a very tight knot. All the money I earned was forwarded directly to the school for tuition, leaving me to become very adept at budgeting a five-dollar stipend my parents sent me once a month. Overall, I had settled into a routine that seemed to be working favorably. I had remained healthy, hadn't missed a class, and my attitude, for the most part, had tended toward the positive. There was, however, one jutting irritation: I was flunking. And after the first marking period, I was placed on academic probation. I ate well, played and slept well, but somewhere in the mix of it all failed to grasp what was most immediate: the strengthening of my mind and the purpose of my being at Edenfield in the first place. At first blush, I thought of it as a mere oversight. The administration, however, took a far less casual view, one that stressed that I was running out of rope … and fast.

Irony of ironies, Harmon Little was my counselor – and my floundering academically prompted both his attention and concern. I sat facing him in much the same way I had with Reverend Mayfield only months before.

"Let me ask," he began. "How are you doing spiritually?" It was always the spirit first. Everything else in due time. It was the order of things.

"Fine," I said, smiling and wide-eyed.

Contemplative seemed to be the only word that fit the wrinkle in his forehead. I sensed he was not satisfied with quick retorts or one-liners. I fidgeted, cleared my throat, and shifted in my seat.

"You know," he said, "often when people experience personal crisis, the underlying causes are not always readily evident." He spoke with some degree of compassion, though what I sensed was an offering to hear my confessions. There could be only one true answer as to why my grades were suffering: I was in a spiritual fog.

"I'm actually doing quite well spiritually," I said, trying to employ the divine without being overtly obvious.

"Good," he said. "Good."

I kept my smile broad and full of love, letting him know that it was okay to move on.

"Tell me," he said, the wrinkle in his brow growing deeper, "do you set aside time for personal devotions each day?"

"Well …" I said, my mind racing for an acceptable lie, "my schedule is so varied, what with classes and working at the mill and all, that I just have to devote whenever I get the chance."

His look went from deep thought to peculiarity. I began to feel warm.

"You know," he said, removing his glasses and massaging the bridge of his nose, "we may want to talk with Dr. Cannon about your situation."

"Ahhh, actually," I said, fumbling for the proper protest, "I wouldn't want to elevate my problem to that level. As a matter of fact, I've already … aahhhh … cut back on my hours at the mill. Yes. Fewer hours. More time for study." I shook my head yes very fast and without let-up, hoping to boost his understanding.

He replaced his glasses, folded his hands on his desk, and said in a tender voice, "I just want you to know that if there's ever a need to talk, to unburden yourself perhaps, please know that I'll always be available." He was squinting now, even though there was no sun. His lips, as always, were pooched as if waiting for a kiss.

After a moment or two it became evident he was waiting for my response. "Oh, yes. Yes. And thank you." I leaned forward to shake his hand. "Thank you ever so much." For a moment, thoughts of Reverend Mayfield and his mildewed office came in a rush … Carol and Cheryl and Bonitasue in its wake.

"You know," he said, not letting go of my hand, "there's a lot we can do. Just the two of us. Working together. Praying together. Helping you to find that personal relationship with God." I heard myself asking for God's help, to be delivered from one of His own.

"Yes," I exclaimed with a stressed smile.

"Good," he said, finally letting go of my hand. "Why don't we have just a word of prayer before you leave."

"Mr. Little," I said in a pleading and confidential tone, "I don't mean to be disrespectful, but I have to use the bathroom. And it's urgent." I bounced for impetus.

"Oh," he said a little surprised, "by all means. We'll pray another time."

I assured him that we would, then darted from his office in a manner I thought consistent for someone with a bowel in spasm. I had no doubt we would pray again.

Gilroy Hall was a huge dorm in the style of an early twentieth century veteran's hospital. It was a dark, institutional brick covered with ivy, and with two very large, ill-fitting doors at its entrance. It housed one hundred and fifty men, fifty to a floor. Directly opposite it was Angel Hall, its mirror image, only for women. Separating the two was The Quad: a huge expanse of lawn with walkways and benches, a fountain, a flagpole, and a huge stone cross.

The Quad was a rallying point and on-going hub of activity. On fair days, it was a place to mingle and sun, and even engage musical instruments. It was also large enough to provide quiet places for those who chose to study or meditate. Flirting and teasing and tossing Frisbees were every bit as common as proselytizing, witnessing, and debate. The Quad was a common arena for a myriad of expressions. That's why it was the ideal place to leave Evda Nica, king of first-floor prayer meetings, bound, gagged, and duct-taped to the base of its big stone cross just before dawn. War was escalating.

The hijinks between the floors became close to intolerable after the incident with Evda Nica. Electricity and water went off at all hours. Wasp nests were hung from light fixtures in the middle of hallways; 'possums, garter snakes, and bullfrogs were released on one floor after another. Bloodcurdling screams, and always in the dead of night, pierced the halls with savagery and scurrilousness ... just for the fun of it. Rooms were trashed with compost, and shoes were dipped in bright red and gold paint. Beards and moustaches were drawn on pictures of girlfriends with permanent markers, and manure heaped with great care onto doorknobs. Toilets were made to back-up, windows were painted over, and textbooks were confiscated and hidden for ransom. The struggle for one-upmanship was endless but brought a certain light to creativity. That is until the first floor became chafed at having to clean up the two dozen eggs that had been broken in brilliant sunburst patterns all over their larger-than-large bathroom.

It was only days before the first floor did the unpardonable: they pulled the fire alarm, but only after they had tied ropes from each of their doorknobs to the one directly across the hall, making it look like they had been victims of a major prank: trapped in their rooms and forced to crawl out their windows.

Dr. Cannon, the entire volunteer fire department, and a sizeable number of faculty – all having been pulled from their beds by the alarm – assembled the entire student body in the chapel auditorium. It was four a.m. and Dr. Cannon's demeanor, as scarlet as the flush on his face, struck with unassailable fury. The wars were over.

Chapter Seventeen
Airy, Sexy, and Fraught with Impulse

Those balmy summer nights were the ones I remembered most, when Bea would pick us up, Kellen and me, outside of town. She preferred it that way. Keeping a distance between herself and Edenfield was something she insisted on maintaining.

"People in Edenfield always want to mind your business for you," she liked to say. The beauty was in the way she said it. It was art in the form of disdain. She had her own way of being cheeky.

It wasn't long after our first meeting that she and Kellen prodded me into tagging along – just the three of us and her Cadillac she called Linda Sue. At first, I protested just enough to be polite, but not enough to refuse altogether. It was the beginning of a friendship I never anticipated. Right from the beginning, right from the very first night, I could sense something special between Bea and me, something kindred, much like what I felt with Kellen. It was intimacy of an endearing kind, nothing that needed nurturing to take root, but one already affixed with a bloom.

After several all-night excursions, allowing ourselves to be vulnerable and sharing secrets I never knew I had the courage to divulge, I began to know Bea as both a playmate and a friend, a connection that grew right along with the liberation I was beginning to feel. Still, there were times when tagging along made me feel very much like a third wheel. So much so that I found myself making excuses not to go. But it was to no avail. I had been adopted. Like it or not, I was part of the team. My feelings of being intrusive were never allowed beyond the time it took Bea to shoot me one of her dagger-eyed disapprovals, and for Kellen to physically toss me into the back seat.

I valued how Kellen and Bea made me feel, how integral a part of their lives I had become in such a short time, despite their bankrupt treatment of my ghoulish nosebleeds. But, as close as I felt to them, I was often confused about what Bea and Kellen were to one another. So often like sweethearts, so often like brother and sister. And though I felt like a brother to Kellen, I had no idea what I was to Bea. I was, obligingly, a friend and confidant – half of whatever it was that caused us to care for one another. But as the weeks passed, I couldn't deny that I wanted it to be more – more than just a friend, and certainly more than a brother. And though the three of us weren't big on much of anything except being together, we embraced what that gave us: a sense of belonging. We laughed and joked and delighted in the idea of being outlaws; full-on with barbs and righteously stalwart in denouncing the games people play without recognizing the ones we played ourselves. We were critical of those with influence and sympathetic to those affected by it. We pitied those bound by misgivings and sat in judgment of those bound by doctrine. In large part, we were malcontents, undefined and without roles, and defiant of pressures that sought to tie us to statutes of any kind. We were committed to making life as simple as we could for ourselves, and we settled for nothing less than it being airy and sexy and fraught with impulse. It was, as far as our understanding could reach, our formula for freedom. We knew it was decadent, and we just knew it would last forever, as incestuous as it may have felt at times.

On Saturdays, it was nothing for us to stay out all night. Linda Sue was like a house on wheels. We would drive hundreds of miles – always too fast and always, weather permitting, with the top down. Kellen and I would tell Harmon we were hitchhiking to my parent's house for the weekend. He was forever insistent on a word of prayer before we left, and I was forever guilty about the lie.

We spent a lot of those summer nights by the river. But my favorites were the ones with a big moon and the way it sent shadows to fill and darken the deep narrow space between Bea's breasts. We were as burlesque as the moons were corruptible, taunting and teasing and sprinting to the river's edge, its sharp-edged reeds knifing against our legs, then hurling ourselves off its bank, crashing and gliding, tense and naked, through its icy waters ... and with the moon casting a light that was as partial to her areolas as it was to her eyes.

But it was somewhere in the excesses of August, and that first-ever jolt of bourbon, that she became fastened to my every thought.

"Here," Bea said, her voice coming out of nowhere.

"Huh?" I was preoccupied with the way the light from the moon made her bare shoulders glow as if they were under a black light.

"Here," she said, holding the bottle out in front of me. It was sour mash. *Blackjack,* she called it. She gave me one of her trademark smiles and pushed it closer to me. I was still wet and shivering from our midnight swim. We all were. But just as I reached for the bottle, our fingers brushed, then lingered for perhaps a second longer than they should have. I felt it long afterwards.

I sat staring at it before taking a swig, conscious that she was watching me, maybe even wondering what to do with me, then took an even bigger swallow, knowing full well I wasn't given to its fieriness. I tried not to grimace. "Smoooooth," I said, despite it burning my throat and chest like one of Mother's onion poultices.

Bea was six years older than me and had attended Edenfield five years earlier, long enough to learn what they expected and who expected it. She left with a sense that there was much more to life than what Edenfield was willing to reveal. Doses of reality hadn't come fast enough for her while she was there, or in big enough chunks, and had left her with more appetite than experience. And since time was quintessential for her, she decided not to devote any more of it to Edenfield. She never returned after her sophomore year.

"Smoooooth," she said mockingly. There was something intense about being close to Bea in the moonlight. Her presence had always been reassuring. Settling. Calming. But tonight was the opposite. There was a worldliness about her, to her gestures, to her simplest moves: the way she rolled her head, hummed snatches of love songs, and toyed with the ends of her hair, even the way she stretched and arched her back as if lifting herself toward the sky, as if making some kind of offering to the moon.

I struggled to keep from becoming obvious, though lust seemed to be gaining an upper hand. I tried to reason that my thoughts were mere collisions of the heart, but I knew in dead earnest that I stood at the brink of my own fire-out-of-control, experiencing a hedonism substantive enough to dwarf my mother's prayers.

Bea sipped at the Blackjack, then waited, her eyes full on me, then swallowed hard, its fire dissolving with a tiny shiver and the trail of sweetness on her breath. I sat forward, propped on the edge of the backseat while she passed the bottle to Kellen. I could smell the river in her hair, see it catching the moon. She was all too inviting, the way she rubbed her shoulders and arms as if with an invisible towel, the way she laughed – the huskiness of it – and the way she liked her lips. She was unhurried, deliberate, beyond flirtation.

The bottle came around again, and then again, until it worked its way through me, warming and triggering my longing to claim Bea as my own. They were base desires, but tantamount to what I sought: the softness of her neck, her hands in my hair; her stretched and taught, wet and warm alongside me. I closed my eyes to the very notion, and for an instant, images of Carol and Cheryl and Bonitasue danced before me – joining the carousel already swirling in my head. I could feel my heart and chest, drum and drummer, pounding, wanting Bea more than air. I wanted to know the full length of her, her flush and swell; wanted the invite to all that lay secreted away and to pull my breath through the numbing scent of her musk. I wanted to scream her name.

"THATCHEROO!" Kellen was animated, energetic – as always – his voice echoing from some far-off place. "THATCH!" His barking was mixed with laughter. Bea's laughter was there too, but softer, throatier.

"Let's set him up," she said.

"I've got a better idea," I heard Kellen say, "Let's let him sleep." There was a moment of severe silence, then a second or two of my own labored attempts to sit upright. After that, things washed to nothingness. The Blackjack and I slept thick and sodden under the blanket of a balmy moon-filled night, the huge backseat of Linda Sue like the belly of a whale.

My longing for Bea was a scenario that played out many times over the summer, right along with the fantasies I kept of her, of us. But it wasn't until months later, during those first days of fall, that I was able to hold them up to the light; those blissful and warm October days before I stopped second guessing myself, before I was truly able to admit what she had become to me. And it wasn't until early November, just before Fall Revival, that I knew, once and for all, that I would be unable to keep it locked up forever.

CHAPTER EIGHTEEN
Fall Revival

Eight weeks into the semester left many of us feeling as though we had acquired at least a veneer of experience, enough so that the glaze of wide-eyed naivety so prevalent on freshman faces was seen with less and less frequency. In its place, though, was a heaviness about the eyes, evidence of insistent regimen and routine. It was a kind of weathering, the hardening to unexpected workloads, prayer meetings, devotions, chapel, Sunday school, church, and the myriad of Christ-oriented, God-fearing assemblage. We had in a very short time found ourselves stomping through the foothills of spiritual and intellectual catechism. Despite it all, even the sermons reminding us that *God could be vengeful,* it hadn't been enough to prepare us for The Fall Revival.

Eight weeks into the semester was enough time to become acclimated, but not yet stymied. It was time enough to feel comfortable, to develop a sense of trust, but not be removed from the shed of vulnerability. This is what made most of us so malleable to Edenfield's principal purpose: the preparation and spiritual conversion of our souls. Soul conversion was an arduous task, but there was little question that we could write our own ticket, both for this life and the one hereafter if we but offered ourselves at the altar ... accept Edenfield's most lauded intention.

To its credit, Edenfield made no misgivings about its purpose, gave no illusions about its being anything other than for the glory of God, and held no truth as sacred as its "first-to-last, always-and-forever" Christian duty to see that its purpose be fulfilled. I suppose it was all a matter of perspective, but as an eighteen-year-old freshman, I was content with simply being housed and fed. The task of preparing for an afterlife was something far-more reaching, even terrorizing, than what I'd been, able to confront. It meant, of course, that in the interim I worried more often than I wanted about dying. I likened it to living without life insurance. Still, there was something intrinsically appealing about charting one's own course despite the constant reminders about the dangers of living without Christ's assurances. The denouement of these reminders, I soon learned, culminated in the workings and celebration of The Fall Revival.

The Fall Revival was always during the first week of November. It was, without compromise, a time of cleansing, a time for the atonement and reconciliation of sins, a time for declaring who and what we were and where our feet were planted. It was a time that denoted where one's house was built – on solid rock or sinking sand – and a time that did as much to divide as it did to unite. The Fall Revival was purposed, a time for the out-and-out acquisition of souls, a harvesting for Christ.

The Church was filled to capacity. Nine hundred of us: students, faculty, and the community at large. So attended that we sat on the balcony steps and stood as many as two deep along the walls. Even the accordion panels dividing the sanctuary from the fellowship hall were collapsed out of the way, freeing up enough space for another two hundred or so. We were, shoulder to shoulder and, row after row, an army for Christ.

Duncan thought it was a good idea if we sat together. There were very few times he didn't think of himself as my big brother. For reasons I couldn't explain, I didn't mind.

When the sanctuary lights began to dim, signaling that the service was about to begin, I gave the congregation a quick look to see if I could spot Kellen. I found him sitting expressionless in the last row of the balcony, staring off into space.

"Do we have to be here?" I asked Duncan in a rough whisper while still looking up at Kellen. Duncan turned and followed my stare. "Every night this week, little brother. Harmon himself personally checks the dorm. Every room." Duncan loved coming across as a purveyor of truth, but moreover, mixing it with doom. It was a salient cunning, something he accepted as his calling.

The choir entered from the rear of the sanctuary with their white-satin gowns radiating under the now brilliant lights and with "The Battle Hymn of The Republic" reverberating softly from their cores. They stepped two-abreast down the center aisle, their cadence slow and in perfect time with an imaginary drumbeat. They were like descending angels. Wave after wave. Thirty of them. Christian soldiers. Bearing toward the cross.

Without breaking stride or compromising a note, they crisscrossed at the end of the aisle, weaving, one in front of the other, and ascended the stairs on either side of the altar. Once on the altar, they crossed in front of each other again, weaving like delicate stitches through intricate fabric. On they went, in perfect harmony and order until they had assembled themselves in the huge choir box behind the pulpit. It was precision personified, and in perfect time for their heaven-shattering crescendo: "HIS...TRUTH...IS...MARCH...ING... OOOOOOOOOOOOOOOOOOON."

A thunder of AMENS and HALLELUJAHS assailed the air. Heads and hands and voices everywhere were raised to the heavens. There was a mountain of gladness, and I couldn't ever remember being so swelled with a feeling of majesty. Fall Revival had begun.

Only seconds later, Edenfield's pastor, Thurmond Ivy, stood at the altar and asked that every head be bowed and every eye closed. A blessing spilled from his lips as divine as if he had descended from a mountain top with a message carved on a stone. It was like being in the presence of a prophet. Joy was in the air.

Within seconds, the lights dimmed again. A spotlight flooded the organist and "Rock My Soul In The Bosom Of Abraham" erupted with living force. In an instant, we were one, rocking back and forth, clapping to an eternal rhythm, vibrating the building's very foundation. Somewhere in the background, tambourines penetrated the air. We were electric; all of God's children, and with voices rolling like thunder. As the song came to an end, shouts of "GLORY" gradually gave way to the daubing of tears and a final stillness. Another prayer, this time for the offering, one that reinforced the gift and the giver, and blessing all who would be generous.

As the plates were passed, I reviewed my program. There was a different evangelist scheduled to speak each night. None of their names were familiar to me. Their credentials, though, read like a who's who of Christendom. Only the most prominent, I had been told, had been invited: evangelists renowned within the Protestant world; evangelists with names that could never be mentioned without accolades and gladness-of-heart; names synonymous with resurrection and salvation; modern-day John-The-Baptists, prophets, and healers of our time; lights cast unto the darkness.

Five nights, five different preachers. The first night belonged to Warfield Good. And as he stepped to the podium, it was evident that he would have little patience with anyone who doubted the seriousness of his mission or the pricelessness of what he had to say. His words were immediate, booming at us even before he'd opened his Bible. Only six words before I realized he was more than a living symbol of God's plan; he was the *core* of God's text.

"LET ME INTRODUCE YOU TO JESUS!" he boomed. Just like that. The gift of Jesus. A lightning bolt. Introduction enough.

"MANY OF YOU PROBABLY THINK YOU ALREADY KNOW JESUS!" His long bony finger did a sweeping point at the entire congregation. "And I'm sure that there are some of you who DO." His smile cut into his cheeks until it fashioned itself into a look of concern. "But I'm just as sure that there are those among you who DON'T." There was a pause while he seemed to make personal eye contact with all nine hundred. "For those of you who think that you have reached the pinnacle of your expression, let me have your attention for just a moment. I'll be brief." He leaned against the podium, resting firmly on one elbow, snuggling up. "YOU COULD KNOW HIM BETTER!...AND THAT'S WHY I'M HERE TONIGHT!" Coughs and throats being cleared mixed and mingled, rose and fell as nerves unraveled in varying degrees. He waited while we returned to a semblance of reverence.

"For those of you who KNOW you don't have a personal relationship with God, come a little closer, I've got a word for you." He leaned out over the podium like an eagle perched and ready to do whatever was necessary to defend its young. "Repentance," he whispered, then smiled as if it had been the cleverest thing. "REPENTANCE," he thundered suddenly, "REPENTANCE!"

No one was exempt from his exhortation, neither those who professed to know The Lord as their personal savior, nor those who didn't. There was no distinction. All had sinned and come short of the glory of God, and, by God, he was going to ferret them out. He was going to wring the sin out of them as surely as one wrings rinse water out of laundry. It was what he did.

Warfield Good was rangy and a bit awkward, and at nearly six and a half feet tall possessed a daring balance of white hair, white shirt, and white socks. His long, bony frame made his black suit look like it was still on a hanger and his wearing it seem like a necessary encumbrance; and little, if any, mind to it when it bunched up under his arms and climbed halfway up his back each time he brandished the Bible over his head. His face was a mask of inquiry, as ponderous as his labored breath and as brooding as the profusion of thick white bristles above his eyes. His lips were swollen and endowed with enough compression to send spittle clear into the third row. And his neck was both long and narrow, as was his nose, but neither were as pronounced as his Adam's apple, a painfully large and sculpted arrowhead that rested on top of the knot in his tie.

"I didn't come here tonight," he said, "just because The Church had enough good sense to ask me." A smattering of laughter trickled here and there. "I came here because God SENT me." AMENS shot like cannon fire from every corner. "I came here because HE told me there is a NEED, a need for LIFE! Let me HEAR from you!" Praises erupted from the front row to the back of the balcony. "I don't know about you," he said, "but I can feel His spirit moving among us." HALLELUJAHS now joined with the AMENS. "Let me tell you, people, GHHAAWWD is in our house tonight!" The congregation rose out of their seats. Jubilation was unloosed. "AMEN!" he echoed. "WE'VE ALL BEEN TOO QUIET TOO LONG." There was a message, and it was beginning to flow. The Kingdom of God was at hand. There was a cadence to Warfield, as if he had volumes to say and only a short time to say them. "GHHAAWWD is working here tonight." I felt myself being drawn forward in my seat. "GHHAAWWD has come HOME tonight." A thousand YESES shattered the air. "To lay HOLD of his children! Hallelujah." Bodies jumped up and down. A look of wildness radiated all the way from Warfield's face and outstretched arms to the battered and tattered Bible held high over his head. He was lightning fast, as if he had learned to preach by watching cats fight. I watched him weave back and forth across the altar, in the spotlight and out, his presence as strong as the message itself. The next thing I knew, he had weighed into us with a testimony about just exactly who his God was, none of which included the watered-down version of *mister nice guy,* who, in the end, sends us all to heaven, but a God of consequences, one who holds us accountable for our choices, choices that had everything to do with where we'd spend eternity.

Forty minutes later, Warfield Good stood slouched in the sweat of his labors. Steam seemed to rise from under his collar, and strands of his hair, sculpted and fastened with the shiny brilliance of Wild Root, separated and fell in sodden strands across his forehead and down the side of his face. He paused for a moment with his eyes closed, as if waiting for restoration. "Let me assure you of one thing," he said softly, "GOD is listening to each and every heart here tonight! You've heard from Him. Now He's waiting to hear from you. Will you keep him waiting?"

I was, at once, along with the rest of the congregation, a target for spiritual self-examination. It was very much like presiding over my own trial where the only possible verdict was guilty. But Warfield Good was not about to turn me or anybody else away. Instead, he gathered us together; told us that being guilty of sin was by itself a burden, but that the reward lay in its forgiveness. The only requirement was recantation, a simple and public revocation of our life as we knew it. And since the only alternative, according to Warfield, was a path of destruction, the choice seemed simple. But either way, he assured us, we were certain to reap what we chose to sow.

About the time my bladder signaled to me that it needed tending to, Warfield seemed to enter a state of having been anointed, first going this way then that across the altar like a prize fighter moving about in the ring. He was zigzagging, stopping short then changing directions, making half-circles, and doubling back. He did everything short of making angels in the snow. "Jesus is calling," he said with a pleading voice. It was then that the choir began to hum "Jesus Is Calling." About that time, my wool pants had joined my body heat and sweat and were on the brink of eating me alive.

Warfield stood alone, center stage, clutching his Bible like a life-giving amulet against his heart. "I want each and every one of you to close your eyes and bow your head," he said. His voice was gentle but commanding. I watched as heads began to bow all around me. There was strength that rose from their connectedness, from their willful obedience. "I want you to think about the darkness you are in at this very minute." He was leading us, unafraid, through the minefields of our sins. The choir now began to sing softly. "I want you to think," he said, "about where you are along life's path." His voice vibrated with a merciful tone. "And then I want you to ask yourself if you want to go the rest of the way without God. I want you to weigh the gravity of your decision; the consequences of rebuking what God is offering should you turn away and continue down that same path you're on …*alone.*" The choir's volume inched upward. "Yes, people," he said, "Jesus is calling." His voice was rimmed with timbre. "Calling for you and for me."

My head was bowed and my eyes were closed, and I could feel tiny beads of sweat inside my wool pants beginning to trickle into my crevices. But just as the tone in his voice reached the pinnacle of consolation, I did the unthinkable: I peeked. Opened my eyes. Looked around. Warfield's hands were clutched to the sides of the podium and his face was marked with indecision as if he were vacillating between going for our jugulars or our hearts, or both. I knew I had to act now or lose my chance forever. I began the hopeless task of trying to bring some degree of air to the crotch of my pants. "Every head bowed, every eye closed," he coaxed.

The breathing was heavy all around me. "I know there are many of you out there who are hurting," Warfield said. "We don't have to be geniuses to know that. And there are many of your brothers and sisters hurting right there alongside you. Hurting to know God. Hurting to know Him better." I looked to Duncan for support. He glared back with a look that seemed to suggest *this just wasn't fun anymore.* "I don't have to tell you who you are," he continued, "but if you can just slip up your hand so I can see it. Just slide it up above your head. I'll see it. But more important, God will see it." Faint whimpering began to dot the air. "Every head bowed, every eye closed," he said. "Yes. God bless you. I see that hand."

The choir's volume pressed upward yet again, this time with resonance and power and all things worthy of God's love. Many wept. All had sinned. "Won't you slip up your hand?" Warfield prompted. I peeked again. Curiosity was my degradation. Throughout the congregation, hands were being raised. One after the other.

Warfield's voice was now softer. "Do I see another hand? Thank you!" He searched the congregation, pausing while the choir painted pictures of lofty spires and stained-glass windows on our hearts. Warfield was a study of veneration; postured in prayer, fingers pressed to the bridge of his nose. "When I hear the stories of young men and women," he said, "so caught up in the pleasures of the world that they are blinded to the gifts of salvation, I am moved to the depths of unrest." The strains of weeping and noses being blown filtered like a carefully timed chorus. Warfield paused, waited. "BUT THEY'RE ONLY FOOLING THEMSELVES," he exploded, large projectiles of spittle sullying the air. He paced out a figure-eight, did a couple of side steps then lunged at the microphone. The podium rocked, but held. "THEY'RE ONLY FOOLING THEMSELVES," he repeated, as if the more he said it, the truer it became. In less time than it took to catch his breath, the expression on his face turned from simple pain to consuming agony. "Oh, dear Jesus," he strained, his face turned upward toward heaven and his hands and arms held high above his head as if expecting to receive God's answer in the form of a package, "send us the courage to say yes." We waited while he wrestled with his anguish. "As I stand before you," he said, "the way I'm standing here tonight, I can't help but think of all the souls that turned away after I offered them the gift of Jesus. I'm thinking if I had only offered *one more time,* it may have made a difference." I could feel the body heat of nine hundred. "So, I intend to see to it that that difference is made here tonight. I intend to offer and *keep* offering *one more time.* I don't intend to let a single lost soul escape tonight, not as long as I can offer *one more time.* " He stopped just long enough to blow his nose on the huge white handkerchief that he yanked from his rear pocket. "I sometimes wonder why I even have to do it," he said. "Why I have to beg you to take hold of Jesus." The choir was now on its feet.

"For those living with that lonely, empty feeling …" Warfield was now peeling back the layers, bringing to light what underscored our darkness, our moments alone, "… and with that knowledge that something is missing, I urge you to rise up out of your seats and come forward … out of the darkness and into the light." The choir's resonation of "Jesus is Calling" suddenly became a powerful magnet. "Make your way to the altar," he said. "Jesus is calling."

Throngs of wrongdoers and offenders of God's laws began rising out of their seats and making their way toward the altar. Some pushed forcibly past their pew mates and fell wailing into the aisles. Others came without a sound, bent and broken and dragging a lifetime of sorrow. Some babbled in tongues, and some came in humbleness with little more than the tear trails that marked their faces. Yet they came. One after another. Each an answer to prayer.

By this time, my shorts had bunched up like a hangman's noose around my privates, and my need to urinate had grown to a state of urgency; my underarms were soaking wet, and my wool pants felt like they were lined with hair. I was well beyond losing refinement.

More and more people made their way into the aisles and toward the altar. I could almost hear their sins being shed, being ripped from their flesh and hurled through the air. "Yes!" Warfield implored, "Come stake your claim for all eternity. Rise up and greet Him now so you can rise up and greet Him proudly on that final day."

Within minutes, space had vanished at the altar and the aisles had filled to overflowing. Some kneeled and some stood shivering as if standing under an icy shower. Some moaned. Some sobbed. A few pulled at their hair. They leaned on each other, embraced, drooled.

"Don't be fooled into thinking that you'll do it later," Warfield railed. "Don't trick yourself into believing that there will be time enough tomorrow. I've known many whose tomorrows never came."

My mouth had the consistency of baked clay. I kept licking my lips, kept sending my tongue in search of moisture. There was none. I was convinced at this point it had all worked its way into my bladder. My need to urinate had now advanced to a state of frenzy.

"If The Holy Spirit is calling your name tonight," Warfield entreated, "and I believe He is, you've got to know that you may never have this opportunity again." The end of the world was coming, and Warfield wanted us to know where we'd be if it came tonight. "There are those here tonight," he said, "who will never know the misery of their own pain until they are made to live without it. So, I implore you," he said, running from one side of the altar to the other, his hands extended as if asking for alms, "REACH OUT TO YOUR NEIGHBORS ... those next to you. And those of you kneeling at the altar, GET UP! Go to your friends struggling with saying YES and bring them back to the altar with you."

I began to feel as though my flanks were exposed, cut off from all means of rescue. I glanced up at Duncan. The ruddiness in his face had changed to a distinct pinkness that clashed with the orange of his hair. He looked like he was about to burst into flame.

I wanted to remove my coat, but the fear of bringing attention to myself was greater than my fear of combustion. But even before I let it become an issue, I saw Harmon Little working frantically through the crowd. He was on a mission. It was Duncan and me. Down front, Evda Nica had risen from the altar, his face soaked with tears (it had been the third time he'd been saved since arriving eight weeks ago) and began working his way back toward us. His eyes were red and raw from crying, but he pushed and squeezed through the wedged and weeping masses. Panting and layered in sweat, he struggled like an animal mired in quicksand, lurching and lunging, desperate to be free, and all the while with his eyes drifting between Duncan and me. He was coming. Harmon Little was coming. The work of The Lord was at hand.

Within seconds, and before either of them had managed to move within striking range, Duncan began nudging me and motioning that the time for us to leave was now. But before I could turn, someone from behind me had leaned over the back of the pew and grabbed me by the arm. It was Dr. Wolsey, Economics and Sociology.

"Weldon," he pleaded, his voice as sorrowful as the choir's hymn, "let me pray with you." I could feel his one hand tighten on my arm while he managed to grab hold of Duncan with the other. I could feel the blood beginning to drain from my head as I watched his lips moving, mouthing words that fell dead and silent before they could reach me. On the other side of Duncan, Zena Ferguson, President of the Women's Guild, had maneuvered herself into his personal zone and postured herself with sisterly love. By this time, Harmon had arrived at our sides. I glanced up in time to see Evda climbing over one pew after another. He reached us wild-eyed and with a heavy line of dried spit across his lips. Duncan and I were surrounded. Evda and Harmon grabbed hold of us, began praying and reminding us that God so loved the world that He gave his only begotten son. Zena Ferguson and Dr. Wolsey each prayed a separate prayer. "Won't you go forward, Duncan? Won't you show Weldon the way?" They were all talking at once. Behind Harmon, I could see someone lying prone across the backs of two pews – it was Etta Pritchett – a human bridge holding onto and pleading with a lost soul.

More and more rose from the altar, the names of loved ones on their lips. They swarmed through the congregation, pushing and pawing, looking for the ones still undecided, looking to bring them into the fold.

Evda's stranglehold on the lapel of my coat was enough to keep me tied to our circle. I was cognizant of being there with them, but my mind was somewhere far away, walled in silence. I let my eyes drift back and forth between them, back and forth between Harmon's large purplish lips working only inches from Duncan's ear and Zena Ferguson praying by his side. Zena's face was wide and flushed to ruby red, laden with servitude and heaped with suffering, confirmation that she was where God intended her to be. Dr. Wolsey had now let go of Duncan and was focused solely on me. He continued to lean over the back of the pew and hold onto my arm as though I was worth so many points if he landed me. With his face carrying a look of abhorrence, he cried for my redemption, his spittle, like microscopic shards of crystal, dotting and stinging my face. Alongside me, Evda's face seemed to contort, going from monster to clown, then back again. His hair was matted and sweat covered him like thick transparent skin. And though his lips were moving, I was aware only of his very hot breath and the insistent clicking and clacking of his tongue. He was entranced, in a state of rapture, alone with God yet hanging onto me. It was a feeding frenzy for the born again.

Between the preaching and the praising and the praying, the clapping and the singing and the shouting, I moved ever closer to overload. My need to urinate had red-lined, had become as intense as the surge of resistance signaling me to bolt and run. I could feel Evda's arms draped over me, cradling me. I could feel Dr. Wolsey's hands, meaty and warm, fastened to my arm and shoulder. Together, they joined to stir the vertigo welling deep within me.

I chanced a quick glance at Duncan. He was pulling away. Side winding; trying to free himself from Harmon and Zena and two members of the Hymn-For-Him quartet. "If I went forward, it would only be for you, not me," Duncan said. His voice was directed toward all the hands that clutched him. "Maybe tomorrow will be different," he said. Duncan was resolute, certain he knew his heart. But Harmon was sure he could change it.

Dr. Wolsey and Evda repositioned themselves, blocking any chance of my escape. Their voices pleading, their breaths stale and sour. I strained to look beyond Dr. Wolsey's all-bald, glow-in-the-dark head; strained to look for Kellen as if the sight of him might somehow give me strength. He was there, in the same place. But no one was reaching for him, praying with him, or trying to bring him to Jesus. Yet all around him people were heaped one on another. I knew he was in his place where no one could reach him; away from life as it became too much to sort.

Duncan continued to inch toward the outside aisle, and I began to feel pangs of abandonment. Whatever composure I had left was beginning to dissipate like vapor into thin air. And whatever was happening to me, I was certain I was losing. But somewhere amidst the coaxing and the pleading, I did what I desperately did not want to do. I buried my face in my hands and began to sob. It came upon me as quickly as a summer storm, and with nearly as much force. Dr. Wolsey and Evda took it as a sign of my turning it over to Jesus and began sobbing alongside me. They sobbed in tandem. We sobbed in unison. I sobbed. They sobbed. We sobbed.

We were so hermetically entwined, their arms wrapped so tightly around me, that I could feel the convulsions from their every breath. Claustrophobia now circled dangerously close, causing me to pull away, but my efforts were met with like resistance as if I were held in check by the strength of heaven. But just as well-defined as my being wrapped and held in the arms of strangers, was my almost un-restrained need to urinate. I was very near the verge of bursting, and it proved to be the ally I needed, the fuel for my weakening reserves.

With the single-mindedness of someone escaping from a water chamber just before the moment of death, I exploded from their grasp. Agonizing groans tore from my throat as I scrambled, ripping and tear-ing past parishioners as if trying to get to the only remaining lifeboat on a sinking ship. I pushed my way to the end of the row, climbing over one parishioner after another, past those crouched and clumped together in weeping masses, past those huddled and blubbering, past the wretched, horror-stricken faces repenting their crimes. On and on toward the outer wall. I never looked back, but I knew Evda was in pursuit. It no longer mattered, only that I get to the exit door and beyond. But in the next instant, I knew I had waited too long.

I felt it as I reached the outer aisle, as I pushed and burrowed through the sounds of contrition. It was searing-hot and coming in short bursts. With no other objective but to try to outrun its wetness and its scent, I clawed my way to the exit door. With one mighty lunge I felt its misaligned hinges give way and the cool night air rush against me as if we were lovers reunited. Behind me, I could hear the bellowing of Evda's voice above the rest of the congregation. It was desperate and unmusical, straining to echo his last sentiment, "DON'T BE AFRAID! I'LL PRAY FOR YOU!"

I sprinted with all my might into the alley behind The Fishes and Loaves and crashed into its trash heap of cardboard boxes. In the same instant, I let go of what was left in me, feeling it flow from me as mighty as a river breaching its banks. My eyes teared, and my sinuses drained full out. I waited, braced by my own tranquility and watched the last trails of steam rise and vanish in the cold night air.

I stood gazing skyward, breathing deeply when the image of Bea came at me out of nowhere. She was just there, unprompted, waiting for the chance to interject herself. There was a sense of assuredness that came from my thoughts of her, something affirming, something that helped me believe that I was no less for failing to grasp all things paradisian. The mere thought of her provided me with a certain strength, something I clung to – covert as it was. Even from the beginning, she let me know we were much the same, kindred spirits behind Edenfield masks. It had been the unspoken, but unmistakable message we shared: that we would be things of refuge to each other. The aftermath of tonight's revival had been sufficient cause to re-connect with her, the antidote to the haze swarming inside my head. But then, like so often – in the reverie of revelry – blood sprung from my nose and flowed down across my lips and chin almost before I realized it, adding its own punch to the night.

Everything in me seemed uncapped; blood flowed from me like an open dam, and I was no longer of the mind or will to do anything about it. Exhausted, I leaned forward and let one giant drop after another fall and burst against the cardboard boxes, each a dazzling starburst in the moonlight. I stayed that way for some time, until the drops became smaller and fewer, and until they ceased altogether, swelling and clotting themselves into a great crystal lump inside my nose.

My clothes and hands were spattered and spotted and streaked with blood. I had no way of knowing what my face looked like, save from it looking battered and beaten. To avoid what was surely to be unending speculation, I stayed in the alley and the shadow of boxes until the auditorium emptied and the congregation thinned to a trickle.

The revival had done anything but revive me, and failed, at least for now, to win me for Jesus. Instead, it had urged me toward comfort of another kind: toward recollections of Bea and the daring that made sense of who and what she was, and who and what she was to me.

When the sidewalks and campus finally had the feel of being deserted, I made my way toward the dorm. The cold night air against my face was as welcome as mother's milk, and I marveled at how clear it made everything seem. I hesitated outside just long enough to consider the hot confining space of my room, then turned and headed toward the soccer field, toward the vastness of the night sky and its canopy of stars. It was the solace I longed for, that and the pale dissident smile of Bea ... the smile that so often tempted and brought me heedlessly close to what I knew was forbidden. That same smile, I was sure, that would follow me to my dreams and give me hope for endless summer nights…just her and me and Linda Sue.

Chapter Nineteen
Fugitive Status

Attendance for the second night of revival was replicate of the first: swelled to overflowing. I couldn't tell that any of the faces were different, though I had ditched Duncan for Kellen. Seats went early, which left Kellen and me standing in the balcony along its outside wall and adjacent to the exit door. With only slight variations, proceedings were much the same right up through the offering. Then, during the prayer immediately following, a prayer of immense proportion, Kellen nudged me from my head-bowed-eyes-closed state of compliance, and with a head nod, motioned for me to follow him. We slipped through the exit door without a ripple. It was extraordinary timing. Within seconds, we had shed the bonds of revival and moved across the concourse and Highway 31, away from streetlights and into the safety of the fields that had become as familiar as home.

What we'd done had been risky, but another night of spiritual entreatment on the level of Warfield Good was beyond our limits of adolescent male tolerance. So, we did the self- respecting thing: we fled.

We spent most of the night backtracking where we had spent half of the summer: in the fields beyond the city markers and down along the banks of the Sands River, places off the beaten track. Though we were in and out of the same old places, they seemed different draped in the decay and rush-turned-hush of autumn. They seemed older, more temporal, more in tune with taking stock of our trespasses.

We settled in Duncan's old campsite, huddled around a fire we built from the wood he'd left behind. We joked about our fugitive status as self-imposed exile. Somehow, labeling it seemed to lessen the sting of turning tail and hiding out.

After settling in, we found ourselves reaching into a sphere of self-examination: from the acquisition of souls to what we thought might be our personal responsibilities to God, or if, in fact, there were responsibilities at all. We tried with flawed-but-youthful passion to fathom the depths of the spirit: to connect the many shifting pieces of an everlasting deity to the scrapheap of mortals He was resolute to love, even daring what we might expect in the way of punishment and reward.

We were deliberately serious, fiery and exuberant, in our reach to know the heart and mind of the God Edenfield guarded with impunity, and if the ravings of Warfield Good were as close as we'd ever get.

We were as relentless as we were random. Just what was man, anyway, besides the highest order on the food chain? Was he, before anything else, a spiritual being who was given a physical body in order to experience things worldly and profane? Was man's time on earth probationary? —a time to prove himself worthy to inherit the kingdom of heaven? And what was his charge, exactly, and how was he to know it? Did he have rites to satisfy? —offerings to make? What precisely did the Creator have in mind for us beyond multiplying and taking dominion over what He had created? And if He truly intended that a purpose be attached to each of us, why did He bury it in such complexity? And why is it that the scriptures are given to so much interpretation? —so much left to dispute? And why do they cause so much division, even amongst believers? And had the things which were once plain and precious to the understanding been lost to man's constricted perspectives? —his persuasions?

The campfire was reassuring, and we churned on and on, finding spiritual significance and giving reverential treatment to even the least of things, yet knowing that we were no closer to their resolutions than we were to solving the meaning of life. They were sessions that lasted four nights in a row. But it was during our last night that things began to repeat. We had gone as far as we could. And though I was sure we had raised enough spiritual issue to keep seminarians the world over confounded well into the next millennium, we gave it up, leaving it to the mystery that was God. Besides, I'd had enough of my own speculation. I needed something more complete, something more tangible than conjecture and hypothesis. I was not only in the mood for things real, but also feeling it as a *need*. Real answers to real questions. Things tactile and sensual, things like the aromas that filtered from my mother's kitchen and the comforting resonance of my father's voice. I needed to feel things like blood coursing through me at the sight of Carol and Cheryl and Bonitasue cartwheeling through the air, and the wincing excitement of Widow Tidewater's foot against my thigh. I needed Kellen to speak to me like a brother and assure me that we were special in the eyes of God, to tell me that even though we may not always do what pleases Him, He knows our hearts. I needed to move back to basics, to Sunday school fundamentals, teachings that not only came with the assurance of God's love but left me knowing I was worthy of it.

"I feel responsible for you missing the revival," Kellen said. It was a second or two before his words registered fully.

"Well," I said, "I appreciate your guilt."

"It's just that I feel like I may have taken you away from something you needed."

I hesitated, thinking it was going to be necessary to parry some plea for forgiveness, but it wasn't. "Well," I said, "it wasn't all you. I certainly had a choice in the matter. Fact is, I feel closer to whatever created us when I'm out here under the stars instead of in that auditorium, and I can't help it if it's misunderstood, even by you."

"Yeah, well it's the Edenfield in me I guess, that pang of conscience that says I should have been more responsible. Not dragged you away."

"To be my brother's keeper?" I said.

"Something like that."

"Well … it's not worth beating yourself up. We're here and I'm glad of it."

"Yeah, but what if you needed more?" he said. His face was pointed toward mine, but his eyes had become lost in the shadows. I could only assume they were on me.

"You mean more of what I got the first night?"

"More or less," he said. "It takes a while to connect. Can't expect to come away with the *fullness of it* after only one night. Takes being there to get what you need."

"And what might that be?"

"The one thing Duncan said we all needed: to get our pumps primed now and again, feel our sweat heavy-up and break loose by giving into *The Word*. Said we needed to feel the swirl of angels so we could feel the grip of the devil loosen up and fall away. He said we needed, at least once, to feel the total collapse of our house, our knees growing weak and our heart pounding right up through our throat. Needed to feel the Holy Spirit, he said; needed the restoration that comes from knowing that there is a power greater than all of us combined. Then he said we needed to lay ourselves, uncompromised and naked-to-the-bone, at the altar; to offer ourselves up, mind, body, and soul, to Jesus. He said we needed to *feel* it if we ever expected to *know* it." He leaned toward me with a thin-flat smile. "Course he was red-eyed with homebrew when he said it. Thing is, he may have been right."

Maybe Duncan was right. Maybe all we needed was to *feel,* to go beyond our penchant for intellectualizing and trying to understand by reason alone. Maybe God's love and gifts were not as complex as I made them out to be. Maybe the whole thing with believing wasn't rooted in reason at all, but in gut feelings and blind faith. Perhaps believing even *defied* reason. Maybe The Church fathers had understood this a long time ago, had discovered that feelings fed emotions, and together provided powerful inroads to the heart. Control them, control the flock. They were, after all, the things most easily identifiable simply because they could be felt. Reason, on the other hand, presented intangibles, things controversial and refutable, never the same from one person to the next. There were simply too many variables: too many theories for each point of view, and, conversely, too many ways to not only prove, but to disprove each of them. Reason alone provided too many ways for mayhem, leaving The Church open to endless assault, and making its posture a forever defensive one. There was no way it could sustain such inquiry. There was simply no place for second-guessing and questioning, no place for the remnants of suspicion and doubt. Believing had to be achieved by faith, and no better way to know faith than to *feel* it. But then, again, maybe Duncan was wrong.

Kellen sat with his back against the woodpile, his legs stretched out toward the fire. "You know this is my last year at Edenfield," he said, his voice coming as an interruption to the hissing embers. He was all at once tired of remembering Duncan's drunken ramblings and the need to feel the power of the Holy Spirit.

"I know," I said, kicking one of the logs just right and sending a flame bursting across its surface. "What's your plan?"

He sat motionless for the longest time; his gaze fixed on the flames nibbling away in silence. I thought he may have been entering into one of his episodes when he finally repositioned himself and said, "I don't have a plan. Never felt like I needed one. I'd just as soon let things take care of themselves. Kind of a destiny and providence thing." He was controlled, in a free verse with himself. "Besides, planning requires organization, and I'm not much on that. Wouldn't know where to begin." He paused as if studying what he'd said. "Although," he said, "I guess maybe the first thing I'd have to do is figure out where I want to end up. But that could take forever. I mean my agenda changes about every time I wake up." He laughed. "Fate and destiny," he said, "they take the worry out of making decisions."

I was having trouble determining his mood and tried baiting him without raising his ire. "Well," I finally said, "there's always the mill." My tone was informative. "However things turn out, with or without a plan, I'm sure you'll always be welcome at the mill."

He rolled his head in my direction. "Is that your solution for me? The *mill?*"

"Either that or The Fishes and Loaves." I had succumbed to imagery. "Imagine you and Becky Summers. Up and down the aisles. In the produce. In the freezer. Together. Packing meat. Making change. It'd be like a little piece of heaven. Better yet, a little piece of America. With one fell swoop you could have a family, a future, and a capitalist profile. It could be yours. Everything. The dairy, the baked goods. Now that's a plan."

He waited until my blank stare had lost its hold. "Well, as grateful as I am for your insight, I don't think Becky Summers has quite the makeup that I'm looking for. And just so you don't get the wrong idea," he paused, lacing his fingers behind his head, "Becky and I would never work. We're simply worlds apart: two renderings of a most complex reality." He rolled his head toward me to see if I understood, or if I even cared to. "She's simply incapable of fulfilling the need I need." His eyes were locked on mine, but then they slowly drifted back to the fire.

I was all at once feeling like I had ventured too close to something too personal. "You see," he said, not recognizing that I wanted to drop it, "I need things beyond the *norm.*" He stopped, pawed at the back of his neck, and let out a big puff of breath like he was having trouble with where he wanted to go. "Becky is, in every sense, traditional," he said, "and, as we both can attest, with passions of her own. But mine are of a different kind. It's passion to be sure, but of a dissimilar amalgam." The night's chill was snappish and began to fill in around his words. "But then we're all dissimilar to a point, angular and seeking in discordant ways a touch of the divine. Even so, I've learned that we're all pretty much alike when it comes to things like *need,* or *want,* or *hunger,* whatever you want to call it…though I often feel like I have more than I can handle: the way it can't ever stop gnawing at me, and me with just enough reserve to keep it pressed down—forever mindful of my *audience.*" His face was, all of a sudden, a study – the firelight amiable and enhancing. "Too red-blooded for my own good my brother used to tell me; all the time too interested in what goes on in bedrooms. But he was wrong about that. I mean as expressive as bedrooms are to relationships, I'm more interested in what goes on *before* and *after.* The *in-between times* I call them…times that count the most…where *real* love takes place." He paused, waiting for my response. When the look on my face told him there wouldn't be one, he said, "In Becky's case, she's infinitely better off with Duncan. Though I don't know if either of them has enough in-between stuff even for compatibility, much less love." I enjoyed Kellen's opinions, but they usually had to be dragged out of him. His volunteering them like this was out of character. "I never saw a lot of *in-between* stuff when I was growing up," he said. "At least nothing that amounted to anything. Unless you want to count contempt as something. I never really gave it much thought, just figured all families were pretty much the same … at least the ones I knew. Didn't know it could be any other way until I went to live with Stone and Judi. Now I know."

I sat hovering inside my jacket, braced by the night's stillness and waiting for the right words to come. I wasn't altogether clear on what Kellen had meant to say or what he intended to leave me with, only that it resonated with a niggling uncertainty. Whether his holding forth was that of conviction or confession was hard to tell. What I did know was that my dredging for deeper meaning would have been pushing the boundaries of my comfort zone, something far too likely to be seen as ambitious. I was more than okay with not taking in the finer points of his struggles; better off, at least for the time, leaving them to the torrents of the unknowable.

"So…," I said at the risk of suspicion and grainy with a need to know, "what about you and Bea? How much of that is *in-between* stuff?"

"All of it," he said, then lay quietly for some time. "It's made us better friends. Regrettably, that's all we can ever be."

I sat frozen, unblinking, the breath nearly sucked out of me and feeling as if there was a god after all. I waited, feigning thought, my tongue thickening, my throat beginning to constrict. "Is it the same with…you know…" I said, motioning with my head in the direction of the Littles. I didn't need to say Gretchen's name. Didn't know if I could, anyway. I only had so much nerve, and I'd gone about as far as I dared.

"There are things you don't understand," he said, his voice soft and trailing.

"You mean like things born out of need and want and hunger?… like Marsha Tidewater?" For a moment I sat reeling from my own sarcasm. Where had it come from? I didn't know. It just popped out and with no more effort than it took to spit in the fire. All I knew was that I'd said it, and it was too late to take it back. I sat waiting in the echo of my own words, in their insensitivity.

"I know what you're thinking," he said, his voice kind, "but it's only part of the truth." A *you've-gotta-believe-me* expression contorted his face. "There are things…" he said, lowering his eyes. It was a gesture that seemed to diminish him.

"What things?" I asked, wanting to know everything, yet at the same time wishing I could reel in my invasiveness.

"Look," he said, working hard for my understanding. "I know I've been…you know…a bit hard to figure out at times, but…" he stopped dead, again. "…All I'm saying is that there are reasons for what might seem odd." He was struggling. "And those women…" he thought for a moment then raised himself up onto one elbow, "they're alone for the most part, desperate, needy, but it's nothing I can help them with beyond what can come from a moment in time." He seemed tired. I waited, not knowing if he was done.

"Needs can be damnable things," he said. "That's why it matters how we tend to them. Providing, of course, we can identify what they are to begin with. I guess that's why I go from here-to-there so much, searching to get at the heart of what haunts. But it's knowing, I mean really knowing what they are that scares me."

He laced his arms across his chest as if warding himself from the night air. "Mine is a restless spirit, Weldon," he said, "always a thing of contention, but never really wanting anything more than contentment. The real kick is I'm never settled enough to know when it comes."

I watched him through the fire's dimming light and thought about how each of us had been branded with notions of need and in-between times. I was never certain of any of them, only their potential. It was all just so much chaff in the wind to me, stuff that just seemed to look for a mind to confound. I had little doubt about my own contentment, or what it would take to bring me closer to it. No mystery there…just the lack of courage to let her (Bea) know. Kellen seemed a far opposite. He had the courage, just not a clear notion of where to direct it.

After that, we sat in silence, watching the flames turn to cinders, taking what we could from the last of their light. His words, though, just seemed to hang there in the night air, thick and resonant and looking for someplace to land," I said, "each of us, if we cared to admit it, seems to want that spark of the divine, that indisputable and unexplainable connection to God…tethered in some way to His mystery, to what He brings in the way of contentment…and peace."

He shifted slightly, uncrossing one foot then crossing the other. "Odd as it is," he said, "as much as I think of God as the embodiment of love and mercy and forgiveness, His peace is still something I know very little about, something that's never quite found its way into the nous of my being."

I wasn't sure I understood the depth of Kellen's lack of peace, but wondered what forces kept him from finding it. "Well," I said, trying to talk around my confusion, "what do you suppose it is, I mean the *one* thing that might give you the peace you're looking for?"

He said nothing, only repositioned himself against the woodpile, adjusting his back to its bark and knots. After a time, his voice broke with certainty. "Acceptance," he said. I said nothing in return, only waited until his voice broke again, only this time it was weak and aimed into the blackness. "I'm talking about *my own*…my acceptance…acceptance of the fact that I'm exactly the way God made me, and every bit the way He intended me to be."

I walked back to the dorm that night wondering about my own acceptance. If I was, in fact, exactly what God intended me to be, what He'd made me to be, and if it might somehow bring me closer to contentment—to *His* peace—and if that might somehow be the bridge I needed for a divine relationship. I was surrounded daily with affirmations from one classmate or another about their relationship with God, with what He'd done for them, and what they were sure He was going to do next. It was a steady barrage of God told me this and God told me that: revelations clear and concise and uninterrupted. *Word* they called it, as in I received *word* from God. I could only marvel at how God was forever showing them such and such, and how He so generously directed them here and there and everywhere. But it wasn't that way for me. My connection was, in and of itself, nonexistent, without configuration or clarity, about as arbitrary as a silk scarf billowing in a strong wind…and just as silent.

My dilemma was that I never had a clear vision of God, and nothing in the way of expectations, His or mine. What made matters worse was that I had no idea how to unlock His mystery. Prayer just seemed to float off into space. I aimed them upward to where I thought God ought to be, but never had the assurance that He received them. I experienced nothing of God on my own, only from those closest to me. Kellen's god, for instance, always seemed to be one of confusion: a god with a maybe-yes-maybe-no disposition, forever with more questions than answers. Harmon Little's god seemed to be one who watched and waited for me to transgress, and where I'd have to pray all the while that he wouldn't search me out and devour me, hair and all. My mother's god was gentle and kind, providing and protecting, and who stood at all times in a meadow of wildflowers surrounded by the likes of little children and lambs. Duncan's god, on the other hand, was a mighty warrior, wrathful and vengeful, making the rivers flow red with the blood of his enemies and doing whatever it took, and by whatever means, to remind us that we would all stand before Him one day to account for every breath He'd allowed us to take.

Whose god did I want? Whose god did I need? —and whose could I afford not to have? And was he, in the final offering, anything other than what we wanted him to be? It was the same for all religions, I imagined. Dad called it brain fodder: balm for the meek. Dad was always good at railing against what was contrary to his thinking. Religion, though, seemed to be at the top of his list. I couldn't help but think he was partly right part of the time but could never quite figure out which part or which time.

So, despite Kellen's campfire revelations and our attempts to bridge what lay between the mind and the spirit, the night still carried a chill that spoke to the divide that lay between Edenfield and me, between God and me. And I had a sense that a binding relationship with either of them still rested in a wind that had yet to reach me. And whether that wind would warm, or cool, or cleanse, only time would tell.

CHAPTER TWENTY
Mister-Granddaddy-Bull-Moose-of-All-Time

The fall revival came and went with mixed, but mostly favorable reviews. It had, with one giant stroke, strengthened Edenfield's Christian base by a favorable margin. Duncan's unofficial tally had the student body at around eighty five percent saved, but only about fifty percent sanctified. Five percent, he figured, were perched on the ledge of indecision, agnostics only for the sake of convenience. Another five percent were complete unknowns, attending Edenfield only at the insistence of their parents, the threat of disinheritance as the ruling factor. And still another unalterable and predictable five percent inextricably on a one-way street to hell. I wasn't sure where Duncan had placed me or even himself, but I was thinking he should have had a category, even at one percent or less, for the confounded.

Harmon was less cynical in his assessment of the rival. In the five-minute time slot reserved for him during Chapel each Friday—presumably for a financial report, which most always turned into a sermonette on how he had once again kept the school from financial ruin through his devotion to the finer nuances of accounting—he gave it to us short and sweet. "The Fall Revival has struck a real chord in the name of salvation," he said, "but this is still a fertile field (at this point, his eyes did a quick dart about the auditorium, then seemed to settle on me) and there is still a lot of work, we as Christians, need to do." He paused, righted himself then began again. "Our first obligation, as always, is still unchanged: to love and honor our Heavenly Father. Without exception, this means living within the precepts of Christ's teachings. This in turn enables us to grow in faith and to be the example He would have us be. One of the ways this is possible, and what personally works for my family, is to live in moderation, to avoid excess. Living moderately and modestly has its roots in obedience, not only to God, but to His institutions." He paused, letting the ensuing silence carry its own emphasis. "After reviewing the books for the third quarter," he said, "I found some disturbing facts, all of which point to *excessiveness,* to our living *immoderately.* To be more exact, the budget for toilet paper has already exceeded what we have allocated for the entire year." There was eye contact all round. Images of excess wiping, as well as looks of accusation, seemed to pass from one to another. "I've asked myself how this could happen. And the only thing I could come up with is that moderation is not being put to the test here at Edenfield."

For those who didn't understand the redemptive powers of guilt, there was sizable laughter followed by dead silence. Harmon's manner and tone were as serious as last rites. His tale of rising costs and how we were tampering with his money was his way of helping us toward perfection, helping us find our way to Jesus in the only way he knew: through the ledgers of debit and credit. All in all, he was as businesslike as we had come to expect, and as calculated as the numbers he was entrusted to keep.

Except for a few insurgent acts, smoke bombs that turned the third-floor hallway into an opaque tunnel, and a series of retaliatory cherry bombs delivered to the first floor between two and four a.m., the following days remained pretty much in the spirit of revival. The new converts, as infusing as they were to the world of Christendom, were, as often as not, impositions to those of us still struggling with things like self-actualization and sexual impenitence. New converts were not only exceptions, but exceptional as well, possessing the same qualities as unannounced exams. They beamed with vigilance at every juncture, like puppies loose from their leashes for the first time: eager to please but lost in the tall grass. They passed out tracts and quoted scripture, mostly to one another, flooded the Missionary Council with applications for the remotest outposts in the world, and popped up out of their seats at every opportunity to give, *still,* another unsolicited account of how Jesus had snatched them from the jaws of hell. As a part of responsible Christian living, they regularly volunteered for community service, reported to their dorm proctors things they perceived as cracks in Edenfield's holy infrastructure, and saw to it that no one was denied a personal introduction to Jesus. They were, for their very own fulfillment, self-appointed missionaries to the campus, as heavenly endowed as they were thorns in the flesh.

Thanksgiving vacation, so far the semester's biggest morale booster, meant going home—time away from the familiar to return to the even more familiar. Aside from Duncan, the entire student body had vacated as if Satan and his army were in hot pursuit. Duncan had decided to stay in Edenfield, celebrate Thanksgiving with the Summers' and work at the mill on Friday and Saturday. He was not in the habit of complicating his life with *time off,* a thing too likely to break his rhythm.

Kellen's plan was to leave Tuesday evening, hitch a ride with his trucking buddy to Chicago, and then hook up with a team of beef haulers who claimed to own the passing lane all the way to Oklahoma City. From there, it was about a two-hundred-mile hitchhiking frenzy, west-southwest, through the dry, wind-whipped flatlands of Oklahoma, and across its dusty, sparsely-traveled two-lanes that connected one gas-pump-diner to the next; remarkable two-lanes that baked and radiated under all-day suns and wound snake-like through the glare of red rocks and clay until they eventually disappeared into infinity and until they eventually led him across the Red River into Texas. He'd made this same trip numerous times and always with time to spare. If things went the way he planned, he figured he'd be there Thursday morning about the time breakfast gravy was hitting the table.

Tuesday evening, Duncan and I walked Kellen to the front of the campus, shook his hand, and patted him on the back before he hustled himself high up into the truck's oversized cab. We yelled to his buddy to be sure to point him in the right direction after dropping him off in Chicago. He yelled back that he didn't think Kellen could get to where he was going from Chicago but was probably dumb enough to try anyway. We laughed loud and made crude but guarded remarks, then stood a little forlorn while his buddy slipped the big rig into low gear – into bulldog – and pulled away, heading toward a world Edenfield prayed would perish before any of us could ever gain knowledge of its existence.

At the top of the rise leading out of town, and just before they began their quick descent beyond its horizon, his buddy let go with his big diesel horn. It filled the autumn air with the sound of Mister-

Granddaddy-Bull-Moose-Of-All-Time ready to mount the cow of his dreams. They were like outlaws on the run with nothing but open roads and blue skies and whatever else that lent breadth and space to a cowboy's world. The heavy diesel smoke lingered longer than usual in the damp November air. But as I stood there watching it dissipate into nothingness, I knew that Kellen was as much of a brother to me than I could ever expect...or ever hope to have.

CHAPTER TWENTY-ONE
Against the Backdrop of a Steel-Gray Sky

Monday morning Chapel was alive and buzzing with a picnic atmosphere. Thanksgiving vacation had done the inevitable: it had rejuvenated, added spark to declining adolescence. Personalities burst forth like an autumn harvest. The whole scene was like a county fair competition for the brightest smile. I felt at home, oddly enough, surrounded by a resurgence of spirit and life. And as I watched the antics unfurl around me, I realized I was doing it with a degree of gladness. I didn't know where it was coming from, but I knew for certain that being here was less of an effort than being at home.

The four-day hiatus with Mom and Dad had been a mixed bag. I was dismayed at the vast tundra that had opened up between them and me and the home I'd left only five months ago. My return was like stumbling into an unfamiliar neighborhood with unenlightened people. Their ways suddenly seemed more offbeat than what I'd come to know at Edenfield. Even the efforts of Freddie Heartland and a shared forty-ounce bottle of Budweiser, passed back and forth and swigged between rough talk and belching, weren't enough to pull me back into the local mindset. I was having trouble being reminded of my raisings, trouble deciding where I belonged and what world I wanted as opposed to what world offered the best fit.

Even high school friends who had gone off to school, and now home for the holiday, were able to offer little in the way of anything new. They were, for the most part, so self-absorbed with either cynicism or depression that their presence alone was an imposition, hardly worth either of our efforts. Even the friends who had decided to tough it out without "all that college claptrap," proved just as uneventful. All their talk about making plans, and their plans to make plans, forced me to an early retreat and back into the precincts of

Mom and Dad. By Sunday evening, though, Mother had whittled me into kindling.

Mother was, for the sake of explanation, compassionate to a fault, sentimentality often besting her, even on her most virulent days. Thanksgiving, however, had not been such a time. She had been exponentially lethal: manipulation as the weapon of choice, control as the ultimate objective. She had, during the course of a single weekend, unearthed every heart rendering, pain wrenching, and emotionally crippling tale she had ever known – just for me. There were the emotional scars from her childhood, the bitterness from living with my father, and the ceaseless, many-syllabled names of her illnesses: Latin names, full of dread and technical jargon. There were the sacrifices she had made throughout her life: things she went without and did without; and the opportunities she let pass her by, all for the sake of her family. It was as if she were duty-bound to undo me. I was, in the most literal sense, a captive audience and the sounding board for a life she interpreted as pain. There was a lifetime of feelings to unload, and, by God, there was no time like the holidays to do it, and no one who could be made to feel more obligated to listen than me. As the only child, I considered it my fate to feel dutiful, responsible. I convinced myself to take it. And I did. But I had no idea it would cling to me with such permanency.

Freddie had sprung for the beer, getting one of the exercise jockeys at the racetrack to buy it for us. It cost him four dollars, two for the jockey and two for the beer. It was robbery, but Freddie was flush. He worked, after all, setting pins at the bowling alley above Helzinger's Hardware. He made fifteen cents a game.

What little time Freddie and I spent together that one night, laughing like hyenas and listening to each other's slurred speech, was as much without substance as it was without airs. We talked with as much bravado as we could and for as long as we could before the cold night sent us on our separate ways—home to our flannel sheets and the mysteries that eluded our understanding. We knew, though, as we walked away, fading into the shadows of one streetlight after another, that there was little need to look back, little need to hope that things would, or could, ever remain the same; that we were headed toward very distinct and separate worlds, and that our times together, and the world we knew growing up, had all but come to an end. I could sense the tundra growing even wider.

Chapel was taking longer than usual to get started, but other than me, no one seemed to notice, or, much less, seem to care. The all-around camaraderie had escalated to the liveliness of a political convention. Finally, and just for the sake of order, Dr. Luteholtz was able to coax the Hymn-For-Him quartet onto the stage. But just as they were sounding their pitch pipe, Dr. Cannon, his face ashen, made his way down the outside aisle toward the stage. Harmon Little was at his side.

There was an immediate hush as everyone hurried to their seats. Dr. Cannon's presence was quite unexpected. It wasn't often that he addressed the student body during Chapel. Within seconds we sat in total and absolute silence. He was stark and began without a greeting. "Today marks a new beginning for us all," he said, his words tender and loving. We waited. His pause was long and conspicuous. "And today," he began again, "we can be sure that angels walk among us." Something was happening. "Today we will realize the significance of celebrating the gift of life. And today we will know the preciousness of our time together and the unfathomable limits of God's everlasting love." Stillness joined the silence. "And today will test the understanding of that love. Today, we will know full well the strength of our love for one another, the strength of our belief in God Almighty, and the strength of our resolve as Christians."

Outside, the wind rushed and pushed against the chapel's ill-fitting doors. "For it is today that I stand with a heavy heart to tell you that we received word, only a short time ago, that Kellen Manly has died."

He went on with details, but they were lost against the insanity inside my head.

". . .killed in a head-on collision. . ."

Prayers that sounded like chanting began to rise all around me.

". . .yesterday. . ."

Hearts, pierced and dying, began their sorrow—that mournful pitch that somehow connects the living to the dead.

". . .apparently on his way back to Edenfield. . ."

Voices, lyrical and tremulous with confusion, and pleading with God that it not be true, wailed like demon dreams.

". . .May God rest his soul. . ."

I watched Duncan's huge frame rise up out of its seat. I stood, not knowing that I could, until his eyes found me. I was suddenly neither here nor there. There was light, but no sound; flailing and contorted faces, weeping and sobbing, but no sounds. Only a deafening drumbeat: my heart, wild and stormed, and numbed in a sea of silence. So quiet.

I watched Duncan push toward the aisle, past those bent and praying. I stood holding to the back of the pew and watching him lumber past me up the aisle, his fingers laced behind his head, his elbows forward like blinders. I wanted to reach out, to touch him, for his sake as well as mine, but just stood there amidst the sea of quiet, contorted faces, while he disappeared somewhere beyond the chapel doors and against the backdrop of a steel-gray sky.

The basement door was never locked. It opened, as it always did, with the same familiar creak. The smell of mildew and laundry soap greeted me like old friends. I stood for a moment in the doorway while my eyes adjusted to the dimness, the faint light from the double layer of clouds squeezing in behind me.

"Hello," I sang, my voice trailing off to nothingness. Somewhere on the other side of the plywood partition, I heard the furnace click on. I shut the door gently behind me. Light labored through its seldom washed glass. Shadows, variegations of blacks and grays, were the only reality, the only dimension to the darkness.

In a head-on collision. Dr. Cannon's voice was still alive in my head. *Apparently on his way back to Edenfield.*

"Hello?" I tried again, my inflection making it sound like a question. I waited like an intruder waiting for some sign of life or some signal that I was not alone. What came back was an echo of emptiness and a feeling of being in a world set apart.

I eased myself about the room, compact and common: a combination kitchen, living room, and study. Kellen's presence was everywhere, on everything: from the dishes in the sink to the books on the table, from his magazines on the sofa to a lone shoe in a corner. Like he'd stepped next door, or just gone to class. Be back in a minute.

His Sam Snead straw with the grosgrain band was perched atop a lamp at the end of the sofa. It looked ready to travel. I stood for several long minutes staring at it, remembering, before I picked it up, before I rolled it over and over in my hands. I tried to think beyond the deadness inside me.

In a head-on collision. The words again. *On his way back to Edenfield.*

How had it happened? —and where, exactly? —somewhere on

some lonely stretch of road with nothing but rocks and boulders and long exasperating minutes between cars? Had it been early in the morning with the sun in his eyes? —or in the afternoon with nothing but the glare of sunspots dotting the sky? Jesus! How long did it take before someone arrived? —before he died? What words, what name on his lips?

I waited for the hurt to wash over me, the grief to consume me, but there was little in me beyond numbness. I wanted to scream and wail and gnash my teeth, kick and curse and feel fury burning inside me. I wanted to be able to lash out at the world, drain myself of this consuming frenzy. I wanted to feel cutoff, stripped of love, wanted to feel hopeless and alone, sapped of life and strength and will. I wanted to grieve myself sick, to pay homage to my friend and brother, to sacrifice a part of myself to his memory. I wanted to feel the void, wanted to collapse. But I couldn't. What was wrong with me?

I moved off toward the bedroom. *Wouldn't it be funny to find him sleeping,* I thought, exhausted from the trip? What a celebration of one hellacious mistake that would be.

A faded red blanket with an Aztec design hung in the doorway. For one fleeting moment I believed he was there behind it and pushed it aside without as much as a sound, careful not to disturb him. A half-light from the window above his bed filtered just enough to add dimension to the room's gray upon gray. My eyes were already adjusted to the dimness and went directly to Mrs. Little. Her eyes peered back, directly into mine. I stopped dead in my tracks. She sat naked on the edge of Kellen's bed, rocking silently to-and-fro, his pillow held tightly against her breast. A sensation of pressure, of fire and ice, pulsed upward through my neck and face. Her hair was uncombed and lay in knots and mats, and her face was puffed and swollen and without the color of life. And her eyes, only empty sockets fastened and staring at something beyond me. I turned, but there was nothing, just a cinderblock wall and a stirring of shadows…and the two of us, her and me, her nakedness, her smooth-upon-smooth skin stretched taut over the swell of her thighs. I wanted to reach to touch her but didn't know how…and there were no words…from either of us… only a tight space…and me and Gretchen Little…and traces of the devil. Her eyes stayed fixed, locked, and unblinking as she continued to rock. In a flash, day had turned to night and left me knowing, then and there, that Kellen wasn't there behind the Indian-blanket door, and that he never would be again; left me knowing, then and there, and with unclouded certainty, that he was gone. Forever.

In a rush of nightmare-turned-to-life, I wheeled and broke like a stallion from a burning barn.

CHAPTER TWENTY-TWO
Beyond the Complexity and the Pain

Everything was a blur, even my running. It never crossed my mind as to where. I simply ran. Still lifes: houses and barns, fields and cross-roads, rocks and fences and trees, endlessly and as far as the eye could see, swept past me without a sound. Nothing moved, only me. No pain. Only running. And no sound except for the rasp of my breathing, and no feeling except for the jarring of my footsteps. There was nothing, only indifference and a sky the color of bad meat, and me ... running. I knew as I ran that Kellen and death were now one and the same, maybe out in front of me waiting around some bend in the road, or maybe running step-for-step behind me. It didn't matter. I knew they were there, and that they would reach out to touch me soon enough.

Castle City erupted around me. It was a mass of color, blurred and skewed and out of rhyme. But I moved through it without the slightest acknowledgment, through its onslaught of noise and aggression, in and out of its traffic like a fox on the run. The interstate bypass intercepted me on the right. I skirted across its eight lanes and then across an open field to Decker Road. It finally dawned on me that I knew where I was headed after all.

Nightfall comes early in late November, and with it comes a descending chill. I wasn't prepared for either. My orange tee shirt and poplin jacket, testimony to my belief that Indian Summer would last forever, were all that separated me from the strains of frost. I was tapped, and my breath erupted with the sounds of croup. I had run too far too fast.

Across the road, the Flamingo Motel sat against a blackened sky. Its pink cinder blocks decorated the landscape like a fly decorates a birthday cake. Its eight connecting units, alive with road-dust and dirt, gave them the appearance of misconceived bomb shelters.

There were no signs or sounds of life except for a red neon "No Vacancy" sign that blinked and stuttered above the office door. I stood with my arms laced across my chest and rocking from side to side waiting for some miracle in my blood to warm me. It was only seconds before the steam inside my jacket turned to icy vapor. I bunched my coat up around my neck, squeezing what warmth I could from its collar, and crossed to the other side.

Bea's living quarters were around back. They ran straight back from the office and rested on a concrete slab. Its hideous, mauve-colored aluminum siding and the blue tin awning over its door made it as austere as the farmlands that stretched for miles beyond it.

Off to the side, Linda Sue sat rusting in a mud hole and looking like she hadn't been moved in days. I hurried to huddle in the slip of Bea's doorway, out of the wind. I hadn't eaten since breakfast, and it was all at once as daunting as the cold and the seven miles back to Edenfield.

I squeezed against the door and stood peering through its tiny pane, trying to ignore a mounting assault by the wind and the sand it hurled against my legs. I could see only part of a room: bathed in an eerie mixture of shadows, undisturbed and mute as a grave.

I knocked without much nerve, then waited. Nothing. I knocked again. "BEA! ARE YOU IN THERE?" My voice was shaky, unfamiliar even to me. "BEA!" I blurted, my voice growing louder along with my knocks. "IT'S ME, WELDON!" I tried the handle. Locked. The awning above me popped and creaked and strained in the wind. I pounded. The sound was angry and aggressive. For just a moment, the image of Gretchen Little rocking in the darkness darted across my mind. I backed away from the door. Did she know? Had someone called? Was she in there, naked, rocking in the darkness? "BEA!" I clamored, sounding like a yelping pup under the awning.

I stood for what seemed like an eternity peering through the web of cracks spiraling through the door's glass pane before I saw her. She looked small, vulnerable, engulfed by a robe that draped clear to the floor. She paused just long enough to peer out at me hovering under her awning. I said nothing, just waited for her to unbolt the door.

The hem of her robe billowed and parted at the sudden gust of wind. Her face was pale and swollen, and for a moment we stood staring without a word before I stepped past her into the unlit room.

Its warmth rushed over me like the blast from an opened oven door.

She closed the door behind me then waited before turning around. Everything about her said she knew. She looked weak, wrung out from crying, broken in a thousand places. We waited in silence, neither of us having the words to comfort. Why had I come? What had possessed me?

"Harmon Little called early this morning," she said, her voice raspy. "He said he thought I would want to know."

I could hear my heart pounding above my own breathing. I felt offended, even violated that Harmon had worked his way into our sorrow. Words continued to escape me, lost to an overriding emptiness. I imagined Harmon's piercing nasality relaying the news.

Then I thought of Mrs. Little sitting there on the edge of Kellen's bed, teetering somewhere between mirth and madness. For a moment I wanted to collapse, ball myself up in one giant heap and cry myself into obscurity. But I couldn't. Why had I come?

"He said I shouldn't forget that death was part of the natural order." She was hoarse. "The necessary progression to our eternal reward." I felt flush despite the chill that wouldn't leave me. "And that death was the outward sign, the renewal of hope for Christians everywhere; something to be exulted as well as mourned."

I stood searching for something recognizable within her dark shapeless frame. "I think he's right," she whispered. "We shouldn't forget."

I'm certain there was nothing I could have said that would have made a difference. It was a time more suited for things like primal screams and wishing we'd never been born, not words; a time more suited for smashing things against walls and for the bite of Blackjack crashing through my brain, not a time for words. Words would come later – from others – to reflect and comfort, and at a time appropriate to the pain. This was not that time.

She began to cry, softly and under her breath. From there, she went quickly, convulsively, giving in to the weight of it all; giving in, I guessed, the way she had most of the day, ever since Harmon's call.

Outside, the wind raced full out, batting itself against all of creation. For a moment, I could almost feel myself being jostled, needing something to hold on to. I wanted it to be Bea, but even though we stood there within arm's length, close enough that I could smell the life on her skin, there was a feeling of incompleteness, as if Kellen needed to be there to make us correct, to make us whole. Still, I reached for her, hoping she would feel my strength, hoping she would want to.

I had never held Bea, not a single time, had never as much as draped my arm over her shoulder…until now. It was her hand that I first reached for. After that, we just sort of fell against one another, holding on for dear life. Yet, in the midst of it, there was a stark sense of something that warned, even forbade. But for the first time, we were pressed in and new, and I was beyond cautioning. Nothing else mattered, not protocol, not boundaries, nothing but the relief and comfort we sought. And, yes, there were stirrings, as soothing as they were shameful, as foreign as they were familiar. Outside of that, I sought only to be healed, and that something…anything…be added to my emptiness. But it was only when she allowed the encircling of my arms that I became awakened to the complexity of her touch, her affirmation. I was a stranger to such complexity, still it was the only manner of life that now seemed to make sense. We were, for a moment in time, together, braced, buoyed by chance and possibility, and beyond wanting to hold back.

"You're so cold," she uttered.

"I ran all the way here," I said, my voice unsteady. Her arms tightened just ever-so, warming me. "I just needed to run," I said. "Just needed to move and keep on moving; to outrun the light of day, life and death and the devil…all of it." My heart was pounding loud enough to hear.

"I'm glad you did," she said. "I'm glad you're here."

I was lighter than light, suspended in that instant burst of fear-and-knowing that comes between tripping and falling; caught in that split second of hurling out of control when the shock of adrenaline freezes the heart and mind; a time when there is no thought, only the sensation of being detached, part of a perpetual and unforgiving vertigo.

We stayed locked against one another: she, full and finite against me, my face buried in the soap and rosemary scent of her hair. Who or what I was, or what I was becoming, no longer mattered. Reality mingled with wonder, and I was content to let them carry me wherever they pleased.

I tightened my arms around her, used what strength I had to hold her. All that registered, and all that I had room for, was the here and now and the sensation of holding her in a way I'd known only in fits of fantasy. It was then that Kellen, as clear as crystal, peered back at me from the shadows. At first, I stood almost ready to speak, but then closed my eyes against his intrusion, against his reach into my soul and my pretense for being here.

All along the mauve colored aluminum siding the wind was without quit, ancient and bare-toothed and full of Kellen straining to lift himself from his death place. I wanted to reach back, grab hold of him, and pull him free. If only I could.

"You're trembling," Bea said, her words seeming to come from far away.

"I'm just cold," I said, looking down on her, our lips within a hairs-breadth of touching. For the longest moment we stayed that way, as nurturing as the darkness around us. But then out of some depth of tenderness, or curiosity, or even despair, she brought her cheek to rest against my own.

"I can warm you," she whispered, her breath faint and bidding. For the first time, I had a sense that she wanted to embrace all that moved and stirred, and all that rose and fell within me. And though she was full and steadfast against me, I knew she was only half there, suspended somewhere between desperation and the hope that comes with a new dawn. Still, she clung, and there was a sense of promise to it, a glimmer of what I longed for.

"I know," I said, not wanting her to pull away, but somehow wishing she would. Images of the day battled for a foothold, first filling me with the want to be lifted and carried away, then urging me to stay.

"I know you know," she whispered, a mix of consolation and grief fitting her even more rapt and sure against me.

There was a voice, a thing both inside and outside of me, telling me that Bea and I were all at once everything I ever imagined: all the things invisible and intangible, all the things that summoned, and that could be held and tasted and touched.

Yielding was how she brought her lips to mine, tasting them, once, twice. Soft upon soft and with the sweetness of all things new. And though she was exact and real in my arms, it was Kellen and his pained expression that stared back at me from the shadows. But before I could begin to understand the fullness of what we were at that moment, before the thought of it sought a level of knowing, she gathered my hands in hers and led me through the darkness to where she slept.

The luridness of a back porch light filtered through the sheers above her bed, casting her silhouette in its glow. We stood for what seemed like eternity, fastened in time, before she reached to undo her robe. I couldn't be sure if Kellen was still there reaching out, only that Bea was now a slow motion, frame-by-frame revelation. It was there in that time and place that we fell, tangled and unfamiliar; there, absorbed in darkness and sweat and affirmations that sought to bring comfort to sorrow; there—pressed and irretrievable and quickened by sounds and scents unrecognizable—that we gave and took and clung to the life that was there for the taking; there, wrapped and laced, flesh upon flesh, that night, in that instant, mercilessly reaching to get beyond the complexity and the pain, that we were changed forever.

CHAPTER TWENTY-THREE
Catch Me If You Can, I'm Dying

Somewhere in the predawn light and the remnant glow of a half-moon, we tried, Bea and I, and in our own quiet way, to make sense of what we had done. We lay close, within arm's reach, within a fragile stillness. Several times I tried gathering her to me, to ease her pain as well as my own, but my touch was hollow and un-redeeming, even to me. The last time I tried, she slowly, almost apologetically, drew her knees into her chest between us, walling me away. For a time afterward, I lay heavy and full of my own loathing, thankful for the darkness. I wanted to tell her I was sorry, and that the blame belonged to me, but there was a distance I couldn't bridge. She cried softly, her stunted breathing coming to me again and again until at last it flowed steady and unbroken. I wanted to beg for her forgiveness, but somewhere within the enormity of my regret, within the echo of Reverend Mayfield's Sunday school anthems, I knew there was nothing that could be said to salve our offense, nothing that could be done to make it right or forgivable. So I lay in stillness and watched as she tried to sleep, watched as she jerked and mumbled and responded to dreams. For some reason, I felt the need to keep vigil over her, as if watching her could make a difference, could give her peace. But somewhere amid my attempt, and in the softening haze of the morning's first light, sleep, at last, came without warning.

I woke just before noon to find Bea gone; her side of the bed so cold that it felt damp. I gathered the covers around me and stumbled my way into the living room, not really knowing what to expect or what I'd find. The house was unusually quiet, and the rooms suffused in a mulish gray, reflecting the color of the sky. The sound of the wind under the eaves whistled with renewed purpose, and I squeezed the covers even tighter around me. I called her name several times before noticing that her car was gone. The mud hole where it had been sitting looked abandoned, the water's surface rippling in the wind. I searched for a sign, a note. Anything. But there was nothing. Maybe it was her way of saying she would be back soon.

I peeked inside her cupboards with a strange sense that I was violating a trust. I hadn't eaten in a day. Still, I felt a twinge of guilt about helping myself, even kept looking over my shoulder to make sure she wouldn't walk in and catch me. Then in a pour of bran flakes and the last of her milk, I ate just enough to dismiss my hunger, and with little impetus afterwards but to go back to bed.

I spread myself, languid and without airs, across the bed and its cool rumpled sheets. Bea's presence still lingered, her pillow alive with her scent, her essence. I drew it close, held it against my face, and once again Bea and I were a beast I did not know. I lay awake provoked by a sense of iniquity and searching for ways to undo what I had done. I don't know how long I lay there before I drifted back to sleep, only that it was nearly midnight when I woke again.

For the longest time I lay in a stupor, my mind rampant with dreams and my hair and pillow wet with sweat. I ached with heaviness. Even blinking was an effort. I imagined Kellen in the shadows, watching me. I could sense him, and even expected him at any second to appear out of nowhere like the first night when he strolled around the end of my bed. I felt naked, as if I'd been caught in the act of betrayal. I wanted to ask his forgiveness for what I'd done for the way I felt about Bea, and for the disquieting sequels I played out whenever she entered my mind, which was often.

I sat upright, trying to focus, trying to make sense of my apparitions and what I was feeling, trying to place myself amongst the unfamiliar objects and their shadows. What had I done to Kellen's memory? What had Bea and I done? What had we accomplished? Destroyed? We were alone now. In different places. All three of us.

The wind had stopped, and the house had quieted to a whisper, but there was still no sign of Bea. I checked for her car, but the driveway was still barren, its mud hole as peaceful as a mountain spring. I called her name anyway. Still nothing. I was filled with a kind of veiled emptiness, like I was part of the hush that had settled over the room. I closed my eyes, traded the night's darkness for my own. I had been left to my own fate: punishment for having moved beyond my world of make-believe, for my act of betrayal.

I didn't dare turn on the light; I'd had enough reality for a while. Yet even in the darkness, the room seemed to take on a life of its own, seemed to loom with what Bea and I had done, seemed to shudder with our churchlessness, with the latitude of our crime. But the thought of her running away, leaving me to endure it alone, left me rummaging for excuses, searching for the justifications of our sin.

I eased myself out of bed and helped myself to one of the cold beers in the fridge, then discovered that sitting alone in the dark was as disturbing as it was comforting. Bea's leaving had been a clear choice: Kellen over me, his memory over all else. Her mourning had been incomplete, and I had interrupted it, skewed it. My attempt to comfort had only added pain to pain. But what did I know except that Kellen's death had been a time that cried out for someone to hold onto? It's not that often that we lose our best friends, not that often that we're undone with disbelief and the god-awful need for relief. What we did was as emotional as it was physical, as caring as it was self-absorbing. And now I could feel the distance between us. But what was done was done. It was that simple. It happened. And I couldn't take it back any more than I could bring Kellen back. It had been a moment in time, and now a part of who we were, even after the mourning.

The beer gradually worked its way into my veins, warming and numbing as it went. With it, thoughts of debts and trespasses slowly faded to a level without relevance. I bathed in it almost until daylight, until I was filled with enough confidence to leave. I tried scribbling a note to Bea, tried making sense of what I was feeling, but it was no use. For the first time, I felt like something to be despised.

I stood for a moment under the creaking sounds of the awning and thought about the long trek back to Edenfield and whether it was any longer a place I wanted to be. But I headed for it anyway. I had no other place to go.

The countryside before dawn was like another world, eerie and full of spirits. Tractors and hulking farm machinery sat crouched and sleeping against the black horizon. It all became ghoul-like in the early light. I ran toward Castle City, trying to outdistance the memories of Kellen, thoughts of Bea, death, disloyalty, betrayal, lust, love. But they stayed with me, stride for stride.

The North End Bridge was one of old steel girders; a two-lanner from the Franklin Roosevelt era that looked like it lacked the wherewithal to bear even the slightest weight beyond its own. Daybreak was kinder to it than the full light of day, but still, its flaking foam-green paint made it look diseased. Its spindly frame spanned the Sands River at its narrowest point and connected Castle City's north end to places like Mickey Dee's Diner, The White Horse Meditation Lounge, and the Flamingo Motel. I approached it like an old friend I hadn't seen for a while.

There was no protection there amongst its girders, yet still I stopped halfway across, as if inescapably tied to the memories of Kellen and the many times he coaxed me to jump from this very spot, to launch myself through the warm summer night and cannonball myself into the Sand's shocking cold waters. It was a twenty-foot fall, and when it came to plunging straight down into a deep fast-running river, I was the king of prudence. I could always rationalize why I shouldn't, why I couldn't: sore foot, kink in my neck, even something about a cousin who had once jumped from just such a spot. "They never found him," I told Kellen. "Some say he was caught and dragged downstream in an old set of bedsprings. Awful thing." But Kellen knew, and it never seemed to matter. He was simply happy for himself, to be able to float through the air in the haze of the moon, to catch the light of a billion stars, plummet and spin and finally crash with the sound of a granite boulder into its icy depths.

The times spent by the river with Kellen and Bea were times inundated with our wanting to be wanted, but, in particular, my wanting Bea. I tried to reason that it was natural that I should wallow and whimper for the taste of her, even hide behind diverted gazes to take her in. When it came to Bea, the years spent in the riddles of Sunday school and its inadvertent disseminations of guilt, had proved inadequate against the fires that burned within me.

Bea was, from the very beginning, the object of my desire, pure and simple. It was an uncomplicated desire, single-purposed and with an obsession so strong at times that it would quicken my breathing, yet I embraced it. Though it was obsession, it was *my* obsession, and I loved the searing, passionate rage it brought to me. I hated it for the way it drained me and occupied my every thought, but I loved its sense of urgency, its intensity. And I loved its unyielding nature and how it made me feel even closer to her, how it filled me with immediacy and heightened my awareness of her affect.

I turned to look over my shoulder, half expecting to see Kellen, saddened and dismayed at what I'd done; then I turned back around and for an instant imagined him poised and ready to dive into the Sands.

"WHERE ARE YOU, DAMN IT?" I screamed, my voice reverberating amongst the girders. "NONE OF THIS WOULD BE HAPPENING IF YOU WEREN'T DEAD!!! DAMN YOU!!!"

I waited, listening to my words echo up and down the bridge. I wasn't accustomed to such a mood. It was as foreign and as unnerving as the dark running water below. What world had I created with Bea? What nightmare? Where was I to run now?

The wind had begun again with a renewed rawness. Below me, the blank unreflecting Sands moved snake-like between its banks, its green-gray mass mirroring the bleakness of the sky, its purging powers seeming to vanish under the siege of November.

I moved off the bridge hunched like a taut knot and stagger-stepping against the grain of the wind. I walked as fast as I could, thinking that quick exaggerated steps would somehow warm me. But it proved too little in the wake of a sunless dawn. Once off the bridge, I turned and headed west into the section of Castle City known as Old Town. Its houses and storefronts were tall and plain, ashen and pockmarked, but it was the shortest route back to Edenfield. Street after street, unlit windows far outnumbered the lighted ones, but somehow I felt akin to its early morning abandonment, how it lay dimly lit and brooding. Occasionally, a car would wind slowly past me as if I were an unavoidable fate, a black cat ready to dart across its path. They were like monsters half asleep; marauders with their lights on low-beam and all too aware of where I had been and what I had done.

On the other side of Old Town, I began to run again. The cold was beginning to bear down on me, and I was desperate for the warmth that running would give. Queen's Hill Road was long and winding with an ever-so-slight upgrade, and the most direct route back to Edenfield. I ran the three miles to its summit where a blinking yellow light flashed nonstop day and night as a caution to its intersecting roads. As I approached, an image of Kellen standing bare chested under its pulsating amber glow, sweaty from the hot summer night and our long walk back from the Empress Lilly, washed over me as intensely as the image of Bea's nakedness in the glow that had filtered from her back porch light. Their images were dauntless and intruding, as permeating as the sheet of angry gray sky.

The intersection was barren and uninviting, and sand devils from the side of the road swirled at me, stinging me up and down my legs and across my half-frozen face. I stood wheezing, trying to catch my breath, and feeling my legs begin to cramp. I turned and headed for a large clump of trees below the crest of the hill, then moved to the leeward side of a huge, jagged fir. Exhaustion pressed in on me, soothing me like a lover. The morning's uncompromising cold and the weight of the night's remembrances were as troublesome as the tears that refused to well. From the summit, down through the trees half empty of leaves, I could make out the houses marking the outskirts of Edenfield. Beyond them, the church's big brass steeple towered amid red and gold leaves like the focal point of a painting. Beyond it all, the Sands River twisted and turned and disappeared several times before vanishing altogether.

All around me, the tops of pines hissed and swayed in the wind, and for a moment I waited for the sweet smell of Bea's perfume or the high pitch of Kellen's laughter to come rushing up the hill on some great gust of wind. I waited but they never came, neither of them. The only smell was that of dried earth and leaves, and the only sound beyond the wind was the repeated hollow crack of some clapboard shutter off in the distance, struggling to be free.

...Actually, Kellen's being gone was no big deal. I mean life would go on. So he wasn't here. So what? What does it change? Everything will be the same except for him. For him it was over. A life lived and gone. Fact of the matter, it was probably for the best. He was so unresolved. Didn't know where he was going or what he wanted to do. He was just Mr. Pretty Boy Big Shot. Well, it was just too damned bad for Mr. Pretty Boy Big Shot. I mean what could he expect? Hitchhiking all around the DAMN country; hopping in one DAMN car after another, with one DAMN stranger after another. STRANGE roads. STRANGE towns. All DAMN day. All DAMN night. He ASKED for it. And, BY-GOD, he GOT it. And now it's OVER! DONE! ARE YOU HAPPY NOW, DAMN YOU?!...

Off in the distance, the bell tower bonged like some patriarchal cock crowing before the first light. Its hollow intonation enveloped me with an unsettling dread. I looked around for Kellen – to tell him I was sorry – but another bong woke me to being knotted and stiff, and that I still had another two miles to go. I pulled myself upright and hobbled about until I could feel the warming sensations of blood in my legs. I waited until I was steady on my feet and until the bonging had faded to nothing but echoes pealing across a landscape readying itself for winter.

I checked my hiding place and thought for a moment that I might stay, but knew that its protective cover would only be temporary, no more lasting than friendships and the days of summer.

In an instant, I turned and bolted in a mindless downhill romp. Down the long winding path through a whirlwind of prattling leaves. Down the narrow, sloping, clay-packed trail and the maze of tall grasses that lurched to touch me as I passed. Down and down, faster and faster until my breath was thick and wheezy, and until I finally merged onto Edenfield Road. Its unblemished asphalt stretched before me like a velvet ribbon, and I glided onto it without breaking stride. One more mile. My legs laboring under the weight of someone twice my size, but I pushed through it, beyond what I thought I was able. Pain squeezed across my chest. I pressed even harder. Kicking. Hurting. Lightheaded. Half a mile. Across the railroad tracks. Past the sign announcing Edenfield and the billboard praising the college, past the field and the trail leading to Duncan's summer camp. On and on, always toward the brass steeple. Edenfield was ahead of me, under me, behind me—as defiant as it was devout. One hundred yards. My chest sucking and wheezing, saliva heavy in the corners of my mouth. The final shunt. A blur. The campus. The chapel doors.

My hair lay dissolved like shreds of wet black silk across my forehead. I flipped up the collar to my jacket and hunched as far into it as I could. I was wilted and clammy, and more than just a little aware of my own odor. I paced back and forth trying to shed the frenzy coursing through me then tried walking with a look of stoicism, deadpanning my way through a throng of familiar faces and their hopeful good mornings.

I hesitated before entering the academic cavity of Voyce Hall and swiped at the tickle inside my nose. Blood. I daubed and inhaled deeply…time and again, time and again…drawing the cold air across whatever had erupted. It held.

I watched as a few latecomers made their way across the quadrangle. They hurried, their heads lowered like icebreakers against the wind. They appeared miniature, dwarfed and colorless against the transparencies of a bleak November.

Voyce Hall was alive and waiting. I turned and lumbered my way into its warm musty tranquility. I was the last of the stragglers and entered through the old wooden doors marked Exit Only. I was barely inside when they banged shut behind me, their loose hardware echoing like a broken tambourine.

Except for the whir of wind rushing under the ill-fitting doors, Voyce Hall was uncommonly quiet and still. The only other sound was a tiny trail of steam escaping from an ornate and aging radiator. I stood surveying the high ceilings and long hollow corridors, half expecting to see something I'd never seen before. I scanned its air of indifference with my own and thought that maybe being here was far less important than I had come to believe.

The hall's warmth was suddenly making me flush, and I turned back around to stare out the doors, debating if I had the will to stay. The sky had grown even darker; even the lights in the hallway seemed dimmer. I leaned against the doors. The coolness from the glass felt good against my face. That's when I became aware that my hair was colder and wetter than it should be. And that's when I began to shiver.

I looked out upon the quadrangle and watched as the wind erupted with renewed intensity, like a Nor'easter gone mad. Leaves were picked up and sent hurling in a temper. Pitching and arching and diving, they swarmed and batted against one another, dipped and banked and climbed in a thousand different tucks and rolls. They were rapturous, jutting and soaring, rising and falling in a chorus of *Catch me if you can, I'm dying.*

I leaned even harder against the doors, but they seemed heavier than usual, refusing to budge. I stood for a time feeling like a shadowless presence, powerless and weak against their weight. That's when I noticed the light all around me growing fainter; and when I looked out through the doors and saw myself running and jumping amid the leaves. And Kellen was there. And Bea. And we screamed and danced and swung each other round and round. And we twirled and spun and let our coats fill with wind until we looked like bats ready to fly. And we laughed until we were hoarse and until we fell on each other in a heap; then rolled and tumbled until we were grass-stained and covered with mud. And we held each other so close that there was a blending of our musks. And we stayed there, locked and entwined, and until we warmed each other with our breaths and a chorus of "When we all ge to Heaven." We shrieked with laughter at the last flat note then peeled away to swarm again with the leaves.

"WELDON!" It was Harmon Little. "WELDON! CAN YOU HEAR ME?" I could tell he was shouting, but there was barely a sound, as if he were far off or deep in a cave.

Somewhere, there were desks and chairs groaning across wooden floors, and the shuffling of feet and muffled voices. And then I was being lifted, carried. There was a flash of faces and lips moving, but there was no sound. If only they would put me down. I needed to catch Kellen and Bea before they disappeared. I could hear them beckoning high up in the wind. Tears welled to overflowing, blinding me as I strained to search them out. All at once, I felt a rush of wind on my face and the vibration of the doors banging shut behind me. Dull voices now mingled with the arms and hands keeping me afloat. Still, I could imagine the soft earth and grass of the quadrangle beneath my feet, heavy and moving in slow motion, each step more ponderous than the last, running until I couldn't run, until I was given out, until I realized that Kellen and Bea were too far ahead of me and that no matter how far or fast I ran, I could never keep up, never catch them. And I knew that what I felt deep within was my own goodbye.

All around me, leaves soared and circled and darkened the sky. In droves they stormed the buildings and grounds, streets and sidewalks; swept past hunched and huddled figures and slithered through the silver-gray mesh hanging dank in the air. I watched with a sense of wonder as they were swooped up and tossed like tailless kites and whipped into a directionless, zigzagging fray. I closed my eyes to their wildness and let myself be lifted along with them, a single leaf awash in a rush of death; part of a rattling flurry; at one with a raspy exaltation of camouflage flaunting the chill; bliss vying for its share of days. *Catch me if you can, I'm dying.*

CHAPTER TWENTY-FOUR
No Cadillac, No Light

I spent the next three days in the infirmary recovering from a hundred-and-three-degree fever. At the end of the third day, the consensus was that I was well enough to go to church, and so discharged. Church was always the yardstick. The following week I dragged myself to and from classes on what reserve strength I had left. But by the end of the week, it too, was gone, and I ended up back in the infirmary for another three days. After the second stay, I was finally strong enough to walk without my legs feeling like they wanted to buckle. I would have left even if it hadn't been the case. Kellen's memorial service was too important to be missed.

I didn't make a point of noticing who was there, though I did look for Bea. When I was convinced she was neither there nor intended to be, I sat alone in the back. I don't remember a lot of detail except for Reverend Ivy sounding lost and muted and far away, and the eight-by-ten glossy of Kellen in his high school cap and gown propped up on a plant stand and surrounded by an array of mums. There was a song, then another, then those who rose to recognize his memory. Harmon was the first. He was skillful, overt in his sorrow and eulogizing Kellen for his sense of community, his desire to learn, and his loving, though often misunderstood, spirituality. Fulton Highlander was after Harmon. And though somber and brief, he was charitable, using phrases like *team player* and *selfless work ethic*.

After a lengthy pause, Dr. Cannon stepped to the podium, his shoulders sagged with the same weariness that was locked into his face. He was slow to start, but intricate and provocative in recognizing Kellen for his ever-endearing presence and the uniqueness he brought to Edenfield. He made it clear that Kellen's life had been a very private and uncommon struggle, and how he hoped that someday his life would be better understood and that it would serve to help bring us all to a higher and more tolerant level of Christianity. He left without returning to his seat, and with his wife clutching his arm. Harmon and Fulton filed out after them with looks of confusion dotting their faces. After that, the entire chapel emptied out, and with barely a word being uttered. I was the last to leave.

It was just before Christmas that I finally conjured the nerve to call Bea. But after only several rings, some recorded voice informed me that the number had been disconnected. I could have almost predicted it.

Without much trouble, I convinced Garth Carrier, my Christmas ride home, to take the north road out of Castle City. I said something about wanting to look at a piece of property—a future business venture—and that his opinion would be a compliment to me. His curiosity made him especially vulnerable to flattery, and within minutes we were easing across the North End Bridge and along the highway toward the Flamingo Motel.

"This is it," I said as it came into view.

"What's it?"

"This here. This motel. This is it." I was talking and pointing at the same time.

He applied the brakes at the last minute and pulled into the drive just far enough to get us off the highway. "This is it?" his voice an octave higher than usual. I glanced at him with a weak smile and sat staring at the chipped and peeling pink paint clinging desperately to the cinder block walls. Boards were nailed over the office windows, and weeds, all the way up to the office door, stood brown and brittle in the snow.

"This is it?" he asked again as if that was all he could think to say.

"Pull around back," I said. He gave me a curious but quizzical look as if not knowing how to say no, then backed off the brake and inched us up the drive toward the back. There was no Cadillac, no light. Only a wall of mauve colored aluminum siding and odd shaped pieces of plywood nailed over the windows and door.

"So this is it?" he asked for the third time.

"Yeah, I guess maybe it's not such a good idea," I said, wanting to be gone.

With nothing but a very long and very tired sigh, Garth eased us down the snowy drive and back onto the highway…due south toward

Chicago and two weeks of family. Garth drove in silence, the headlights of his rust-infected, 1952 slime-green, Chevy Bel Air coupe dim and dingy on the highway in front of us. I huddled deep inside my jacket and resigned myself to the draft from the floorboard and the whine of the transmission unable to shift into high gear. It would be a long night and a long ride—much like the kind, I'm sure, hitchhikers know all too well.

CHAPTER TWENTY-FIVE
Within the Flock

The winter semester was altogether brutal. Inharmoniousness and little in me beyond apathy had become my bedfellows. Minnesota's bleak and somber winter days didn't do much to help matters. My grades, which I had managed to raise to a level of mediocrity, hovered dismally in the same lot as my disposition. The church, the mill, the college, and the endless cold-gray days, however, seemed to be in perfect agreement, seemed to meld inseparably, knit and intertwine in much the same way as mule dung does with hay.

Memories of Kellen still hounded with a sense of finality, wearing on me in the similar fashion of Minnesota's six-month winter. I stayed to myself most of the time, certain that no one could comprehend the depth of my despair. In almost every regard, I saw myself as the last of the holdouts, the only one not resigned to death having the upper hand. To me, death had presented itself as a coward. Faceless. Invisible. The end of color and light and love. ...nothing less than the purest form of cruelty. Becky Summers said it best: said that the *time* of its coming best defines it. When it comes at long last to the suffering, it's a "merciful angel," but when it comes without warning to the young and the healthy, it's an "emissary from hell."

The two weeks at home with Mother during Christmas had helped to establish once again that life was not fair, as if I needed to be reminded. But like so many of Mother's aversions, she had to reassure me of the dark side, to make sure I understood the ramifications and pitfalls inherent in the real world. It was her way of walking me through life. "If you don't know about these things," she said, "then how can you ever expect to steer clear of them?" It was her own slice of Zen.

By Mother's account, death was just such an obstacle, as was emotional and physical pain, as was fear, superstition, prejudice, anger, and depression. And they were all out there waiting to have at me. And as fortune would have it, she wasted no time, minced no words, and spared precious little in her detailed accounts of each. The accounts were, of course, personalized, and left me knowing infinitely more about her than I ever wanted. My despair over Kellen's death, however, never seemed to give her much concern. "You're young," she said. "You'll get over it." It was the summation of her comfort. I realized then that her palmistry was predicated solely on needing someone to listen, and it was evident that my father had stopped long ago. Still, my pain had eluded her, had paled in the shadow of her own.

It wasn't until Merle Ethridge, a ministerial student from Byesville, Ohio, presented a chapel message about loss and suffering, and about how they could often be blended into strengths of hope and faith, that I was able to loosen my mind's grip on death and its sting. As a testimony to this very notion, my roommate, Erlin, organized a special roundtable of open confession so that each of us might know the sufferings of his brothers, and might come to know that we were not alone in times of trouble. It was a worthy concept, received and sanctioned by The Dorm Council. But when Jonas Wheeler, a balding freshman and Sunday school attendance-taker, told of his suffering when he, by accident, dropped and broke his gift-jar of peanut butter while on a sixth-grade field trip, I began to sense that suffering was not without its variants, and was by no means the same for everybody. And when Erlin, seized and made to stand up by the Holy Spirit, told us about his suffering because of the incessant urge to masturbate, to the tune of two and three times a day, I had the unsettling impression that the forum had somehow taken on a vague elasticity, one that stretched into realms not formatted for newness of strength or the warrants of rebirth.

The belief that confession was good for the soul—public confession in particular—kept The Church abreast of what the current sins were within the flock, and in turn enabled them to track trends and implement strategies for their restitution. But Erlin, in one uncontested revelation, had brought the room to its knees. He had seen self-conflict and inner struggle as man versus orgasmic need. And like any conscientious Christian, opened himself up to confession, letting its bite march as naked as the first day of spring down the halls and into the hearts and minds of all who were under the same condemnation. It caught and spread like wildfire. No one, it seemed, was without his indulgence. One after another they rose. Each a fallen angel, each with his head a little lower than the last. Tales of lust and orgasmic bondage aviated from rug to rafter. It was sin. They knew it and, by all the martyrs in heaven, were there to own up to it.

After a while, the image of all that semen spewing through the air, or into a sock, and from creatures with eyes rolled back and lost behind their lids, left me feeling a little like I was heading north in a south-bound lane. And even though I sat there amongst them, I was removed. Still, they rose, each a flushed and sweaty crimson, each with his own account of his concupiscence. I eased out of my chair at the back of the room and inched my way toward the door. I left knowing, and as deep inside me as I could reach, that I was not, nor ever could be, like them. I did not fit the mold of a public confessor. I would need to acknowledge my sins and my creator in some other way.

The deep and genuine flushing of sin, of bringing it to the surface—lust in particular—was the key to holiness according to Erlin. The outward sign of contrition not only revealed a deep sense of shame, but broadcast to the world a firm resolve never to sin again. It was an expression that brought The Church and the sinner into agreement, and a demonstration of the effectiveness of guilt and remorse, without which The Church would be more than a little compromised. Conceptually, it was solid…right up until the time lust came rushing back to reassert itself. And come rushing back it did, over and again, its consuming sway refusing to be ignored, even in the most resolute.

The Church made it quite clear that God could not abide sin, nor condone where it resided. So, the majority pressed upward toward the mark of excellence, denying what was natural for the sake of securing a place in the hereafter. And after a time, there was the understanding that the holier we became, the worse we'd feel the next time we sinned, and sin we would. Lust—Siren and temptress that it was—all but guaranteed it. As urgent and natural as it was, lust came with the irony of sin. And so, as often as necessity dictated, the redemptive process was revisited and renewed. Round and round, the familiar cycle of sin, sorrow, contrition, and the restoration to sanctity became as customary and as expected as the hourly bongs from The Church's big bell tower.

The whole process of our assimilation into Edenfield became quite simple once The Church convinced us that we were shameless sinners. Once accomplished, the only remaining requirement was an abandonment of our former selves. And since most of us hadn't the vaguest idea of who we were to begin with, it wasn't difficult to understand why we were such easy marks for an army of zealots driven by a mindset that it was only through The Church that truth could ever be rightfully known. They were pursuers determined to turn us toward Jesus. And we soon learned the one thing they already knew: that if we were held captive long enough, we would agree to most anything. But at the time, a life riveted to self-denial rested for me within the realm of the absurd. Lust, the principal pestilence, I figured, was in me for a reason and every bit as essential as, say, peristalsis. As far as I knew, I could see no way to reverse or undo what evolution had provided. And so, for the time being, I chose to remain unchanged, flawed as I was.

I lay awake that night listening to Erlin's breathing, thinking how the sorrow of his sin, coupled with public confession, had for the time freed him from his iniquity. The moonlight from the window illuminated his side of the room and cast him in a kind of celestial iridescence. I took it as a sign from God, one that said He was pleased. I knew only somewhat of God's light; sometimes coming as a ray of hope, an illumination to an otherwise darkened path; sometimes as a lighthouse beacon full of warning. I saw them as reflections of our efforts and in proportion to our wanting to draw near to Him. The one thing I knew for sure was that Erlin's effort was constant, striving night and day to be virtuous enough for eternal rewards. Duncan said being virtuous enough for God was far too unreasonable a thing to expect of ourselves, and that it wasn't God, after all, that was so tough to please as much as it was The Church.

"That's where the real slag comes from," he said. "Hell, they got everything wrapped up so tight in guilt they'll have people like Erlin Shadwell barking at the moon by the time they leave here. It's religion, Weldon. It ain't God."

For all I knew, Duncan may have been right. The Church did remind us on a regular basis that we were conceived in sin, shaped in iniquity, and that there was not one good among us…no, not one. It was standard exhortation. The real sorrow, for me anyway, lay in the fact that there was a growing number who had moved closer to believing it.

CHAPTER TWENTY-SIX
In a Rage of Silence

The high grass and weeds in the field behind the house were thicker now, the path narrower and less packed since last fall. I tried to imagine the spot where Harmony had waited for me, but then dismissed it like so many of her other *unpredictabilities.* Still, she was a force to be reckoned with even after I'd moved out nearly eight months ago. Whether sending me letters through the mail or calling the dorm proctor pretending to be my sister, she always found ways to showcase her ever-burgeoning libido: her sultry stares, breathy hellos, and the wistful pantomime for older and more mature prospects such as myself. Whatever Harmony's fascination with me, it was not one she chose to hide, even in church, even with all the eyes so roving and quick to judge. And though she often held me throughout the service with that same stare she used during evening devotions, I was somehow able to avoid its pull, even after she flared her nostrils and dangled her shoe from the end of her toes. I had an idea that what burned deep inside Harmony was every bit as real as what burned inside me. It was unnerving enough to want to keep a block of the most faithful between us. I saw it as righteous interference against the intemperance that sought day and night to satisfy the very thing we both had in mind. I was just thankful I couldn't see past her being anything but fourteen.

The basement door was unlocked as usual, and the musty smell of plywood greeted me outright, welcoming me back. I waited with the door open, until I was at ease with the dark and the vastness it brought to a room now half empty. As always, the refrigerator vibrated and hummed; and overhead, the floorboards squeaked and creaked, following the Littles from room to room. The sounds of Kellen were there, too, as I knew they would be, ricocheting from wall to wall.

I was still not beyond thinking that he might at any moment flip on the light. SURPRISE! I could imagine his high-pitched laughter at having caught me unawares.

I had come for the hat: his Sam Snead straw with the grosgrain band. It was all I wanted. It had become an obsession in recent weeks, something I thought would best secure his memory. I felt comfortable wanting it. I knew he'd want me to have it, even though I had to steal it.

Voices, softer than I remember, muffled their way down through the floorboards, ending in sodden tones just before Mrs. Little began her nightly piano serenade. I stopped to listen, but it was a serenade I didn't recognize, one that was slow and plodding and from the low end of the scale; one that seemed to swirl downward and out of bounds, a thing deliberate, grating, and fitful, leaching its way through the joists and past the pipes, and into my core.

"GRETCHEN! PLEASE!" The words were Harmon's, and they came rising above her playing. "WILL YOU EVER STOP?" It stopped. Sharp and pained and sour. Fists on keys. Sudden. Crazed. "WILL YOU EVER LET HIM DIE?"

I waited for the next sounds, but they never came. None but some stuttered footsteps and doors being closed for what seemed like a final time. Then came the sobbing. Harmon's. Full and weighty, and in a flood.

My hand was still on the doorknob, reminding me that I was in a place uninvited and listening to what was sacred between a husband and wife. I didn't bother locking the door behind me, just left it as it was and slipped back into the night without a sound, without a word…and without the hat.

Midterms had come and gone with only minor impediments, but my motivation had tanked, plummeted with the velocity of rocks falling down an open well. My devotion to studies just couldn't compete with the blue skies and dry warm winds of an early spring.

At first, the resurgence of differences between the floors took on an air of friendly fire, just light-hearted pranks, nothing that would create concern from classmates or faculty. They were pranks with the monotony of summer camp: a short-sheeted bed, someone's alarm clock going off at three a.m., shaving cream in someone's shoe. Just good-natured boys trying their best to stay that way. But almost without warning there was an escalation of activity, and once again pranks rose to one-upmanship. One-upmanship, however, then spiraled, as it most always did, to get-even, and get-even seguing into revenge. And before long, battle lines were once again drawn, and wars were once again being waged. Testosterone levels had risen right along with the path of the sun.

Empty pop cans spelling out FIRST FLOOR SUCKS were arranged in giant block letters in front of the administration building. Heads of chickens were left in front of everyone's door on the second floor. Voodoo dolls, complete with names and strategically placed pins, were sent to those on the first floor. A giant pentagram was chalked in the middle of the quadrangle and surrounded by orange and black luminaries. Next to it was an inscription declaring THIRD FLOOR WILL FALL. It had gone too far…once again.

The pronouncement from the Chapel pulpit by President Cannon was singular and predictably ill fated. He had turned the other cheek for the last time and announced in a staccato cadence that another single incident that even had a vague resemblance to sophomoric *moronism* would mean certain and irrevocable expulsion for those responsible. He had had it and left the platform in a rage of silence.

That night, while every window was open to the wonder and balm of a spring breeze, the public address system from The Church's main sanctuary exploded with pipe-organ horror. The sound was harsh and venomous and reverberated from the bell tower with enough volume to wake the whole town. It was a dirge of titanic proportion, a hymn from hell, strained and flat and crazed. I tried to imagine who would have the grit or the insolence to go against Dr. Cannon's decree. But by the time the pastor and the resident advisors had made their way to the sanctuary, Harmon Little was already leading Gretchen away.

Chapter Twenty-Seven
Catherine Ivy

I hadn't intended to study on Saturday night despite the fact that I was skating near the edge of academic probation…again. What was the point, anyway? —all this ceaseless inquiry? —all this academia? How had it benefited Kellen? Death made no concessions to the learned; it called and we went, regardless of how long or how hard we studied. It just didn't seem quite worth the effort anymore. Still, here I was, marching up the steps of the library, trying to honor some waning sense of responsibility. My efforts had been dismal even before I caught sight of Catherine Ivy. After that, they were reduced to rubble. I couldn't help but think that fate was at work to save me from a night of perilous obligation.

I'd gotten only as far as the reference desk when I first spotted her. She was sitting alone, her bare feet propped up on the chair next to her, her sandals askew on the floor beside her. She seemed transfixed; absorbed by the pages she flipped with the eraser end of her pencil.

My action was immediate, instinctive. Something powerful puffed me up and marched me across the library floor as if I had been conferred with full wit. I didn't bother looking left or right but headed straight to the card catalog pretending to be caught up in the heat of research. I wasted no time with my theatrics, but went straight to posturing and making believe, feigning to select the appropriate drawer, then rifling through its contents. I became a symposium of dedication: caring and artful, and with looks of inquiry wrinkled just so in my brow. When I finally gave a glance in her direction, I discovered I had been blocked from her view all the while. A display case fragmented with paleontology oddments rose up between us like some misplaced albatross. I was forced to abandon the entire facade.

"May I?" I asked, my voice as airy as I could make it. She looked up, took a second to realize that I was talking to her then looked around to see if maybe she should ask someone before answering. The library was empty except for a few stragglers huddled in sparse little cubicles around the outside walls. "This chair," I said, my voice rising, preparing for a question, "is it taken?" A slightly startled look joined the wonder on her face, her freckles suddenly taking on a deeper, darker tone.

"No," she answered, clearing her throat, a half-smile lingering. She left me feeling meek, temperate.

The chair was opposite her at the end of a long oak table, and I slid into it without excuse. Just as I did, she reached and fumbled with her papers, gathering them closer to her. "I'm Weldon Thatcher," I said in a half whisper, considerate of the library. I waited a moment then extended my hand.

Her hand was warm, and I could feel its delicate bones. She swallowed hard. "I know," she said in the same quiet tone, "I'm Catherine Ivy."

I hesitated, ingratiated by her touch. "Yes, I know," I said. "It's nice to finally meet you."

"Likewise," she uttered. We both managed smiles before becoming part of the library's silence, its book silence. She then returned to her reading and dallied with her pencil, tapping it against the pages of her book and rolling it between her fingers. Her thick dark hair curled and dangled in frizzy strands in front of her eyes, hiding them as she read. I allowed myself furtive glances over the top of my book, determined that there would be no eye contact. My fascination with her had been the same ever since I first arrived in Edenfield, ever since I noticed her maneuvering in and about town, in and amongst The Church's congregation each Sunday, and ever since I noticed how she noticed me. On Kellen's advice, I let it stand as fascination. Nothing more. She was a senior in high school and Reverend Ivy's daughter.

"No need to waste your time," had been Duncan's unsolicited advice. "Preacher's kid," he'd said in between sucking at his molars. "Too full of complications."

"Pardon me?" Catherine said suddenly. I looked up, then glanced over my shoulder to see if maybe she was addressing someone else. She wasn't.

I pointed to myself; my eyebrows raised in surprise. "Me?" I asked, caught off guard.

"I thought you said something," she whispered. Her mouth was small, but her lips were full, and I felt myself begin to derail just ever so.

"No," I whispered back, shaking my head. I wondered if I had maybe muttered something aloud. She returned to her reading.

Intrigue emanated from Catherine Ivy's every pore. It had only been in the last couple of months that I had been able to identify intrigue as one of those nuances I was so helpless to resist. I likened it to my self-imposed Bohemian life, the one that kept me cloistered during the hard months of winter and helped me to see myself as a poet – or hedonist – I didn't know which. But there had been an epiphany, something that had opened me up to the infinite number of galaxies in the wake of Kellen's death; galaxies with pitch and tone, angle and dimension, the ones I had been so blind to because my focus had been so narow, so self absorbing. Then again, maybe my epiphany was as simple a thing as growing, questioning, self-examining, the trips back and forth to my heart. But then again, maybe it was losing Bea and being stripped of what I treasured most that helped me know what was most precious. But in the wake of it all, there was perspective, things with composition unique to certain light and time of day, things I had failed to see, mostly the intricacies of the coeds that surrounded me. I could see it in the arcane and the pious, the fallow and the formal; those determined to be frigid and those destined to be frail. I could even see it in Etta Pritchett. But Catherine Ivy was altogether different. She had intrigue. And that made her readily distinguishable as art. She was by no means glory defined, but was straightaway possessing of something that connected her to the earth, to its primitive shapes and forms. She was gestures and mannerisms come to life: the way she tussled with her hair, wound it through her fingers, pulled at it just enough to tease. And then, too, there were those hazel eyes that never seemed to be fully open, and her eyebrows, thick and black, and her skin, freckled and fair, perfect in whatever light. And there was the very deliberate way she pushed her tongue into her cheek, and the way she glanced at me as if she wished I could read her mind; and the way she preened, like a cat on a back-porch swing, curious and full of mystery. And though she was a little to the left of precise, perhaps a tad Ruben-esque, she was a universe beyond plain, something new passing from bud to bloom…a *bouquet* of intrigue.

Catherine no longer used her pencil to turn the pages. Instead, she licked the tip of her finger, time and again, page after page. I cleared my throat louder than I intended. She looked up, and for a moment there was eye contact. Caught. "My throat," I whispered, pointing toward my Adam's apple. She smiled and nodded, lowering her eyes and touching her finger to her tongue once again.

There were times when Carol and Cheryl and Bonitasue still lingered life-like, still jumped and twirled in a mass of pleated skirts and pom-poms, still pranced and danced within the perimeters of my imagination. They were indelible, irrepressible images. Inescapable fantasies. Bea lingered there too, complete and inescapable. There had been very few times since our last night together that she hadn't been a part of me, hadn't lain beside me in my dreams. Often it was beyond what I wanted to entertain. And yet there were those times when I would search my mind for her, try in some unfathomable way to reach her, gather her to me … and even times when she would allow it, toy with my hunger. It wasn't all that surprising why she haunted me, or why I let her. And it wasn't until that very moment, sitting within the aura of Catherine Ivy, that I even had a sense of wanting to let her go.

The overhead lights dimmed their silent warning. Ten minutes before closing. Ten minutes to pack up and check out. Catherine hurried into her sandals.

"Calling it a night?" I managed to say, my voice cracking at the end. I could feel my face flush: hints of raspberry and cherry.

She smiled then shrugged, leaving her intentions open-ended. I stood dumbfounded while she gathered her belongings.

"Want to grab a Coke?" she said all sudden like.

I felt the blood rush from my head. I bit my lips, puffed out my cheeks, and stabbed at the table with my pencil. "Sure," I said, feeling my throat begin to close and my face go from cherry to scarlet to crimson.

"I'll be a few minutes," she said.

"I'll meet you outside," I said as I stumbled toward the door. Deep breaths. Deep-deep breaths. The air was balmy, and I was having trouble pulling it deep into my lungs. Was this a date? Deep breaths. What if she wanted to give thanks beforehand? Deeper breaths. What if she wanted me to be the one to pray? Inhale. Exhale. Who was she, anyway? Who was I? Breath. I needed breath.

"Ready?" I heard her say behind me.

We bought Cokes from the pop machine in front of The Fishes and Loaves, bought them in relative silence under a dingy fluorescent light that sputtered from the overhang. We gave each other what we thought were appropriate smiles all the while despite the moths and gnats that swarmed in frenzied circles.

"Well, here's to Edenfield," I said, clinking my bottle against hers. I drank without tasting, my thoughts busy for something to say.

"Well, hello there," a voice rang out from beyond the glow of the fluorescent light.

"Good evening," I said looking up to see Pincus Hoenaeker and his wife Hazel, obese and waddling toward us from the shadows.

"Lovely evening," Catherine said.

"Yes! Praise The Lord!" declared Hazel, stepping soldierly into the light.

We kept our smiles fixed as Pincus used his handkerchief to daub his brow. Before he finished, Hazel snatched it away and began using it like a bath towel, swiping and mopping up and down her arms and across her face, her pasty-white flesh rolling unsparingly under each soulful swab.

"You two are out late," said Pincus, unable to separate from his self-proclaimed role as citizen-father.

"Cokes," I said quickly. "Needed something to go with this balmy evening." My face strained to hold its smile.

"Well, they do look inviting," he said without ever taking his eyes off Catherine.

"All cold and wet," piped Hazel.

"Yes, cold and wet," quipped Pincus, "two things we try to avoid outside of winter."

"Yes, praise God, isn't that the truth," I added then waited while we all exchanged smiles and the substrata of Christian civility.

"Well, let's get at those drinks," Pincus said to Hazel. Hazel squealed like a stuck pig. I supposed it was her way of letting Pincus know just how in-tune she was with her feelings. Oddly, it forced me to see her in a diverse light: mainly how she, in the throes of passion, would likely buck the snot right out of Pincus while giving thanks to God with each grunting breath. It was, after all, hers to enjoy; the one thing she knew in her heart that God had reserved exclusively for husbands and wives.

I could feel Catherine retreating, inching away, the gentle squeeze of her hand urging me to follow. We said our goodbyes as we back peddled from under the overhanging fluorescence, wishing God's blessings on them both as we went. The sunken look on Pincus' face followed us for several long minutes, well beyond where the sound of our voices could be heard. Over our shoulders we watched them move about on what seemed like a lighted stage then disappear into the distant light of a quarter moon.

"What do you make of them?" Catherine asked. The darkness prevented her from grasping the fullness of my pained expression. I wanted to say they were where they belonged and that I couldn't imagine them outside of Edenfield. Instead, I said "They're different," my words emptying out into the darkness. She left them there, unexplored.

We walked with ease in and about Edenfield, letting the first rites of spring take the reins – Pincus and Hazel long forgotten. Catherine was far more animated and candid than I had imagined. We talked about the stars and how liberated the night made us feel; about eternity and the vastness of the heavens; about spirits and angels and God.

"I suppose you'll be enrolling here in the fall," I said.

"Actually, I'll be going to Mexico," she said. I slowed my steps and rolled my head in her direction. "It's true. I'm going to be a missionary. It's the message God has been speaking to me, what He's called me to do."

I could feel the same old familiar agitation beginning to seethe behind my breastbone. I couldn't have cared less about her going to Mexico, but I'd had it with trying to understand how everyone but me could have a spoken relationship with God. I was at the end of my emotional rope with it, tired of being tethered to its concept without ever a result.

"So, how does that work?" I asked, trying to talk above my agitation.

"How does what work?" she asked.

"Talking with God, getting Him to listen and to talk back, and then knowing what He says when He does." She gazed upward in my direction, her eyes wide and amazing, full of the shadows that only a quarter moon could cast. "How do you know," I said "that you're not imagining things when you say He speaks to you? How do you know that you're not just so full of hope that you believe what you want to believe?"

"You really don't know, do you?" she said. My silence was confirmation that I didn't. "It's not actually a voice," she said in a tutorial tone. "At least not the kind you're used to." She gave a quick touch to my arm. "It's more of a feeling," she said without losing stride. "Deep inside. In your soul. In your heart. It's either confirming or not…depending on which way God intends to lead you; depending on what He puts in your heart to desire." Her innocence was matched by her conviction. "I don't know what else to tell you," she said.

We walked for several long minutes without talking. I wasn't clear about a lot of things, but felt disposed to reaching out to her as if she were my last hope for resolution. "I'm not really sure what I need to know," I said. "God's ways become more of a mystery to me by the day. Seems the more I learn about His ways, the more estranged He becomes. Makes me wonder if it was His intention to be so complex." I needed her to know my confusion, and nothing would do except to lay it all out for her, let her sort through it in her own way. "I think about all that time in Sunday school," I said, "...all that time in agreement with what was taught. Now I just think about how it so often seems like a kettle of spinach."

Catherine was an attentive listener and waited while I rattled on about simpler times and in the straightforward, unhurried fashion of "Jesus loves me yes I know, for the Bible tells me so."

"Do you ever pray?" she asked with a voice glazed in meekness, as if she had been embarrassed for having asked it.

"I try to pray," I said, not knowing that my efforts were ever wholly sincere, "but mostly it's been a colossal waste of time."

"Because you don't get what you ask for?" she said.

"No," I said, "because I never know what to say. And on those rare occasions when I do think of something, it comes out like it's wooden. They're just words that sort of fall out of my mouth and onto the floor. I don't claim to know the first thing about prayer, but I know when it's not working."

"Well," Catherine said without looking at me, "my daddy says prayer isn't so much what we SAY to God as it is the condition of our heart when we come before Him." She smiled as if she knew the truth of the matter. "I mean, it's being mindful of Him that prompts us toward the intimacy of prayer in the first place." She hesitated just long enough to ask if I thought that made sense, though I suspected she was really asking if I believed it. I told her yes. "I don't always *decide* to pray as much as I'm *directed* to pray," she said. "My desire is simply to be *near* God, to have a heart-to-heart intimacy. It's really an act of dependence and adoration, being open to His Spirit, or to His voice if you will, that makes us willing to enter into His presence. Prayer is simply a response to love."

I felt myself being pulled along by her assurance. Her voice on the night air reminded me of the nights with Kellen and Bea, how their voices resounded in the moonlight, and in the rush of the wind and river. We sauntered without regard to time or place, daring now and again to lean too close, to touch. And even though there was effortless sharing and imagined freedom, it was the occasional silence that made me most aware of the harmony between us; that made me most aware of the pleasure in simply listening to our footsteps on the gravel roads.

The parsonage was well lit. First floor lights were on throughout, and the porch light was on high beam. "Wait here," Catherine whispered, "I won't be long." In the next instant she was across the lawn and onto the porch. It was only minutes before one room after another went to black, even the porch light. With a watertight certainty, she had closed the parsonage for the night. Except for a tiny amber light that glowed like a candle in the living room window, the parsonage was cloaked in darkness. Minutes later she stood as a mere shadow in the doorway, barely a silhouette in the nightlight's amber glow.

Slowly. Slowly. Without a sound, she pulled the door shut behind her. Then, and in her bare feet, led me by the hand to the darker-than-dark garage behind her house.

"Are you sure this is a good idea?" I whispered.

"Shhhhhhhhh," she warned, her finger upright against her lips.

We waited, silent and wide-eyed, fixed in the coalmine darkness of her garage. "Are you scared?" she whispered.

"No," I said through a dry mouth…a lie that only amplified the Brobdingnagian pounding in my chest.

"What do you think?" she asked, leaning into me, her breath feather soft against my cheek.

Almost at once, I could feel her arms closing around me, her hands on my back, the stab of her breasts dense and eager on my chest. In the charcoal darkness I could feel her thighs trembling and her hips full and strong against my own. All that was left to the imagination dissolved in an instant when she guided me to where she wanted to be: inside her daddy's car.

In less time than it took to close the door, we were one, single, indistinguishable and inseparable, smothering under each other's might. We were all and everything, chaotic and convulsive, inflamed and bestial; mere things without compromise or composure, left to know each other only by feel. We were unknowns. Undone. Ungodly.

It was then that a light —kitchen? —shot like a lightning bolt through the garage window. We froze, seared to the seat, sweating like pigs ready for slaughter. For a single moment, I was seized by the thought that this was the preacher's daughter, and not just any preacher's daughter, but the preacher of Edenfield, and that we were both unbuttoned inside his car. Even if we didn't get caught, God would know. Could the road to hell be any shorter? I sat there gasping, looking at the air freshener with the face of Jesus hanging from the rearview mirror.

Just then the light turned to darkness. Reprieve.

"I have to go," I wheezed.

"No," she said, "Not yet." I could feel her body tense, mine weaken. Instantly my mind was wild with needing to be anywhere but here. But then there was that all-pervasive knowing that told me I needed to be still, to ready myself for the tiniest sound, for the slightest movement, for the next lightning bolt that would surely greet us with the fate of a Judas kiss. My sweat began to thicken.

"I really need to go," I said.

"No," she said, "that's probably not what you REALLY need… or want."

"How could you possibly know what I want?"

"Because you're a *guy*. And I'm not naïve. You want what all the others want."

"I'm not like all the others," I said. "I don't want what all the others want."

Her eyes glanced up at me in the darkness. "Not even the *smudge* of me?"

I'm not sure how long or how far I ran before heading back to the dorm, only that there was a stitch in my side by the time I got there. When I got to the room, Erlin's snoring was light and steady, and the hands on his glow-in-the-dark alarm clock pointed straight up at midnight. I was too wired to sleep, and the run had done nothing to help. So I lay atop my covers trying to sort through the images of the night and the anomalies of Catherine Ivy, farce and corruptibility leaving little room for anything else.

I can't say what it was exactly that caused me to bolt and run, only that I did. Fear and anxiety, I suppose, and the suddenness of my most coveted fantasy being offered without condition. Then again, maybe it was just cowardice. But it didn't matter. All I knew was that putting distance between her and me seemed to be something far less likely to cause pain than if I'd stayed.

I hadn't expected anything from Catherine beyond what comes from the casualness of infatuation. I simply hadn't anticipated her intensity—or her defiance for that matter—to the things of *thou shalt not.*

She was so alive: courtesies and endearments, curiosity and spiritual discernment. But then there was that final suggestion, her whispered breath like an oven blast against my face. And even though I resisted, there was still that very real part of me that wanted what she offered. Even now it urged me to go back, throw a stone at her window and ask if we could pick up where we left off. But then there was the other part that wanted to keep running.

Erlin's breathing had become sonorous, as if he were laboring up-hill under a heavy load. It seemed a fitting lullaby to my dissonance.

How had I resisted Catherine, anyway? —set aside my own carnality? I'd had no such reservations with Bea. But I was certain there were remnants of love with Bea. Had it been the only difference? If so, I wondered if God had seen my running as a sign of righteousness. It was a stretch, but one with possibilities, one that might establish the beginnings of a personal relationship. Still, there was that part of me that wanted to retrace my steps, go back, throw that stone.

Erlin had grown increasingly uneasy with my frequent lapses of faith, with my inability to establish a spiritual bond with The Almighty and came right out and said that God had already established a relationship with me, whether I knew it or not. It was just my *flesh* that kept getting in the way; that kept it from becoming aligned. And no matter how hard I tried to think it through, the carnal part of me was not equipped to handle it because a personal relationship with God was simply nothing known to the secular world, but something supernatural—something belonging to the spirit—nothing that would satisfy the precepts of reason and intellect.

If that were the case, could my running from Catherine Ivy have been prompted by the spirit? Had God been able to work through my spirit and do for me what I could not do for myself? Was that part of the relationship?

There was a hush to the streetlight filtering through the trees and onto the wall above my bed, a hush to its abstract shadows of leaves and branches dancing in the quiet of night. It reminded me of an Edenfield holding its breath, waiting to exhale, much like me in the aftermath of Catherine Ivy.

Outside, voices in low talk filtered through my window then faded, inching into the night. I wondered if Catherine had heard them; wondered if she was lying awake this very minute staring wide-eyed into the darkness and thinking about me running away, about my rejection? I was never clear about preachers' kids except that they were somehow a breed apart, nothing that seemed to fit a mold except for maybe an inordinate mix of rectitude and onus. I tried looking beyond that mold but kept coming back to Catherine as a product of a thousand different sermons and as many entreaties; kept coming back to her as being summarily scrunched and packed and tamped into a ball of repressed desires, even resentment. I should have learned as much from Duncan.

Erlin's snoring continued its upward spiral till it reached a level of distress, something akin to a steel rake being drawn through gravel, and something that brought me further into wakefulness with each inhalation. It was nearly two o'clock before he changed gears and lapsed into a slow melodic rhythm, and before the jolt of Catherine's final words began to wane, before I finally slipped past them into the blessedness of sleep.

CHAPTER TWENTY-EIGHT
Duncan, Mother, and the Big Silver Quonset Hut

Duncan was noticeably upset that I decided to leave Edenfield for the summer. He had extended one invitation after another to stay with him at his camp, but the camp seemed to lack the respite I thought I needed. His final plea came just before my last exam. It was in the form of a declaration with a number of promises as enticements— the old carrot-on-a-stick ruse. He not only swore he would dig a new latrine, but even promised to maintain it. "Got plenty of toilet paper," he said. "No problem there. And we can always get more." This I knew to be true. He assured me that we were guaranteed a steady supply of fresh vegetables from his uncle's garden, and that he'd personally steal all the apples and corn we wanted, whenever we wanted them. When the look on my face told him he needed to up the ante, he said he would do all the cooking, and that I wouldn't have to pay rent. When I still hesitated, he had no choice but to use his trump card, his ace in the hole. In one gigantic facial wince, he shifted a thoroughly ripened chaw from one side of his mouth to the other, spit out the bits and pieces that came loose during the transfer, then, after a rather lubricious tug at his crotch and a quick look over his shoulder, told me in a hushed tone that he was working on a system using an old generator to pump water straight from the river to the camp—and even to heat it. He said it was the sort of thing he didn't feel comfortable broadcasting, because if people knew about it they'd more than likely be wanting to get the health department in on it. And it was just the kind of red tape he didn't need to be bothered with. Though he did add that the water probably wouldn't be up to drinking, and that we really ought not consider it for cooking either, but he was just as quick to add that it would be good for everything else.

When he was finished talking, he contorted the muscles in his face to squeeze off a ferocious amount of tobacco juice which he let overflow his bottom lip and spill unaided alongside one of his boots. "So, what do you think?" he said, wiping his lips with the back of his hand. I shrugged, hemmed, and hawed. Finally, he gave me a look that said he was losing patience. It was a look tinged with bewilderment as to why anybody would hesitate, even for a minute, at such an offer. I said that I was appreciative of his invitation but felt what I really needed was to be away from Edenfield for a while. He just stood there with his lips pursed and snorting through his nose. After he studied me with some degree of disgust, he scratched and pawed at himself and finally said that he thought all I really needed was a swift kick in the ass. He left without another word, the smell of Beechnut lingering in his wake.

Badgering me came all too easy for Duncan. He thought that calling me names like Faint Heart and Milksop would somehow win me over. It didn't. And two days later I was back home with Mother.

After the first weekend at home, I was convinced that being with Mother was not the change I needed after all. Her world, over the course of a year, had been reduced to the confines of her house and the irrepressible memories of dead relatives: brothers and sisters, third and fourth cousins three and four times removed; great aunts and uncles I'd never heard of, and even some she'd never even met. There were stories that had been passed from one generation to the next about this one and that one; about Cousin Esther and Uncle Bill and the cow they stole and kept in the house all winter, about how somebody had danced off the end of Grandmaw Ann's porch and broke his neck, and even about somebody's half-sister being their mother. There were endless accounts about the heroics of suffering and the ingenuity of survival; stories about natural disasters, about creeks overflowing and babies and snakes and houses all being washed to the river together; about Uncle Aaron and how he would be fetched in the middle of the night to lay his hands on the sick and fevered, and pray and chant in inaudible tones and heal by faith; stories about Grandpaw Winright and how he would in drunken rages chase the whole family from their beds with his shotgun and make them sleep out the night in the orchard; about Uncle Reece's one-eyed rooster that was possessed by the devil and how it had jumped up and cut the throat of a man named Turner something-or-other; and about a neighbor's bull that broke through the lower bottom fence and gored and killed their one and only mule named Ole John, and how Ole John's ghost would come back and run round and round the ceiling of the back bedroom on nights without a moon. It was all there within her. And for reasons known only to her, she felt compelled to dispense it all to me.

Mother had also taken to singing a lot, mostly at night and always from her rocking chair. "We Shall Gather at The River," "How Great Thou Art," and "Amazing Grace" were mainstays, her link to kingdom come. She also spoke of Armageddon with consistency and a deepening sense of joy. And she spoke of how the scriptures had made it all very clear to her what path my life should take – none of which was subject to debate – and how glad she was that she had the entire summer to reveal it all to me. One week and a severe nosebleed later I was back in Edenfield, encamped within the sanctuary of Duncan's wilderness compound.

Each morning, the inside of Duncan's tent held tight to a dank musk and a dew-like chill as if it had overnight become part of the river bottom. Waking meant suffering with muscle soreness and a sinus headache, the sort of things we needed, according to Duncan, to make us feel alive. Even the early morning sun was useless until it came full view over the eastern rise. Then it was only minutes before it converted the dew-soaked canvas into an oxygen-starved oven.

Spiders knew the tent as home more than I did. They worked openly, night and day, to attach themselves to whatever was unwitting enough to be in one place too long. And where I devoted myself to destroying their handiwork, Duncan worked to protect it. He considered himself an ecological savant, adamant about living compliantly with nature and letting spiders and all things with digestive systems assume their natural place without interference from the likes of us, though he did take exception to mosquitoes.

After about a week's worth of river baths, sleeping on a surplus Army cot, and the alternating torridity and hoarfrost, I began to question the soundness of my decision. But after the first heavy rain left me and everything I owned smelling like an outhouse mop, I decided to risk what was surely to be a scarred reputation for the sweep and swell of the big silver Quonset hut that sat adjacent to the soccer field.

The Quonset hut had once served as the campus laundry, but had been converted into living quarters for students working at the mill during the summer. As a qualifier, I wasted no time in exercising my option.

Duncan took my departure to heart. Why anyone in his right mind would want to leave his personally crafted Mecca was beyond him. He accused me of being too coddled to understand or appreciate what real men feel. He was offended and did the one sure thing to let me know it. He shot a long silky stream of tobacco juice into the dust between my feet, the spray landing across the tops of my shoes. Then in a final gesture, waved me off and disappeared behind the burlap curtain surrounding the latrine. It was only minutes before I slung what little I owned over my shoulder and worked my way in the direction of the Quonset hut and the tangerine-colored sun-ball sinking beyond the horizon. It wasn't until I settled in that I realized that ninety percent of the Quonset hut's summer residents were devotedly committed seminarians.

Catherine Ivy departed for the mission fields that summer—a two-year commitment near Manzanillo, Mexico. When her father announced it at Sunday services, it brought a round of praise from the entire congregation. Reverend Ivy stood broad chested and deep in his own smile, proud that Catherine had so much love to share.

Mrs. Little was rumored to be doing much better since the night of her bell tower prelude. Harmon offered words of assurance that she was receiving the help she needed and was progressing with God's speed. I didn't see much of Harmon that summer, only an occasional glimpse of him chasing here and there in his Volkswagen bus, the long strands of his comb-over caught in the back draft and trailing like the tail of a kite out his side window.

For the most part, things at the mill were unchanged and Fulton Highlander was there as an icon of perseverance to make sure of it. Unlike Fulton, however, my bunkmates and future seminarians were of the same persevering mind, the Bible, as ever, their mantle and guiding light. They read it and slept with it; debated and discussed it; brainstormed, pondered, challenged, and questioned it; preached, sang, and prayed over it; and interpreted, compared, concluded, and testified on its behalf. They were a dogged lot, always trawling as deep and as far as the Holy Spirit would take them. Their pursuit for the truth carried on each night well after the lights were out, and on many occasions began again even before Floyd Hanna's roosters started their morning anthems. Scripture was what sustained them on their way to the mill, at the mill, and on their way home. It was milk and honey for their souls; the thing discussed at breakfast and over supper; what was dissected while standing next to each other at the urinals and in the showers. But it was especially intimate and exaggerated while they sat next to one another on the commodes. There were no stalls or partitions in the hut's lavatory, only a conspicuous line of commodes where each of us shamelessly recycled his meals in full view of the others. It was just the way it was. And without any means to change it, it grew to be a favored place for the longest and most intense scripture sessions. It was unthinkable to do a sit-down without at least a copy of *The New Testament* and the time to fellowship. It was just another way of doing battle for The Lord.

Duncan and I still worked out back in the Hinterlands, even though he made sure he hissed at me whenever we got within proximity. He kept saying I had "broke camp" as if I had turned tail and run after encountering the enemy. But after about a week, the pretense of being at odds became too draining. We were simply missing too many opportunities for foolery. In a parlance of *let by-gones be by-gones,* we returned to our rightful selves. Besides, Duncan was my sole supplier of apples, pilfered or not.

Chapter Twenty-Nine
Gold Leaf Envelope

The latest in a series of shop foremen was R. T. Hammersmith. He was blind in one eye and about as wide as he was tall. His disposition forever suggested that he had just crawled out from under a rock, and the permanent scowl attached to his face was his implicit badge. He was bowlegged, most likely from having to support the equivalent of two torsos, and his voice was so deep and gravelly that everyone called him *Balls*.

With Balls sending us one reject after another, the biggest part of our summer was spent in trying to train them without getting them maimed. To a man, they were more hindrance than help, forever stumbling and falling, smashing their hands, straining their backs; always complaining about the heat, the noise, the bugs, the smell; always late, always needing something to drink, and spending half of the time in the toilet. They all wanted jobs, but none of them wanted to work. Duncan figured they had spent too much time in arts and crafts classes, too accustomed to the intricacies of cutout dolls and what could be composed with colored pencils. After a time, Duncan began sending them back about as fast as Balls sent them to us. Even Cleveland had taken to throwing sticks at them. After about five weeks, we got some scrawny looking misfit by the name of Billy Screws. He stood just a little over five feet tall, weighed about as much as Duncan could pick up with one hand, and paraded around like a bantam rooster. He had long blond hair that he kept greased up high on his head and slicked back behind his ears into a ducktail. He let us know right off that he was from Castle City and wasn't about to take any flap from that countrified, preacher-looking interrogator by the name of Fulton Highlander. Duncan and I were both very supportive and even reinforced how fair and noble we thought his thinking was. Balls said Billy was the last of the *organisms* that Fulton intended to hire, and we could either train him or do without. He said at this point it really didn't matter much to him one way or the other because come September the Hinterland saw operation would be nothing but history anyway.

Billy was another one who didn't much care one-way or the other. Despite our insistence that he follow the established safety rules and procedures, he was determined to do things his way, even though he came close to killing himself on several occasions. He seemed to have a mindset that the hard way was the only way. The one thing, however, he did care about was the fact that he had landed a job, his first one as a matter of fact, and, by God, nobody had better try and take it away from him. He was here to stay, to work and to earn his way. As obnoxious and unsafe as he was, there was really no choice but to keep him (it was either him or nobody), and so we allowed ourselves to become accustomed to him, which was, in the main, pointedly better than becoming attached to him. We were, without our usual resistance, resigned that he was to be permanently ours, and rationalized that what he lacked in smarts he made up for in tenacity. He was nothing less than a bull terrier fast at a rat hole. And to his credit, and to Duncan's and Cleveland's delight, he loved to spit Beechnut.

Within weeks, Balls' words about our saw operation began to take on meaning. Huge flatbeds began delivering machinery and equipment. And shortly thereafter, contractors and engineers of all sorts began converging on the mill. They wore hard hats, carried blueprints, and swarmed around as stiff and clean as military officers. There were crews dismantling and removing old equipment, clearing huge areas of floor space, jack hammering out old footings and pouring in new. It was a show of progress, planning, and imagination. It was ingenuity and teamwork, all the things that left awe-inspiring impressions on the sweat-stained labor force of the mill.

For weeks-on-end, a monstrous piece of equipment was laid out, assembled, modified, programmed, tuned, and debugged. It finally emerged looking like a fancy, shiny miracle. It stretched almost from one end of the mill to the other. It was a combination saw, riveter, and stacker, and had an output of what eight men could do. It was twice the length and size of the Hinterland saw, twice as bright, twice as fast, and was operated by the push of a button. It even had a vacuum system that sucked up every bit of sawdust from every cut, and blew it clear beyond where the old Hinterland saw now sat as nothing more than a relic. Automation had come to the mill, and it was Fulton Highlander's finest hour. But it wasn't until it was fully operational that we came to understand its impact.

The Friday before Labor Day Weekend, Fulton took it on himself to sound the quit bell an hour early. He was anxious to assemble everybody for his inevitable announcement which started with a prayer, though mumbled and irritatingly short. I was left feeling corrupted simply by its insincerity. But to Fulton, everything had taken on a posture of insignificance next to his new saw. To say he was merely excited would not do him justice. It was more like his entire persona had been injected with enthusiasm. His talk began in just the same way, but then dwindled to platitudes about sacrifice and cooperation, and about being competitive in an ever-changing and ever-growing industry. He was riding a high horse and feeling confident that that's where he belonged when he announced that the new saw meant the elimination of a number of jobs. However, he wanted us to know that he had a moral responsibility to the mill and could not let the loss of a few jobs stand in the way of progress or profit. He let us know how he had for weeks wrestled with this dilemma, how he had prayed about it and at last came to accept that it was not only the right decision, but the Lord's will. His gargantuan smile was his reassurance to us all that his decision was as nonnegotiable as it was right.

Cleveland stood beside me, his shoulders slumped, making him appear even smaller than he was. He had read Fulton's lips without error. For an instant his eyes scanned up at me, and I noticed his cud sitting dry and lifeless in his jaw as if it had lost all flavor and purpose.

Without missing a beat, Fulton went right into thanking all of us for helping make the transition to the new saw a success. But then gave a *special thanks* to those who would, after today, no longer be toiling alongside us.

"Please know that we will not forget you or the contributions you have made," he said. "We will always consider you as part of our mill family, and please know that you are always welcome to come back and visit." He paused, the silence around him deadening. "We hope that these special envelopes reflect our appreciation for all that you've done. They're not gold leaf for nothing, you know." There was a trickle of laughter, but only a trickle. Still, he paused, waiting for reassurance and approval of his humor and humanity. But there was only dead air, and he seemed to hang there, motionless in his three-piece suit, suspended only by his smile. "I'm sure," he continued, but with a more dampened tone, "that those of you who will be leaving are destined for bigger and greater challenges, and along with it even bigger and greater rewards." There was no sound except for the inadvertent rattling of a few lunch boxes and some throats being cleared.

With a voice as flat as the floor under our feet, Fulton began calling out the names of those receiving their last paychecks. One by one they filed past him, some with a look of bewilderment, others blank and expressionless. Fulton handed them their severance pay with a tentative smile and an even more tentative handshake.

Billy Screws heard his name and moved to the front where Fulton shook his hand and handed him one of the gold-leafed envelopes. "Billy has only been with us a little over two months. Two hot months I might add." There was no laughter. Still, Fulton smiled widely into a sea of blank faces. "Well, anyway, Billy has done a great job for us filling the spot left by Kellen Manly." Billy looked confused. "Good luck, Billy," Fulton said, "wherever God may lead you."

Billy paused, puzzling over the gold-leafed envelope. "What do you mean 'Good luck and about God leading me'? What's this all about?" Billy was oblivious to his fate. Nothing had registered. There was chuckling from the assembly. "Wait…wait a minute," Billy said. "Just hold on a minute here," his look going from puzzled to concerned. More chuckling.

"Billy, please, we have to move along here," Fulton said, his voice nerved. Billy moved slowly away, dazed. The chuckling grew to scattered laughter and guffaws.

"Well then," Fulton said, trying to regain control – the work force having trouble quieting its buzz after Billy. "CLEVELAND YATES!" Fulton bellowed, the work force stiffening, returning to quiet. "WHERE ARE YOU CLEVELAND?" He spotted him with the help of some of the others. "COME ON UP HERE OL' BUDDY!" The hush that filled the air reflected the somber look on everybody's face. Cleveland hesitated, his jaw slack, then stepped forward after being nudged by those who knew him best. He shuffled up to the front and stood looking withered alongside Fulton. His head hung so low that we couldn't see his face, only the top of his hat. Fulton was then handed a special gold leaf envelope by the sumptuously top-heavy Sara Bennett. "You know, boys," Fulton said, "I could say a lot about ol' Cleve here. I could go on about his forty-odd years of service and about his never missing a day, about his production records, and about him never getting hurt, but all that stuff's neither here nor there. Besides, we've heard it all before. But just for the record, let me say that Yates here is one of the best darn saw operators this mill has ever had, and doggone it, we're gonna miss him." That was it. Fulton smiled from ear to ear, handed Cleveland his last paycheck, and patted him on the back while Sara snapped a Polaroid. The flash triggered a smattering of clapping. "Now let's have some CAKE," echoed Fulton. His smile was never bigger.

Cleveland never looked up, just stood there fingering the gold leaf envelope, lost behind his hat and forty-odd years of memories; lost to the silent clamoring and scrambling for the chocolate sheet cake with its blue icing salutation: HAPPY DAYS!

Most everybody shook Cleveland's hand, then left him standing alone until he shuffled quiet and alone out the door. Duncan and I followed and walked with him to his old pickup. We stood huddled there alongside its rusty, faded greenness, its sagging frame, and the smell of hog shit filtering from its bed. We stood in silence, transfixed, waiting for Cleveland to look up, to make eye contact. I fixed my mouth to say something, anything, but nothing came. We all tried smiling, then stood scratching at the gravel with our boots. We were stymied, caught in the constraints of good-bye, when Duncan reached past me and handed Cleveland a remaining half pack of Beechnut, placed it in his hand with a gentleness I'd never seen. Cleveland stood staring at it for some time, then nodded.

The door of his pickup creaked from its years without oil then closed with a thud. He gave us a long but faraway look, the tip of his tongue gently daubing and searching for the taste of Beechnut cradled in his cheek. Then with a heaving breath, pulled out of the graveled lot for the final time, the back of his head and the silhouette of his old felt hat gradually fading along with his truck and its trail of dust. It was a long goodbye.

Chapter Thirty
Billy Screws

Over the summer, the college had purchased a number of houses adjacent to the campus. The increase in enrollment had made it necessary. Right away Duncan saw the added housing as a chance to live *off campus,* which equated to more freedom, which, when broken down, simply meant less chance of getting caught at whatever he might concoct. In a word, he was euphoric, and plowed through each of the houses and each of the rooms with a measuring tape. To Duncan, bigger was better, and there was no doubt that the biggest room was going to be his. There would be no standing in line and taking chances. To Duncan it was a done deal: he was an upperclassman and bigger than everybody else. Case closed. Besides, he decided that taking care of his housing in advance would be tantamount to doing the school a service by lessening the stumbling blocks of confusion during registration. And while he was at it, and to avoid even further confusion, he told me I was going to be his roommate (another done deal). It only took him about six seconds to convince Housing Officer Miles Pentler, rejected from working at the mill due to personal frailties, to approve the necessary paperwork.

Outside of attending church, Duncan and I spent the biggest part of Labor Day weekend dismantling his camp, packing, moving, and setting up house. Our room was gigantic. It had to be the only over-sized bedroom in the entire town, and it was ours. But by the time we had stocked and supplied it with everything Duncan thought we needed, the room turned out to be eighty percent his. Basically, I still clung to my one cardboard box of books and just enough clothes to fill one suitcase. With my bed and desk jammed together in a far corner, twenty percent seemed to fit me just fine.

Registration began that Tuesday. Duncan and I were the first ones there and were in and out before it began to heavy up. By ten o'clock we were at the mill. We hadn't the slightest idea what we'd be doing or where we'd be working, but it didn't really matter much anymore. What once was, was gone; the ashes of our team and playing field scattered to the wind. Our message to Balls: *Put us where you will.* Work was work, and we were there simply to satisfy the tuition ledger sheets of Harmon Little.

We wondered why the parking lot was empty, but we no sooner came through the door than a stench as foul as God had gall to create, hit us head on. Heavy. Oxygen robbing. Plain ole eye-watering, breath-holding putrid. "Lord have mercy," I heard Duncan say, "HOOOO-WEEEE!" And the next thing I knew we were fighting our way back out the same door we just came in. Balls was right behind us.

"If I ever get my hands on the ORGANISM who done this, I'll debone him!" Balls was talking to the wind, his words for anybody who would listen.

"What in the name of the Almighty happened?" Duncan pleaded.

"Somebody went and filled socks with honey dip, then used'em to beat hell out of everything in the mill!" Balls never pretended to be eloquent.

"WHAT?" shrieked Duncan.

"You heard me," growled Balls, "Beat desks, typewriters, telephones—anything that didn't move. Wasn't nothing spared. He even beat the coffee cups. Wasn't a place or thing that was missed: windows, walls…hell, even the bathroom stalls. Every piece of equipment in the plant got it. Everything's got to be steam cleaned and disinfected. Health department's already been here and gone. Sent everybody home. I'm just waiting on some cleanup crew from Castle City to get here. Gotta disinfect the whole plant, offices too. Then we have to wait for the Health Department to come back and give us an okay. Hell, this whole thing might take a week."

"When do you figure it happened?" Duncan was grinning, pretending he was squinting from the sun.

"Figure sometime last night cause a lot of the dip is still soft. Fresh. You know."

"You say he beat on everything in the plant?"

"EVERYTHING!"

"And you say it was socks he used?"

Balls stared past both of us into the brilliance of a blue diamond sky. "Socks," he uttered with a grimace, the mere word seeming to leave a bad taste.

"Must have used more than just one!" Duncan was in his glory. Agitating.

"Found over fifty already," Balls said. "Me and Orlo been here all morning."

"Where do you think he got all the dip to fill 'em with?"

"Saved it up! Borrowed it from friends! How in hell do I know?" Balls waved his arms like he was trying to blot out the whole thing.

"How about the new saw?" Duncan asked guardedly.

Balls hesitated, then hiked at his britches and made big swiping motions with his handkerchief across his forehead and the back of his neck. "Hardest hit of all," he said. "Gear boxes, conveyors, electrical panels, even the catwalk. Like it was the main target."

"Damned shame," said Duncan, his eyes darting from me to Balls.

"How's Fulton handling it?" It was Duncan's final jab.

"He's so mad he can't get his teeth unclenched." Balls had a worried look. "Left outta' here spewing something about killin' n' eatin' somebody. Sprayed gravel all over the lot with that Caddy of his."

We shook our heads and made all the necessary gestures we thought would best demonstrate our disgust, then made our way back to the campus to check out what we trusted would be a promising crop of co-eds. For the first minute or so we didn't say a word, just kept glancing over our shoulders and smiling at one another. But once we crossed the road, Duncan spit out his chaw and bought me an ice-cold soda pop from the cooler in front of The Fishes and Loaves. But before I took a sip, I hesitated just long enough to clink my bottle against his. "To Billy Screws," I said. He stared at me cockeyed and with a held breath before bursting into a howling jig-dancing fool. He looked and sounded like he'd just discovered gold. He finally gathered himself long enough to wipe his eyes with the sleeve of his shirt, and his lips with the back of his hand. Then, without another second's hesitation, clinked his bottle against mine and added very formally, "And to the back seat he was conceived in." We both waited, open-mouthed and wide-eyed, before shattering the silence that hung like an invisible bubble between us. We figured Billy Screws finally figured out what that gold leaf envelope was all about.

CHAPTER THIRTY-ONE
Becky and the Beanstalk

Summer with the seminarians had passed pretty much without incident. Aside from an occasional misunderstanding about my choice of radio stations, my erratic Sunday school attendance, and the off-scouring from a now-and-again nosebleed, we were able to establish somewhat of a brotherly relationship. And though I walked without a declaration of sanctification, I was never lost to its precepts, or the fervent and endless petitions of prayer offered on my behalf. And though I could never, even with the slightest conviction, defend my path of non-commitment, I remained hard pressed to do anything about it. But over the course of those ten weeks, the strength of their faith became a revelation of what I lacked, and of the hunger that remained unfed within me.

I had also spent a lot of time with Duncan that summer, at work and at his campsite, despite his being chafed by my choice of living arrangements. But I also found myself spending more and more time alone, meandering through the fields I had come to know as places of refuge. Kellen was with me most of those times. There was little I could do about it, or to lessen his memory. Time was not yet on my side.

The house Duncan had chosen for us to live in was a large one-and-a-half story bungalow with a lopsided porch across its front with loose cinderblocks stacked in a zigzag for steps. The steps were also lopsided, but in the opposite direction of the porch, and rocked and shifted each time weight was brought to bear. The house had been freshly painted: white with Kelly-green shutters and doors, and carried with it the name of the previous owners: Glasscock. We lived in Glasscock House.

Besides the living room, there were three additional rooms on the first level, each with provisions for double occupancy. The living room remained as the common area, and was used for lounging, prayer meetings, and late-night studying. There was only one room on the second floor, and it belonged to Duncan and me. It was a huge, oversized bedroom that the school had planned to partition into two smaller rooms, but for some reason had failed to do so before the fall semester began. So, at least for the time, it was ours—all of it. The only thing we lacked was a private entrance. Until Duncan could devise something different, the only way in and out was by the front door, and the only way up to our room was the staircase via the living room. This presented Duncan with the near impossible task of sneaking Becky Summers in and out undetected. From the outset, it was his monumental obsession, which by way of association, became a monumental nightmare for me.

The influx of co-eds for the fall semester had been generous in numbers only. And other than *those few* (there were always *those few*…those possessed with the attributes of silver-screen idols and homecoming queens), the fairness issue remained an open sore. I had, however, grown to where I was unshaken by it, even accepting of it, and even tried explaining to Duncan how I believed I had developed the sensitivity to recognize qualities that went beyond what first meets the eye – the crux being simply a matter of caring enough to look for those deeper qualities in the first place. Duncan believed that such acute sensitivity was a danger sign, and that anyone possessed of it, other than mothers and ministers, ought to consider having breakfast across the table from Etta Pritchett. But then this was coming from someone who saw Becky Summers in the likeness of Mona Lisa.

Becky was only partway harnessed when Duncan realized that the block-and-tackle he was using was just plain silly. Her being hoisted to the second floor in this manner was not the answer. So, under the cover of night, Duncan and I worked to cut notches in the trunk of the large silver maple out behind the house, its sole purpose being for Becky's convenience, so she could climb her mountainous bucket up to our bedroom window. We called it *Operation Becky and the Beanstalk.*

It was never my intention to become involved in Duncan's satiric activities, but in his unsuccessful attempts to get Becky up to the second floor and into his bed, his disposition had gone from enmity to distress, and with his hormones leaving heady muscadine trails. And even though I was pretty sure Mother and Reverend Mayfield were certain to invade my dreams and plant their shame, I still felt, in some novel way, as if maybe I should lend Duncan and Becky even more of a hand. I was squeamish about the soundness of it, even from the beginning, and had no misgivings about its moral and ethical implications, or of it being a rule violation on the grandest scale, one that would most certainly call for our being immediately shortlisted, if not altogether expelled. But then I was duly persuaded when Becky promised to supply me with an altogether charitable and free-flowing quantity of Honey Buns and Mallo Cups from The Fishes and Loaves. It was a sealed deal. I was in for the long haul, albeit to my detriment should things go awry.

There were no lights behind the house, so Becky being detected was not a high-priority concern. After she made several heroic-but-unsuccessful attempts at scaling the *beanstalk,* we spent the next couple of days enlarging the notches and adding footholds. It still wasn't enough. Days later, the maple tree looked like it came equipped with a staircase and a banister. Duncan attempted to camouflage the whole thing by transplanting large snowball bushes from the front of the house. No one ever asked Duncan what he was doing, or why he did the things he did. It was too much like a dare. Not the safe thing to do. Most of the time what Duncan did was simply too obscure for anyone to care anyway. The attitude was always one of ambivalence. After all, "It was only Duncan."

Once we got Becky up in the tree, the plan called for her to toss the end of a small line about ten feet to where Duncan would be waiting in the room's darkened window. The line was tied to the front end of a heavy rope bridge, the trail end of the bridge tied to the tree. Once Duncan had hold of the line, he was to pull the rope bridge till it was taut then tie it to the radiator in our room. Simple. Except for one thing. Whoever thought Becky could balance herself across a rope bridge fourteen feet up in the air was not anywhere as astute as I liked to imagine. Duncan blamed me. Apparently, being an outlet for his frustrations was one of the roles I was expected to play. Vexation, not Becky, was thus-far the only bedfellow Duncan had come to know.

CHAPTER THIRTY-TWO
O' Shock of Silver

O' Shock of silver come lighting,
Come lighting pure as snow,
Come lighting the young men a'roving,
Away and ago.

Elizabeth Llewellyn DeForte', Doctor De, Lizzy, had returned from sabbatical. The first time I saw her was in the old reception hall, a great room with high ceilings and French doors along the length of the north wall. The hall had been converted into a large classroom for Humanities, and with a dais raised to just a single step stretching from wall to wall across its front. It was there where Dr. DeForte' dispensed the requisites of Lit and Letters. She was my English professor.

From the very first moment my eyes fell upon her shock of silver hair, Dr. Elizabeth Llewellyn DeForte' became the mainstay of my desires. Even then, as fantasized as she was, there was the certainty that she would never be anything more; that the pairing of *student/ teacher* would forever be the extent of our relationship. Still there were fanciful notions that lingered to my discredit. And so it was, even in those first few days, that I saw her in an ever-increasing light, resolute in her path, representative of things revered, pastoral. From the lithe, silken skin of her neck to the pencil-fine features of her face; and from her sculpted back and hips to the breasts that bore her fame, she was the embodiment of both woman and womanhood.

Duncan soon became the consummate general, barking orders at me as if I were under some strict obligation to carry them out. Getting Becky onto the second floor undetected had become monumental headwork driven by angst, and the inability to do it expeditiously only fueled his frustration. It had been effort without reward, a profusion of failed attempts, and in direct proportion to Duncan's foundering morale. Erosion was afoot.

I saw the whole debacle as being Becky's problem, its roots being her lack of agility and an ardent willingness to point blame, mostly at me. Not only had she failed to come up with any ideas of her own, something I was quick to point out, but had flatly refused to supply me with the promised odds and ends of junk food. "Not until I have been delivered and returned safely," she said to me. She had unilaterally placed me on commission. None of us were happy.

O' Shock of Silver come lighting,
Come lighting though dark it seems,
Come fair of foot and wanting
With promises and the stuff of dreams.

I realized, after a short while, that Dr. Elizabeth Llewellyn DeForte' was destined to be a part of me, but only as a personal and protected keepsake…never allowing myself anything but the least of fantasies. It was even difficult for me to exchange eye contact with her. I was certain my thoughts would be too transparent, and that she would be able to read me like a neon sign, see me in a vicarious state enjoying her like a rooting hog. So, eye contact was out of the question, far too risky a proposition.

Still, it never stopped me from wanting her, from her premature gray and forever-fastened Gibson-girl hairdo to the arch that rose high into her instep; from the pink of her cameo profile to the culture of her aphrodisiac salts; and from her figurine delicacy to her bosom that drove upward and outward, straining against the fabric of her bustier with the same intensity as they strained against the fabric of my desire. She was all that was necessary to lock me in self-imposed bondage. So penetrating was my captivation—my out-of-breath and tongue-tied responses, my blush and pitiable eyes, the way I squirmed and pawed even at her briefest glance—that it was difficult to imagine she was unaware of it.

Out of sheer frustration, Duncan built a trellis on the back of the house. His story was that he was on a beautification campaign, building a trellis for the likes of clematis and wisteria and morning glory. But it was a story he never had to tell because nobody asked. Nobody cared. "It was only Duncan."

He built the trellis out of two-by-fours, from the ground straight up to our window, and he hammered it to the house with sixteen-penny nails. The finished product was anything but beautifying but attested to the fact that it was built to withstand the test of time and the bulk and heft of Becky Summers, even after an all-you-can-eat buffet dinner.

But building the trellis was only half the battle. The other half was getting Becky to the top of it. So, with a plow line tied in a double knot around her waist, and with the determination that only hormones-out-of-control can provide, she decided to give it a try. I was the lookout, sworn to head off anyone who might otherwise impede her long and arduous journey upwards. Duncan kept the necessary tension on the line so Becky could climb from one rung to the next without the risk of falling backwards and ostensibly bursting. After nearly ten-minutes of wheezing, and after nearly losing her hold on several of the higher rungs, Duncan was finally able to maneuver her leaden torso through the window and into his arms. Victory had at long last come to Glasscock House.

Becky's trip down, however, was far and away less eventful. It was about fifteen seconds worth of Duncan muscling the rope hand-over-hand until she landed. Hard. With a thud. And in a heap. We waited in silence while she untangled herself and signaled to us that she was okay. We all gave sighs of relief before she limped off into the night, toward home and the loving parents who praised her often for never staying out past her curfew.

⚬⚬⚬

> *O'Shock of Silver come lighting,*
> *Come lighting as you will,*
> *Come softly while the night lies sleeping*
> *And the moon is still.*

There was never a time, never a minute, that I didn't long to be swallowed up by Dr. Elizabeth Llewellyn DeForte. It bordered on lust, to be sure, but infused with gentility and things that transcended base desires. I felt profound in her presence, as if emerging from some baseline half-man/half-beast into something more attending and self-sacrificing. Her mere presence pulled it from me. And it wasn't so much that she demanded it, but that she commanded it.

More and more I found myself lost in her wonderment, wanting her adulation, longing to be the sole recipient of her attentions. For long entranced minutes I imagined her preparing her lessons with only me in mind; imagined her dressing, smoothing, and combing herself like a cat just for my benefit; imagined her fastening the shock of her silver hair so that its most delicate strands, those entrails of fine silk that stir in the most temperate breezes, would fall and sweep against her cheeks with never a thought except of me. Although I knew her hold on me was of my own making, I never gave up hoping that she would somehow sense that I was perched and waiting on the edge of lover's leap for her to join me.

> *O' Shock of silver come lighting,*
> *Come lighting fast you can,*
> *Come light the hunted and the hunter*
> *Before you away again.*

Chapter Thirty-Three
Stone and Judi Remington

I wrote no letters, nor did I ever expect to receive any. So, when one with my name on it came sliding at me from under my door, it was a long several minutes before I picked it up. I turned it over and over, marveled at the postmark and the Texas return address. It was from Stone and Judi Remington.

Dear Weldon Thatcher,

We hope you don't feel like we've jumped into your mailbox uninvited, but for months we have intended to introduce ourselves. We hope you can accept how we've chosen to do it. We are Stone and Judi Remington, Kellen's adopted parents, and we hope this letter finds you well.

As you very well know, it's been almost a year since Kellen died (I find it hard to even write the word), and it's taken us almost that long to fully acknowledge it. Even now we don't talk about it the way we'd like. You might say this letter is part of coming to grips with our grief. I hope you understand.

Kellen touched a lot of hearts in his own way, and I'm sure we're not the only ones who suffer from his passing. That's why we thought you might like to know that Kellen often spoke of you. So often, in fact, that we feel almost like we know you. During his last trip home, he took to saying how he was planning on bringing you out to visit with us (you and a big red-haired fellow named Duncan). We told him you boys were always welcome. And you still are. We're just sorry that Kellen won't have the chance to be a part of it. We know it will never be quite the same without him, but we just wanted you to know that if you ever take the notion to come this way, we would be proud and honored to have you. He considered you a true friend.

The school sent us all of Kellen's things and it seems like we spend an awful lot of time just going through them. I can't believe how many memories are conjured just by their sight alone. I guess that's why we're hoping that one day we can come together and help each other know him better. He was with us for such a short time. We're just thankful we got to share what time there was and give what love we had. We've always felt that with a family's love, a person is a lot more likely to be at peace. I don't think we're wrong about that. I think Kellen left with a stronger heart than the one he came here with. It's because of Kellen that Judi and I both can now understand that there is more than just one kind of sunset. And that's a good thing.

Affectionately,
Stone and Judi Remington.

CHAPTER THIRTY-FOUR
Unrequited Affection

As of late, I had become more and more restless about Bea and her leaving the way she had. Without a word. Like I hadn't mattered even as a friend, even after what we'd shared. I knew it wasn't by accident that I had turned to Bea when Kellen died. I was struggling with all I had in me to feel even the rudiments of life, to fill the void left by death, and there was no one I trusted more than Bea to help me through it. I wanted more than anything to trust God, but at the time, *God as Comforter* was an idea that eluded me, that stayed buried within the fog of my resentment. After Kellen's death, God was simply someone to blame.

I loved Kellen as much as I loved Bea, but as much as I tried, I could never understand why he was so often distant with her, struggling to return even her slightest affections. I saw these times as his being on the brink of an episode, but somehow, he always managed to keep it in check, never letting his mood go beyond simple detachment. Still, his lack of interest in her seemed to be rooted in something far deeper than simple boredom, something so pervasive that it oftentimes left the three of us feeling separate and alone.

I often wondered how Kellen interpreted his life, if ever he thought of it as disappointing. I often got the impression that he thought of it as being *just not big enough,* and that his alienations from Bea were mere expressions of his discontent. But there is no way of ever really knowing what it was that pushed him away from her at the oddest times, or what it was he really longed for, or searched for, night-after-night.

In his own right, Kellen was a marvel: poetry and balladry all rolled into one. In many ways he was an expression of perfection. It was no wonder that so many of us were taken with him despite his occasional un-churched disposition. It was enough at times just to be in his presence, but too often I could sense Bea's frustration at his unrequited affection. I wanted desperately to fill the void he left in her. In my heart I knew she wanted devotion, but at the same time, I sensed she was willing to live forever without it if it couldn't come from Kellen.

be in his presence, but too often I could sense Bea's frustration at his unrequited affection. I wanted desperately to fill the void he left in her. In my heart I knew she wanted devotion, but at the same time, I sensed she was willing to live forever without it if it couldn't come from Kellen.

CHAPTER THIRTY-FIVE
Dr. De (Lizzy)

There was nothing quite as intoxicating as the afternoon suns of late summer and how they would just hang there in the blue and bake everything into stillness, and how they would warm me and leave me limp and lingering in daydreams. It was just such a day when Dr. DeForte' came striding up the side aisle, as inviting as the sun streaming down on me through the big French doors. From her very first day, she had been everybody's all-in-all. Today was no different except that the arch and angle of her eyes were, for the longest moment, aimed unerringly at me, daydreams and all. It was more than just casual eye contact, yet subtle enough to be dismissed as a passing glance. There one minute, gone the next, rooting me once again into the stuff of vagary.

As usual, a twinge of excitement, as alive as the crack of her footsteps on the oak floor, accompanied her all the way to the front of the room. And, as usual, her sense of magic and spirit settled us into a hush.

"Let us pray," she said, her eyes seeming to find me just before she bowed her head. She was anything but brief. Prayer and servitude, after all, were the major ordinances of her faith, and the most indispensable purpose for her being.

Dr. DeForte' had been schooled by The Church in its totality, emerging as both a leader and a follower of the faith. She was both teacher and student, a spirit undaunted by the ways of the world, and the result and gift of God's everlasting love. She was, in essence, above the mark, delicate of both matter and manner, both consecrated and earthen. And even though her physical attributes were, in every regard, the abundance of milk and honey, and the things that prompted me straightaway to think of her as temptress as much as teacher, it was her distinction as a scholar and her claim of being *born-again* that made her so especially halting.

"Amen." First hers. Then ours.

We waited, letting the quiet aftermath of her prayer settle over us. Without a word, she surveyed our faces. Most of us were still new to her. Her smile was tender and approving, and there was every indication that she knew precisely who she was and what was expected of her.

And, so it was, during those soft thinning days of summer: me, sieved and dubious; she, with the compassion and insight that comes from living without the worry of tomorrow. Such were the times, sitting in adulation of her, rapt and intrigued as I was, that I came to understand that intellect and tenderness of spirit were the purest allures.

By the end of the first week was when the earth began to shift beneath my feet. It was on a Friday, right when the final bell sounded, that I realized the hour had passed without me; evidence being my note pad, as blank as when I first opened it. But it was then, at the apex of a student body rushing toward the weekend, that my name came riding on the air. "MR. THATCHER!" I turned to see Dr. DeForte' motioning for my attention. "MAY I SEE YOU FOR A MOMENT?" Could she actually be addressing me? I raised my eyebrows and smiled, waiflike and elfin, before moving toward her. Then came the hush, then the numbness in my legs, then a tremor of nausea. I waited close-by while she attended to those with specific needs.

She was welcoming without a handshake. "Mr. Thatcher," she said through a smile and a hint of talcum, "I'm sorry to have kept you waiting." She was precise. Pale, yet colorful.

"Not a problem," I said, the words escaping without enough breath.

"Nevertheless, thank you for your patience." She was both ingratiating and sincere. "Let me, for your sake, come directly to the point." I wish I could have been but one of the words she mouthed. "I was wondering if you'd be available to work for me this Saturday. Tomorrow." All at once there were hackles of pain: neck, forehead, molars. "I desperately need to get my office moved and in order, and I'm not up to doing it by myself." More pain: base of skull, temples, left eye. "I can't imagine either of us not working up a good sweat, if you'll pardon the double negative, but I can imagine you saying no at such a late request."

"Not a problem," I said again, feeling as if I'd exhausted my entire vocabulary.

"Does that mean you will?" she asked.

"Yes, it do," I said. "I mean, I do. Will."

She gave me a look as if I might be choking. "Well then," she said. "I'll see you in the morning."

I turned and stepped away, forgetting to say goodbye, or thank you, or what time of the morning she expected me, or even where I was supposed to be.

"About eight o'clock," she said to my back as I was about to exit. "Right here if that's okay with you?"

It was.

It was one of those perfect azure-sky days where everything seemed to reflect warmer and brighter than it was. It was dry and still, as if daylight had come hours earlier than expected and the roosters had been robbed of their chance to crow.

Dr. De (shortened at her insistence) and I used a pickup truck to haul what she needed to her new office. It was a truck that looked a lot like the one belonging to Cleveland Yates, weathered and scaly, and bleached by the sun. She'd borrowed it from Homer Witten, one of the school's maintenance workers, with the stipulation that we have it back by four o'clock. That's when Homer went home. But by the time we cleaned out the back and hosed away the goat manure and straw, we were already beginning to feel the effects of a dog day in the making.

Dr. De lived about a half mile from campus in the very last house on Edenfield's only dead-end street. It was an ancient-looking, two-story clapboard with a cupola that sagged over a huge wraparound porch. Its once white exterior had peeled and faded so that from a distance it took on the color of seagulls, the gray ones that carry a hint of blue. Thick lilac bushes nearly twice my height formed a wall between the yard and the dusty dirt road. From the mailbox at the road's edge, a red brick path, crippled from years of heat and frost and rain, angled its way under the lilacs and across the yard to the front porch steps. Morning glories stretched from the porch rails clear to the roof, and huge wicker rockers lolled in their shade. It was its own little world of solitude, and a place I imagined unaffected by ill will or bad intent.

She lived there alone.

We had worked most of the morning loading and unloading, hauling, and rearranging. By the end of the afternoon, we had made enough trips back and forth between her house and her office that I was sure the pickup could have found its way back without us. It had been a long morning and an even longer afternoon, dry and dusty and with only a single break, just long enough for peanut butter sandwiches and sun tea. We had grown weary together.

It wasn't until the last trip that I became dispirited with the thought of having to leave her. I sat motionless, staring through the fine dust film on the windshield, my mind on nothing but the soft bumping sound of the tires on the gravel road.

It was three o'clock by the time we finished, a full hour before we had to return the truck. "Well," she said, "I'd say this calls for a celebration." She disappeared just long enough to return with two tall glasses cloudy with lemonade and tinkling with ice. We gave in without the slightest resistance and settled bone tired into the rockers. She sipped demurely. I strained to keep from draining the entire glass at once.

A hint of a breeze pushed at us through the vines and across the porch, just enough to soothe my prickly skin. Dr. De fished an ice cube from her glass and rubbed it back and forth against her breast-bone. She rocked, half asleep, her face a picture of peace and grace, while big drops of water trickled and disappeared down the front of her shirt. I wanted to reach out to her, to smooth back her hair, to whisper things blushing and poetic. Instead, I joined her in her place of meditation.

The giant rockers creaked their own peaceful song along with the resonance of a thousand katydids from the fields around us. They were the last things I remembered before she woke me with the touch of her hand on mine. At first, I thought she was part of a dream, then realized it was really her, leaning toward me, smiling.

"I want you to know something," she said, her voice a husky whisper, her look dreamy and affected. I let her know I was listening. "I'm in love," she said, beaming with all the light of the world.

Her words left me in heroic flight, caroling inward. She squeezed my hand and pulled it to her, her smile widening, her eyes intense and on mine. I drew a great breath from the porch's cool, scented, morning-glory air and for the first time knew what my Mormon Uncle, Ephram, meant when he said, "Man *is* that he might have joy."

"It's Jesus," she said adoringly, breathlessly. "I'm in love with Jesus!"

Dr. De was forever awash in a look of refinement, and the following Monday was no exception. Alive in her morning dance, she came across the quad starched in a self-contained atmosphere of gladness, her footsteps precise, her spine straight as a poplar … as if she were tethered to the one and only string of sanctification. She was grand in the way she attended the dry morning air, confident that her virtue alone was enough to cleanse the very ground she walked on.

She caught me out of the corner of her eye as I came diagonally across the quad. She slowed then came to a halt waiting for me to join her. "Mr. Thatcher!" She greeted me with eyes and a voice full of cheer. She always called me Mr. Thatcher, careful never to give in to the smack of familiarity. Anything else could too easily be construed as coloring outside the lines … a real toehold for the devil.

"Good Monday on you, Dr. De." I did my best to be formal without being formal.

"I take it you've recovered?" she said, her smile remarkable and inviting.

"Somewhat, I suppose, but certainly not enough to stay awake in class." She laughed, and we talked as we walked: the weather, Mondays, God's love. I felt light.

"Mr. Thatcher," she said as we were about to head off in different directions, "Can you type?" Her face was squared with mine, her eyes penetrating.

"Yes," I said with a degree of accomplishment.

"Well then, would you be interested in working for me? Odds-and-ends. Typing mostly. Nothing extensive. And only when your schedule would permit. I can pay you a dollar an hour." Despite my not wanting to appear too eager, I began nodding, then blurted yes sooner than I intended.

"Fine then," she cooed, "If you'll see me after class this afternoon, we can compare schedules." And that was that except for the acid in my stomach attacking the Hershey bar I had eaten for breakfast.

Dr. De's office was as kempt as her person, as precise as the lace and silks that attended her. But what with cabinets and desks, books and typewriters and sundry paraphernalia, there was hardly enough room to swing a cat. Rather, it was an office given to order, in the same convention as her life.

Most days, Dr. De was a sea of motion, sunlit and lissome, a scholar embraced by tradition. From my own quiet corner of the world, I saw her as poetry, only heaped with images of me at her side: just the two of us, barefoot and breathless, wet with sweat and morning dew. Then, too, I embraced her as foundational for wellness and joy; things that added light to otherwise darkened rooms, things that added sustenance to my moments alone.

From the outset, Dr. De and I were like objects made obstacles in the stingy space of her office. But in light of our being polite and accepting, it was a hindrance made tolerable. My role was strictly that of the proletariat, an honest worker doing what he does for honest pay. I made sure I was always the model of punctuality, in part to ensure my tenure, and partly to detract from my shortcomings. She, in turn, was forever respectful of my efforts and never withholding with her compliments. We seemed to revel in the pleasure we brought to one another.

We soon discovered that whatever we had, and whatever it was we gave to one another, worked. We were a team. And though I became less and less inhibited in her presence, I never lost sight of our *student/ teacher* relationship. Our stations were never left to doubt, though I began to think of her more as Lizzy than Dr. De, though I was forever removed from ever uttering it. I reckoned it to the close confinement of the office, and her, with increased frequency, calling me Weldon.

If my behavior around her was discrete, then my observations of her were even more so. Though I was anything but obvious, observing her was something I was incapable of denying myself. She was the possessor of qualities capable of leaving sinkholes in most men's Christian orientation. I was no exception. I loved the way she occupied space and the way her presence lingered long after she left the room. And I loved the way she pawed at herself, arched her back and opened her mouth to yawn; the way she was able to communicate with me without as much as a word. And I loved the way she looked at me without actually looking at me, and how she closed her eyes, sometimes for only a second, perhaps to dream.

As a matter of course, Lizzy loved to challenge me with scripture.

To her, it was fun beyond description. Stumping me was an altogether bigger thrill. But I was a willing subject, unafraid to be baffled. I enjoyed it, if for nothing more than the sound of her laughter. *Laughter with an appetite* I called it, a pure fascination with the heart. It was a joyous entreatment of the soul, a tendered sweetness that had no longing of its own, just a notion of what it was like to be free.

Our times in the office often ran beyond dark, and many times were spent just in talking. She consoled by saying that such times served her well, made sorting her thoughts less troublesome. Over the course of weeks, our intimacy grew right along with her willingness to share her sophistication. I was, more often than not, gripped by her depth of knowledge. Aside from the scriptures, English literature was her academic love. She could talk without end it seemed on such things as tone and meter, style and form, plot, and character. They were all part of her embrace. And as the weeks passed, she became bolder, began drawing parallels between the motifs of various literary works and modern-day religions, began pressing toward things Freudian and Oedipal, began deploying terms such as *ethos* and *pathos*. It was all so learned, and I basked in her light. There was obvious joy in her lifting me up, seeing me hang on every word, so she delved headlong, day after day, into works fraught with symbolism, works that foreshadowed death and themes that returned us to the womb. There were subjects about adultery and fornication, lust and incest, and after a while I realized there were no boundaries, no fences, and I began to feel worthy of her tutelage. But no matter how far afield she would go, or how deep she chose to take me, she would always bring me back into the King James sector of her world, and always end with prayer.

Her prayers were seldom short or simple, and never without intensity. Routinely, she would cradle my face in her hands as she began, then, after roiling with warmer and warmer breath, move them onto my shoulders and then down to my hands where she would gather them in hers and press them hard into her lap just before whispering an exhausted Amen.

The Friday night before Fall Revival, we had worked long and hard grading test papers. It was late when we finished the last of them, and I was more than ready to forego the goodbye prayer. But knowing that that was impossible, I closed my eyes and waited for her blessing. Her routine, however, was not the same. She went directly to gathering my hands into hers, then resting them not into her lap, but into mine. All four hands together, squeezed and pressed into all that nested against my inseam. And this is where they stayed while she rocked back and forth in prayer. I had no recollection of time, only the irrevocable surge that finally froze me in spasm, seized me and locked me against the four hands fist-rocking in my lap. It was a surge I felt all the way from my stomach to my knees, and one, I do believe, that made me utter something unrecognizable, perhaps in an unknown tongue. It was a surge that left me drained and wet and nearly in tears, empty and close to dead with trouble and confusion. It was a surge that sent me running from her office and into the night without my jacket or waiting for her Amen.

CHAPTER THIRTY-SIX
The Ultimate Means to the Ultimate End

During revival week, faculty members were charged with bearing the full armor of righteousness even more than usual and seeing to it that a prayerful vigil throughout the campus was as all-consuming as possible. Even homework assignments were purposely light so that greater attention could be given to prayer and meditation. The hope was that the student body would come to understand and embrace revival as the ultimate means to the ultimate end. It was also a time when student work activity was minimized, even for those working at the mill. Considering what had transpired between Dr. De and me during our last session, I was grateful for the reduced workload and the hiatus it afforded. It was difficult enough sitting in the same classroom with her, watching her parade round and about the dais, back and forth in a blush, pretending nothing had happened. I couldn't be sure if it was a case of her being oblivious, or if she had chosen naivety for the sake of convenience.

Unlike the year before, I was unable to escape the revival's nightly rigor. Dr. De monitored my attendance as if she had a personal stake in my salvation. I hadn't minded her attention, but I had a sense of being shanghaied when she insisted we sit together on the final night.

For four nights running, the revival had been packed to the rafters, and tonight was no exception. Still, there were souls who hadn't gone forward, hadn't bent a knee at the altar. Stiff-necked souls. Souls with conflicted hearts. Souls like me.

Dr. De was, in every detail, radiant in the sanctuary's soft light. She was in her element, in the bosom of Abraham, and in full agreement with the choir's Hallelujah Chorus as they marched down the center aisle. We sat with a hymnal wedged between us.

There was a prayer, then more singing, then an offering and still another prayer before Reverend Virgil Epps, a short round man with a crew cut and wide spaces between his teeth, stepped to the podium. His thick, black-rimmed glasses were a perfect match for his black suit and tie, and his fixed squint and pained expression an exact manifestation of the gravity and complexity of his text. From the outset, he was as forthcoming as he was without eloquence, and never yielded on the fact that the things of God, and even God Himself, were steeped in mystery. There were things, he said, that God purposely withholds from us, things He keeps from our understanding, things we are simply not meant to know until the appointed time. Secrecy, according to Virgil, was an integral part of God, part of His wonder.

Things hidden, things kept secret, things unknown. It was the sort of message that kept me in a spiritual tailspin. What I needed was not so much a reminder of the mystery, but a light to illuminate it, some offering of hope beyond faith. But then faith was the light. Nothing else could abide such obscurity.

Dr. De sat as still as a gravestone, and with a fixed and illuminating smile. It didn't take long for Virgil to build up a full head of steam, and for the shotgun blasts of his voice to equal the sound of his fist on the podium. With each hammering blow, I felt a growing need to strategize an escape route. But I had barely put the pieces together when the sermon came to an abrupt close, its ending and invitation to come forward done with nearly the same breath. Almost at once, people began leaving their seats and heading toward the altar. Many of the same people who had gone forward on nights before, went again. For some, it was their fifth night in a row. It was a small price to pay for the reward, smaller yet when pitted against the consequences of not going at all.

Virgil's petitions strengthened by the minute, urging us to our feet, urging us to join those choir voices reaching and connecting us to heaven. "Just As I Am," with all the choral sounds and as tender as a broken heart, poured through us with the softness of clouds and warm summer rains.

The thought of a single soul walking away without the protection of redemption was cause for Virgil to make one renewed offensive after another, each time a little faster, a little louder, an octave higher—words and rhythms, rhythmic words, working to quicken us to something loftier and more ideal; words with such travail that they left me with a burning, even a longing, deep in my chest. Dr. De must have sensed it and leaned in close to me. "Don't deny the Holy Spirit, Weldon," she said, her voice low and her hand resting on my shoulder. I felt myself becoming heavy, almost unable to stand. Such heaviness.

She prayed in a whisper—her face pressed close to mine. "Let it out, Weldon," she said. "Just say it: 'Just as I am, I come to thee.'" Inside me, what I reckoned to be the Holy Spirit, echoed the voices all around me: those in front of me, alongside me, behind me; voices rising and swelling, convicting, and vexing. And in their midst, the attar of Dr. De and the recollection of her hands in my lap.

For the first time, I could sense my shell beginning to crack, my ghosts beginning to contract, weaken. Dr. De leaned in upon me, her hair, her breasts, her voice—all seeming to come together, consoling—all fixed on me knowing my heart. In the background, the choir droned, 'Just as I am, without one plea, but that thy blood was shed for me, and that thou bidst me come to thee, O Lamb of God, I come…I come.' My mind was spinning, loose and adrift: on a hilltop, in a valley, in a deep dark hollow.

"Weldon," I heard Dr. De say, "Just as you are…" She was entreating, the preacher admonishing, the Holy Ghost calling. Somewhere in the middle of it all, in the rabid flushing of souls and the effort to shed the weight of faithlessness, my legs buckled, no longer able to hold me. I could feel Dr. De kneeling next to me, her arm draped around my shoulders, her prayer soft and heaving. It was then and there, and by the power of heaven, that my sins had found me out. My remorse bore me like a weeping sore. I had been captured by the power of the Holy Ghost, given over to the will of God, and I surrendered to it with all that was in me.

With the clarity that sunshine brings to a cloudless day, I realized my face was not only wet with tears but resting on the hillocks of Dr. De's bosom. I slumped against her, not wanting to move, clinging to her partially out of being new and untried, and partially out of some unrecognizable need. We were enmeshed, huddled amidst a cacophony of weeping, and me clinging to her whispered assurances as if she alone had pulled me from the fires of damnation.

It was sometime later that we rose and celebrated with the others in the aisles and at the altar. It was joyous reconciliation, a change of status for the spirit, a covenant with God, a crucifixion of sin and a dying away of things that pertained to the world. I was born again.

The chapel was slow to empty. It had been a long night, but fruitful, and Dr. De and I were among the last to leave. We had waited in quiet for what seemed like hours, preferring the presence of the Almighty to any other. Finally, we made our way to the door and left as we had come…together.

CHAPTER THIRTY-SEVEN
The Paradisiacal Latch

Outside, we walked braced by the night air, Dr. De and me. Arm in arm. A frosty breath for each step; all the way to the end of her gravel road. We stood for some time with our arms locked, gazing up through the crystal-clear darkness before she guided me inside, away from the profusion of stars.

Her front room had a discernable fragrance, one that I could only think of as *Lizzy.* It was nothing loud or purposeful, but faint and ambrosial, an essence of dusting powder and freshly cut lilacs. It was a sharp contrast to the giant tapestry of dark reds and burgundies above the fireplace. I let its sense of mystery buoy me while she moved off toward the kitchen. My eyes drifted from one object to another, between the shadows and the colors and the light. I felt like I had been given permission to revel in its numina.

The ceiling was beadboard. Dark cherry. Darker yet with age. It was like a deep infinite universe without the stars, and low enough to touch if I stood on my toes. The floors were darker yet. Planks. Black and polished and covered with Persian rugs. And the windows were covered with heavy wine-colored drapes and swagged onto the floor.

The fireplace looked like it hadn't been used in my lifetime, and a thick rug, intricately blended in fusions of red, had been fastened over its opening. All around the room were lamps with glass shades and beads, and one with a velvet shade and long dangling fringe.

On the wall opposite the fireplace was a large painting in the style of Rubens, and under it a fainting couch, dark reds on dark reds. In a far corner, a small writing desk, delicate in form and fashion, sat lady-like as if it had never known the discomfort of anything beyond the pressure of her pen. Across its top was a stout volume of *Pilgrim's Progress* and a tattered copy of *The Scarlet Letter.* They stood upright, braced against one another like sentinels assigned to keep watch and stir the fires of curiosity. A Bible, black and leathery, lay next to them.

Through a large archway, light from the living room filtered weakly into the kitchen. Dr. De stood by the stove, comfortable in the dim light and the blue gas flame glowing from under the kettle. She was brewing tea.

Except for the sounds of her rummaging in and out of cupboards and drawers, her tea making was done without a word, the way, I suspected, she made it most days: in the habit of silence. I wasn't used to her being so quiet, so focused as not to talk. But then there was something assuring about it all: about cupboard doors opening and closing, about the clack of cups against saucers and water being brought to a boil, something ingratiating about her willingness to stir and brew and serve.

"Do you use sugar?" Her voice startled me. She was standing in the dim light of the archway and looking somewhat provocative, even enticing, even more so than usual. I reasoned that it was the light.

"Yes," I said, all at once ashamed of my thoughts, and glad she couldn't know them.

"Tea will be ready soon," she said as if to ease my mind.

"I don't mean to be academic at such a time," I said, "but I was hoping you could help me sort through some things."

"What sort of things?" she asked.

"*God* things" I said. "Things about God." I was having trouble unfolding my thoughts. "And me…God and me…those sorts of things."

A glow seemed to fill the space around her. "I would say you're wanting to be more spiritual than academic," she said. And with that, she turned back toward the kitchen, making quick work of readying the teapot and arranging a show of finger cakes.

"I think we'll be more comfortable in the living room," she said all at once, "…if you don't mind." And with that we went off to the fainting couch, the tray of tea and finger cakes coming to rest on the coffee table in front of us. She sat next to me: close enough so that I could know without a shred of doubt that she was vital, and warm, and woman.

I waited, following her lead, sipping with caution, and taking in more air than tea.

"So now," she finally said, "tell me what sort of *God things* seem to be so troubling."

"It's prayer," I said. "I need to know about prayer." My voice seemed to resound and bounce around inside my head. "...and faith...and how they influence what I am to God."

She looked at me with thoughtful eyes, ready and resilient. "That's quite profound," she said, stirring her tea. "It's the sort of question that plagues theologians the world over, I suspect." She smiled in a way that said what I wanted to know had limitless possibilities, none of which were absolutes. "But," she said, "you may be wasting your time asking me for answers that can only come from within *you.* The whole thing between God and man, after all, is about *relationship* and our longing to know Him as He would *want* us to know Him. It's the ultimate intimacy, Weldon. Something we all seek."

I nodded, only partially sure that I understood. "I'm sure," she said, "that it's not God's intention to be complex." She paused, her expression almost apologetic for having to rescue me from confusion. I was almost ready to ask if she thought it was God's intention to seem contradictory, when she said, "We also know what He's declared. The scriptures are quite clear on that. And from them, we can know what He expects. It would seem that your wanting to know Him better would start there." I could feel the creases in my forehead relax. She bit lovingly into a teacake.

"The rest," she said, "will come as you draw nearer to God, as your walk with Him matures. And though we can never fully know the mind of God, we can, as good and faithful stewards, know the *heart* of God. It's then that we can begin to align ourselves with His will." Right then, a small cascade of crumbs spilled from the napkin she held under her chin, landing with the silence of snowflakes across her bosom. She brushed at them as if I wasn't there.

I sat wondering if it was every man's journey to seek the will and purpose of God. Was it part of our spiritual density? —part of our God-given genesis? —or was it just part of the Edenfield experience? I couldn't imagine there being so many pieces to the truth.

My father had refused to let the things of God become complicated for him. He'd whittled the whole thing (God, religion, faith, spirituality) down to "The most important job in our lives is to get our children into heaven," and he left it at that. It was the sole claim to his spirituality. Those few words. And he believed them enough to drive Freddie Heartland and me to Sunday school every Sunday morning, come rain or shine, and then come back and pick us up afterwards. His was a simple faith.

"You understand, of course, that prayer is the preeminent vehicle that brings you into that intimate relationship."

"That's the thing," I said.

"What's the thing?" she asked.

"Prayer. Praying. What to say and how to say it."

Her look was perplexed, as if considering how elementary she needed to be. "I don't know that I'd be all that concerned about it," she said, "especially when we consider that Jesus, Himself, told us we don't know how to pray in the first place. Not only that, but that God knows what we need even before we ask."

"Then how is it that scripture admonishes us to pray always?"

Her smile became wide and warm and obvious. "I don't mean to be preachy, Weldon, but I think you'll find that 'praying always' simply means staying in the spirit of prayer. Always presenting yourself reverently and respectfully, so that your life will be reflective of God's love." She stopped just long enough to satisfy herself that I was with her. "In that way," she said, "your life will be the kind that blesses others, and in turn, will become a blessing to God." She sipped demurely at her tea, then pursed her lips and looked me dead in the eye. "You see, Weldon, it's not what you say, necessarily, but the spirit you bring to your life. That is your prayer. It's what brings you into God's presence. And the fact that you're seeking to do just that, to move closer to Him, reveals a thing most crucial about you: that you've welcomed the precepts of discipleship…even servitude… the things most germane to His teachings."

She was a marvelous teacher, Dr. De was, far and away above anything I could have hoped for in a tutor, much less a mentor. And though I couldn't be sure that I would ever be a blessing to God, I was willing to believe that my going to the altar was the beginning of me realizing something higher in myself, something that sought to align itself with the mystery I knew nothing about.

For several long moments we sat staring into our cups. Then, as if on cue, sipped in unison.

"Does any of this carry the ring of truth for you?" she asked.

Oddly, it did. But what I couldn't bring myself to say was that I was ratcheted so far down with opposing views and theories, with conjecture and opinion, with ideologies and doctrine, and just so much from so many, that each of its parts made perfect sense right up till the time I tried piecing them all together. Then it became a thing of chaos and muddle. "Yes," I said. "Perfect truth."

"Then I will tell you this," she said, her voice rising with the passion of one on the brink of revelation, "though prayer is a profound expression of our wanting to be connected to God, our ultimate destiny can only be achieved through a life of faith." She had assumed high ground. "Because, like prayer, faith is a condition of being, a profound response to what lives within us. And it's allowing its governance that we're introduced to the spiritual, the supernatural. It's then that faith becomes more than just a willingness to believe. It becomes a compelling force for life."

She sat in the ensuing lull, sipping at her tea and smiling at what she knew as truth. I nodded then fell in with her…once again…sip for sip.

I couldn't help but see her as faultless, despite the one incident of weakness she had loosened in us. I guess maybe I saw her as God saw her, only through the eyes of vulnerability.

"I'm overcome with joy for you," she said leaning toward me. "Actually, I don't think I could be more proud of you if I tried."

"Thank you," I said, not knowing if I felt the same. We sat not talking for a time, her gaze drifting from my eyes to my arms to my hands, then back again. "How wonderful it is when two people can sit quietly together and not feel estranged," she said. I nodded my agreement and my appreciation of her having thought enough to say as much. "Whatever shall I do with you?" she said. I fidgeted then downed the last of my tea.

"Soooo," I said, not sure that I was ready for more reckoning.

"Yes…so," she countered, and with that, gathered herself and the tray, then headed off toward the kitchen.

"I don't know," I said following her, "that I've done anything to make you proud."

"Oh, but you have," she said, setting the cups and saucers in the sink, then turning to face me. "You took a step of faith tonight for all the world to see." Her smile was attending.

"I suppose I did," I said.

"Of course you did," she said. "The commitment you made at the altar was a living testimony of faith." She stepped toward me and placed her hands on my shoulders, aligning herself so that we stood face to face. "A walk of faith, Weldon, is by its very nature, a walk in the light of understanding. But it's through that sort of faith that we come to believe … and through believing that we are accounted righteous unto God." As usual, she was precise: every syllable anointed, practiced, clear. "It's the foundation," she said, "to what you've been seeking: a covenant with God." It was difficult to concentrate. She was so close. "And anytime faith moves one to answer the call of his heart, I see it as courageous. And, so, yes, I am proud." I tried listening as she told me how much more of a man she thought I was now that I had demonstrated such strength of conviction. I was humbled, even quieted, by her flattery … but she was so close. But it was when her hands drifted upward and cupped my face that I lost the essence of what she was saying altogether. In an instant, or so it seemed, she leaned in and kissed me lightly on the cheek, then the other.

"So proud," she whispered. "Shall I pray for us?"

"Yes," I whispered. "Pray."

With as much instinct as love, I raised my hands to cover hers. And it was then that she moved straight into me, her arms encircling me, her breasts angling to seat themselves against my chest. "Heavenly Father," she began. From there, her words drifted far from me, as my very own so often do in prayer. Only now and again was I aware of the inflections in her voice, rising and falling, tangling and colliding into a collage of thanks and praise. I was adrift, filled with the lilac incense of her skin, the warmth of her breath, and the darkness of the kitchen pressing in around us. I had no sense of where she was taking us, only that her uneven breath was as persuasive as her hands on my back. It was only a heartbeat before I felt the same give and take, before I sensed the searing torch of hellfire reaching with passions of its own. Beyond her, beyond us, I heard the voice of Virgil Epps, but it was far off and no longer mattered. Nothing mattered, only the thunderclap of her AMEN and the jolt of being crushed together without apology. We stayed that way, locked and frozen, not wanting to move. Time and space had no place. We were out of bounds, in a universe without laws, in our own Garden of Eden. "So proud," she whispered, her lips feather-soft against my cheeks, first one then the other—lingering, fostering—until she finally guided them, soft and yielding, onto my own. I was straightaway shunted, in a cloudbank of nothing but the here and now; livened to an intractable yearning, to things, warm and unfamiliar, probing for what was life…and for all that was missing in it.

We were, that very moment and without regard, scandal come to life, clinging to each other as if for life support, groping and stumbling like a couple of drunks into the kitchen table, and without ever once breaking our hold or our kiss. In less than a heartbeat the table gave way, shot out from under us and sent us sprawling across several of the kitchen chairs. We went down hard, along with the chairs, in a thunderous heap. There was pain—left shoulder, right knee—but it was only seconds before we found each other again, before we were fastened into a double-backed beast. We wheezed and panted, clutched and grappled at every body part we could reach. We struggled to right ourselves, to untangle ourselves from the overturned table and chairs, and from a shattered cookie jar with its store of shortbreads; clawing and thrashing about for stability and something solid to hold onto, and without allowing even a hint of air to come between us. We slipped, over and again, but were never deterred. There was a bump to the head, a lost shoe, numbness in my lips, and pressure in my chest. Our world had turned into an inferno, an enraged and enflamed determination to find and undo hooks and buttons and zippers, suffering to get at the prizes that lay beneath them. We were like two freshly charged magnets, never unlocking our lips except to gasp for deeper breaths. Then, like a prolonged aria coming mercifully to an end, fabric and fasteners gave way to the culmination of strength and mania, pressure, and desire. Then, as if being summoned by angels, she began to pray. She thanked the Lord in rapid fire for allowing us this expression of love, her tongue rolling and trilling in flute-like precision, beating against the roof of her mouth like sticks against a hollow log. Then in one giant, uplifting surge – in one final, desperate, winded reach, she contorted into a rising, seething swell to undo the paradisiacal latch. And in that instant, all that was sacred to her torso, tumbled free, fell, and rolled beyond the bonds of captivity. It was then and there that I was sentenced to know the depth of our corruption, that I was upended with the weight of Adam and Eve and the venality they brought to Eden…and all of it coming with a torrent of blood gushing from my nose.

It was the taste that first signaled me: sour and salty. I bolted upright, sat back. The sight screamed of the macabre, her neck and breasts painted in scarlet, like she'd been the victim of a slasher. I looked down, my chest was that of a hobgoblin, nightmarish, flesh and blood. She blinked, waited, her face going from fright to terror, her eyes to panic.

In an instant, we scooted backwards across the floor, away from one another as if each were a fiend from hell. We didn't stop until we were on opposite sides of the room, then waited, frozen, surveying the carnage. It was butchery, and it all fell to me. Even then the flow continued unchecked, surging, running, dripping. I took long swipes with the back of my hand, rich red trails staining with each pass. We were clowns, sad and tragic, even ghoulish. I raised myself up without a word and stumbled to the sink. Then with the nous of urgency, she was by my side, half crying, trembling. In the next instant, she was away then back with towels, helping, but then all at once leaving me to tend to myself. It was a gusher and clotted only after many cold compresses. I looked about, but she had gone off to be alone; still I could hear her, somewhere, praying, rending the air with lamentation. Her wailing eventually gave way to sobbing, the pure and brokenhearted kind, the kind that only time could console, the kind that only prayer could heal. My shirt and coat were easy work. I left by the back door.

Chapter Thirty-Eight
I'll Repent Tomorrow

The cold night air hit me like renewed life; so rejuvenating that I left my jacket open, hoping somehow that the chill would settle me. My breath was silvery in the moonlight, and I walked with quick but quiet steps to the field alongside the infirmary then took its briar-infested shortcut back to Glasscock House. Lights were out everywhere except for the streetlights and the ominous shadows they cast. I couldn't remember the campus ever having been so dark, so still, so enmeshed in solitude.

Everyone in Glasscock House was asleep. The only sounds were muffled snores and the reassuring rumble of the furnace. My footsteps on the creaking stairs weren't enough to disturb Duncan, his breathing steady and deep. My nose was full of blood and so clotted and tight that it felt swollen. But I was too tired to care. All I wanted was sleep.

Had it been the hand of God that had started my nose to bleed? — that kept the two us from free-falling our way straight into the fires of hell? It was a preposterous thought, but I was sure that Dr. De, as a means of repentance if nothing else, would help convince me of its validity.

My nose continued to throb from the clotting long after I was deep into my covers. And it was just before I fell asleep that the smell of popcorn worked its way past the clot. It left me wanting.

Saturday came in a torrent of rain, heaping and slopping against the room's only window in a mottled, silver luster. I lay huddled in the center of my bed, shivering under what seemed like a blanket of dampness.

Despite the rain, I could hear Duncan's alarm clock ticking from across the room, and even though I was quite sure it was still morning, I had no particular reason to check. My only thought was of the breakfast I had missed and the empty gnawing in my stomach.

With considerable effort, I peeked across the room. Duncan was gone. He was never obliged to say goodbye, only a gone-to-someplace note scribbled conveniently on whatever was born with a flat surface, and then only when he felt like it. Lately, he seemed less and less obliged to ask me to tag along, and I was impressionable enough to take it personally—as though I had done something wrong. It was a feeling that tended to stick with me, eliminating any chance I had for enjoying the quietness of his absence. But today was different. I was feeling surly enough to disregard feeling sorry for myself. Instead, and in an act of sheer defiance, I leaped onto the cold floor, added Duncan's covers to mine, and claimed what was left in his popcorn bowl. I picked through its dregs of oil and salt to get to the kernels half-popped and burnt. It was a taste that did more to antagonize than to gratify but did manage to squelch the foulness of my morning mouth.

The rain continued pelting the window. Thoughts of the night before came with its own torrent of self-loathing: spiritual conversion one-minute, moral debauchery the next. I felt like declaring excommunication, as if my desire for Dr. De was beyond my control, as if she were the embodiment of temptation and beyond anything I was able to withstand. But there was something infernal about her—about us—something that caused me to burn at the sheer thought of whetting my hunger in her never-married, middle-aging loneliness. Although I knew I was, in many ways, as sensitive and knowing as the magic that ran through her, I was, at the same time, aware of the fear that kept it suppressed. And I knew the different levels at which we lived and believed, and which kept our worlds at bay. And I also knew the insurmountable leap it would take to fuse them, a leap that neither of us would ever dare take except behind closed doors. It seemed so pointless to make concessions for my lust, but I made them anyway. I made the only concession I could, the concession I always made: I would repent tomorrow. I felt reasonably confident that repentance would always be available. With that, it became simple: I would atone, but later. Afterwards. Tomorrow.

I figured Dr. De's struggle with desire wasn't much different than my own. And I couldn't help but believe that the lion's share of it was natural, evidence that we were robust, vital...*healthy.* And if there was to be any sin attached to what took place, it had to be in the intent, and the intent predicated on evil. That not being the case, I saw it more as a manifestation of things left to the senses, things rooted in the uncertainties of hedonism as much as the obscurities of theology. What happened between us was not intended to diminish my revival experience. It was only a response to some heightened sense of subjugation we felt for one another. It was another stretch, to be sure, but not enough to prevent me from entertaining its probability. If there was any sin at all, it was from lack of restraint.

I sat upright, letting the chill of the room settle over me. It felt oddly cleansing, despite the room looming like a huge warehouse, messy and tasteless. Duncan's paraphernalia only made it more so. Like the two stereo speakers he'd made from orange crates and hung from the ceiling with baling wire; and the chrome ashtray stand with the gilded-framed picture of himself in his high school football uniform; and the wilting and indestructible grocery bag he used for his dirty laundry. They sat as permanent fixtures, perpetual and prolific, vintage artifacts waiting for their time to come. Duncan had a way of destroying my solitude, even with his absence.

The rain continued, but my surliness welcomed it. I wondered what difference it would make if Duncan were here, save the possibility of making it worse. So, without the first thought of consequences, I drugged myself with three aspirin, gave in to the ranks of self-pity, and coasted obligingly back into the arms of sleep. I would repent tomorrow.

Chapter Thirty-Nine
Bent Like a Willow

I was reading when Duncan came in. It was past midnight, and though he was stumbling, he was quiet enough. He didn't say anything, just munched at the row of raw hot dogs he had speared on the end of a stick. He smelled sour, like the concoction of apples and raisins and barley he called *homebrew*. I had tasted it once and it was mustard-seed bitter. But after a few swallows, I remember it leaving me feeling free of every inhibition I ever had.

Besides his hot dogs on a stick, he was carrying a paper bag half-full of golf balls – the kind encircled with a red stripe – the kind that just seems to call out your name when you walk past a golf range after dark.

Near the doorway, and within the glare of our room's curtainless windows, he stripped naked, and with a number-two iron, drove one golf ball after another into the plaster wall above his bed…WHOOP-CLICK-KROCK…the lid from a Clorox bottle as his tee. In no time, there were thirty or forty holes, each ranging in size from a quarter to a silver dollar, and each with a wire-mesh center…WHOOP… and filtering…CLICK…the smell of cheap, ineffective insulation… KROCK. We said nothing to each other. Not an utterance. Just marveled at the hammer and the kill, the strength of it, the sound of it… WHOOP-CLICK-KROCK…and the anus looking eruptions that exploded through the plaster.

Plaster dust drifted as light as air and covered everything, including the both of us, with a fine coat of chalky grit. The stench of it settled with its own distinct pungency. It was nearly one a.m. when he finally lay passed out across his bed. I crossed the room and pulled the covers up over him. I had no explanation for what he had done, only an outlandish delight in having witnessed it…and the unsettling dread of the cockroaches he had summoned.

I woke with Duncan sitting on the edge of my bed, still naked as a jaybird, and with the sun spilling pale and yellow across the floor. We stared at each other without saying a word. I could feel the scale of plaster dust thick and dry inside my nose, and the taste of it on my lips. The longer I stared at him, the more I realized I was his mirror image. His hair carried the residue of ash, and his eyebrows and eyelashes looked like they had been sprayed with frost. There was a white ring on the inside of his nostrils and a white line where his lips came together. The heavier particulates had settled overnight, but the dust still stirred weightlessly in the sunlight.

"You don't have to worry about it," he said, "I'll pay for everything."

I sat upright, blew my nose, and tried to focus. "What was that all about anyway?" I asked.

He shrugged, his shoulders heavy and lifeless. "Celebration, I guess."

"Some celebration," I said. I waited but got no response. Finally, I asked, "Where'd you get the brew?"

"Had it saved up. In case I ever had a want ... or a need." We both sat very still, surveying the destruction.

"What were you celebrating anyway?" I asked.

"The embryo growing deep within Becky's womb."

My mouth became dryer, the taste on my tongue more bitter. "You mean, Becky's...?"

"Yep," he said, his massive frame bent like a willow.

CHAPTER FORTY
A Slagheap of Forfeiture

I waited for Dr. De after class, off to the side, making myself as inconspicuous as I could. She glanced up once to see me waiting, then returned to the regular after-class, hangers-on. She hurried them along but seemed to linger out of a sense of mercy with the last one, a red-haired girl who seemed distraught, tested. I was in no particular hurry and waited while red hair daubed at her eyes and petitioned with her tears, waited until she gathered herself and her belongings, then waited for the bang of the door behind her.

"I'm sorry I took so long," she said, not moving out from behind her desk, "But I'm glad you stayed." I smiled, but with much effort. "Are you feeling well?" she asked. I was having difficulty making eye contact but managed a dispassionate nod. "I missed you in church yesterday," she said. "And today you sat with your head down through most of the class." She stared at me, trying, I thought, to find signs beyond my melancholy.

"I can't work for you anymore," I said. She said nothing, only waited. We both waited.

"I need to work more at the mill," I said, sounding apologetic. "It pays more, and I need the money." There was brief eye contact, and I was nodding as if what I was saying was undeniable. "It's just better for me."

I waited in dead silence and with my eyes glued to the floor. Dead silence was all that came back. After several deep breaths, I turned and wound my way toward the door. I stopped before leaving. "Thank you," I said, "...for the job. For letting me work alongside you. I learned a lot." She was as sober as stone china, her stare focused somewhere beyond me, as if she hadn't heard. I turned, pushed my way through the door, leaving her silent and alone.

I dropped Dr. De's class the following day. My excuse being that the workload was too great, and that I was sure to improve my academic standing with one less class. My fascination with her had become a preoccupation, and I knew in my heart of hearts that something had to give. Still, I couldn't pull away altogether. There was that thread I just couldn't cut. And it kept me dangling and alone, without moorings and wondering if there was anybody or any place not tied to a slagheap of forfeiture.

I wasn't helped by the fact that it was Thanksgiving, the anniversary of Kellen's death and the vast emptiness left by Bea. I couldn't help but think of it without a sense of loss, nor imagine it being any worse until the news…the kind born by a cold dark stranger limping and dragging his way across a frozen and godless earth: John F. Kennedy had been shot down. Lord have mercy…John F. Kennedy was dead.

CHAPTER FORTY-ONE
Plateaus

John F. Kennedy's death had cut the ground from under us. Blighted hope and a somber world, it seemed, were the only things that remained to brace us. Like so many, we saw him as our brother, and mourned in both sorrow and bitterness as if it were our spiritual due. Mother was especially stricken, harder hit than any of us. The President's allure and zest for life had helped her to see the world, of late, as Camelot. But I soon realized that it had also added to her cache of neuroses. Her regular uses of guilt-by-martyrdom had been expanded to include a social conscience suggestive of both Don Quixote and Mahatma Gandhi. Which was which being anybody's guess. What I knew for sure, though, was that it was open only minimally to discussion and even less to reason.

Mother had enrolled herself in night school and then joined some movement called Students for a Democratic Society. From there, she took to writing poetry with varying themes of protest, none of which were without ferocity, though insisting that her motivation was rooted in peace and love. Overnight, she became a groundswell of freeform that did much to rankle the hearts and minds of Reverend Mayfield and his congregation.

Mother seemed tireless. Possessed. She marched in support of Civil Rights, rallied in support of the Nuclear Test Ban Treaty, was vigilant in helping bring relief to the poor in Appalachia, and demonstrated her conviction for social reform by participating in sit-ins and smoking marijuana. The final straw for my dad came when she announced her intention to join the Peace Corps. It was her way of memorializing President Kennedy's legacy. "Somebody has to care," was her favorite comeback whenever we asked why she was becoming so worked up, so involved. It all boiled down to her being convinced that she had a calling. Caring for causes seemed to give her meaning, what she claimed to need for fulfillment.

She called it "newfound freedom." Dad called it "newfound bondage." In her more excitable moments, Dad liked to announce out loud and to whomever, "What you see, everyone, is a woman in complete control of being out of control."

Dad was on the job every morning at six o'clock stamping out fenders for General Motors. At night he rested in front of the television. Dad was uncomplicated mainstream and saw causes as being things for people who didn't have jobs. For Mother, though, he made an exception so long as she made his dinner.

On Thanksgiving Day, mother volunteered us to help serve dinners at a downtown soup kitchen. Later, we ate what was left over and stayed until almost midnight washing pots and mopping floors. Though most of the known world continued to mourn the death of President Kennedy, I was still able to muster enough selfishness to unload what was burdening me.

I waited for the somewhat relaxed atmosphere of Sunday dinner, then segued into telling Mom and Dad that I had no intentions of returning to Edenfield, that I was quitting, dropping out. I told them I felt as though there was nothing to go back to. The memory of Kellen and his death still haunted me. Bea had dropped off the face of the earth and could be dead for all I knew. Duncan was sure to be gone at the end of the semester, and Dr. De (though I said nothing to them about her) had given me cause for psychotherapy. Even poor Cleveland Yates was gone. Anybody who had meant anything to me was either gone or making plans to go.

Except for a moment or two of silverware clinking against the plates and the disquieting sounds of chewing, there was the anguished wait while Mother readied herself for rebuttal. Dad was always Mother's backup, punctuating her views with final authority, but he always had to wait for what she said to know what to support.

Mother was quick, bypassing all other forms of emotion and going directly to breakdown. Her words came through thick angry sobs. She made me see that dropping out would put me right back into a no-win situation with the Army. And how could I be so stupid? Didn't I know the government and the Army and all those pentagon people were at that very minute sending military advisors clear to the other side of the world to some God-awful place called Vietnam? And that it was just a matter of time before they started sending all our blessed baby boys over there just so they could come back in body bags. And hadn't her brother, Trevor, being killed in Korea been enough for one family? And if what I was really trying to do was kill her, why didn't I just take a knife right then and there and cut her head off. From her first syllable to her last, she was the mother of every boy who had ever donned a uniform, or who was about to.

Silence had never been so silent after she left the room. Dad and I sat for a long time, each of us staring off in a different direction, not paying attention to much of anything but the words which she had left hanging with her leveraged brand of love.

It was a long time before Dad said anything, and then it was only to ask if I wanted coffee. I said no, but he moved off to the kitchen anyway. I suspected it was to give himself time to think. I watched him move about in thought, busying himself with this and that. His words, at last, came in low tones … words meant for me and me alone. He talked over his shoulder while he wiped and cleaned. It was easier that way. No eye-to-eye standoff. No face-to-face confrontation. Just him talking. Just me listening.

"Plateaus," he said, edging a knife back and forth through a chocolate sheet cake. "They're a part of life." He hesitated. He liked to hesitate between points. "That's where you are, you know ... on a plateau." I said nothing, just waited for the rest. "Been there myself more times than I care to say. Feeling stranded. Going nowhere. But the thing you got to keep in mind is that plateaus are only resting places, places to catch a second wind so you can move forward when the time is right." He paused, staring at the cake that neither of us wanted. "Question is how long do you want to stay there? Do you want to make it a stopping-off place or a home? It's up to you. But I'll tell you one thing," he said, turning to face me. "You can only stay so long before you start losing ground, can only feel sorry for yourself just so long before the grounds gives way."

I returned to Edenfield the very next day, Dad driving, Mom holding fast to her certitudes. Before we said goodbye, Dad pressed a five-dollar bill into my hand. It was always his way of loving. And though I still had leanings contrary to their good intentions, I knew it was impossible, at least for now, to deny such noble hearts.

Chapter Forty-Two
The Last Goodbye

Duncan was quiet at the mill. He came and went with his head down and said little in between. Our new job was nailing huge shipping crates together, and Duncan did it more with venom than vigor. What little time he spent in our room was, for the most part, done in silence, eating long loaves of white bread…slowly and one slice at a time.

Becky had stopped climbing the trellis, insisting that it was far too reckless a task given her condition. Still, Duncan prodded her, saying that such exercise would make her and the baby stronger. But then Duncan never came across as embracing good sense or rational thinking…like the times he would sleep with Becky's applecart-sized panties pulled over his face, or the times he would urinate out our upstairs window. But for those of us who knew him best, his mood swings and the need to feel unique were the things that made him important to us. Whether his antics amounted to shock or diversion made no difference. He simply felt the need to misbehave more than most. It was what separated him, gave him identity. It was also the thing that so often pushed him to the edge of sublimity, to places of aloneness and indifference, and left him there to find his own way back.

The situation Duncan found himself in with Becky, however, evoked a darkness I hadn't ever seen in him. He even took to saying that the idea of death seemed sensuous, a rapturous and painless respite from the torture chamber we knew as life. I couldn't be sure if it was just another attempt to elicit just another response, but I do know that I heard him one night babbling in his sleep then crying out, "NOT YET! DON'T TAKE ME YET!" It left me feeling as though I had by chance discovered a dirty little secret: that fear, as much as anything else, lay at the heart of his darkness.

December surrounded us in deep dampness, slush, and railing winds. The furnace in Glasscock House had run nonstop since Thanksgiving. It was old and made very loud banging noises but was effective enough to keep us from seeing our breath. Still, it was our own murky anxieties that became the most intractable obstacles. Through it all, Duncan and I continued to plod our way back and forth between classes and the mill, continued to expend what energies we had on what we both suspected would be our final days at Edenfield. Becky was not yet suspected of pregnancy, and she and Duncan were confident they could hide their news until at least the end of the semester. Besides me, no one knew.

The fact that Duncan knew his days were short, made it more difficult than ever for him to cope with the reality of his fate. He went about as if his destiny had proved to be a large and bitter pill, convinced that life had dealt him an unfair hand. What made matters worse was that he couldn't, for the life of him, understand why God had allowed Becky's pregnancy in the first place—as if his and Becky's free will had played no part. Bitterness was not so much his nemesis, but naivety. He finally quit the mill halfway through December.

Mrs. Little returned a week before Christmas recess. In her absence, prayers, regularly and in abundance, were offered on her behalf. She had not been forgotten or abandoned by her fellow parishioners. Except for the community grapevine, her homecoming was unannounced. And for days that followed, the casserole brigade was a worthy and timeless work of selflessness. Edenfield was a community steadfast and well-structured on taking care of its own.

All had gone well for Mrs. Little, though her time away had been quite a bit longer than expected. But through it all, she had gained considerable strength, and though not yet back on the circuit of Sunday School and Church, Vespers, and Choir, she was, according to Harmon, on track with her music…as God intended it. Of this he was certain.

Visitation to the Little's was restricted to Pastor Ivy and Mildred Gunderson, President of the Christian Women's League. But it wasn't until Gretchen made her debut at the Christmas cantata, reinstating herself at the keyboard of the church organ, that she was fully understood; not until she emerged from behind the side curtains and strode across the altar to face the entire congregation for the first time in almost seven months, was there any indication, outside of Harmon's accounts, as to her certainty.

It was the final tribute to the season before Christmas break, and the entire sanctuary was packed to overflowing. From the moment Gretchen appeared, she was magnificent. Radiant. Alive with love and forbearance: Eve before her yielding to temptation. Truly a spectacle of beauty and a wonder of God's love, and, notwithstanding the strapless glass pumps that clung almost invisibly to her feet, as naked as the moment she was born.

Duncan was gone when I got back to the room, along with most of his clothes and his huge Army duffle bag. He had skipped the Christmas cantata. There was no note. No goodbye. No Merry Christmas or see you later. He was just gone. So typical.

I stood surveying the room, wondering if I would ever see him again, knowing that there was a better than average chance I wouldn't. I stood quiet and alone in our warehouse of a room feeling the pang of rejection flooding over me like someone who had made it to the top of the mountain only to find that there was nothing there but dirt. What had been the gain from Edenfield, I wondered? It was the one question that kept repeating. What had been its comfort, save faith? And where was the salve in faith when all I really wanted was to regain those I had lost?

I continued working at the mill right up until Christmas break even though it was difficult to feel good about all the changes that had been made. The only consolation the mill held anymore was legitimizing my time away from study. I don't know if it was the season or the particular state of loneliness I had succumbed to, but I still kept waiting for Kellen to come bounding up one of the aisles at any minute or come flying around one of the corners full of muscle and laughter. I couldn't stop my mind from going back to those times, wanting things the way they used to be. It was difficult to imagine the mill without Cleveland and Buzz Dithers, without the likes of Marblehead and Billy Screws, and without the Hinterlands and Kellen and Duncan. Even Balls had hung it up. Things just weren't what they once were… or in my estimation what they should be. There were too many new faces: strange and unfamiliar, concentrated and serious. Everything was different: newer, brighter, faster…and it all chafed. Everything. It had been too much, and it had come much too fast.

I worked right on past quitting time that last day; just kept working even after the whistle signaled the end of the day, even after the others had made their way to the exit. I'd caught a second wind and suddenly work felt good, so good I felt a surge of energy. I felt alive. Working. Nailing. Lifting. Stacking. It was all so effortless, and I couldn't bring myself to stop until the new foreman made his way back to where I was. At first, he seemed confused, even frightened, as to why I was crying. But after a few minutes, and after I had hammered one of the pallet boards into splinters, he helped ease the hammer out of my hand then walked with me to the door. I don't remember us saying much, just him patting me on my shoulder and reminding me that it was Christmas. It was snowing hard when he swung the door open for me. I never went back.

I slept the biggest part of the following day, then called and lied to Mother that I'd be working at the mill for the next few days. Then lied again about being invited to spend some time at a friend's before coming home. I felt unclean about lying, even guilty, but my need to be alone had surpassed any sense of remorse.

The next day, people started clearing out, heading home for the holidays. By that evening, everyone was gone. Everyone except me. I don't think anyone from the school realized I was still there in Glasscock House. Lights were out everywhere. The buildings were locked and the campus was barren, leaving the appearance of lights being out all over the world.

A lot had happened since I first arrived in Edenfield, things that were altogether impossible for me to understand with any real clarity. But I was sure that going home wouldn't bring me closer to understanding any of it. So, I joined the exodus and stuffed what clothes I had into my suitcase, tied a rope around its middle to guard against its flimsy lock, and made a vain attempt to write something meaningful to Duncan. I told him I thought I had been running faster than Edenfield had intended, and that I was suddenly without the means to keep it up. I tried to explain that I simply hadn't been ready for most of the things that had come at me, and that I knew enough to know when I was in over my head.

Before I left, I read what I'd written several times over. Each time it sounded more convoluted than the last, but I put a stamp on it anyway, hoping that his current frame of mind might somehow lend itself to understanding.

I knew as I stood there that I was looking at our room for the last time. And I also knew, for my own sake, that I couldn't go home; knew that I was far from ready to espouse Mother's compulsions, the bees in her bonnet. My one sustaining comfort was the fifty dollars I'd earned working for Dr. De and its assurance of a bus ticket to Texas. The invite of Stone and Julie Remington loomed large. Beyond that, my only thought was to make myself known to Uncle Sam.

PART II

Chapter Forty-Three
Dr. Cannon

Edenfield's fight song burst into the loudspeakers at a deafening volume, startling and upending my ruminations. Above me, portly thighs and hind sides, like random cuts of meat, rose to acknowledge the end of the welcoming ceremonies. It was an unnerving sight, a manifestation of too many jelly donuts and lard-fried dinners scrambling to shed the hot hard planks of the bleachers. I waited for their plodding exit then found Holly in short order, then found Harris straining to find us. The day had turned to carnival, more like graduation than orientation. Harris was full of anticipation and introduced us to several names and faces we were doomed never to remember. But it didn't matter. There was love and the promise of time and ties, and we were held by it until the throng had thinned and we had had our fill.

The sun was still high when we returned from a late lunch, but the dorm room where Harris had been assigned was cool and inviting enough for a nap. I declined, opting for a walk instead, something I had planned all along. Time just for myself. For me alone. And so I left, leaving Harris and Holly groaning about their tight stomachs and aching feet, sighing the pleasures of the dorm's surprising quietness and the cool breeze wafting through the window. I was off to look for my youth.

The day still clung to its warmth, enough so that I left my coat behind. A jolt of excitement ran through me, filled me the same way it had thirty years ago when I ran and dove into the cold dark waters of the Sands River for the first time.

I walked with unhurried freedom. First, past the vacant lot where Glasscock House *used* to be ... even the big silver maple was gone, stump and all. A large sign with a modernistic architectural rendering declared it as the new site for the science and engineering building. The future was upon us, like it or not. From there, I turned and headed south, strolling under the huge elms that lined the street in front of the rectory. I paused to think of Catherine Ivy and our one infamous night together, and how we had chanced the curse of God right there on the front seat of her daddy's car. The memory of us there in that darkened garage stayed with me all these years, never letting me put it aside long enough to celebrate the good she did in the mission fields. To my own disgust, I couldn't picture her apart from that night. But the untold nights her father visited me in my dreams, seeking revenge against my offense…for being in his car in the first place…always jolted me from my sleep with enough fear to make me promise that I'd never again think of her *in that way.* But I did. And I do.

From the rectory, I made my way to the front of the campus and its wide concourse of grass and maples and shade, unchanged save for it being even denser and greener. I could almost make out familiar voices and the clank of the old loose hardware on the chapel doors. Other than that, change greeted me from all directions. The Fishes and Loaves was gone. In its place was a coin laundry. Pauline's Diner had given way to the new post office, and Celestine Tucker's secondhand shop was now a very smart-looking real estate office. The streets were paved, and there were curbs and sidewalks, and the mill was a looming, empty shell with broken windows and surrounded by its own thick forest of weeds and vines. I walked as if seeing Edenfield for the first time.

The classrooms and buildings hadn't changed except for new windows and fresh paint, and I took as much of it in as I could, remembering. Kellen was there, as always, shimmying his way up the tile drainpipe to the roof of the gymnasium, the way he had so many times, picking his way from drainpipe to window ledge, from window ledge to trellis until he was on the roof, perched at the summit and sizing up all that would be his.

I stood remembering how he would talk to himself as he climbed and laughed at nearly everything he said. He was his own best audience at such times, even his own best friend. It was easier that way. No obligations to anyone but himself. Nothing to cloud his freedom. Nothing but him and his own sheer will. Those were his moments. Unburdened and with a spiritual detachment to anything that might cause fear. Maybe it was just that simple for him. Maybe it was, more than anything else, that single ingredient of not having to rely on anyone but himself that kept him so in control.

For Kellen, it mattered that he was able to see the world from the tops of buildings and the crests of mountains. But to him the thing most valuable was getting there, the journey; journeys he made every minute of every day, whether in his mind or in his indefinable world; journeys he was powerless to refute or refuse; journeys, many of which were doomed from the beginning because they lacked destination.

That first time when he called out to me from the top of the gymnasium to "COME ON UP," I was sure he could smell my fear even though he was three stories up, because it was only seconds later that he said, "No, don't! It's too dark." Somehow, he knew my blood had turned to ice, that I was unable to move. But it was okay with him – enough to never mention it again, enough to never let it make a difference between us. He was always forgiving of the weaknesses in others, like the times I could never jump off the North End Bridge. My fear simply didn't matter to him. He just couldn't ever forgive it in himself, even a hint of it.

From the concourse, I cut across an expansive parking lot where the infirmary used to be, to the road that led to Lizzy's. I liked that it was still the same dusty hard-packed dirt and gravel that crunched under my feet. Even so, it had been opened up, no longer a dead end. Houses dotted the landscape far beyond where the road used to stop.

From the middle of the road, Lizzy's house rose like a giant icon against the late afternoon sun. Nothing was square. No straight lines anywhere. It sagged and dipped and listed and caused the wind to make shuttering sounds against its dried and dying sleep. It was beyond gray, weathered beyond anything that paint could mend, beyond the efforts of what craftsmen might do. Between its look of lament and its being ravaged by the seasons, there appeared to be nothing left except fond farewells. I stood confounded by its power to evoke memories, of Lizzy and me and our last night together. Who did I become that night, anyway? What had I expected of her? She of me? What did we ever dream would come from such fermentation? I don't know as I ever gave it much thought beyond the flush of lust; still there was the notion that I could live without ever having to atone for it. I simply thought of it as having been caught in a collision between want and need, and being full of an eagerness to jump from adolescence to manhood in one commanding leap. Then, too, there was the quest for the unknown: the idea of forbidden fruit and every young man's fantasy of an older woman. I only wish that my patience had been as acute as my desperation.

I turned and backtracked to the campus. Traffic was heavy on the highway, and I waited at the blinking light before crossing and heading into the field leading to the Littles'. About halfway across the field, I could make out a swing set and a tricycle in the back yard. As I got nearer, I could see a wading pool and a sand box, but not a solitary soul anywhere, no stirring of any kind. I walked past it, then down the driveway to the front yard, but still there was no one despite the front door standing open. I gave a timid knock, then backed away. I didn't know who I expected to answer but had hoped to muster the courage to ask if I could maybe glimpse at the basement, stand for a moment in its spell. It had been thirty long years, but I knew it held significance for me. I had left a lot of things there.

After a few minutes, it was evident that there was no one home. With reluctance I walked away. But when I reached the road, I turned to let its un-panoramic landscape take hold for a final time. I studied how things hadn't changed all that much, even after all the years. The driveway still lay filled with white gravel, and the house was still the same dull gray. The trees in the yard, however, had grown to gargantuan heights. They were majestic and cast an unusual depth of shade, keeping the house and the yard colorless and flowerless and plain. Still, they didn't detract from the memories of that first summer. I had only to close my eyes to be there again.

As I walked away, I couldn't help but look over my shoulder time and again, unable to quite let go. The road had a slight incline, giving me the perfect excuse for walking slow. Just as I neared the top of the rise, I turned for a final time, my indulgence turning to daydream, and imagined the notes from Gretchen's piano drifting after me. I stood not wanting to move until the memories of Harmon and Harmony's stringed duets came scraping and scratching on the thin September air. I tried to imagine what Kellen might say if he were here, what thoughts he might have to drive his laughter or add to my illusions.

Within minutes, the Littles' house was lost to the cover of trees and the sweeping turns in the road. I walked only half remembering the houses and the slope of the land, waiting for things to jog my memory. It was almost by accident that I caught the far corner of Marsha Tidewater's house and pool. Houses had sprung up all around it, had relegated it by proximity to the suburbs. But it was the surrounding fields that I missed more than anything, fields that went on forever with Queen Anne's lace and the smell of milkweed. There was nothing but houses now, from one horizon to the next.

I veered at the first crossroad and headed in what I believed to be the direction of Duncan's old campsite. The road was more of a lane than anything else, wide enough for only one car. I walked for several long minutes before a white picket fence laced with climbing roses came into view. Beyond the fence, a faded red roof peeked above a giant arbor of wisteria. From afar, I could see that it was the only house on the lane, but as I drew nearer, it began to take on a vague familiarity. I could hear what I thought was scratching and digging, so I approached with humming and whistling as a way of announcing myself. As I got close, I heard the digging stop. An older man rose and peered from behind the roses. He was thin with alert intelligent eyes and squinted at me from the shadow of a canvas hat. He wore cotton gloves, and the knees of his pants were caked with loam. The sweat drop on the end of his nose told me he had been working for a while. It was small, unlike the ones the size of peach seeds that oozed from his temples and down the side of his face.

He gave me an inviting hello and a bit of a head cock that suggested I looked familiar. I gave him my family's own brand of southern howdy and said something inconsequential about the weather. He kept his smile, uttered something with an agreeable tone and removed his gloves, a gesture that suggested he was ready to either shake hands or take a break.

"I think I've had about enough for today," he said with a grin, motioning toward the long row of newly planted flowers spaced just-so along the length of the fence. "Mums," he said.

I nodded, recognizing his labors. "There's something cleansing about nature's colors and the smell of freshly turned earth," I said.

"Yes," he replied, "there's sturdiness to it. A sweetness not quite like anything else." He was staring down at his diggings. "And sweeter still when you can get your hands into it. Don't you think?" He looked me in the eyes, then smiled broadly. "Do I know you?" he asked.

"I don't think so," I said. "Though I did live here some thirty years ago. Worked at the mill, or what used to be the mill. Went to school at the college for a while."

"Do tell," he said, removing his hat and wiping its band with the backside of his gloves. "Lived at the Littles' for a while, as I recall."

My shock was immediate. He had taken me without warning, and I stared at him as if under a spell. I searched for something that would give me a clue. His white hair, short and neat. His blue eyes, penetrating. I leaned back, squinted, and tried to take away thirty years.

"Doctor Cannon?" I queried.

"You look stunned," he said.

"Speechless, actually."

"Is it because I'm so much older, or because *you* are?"

We laughed a good laugh. "A little of both, I suspect, but mostly that you would remember me. I knew this house only somewhat from when I was here, but never realized it was you who lived in it."

"For thirty-five years, now," he said. "The last ten of them alone."

I hesitated, then realized his implication. "I'm sorry," I said.

"No need to be," he said. "It happens— death as well as life." Before I could say anything, he said, "Join me for lemonade?"

I was on the verge of saying I had to be going, but he had already turned and headed toward the house. "It's already made," he said over his shoulder. "Make yourself comfortable here on the porch. We'll catch the last of the sun."

CHAPTER FORTY-FOUR
The Prophet Jeremiah

He had turned and was already through the front door as I opened the gate. The front porch faced west and had already lost its shade for the day. The field across the road and the woods beyond were unmarred except for a small clearing and a garden just big enough for one.

"Here we go," he said, setting the pitcher and glasses on a small table between us. He poured and we toasted without clinking glasses. "To coming together," he said.

"Without coincidence," I added. We drank deeply and sat for a few minutes enjoying the last of the day's warmth.

"You left Edenfield early," he said, reflecting.

I waited for the taste of lemonade to even itself out across my tongue. "Yes," I said. "I think it was having reached an understanding of the square peg in the round hole dilemma." I paused, deciding not to elaborate, but added, "I was young and impetuous, and basically unprepared for the things life had handed me. So, I did what I thought would cause me the least amount of pain. I left."

We sat without looking at one another, talking into the very low sun. "That was," he said, "right about the time Duncan Skinner and Clovis Summers' daughter, Becky, dropped out of school and started a family."

"Yes," I said, pretending to know more than I did. "That seems about right. I'm afraid I didn't stay in touch like I should have. It was quite a transitional time for me: *adolescent ambiguity* for lack of a better term, that and an incessant curiosity that led me straight into a three-year stent with the Army." I smiled, remembering my naivety, before asking, "Do you ever hear anything about them? About Duncan and Becky?"

"From time to time," he said. "They live right here, you know, just west of town. Far as they ever got. Had a baby girl sometime after you left, then went on to have five boys. Every one of them a redhead. What a brood. The girl was the only one who attended college here. The rest of them went here and there and God only knows. I don't think any of them ever finished except for the girl." He smiled as though they were family. "Becky never did much of anything outside of mothering, including Duncan." He laughed at his own cleverness. "Duncan, though, owns his own business. Digs basements, pours foundations, drills wells. Got both of his youngest working with him right now. They've all had a stint working with him at one time or another, even the girl. Duncan was always good about keeping things in the family. Gave him *control,* especially over the finances. It's a God complex of sorts, I suppose, but he seems to have done all right by it." He gave me a big fatherly smile. I gave it back.

"You've got to admire Duncan, though," he said. "He taught those kids what tough was all about. Let them know flat-out that they needed to pull their own weight if they expected to eat at his table. I don't believe it hurt them any. Might have even toughened the weaker ones and took some of the edge off the tougher ones." I nodded my understanding. "Got to give ole Duncan his due," he said. "One thing for sure, he knew how to keep them busy. If you worked for Duncan, you worked long and hard. No question about it." He paused, thought for a second or two, then added, "I don't know how he's done it all these years—working the way he does—but he just finished building Becky her dream home, or so he likes to say. But she says he never consulted her on a single thing. Besides that, she said she never wanted it in the first place." We both laughed, knowing the truth of what he'd said.

"It's out Edenfield Road," he said, "just past Floyd Hanna's chicken farm." He chuckled. "Did most of the work himself. Put it right smack in the middle of twenty acres. Woods all around it. Can't even see it from the road." He paused again, rubbing the condensation on his glass. "He always liked his privacy, Duncan did. Course I should talk. But in Duncan's own style, he waited until all his kids were grown and gone before he built it, just when they didn't need it." We exchanged looks. His look asked if I knew what he meant. My look assured him I did.

"Anyway, I saw him at the barber shop about a month ago and he said that he built it big enough so all the kids and grandkids could come and stay during holidays. I figure it won't take too many holidays before he's sorry he ever had that idea. But other than a chance meeting now and again, I never see much of him. Not even in church."

I sat listening, trying to imagine Duncan as a husband and father. I couldn't help but wonder if he was satisfied with his life. Couldn't help but wonder where he was with God, or if he had allowed room for Him at all. If he had, it would certainly have to be on Duncan's terms. I thought I might like to see Duncan, but somehow knew I wouldn't know the first thing to say. I couldn't help but feel it would be the same for him. Years had a way of eroding what we allow as memories, what we necessitate for our own fulfillment.

We sat in silence for a while, enjoying each other's presence. Finally, I asked whatever became of the Littles. He continued to stare out across the field long after my question. I was about to ask him again when he cleared his throat and said in the direction of his glass, "After Mrs. Little's appearance at the sixty-three Christmas cantata…"

"I was there," I interjected.

"Well then! Not much needs to be said other than she began an even steeper decline after that. After about six months or so, and somewhere in between states of confusion and euphoria, she stayed confined in one of the state hospitals until about nineteen seventy-five. Then, due to bureaucracy and budget cuts, she was released and sent to live with her sister in St. Louis. She died six years later not knowing a soul. Her sister said she was pitifully sad and alone even during her best times. As far as we know, that's what finally took her. I suspect that there came a time when she just gave up." He paused in what seemed like respect, then asked, "Do you believe someone can die from loneliness, Mr. Thatcher? From a broken heart, perhaps?"

"Yes, I do," I said without hesitation.

He stared hard at me, and at some length, then added, "I remember the day well. It was the very day after my sixtieth birthday." He went silent after that. I sat without a word, remembering Gretchen, trying hard not to think of her suffering – some of which I'd witnessed in her very own basement right after the news of Kellen. I chose not to bring it up.

We sat for some time without a word passing between us, long enough, I felt, for me to ask what I thought to be the obvious question.

"Why was she released to her sister and not Harmon?"

The question seemed to hang in the air like it was out of place, or maybe the wrong time for it. Dr. Cannon stared at me as if debating what to say, or even if he should say anything at all. I waited with as innocent an expression as I could manage. He sipped at his lemonade without the appearance of enjoying it then stretched his lips across his teeth without smiling. "I'm told," he said, "that while she was a ward of the State, she never responded to visits from Harmon and Harmony. Just sat there, lost to the world, like she never knew them." He sipped again, annoyed at what he knew, what he could not forget.

"I don't know how much you know," he went on, "but I'll be as brief and as impartial as I can." He paused again while he pondered what to say. "It was a number of years after she had been confined that it became evident that she was not a good candidate for complete recovery, or even a partial one. The prognosis was continually poor, and the likelihood of her being released grew more improbable by the day. But if such a day were to ever come, she would never be beyond needing round-the-clock care." He sipped, wiped his lips. I drank deeply. "I guess," he said as he refilled my glass, "it wasn't the sort of news Harmon was ready to hear, and I believe that's what changed him forever." He leaned toward me, "You see," he said, "as the college's comptroller, Harmon was the ideal employee: God-fearing, conservative, competent. There was never a question about his handling of the college's money: tuitions, grants, loans, investments, even the payroll. He was a one-man show with an impeccable talent for keeping us in the black. Now I'd be the first to admit that he was a bit left of center – maybe even more than a bit – but unquestionably accommodating in the way we needed him."

I sat wondering where he was taking me. "I admire competency," I interjected. "I also find it interesting that you saw the other side of him."

"You mean him as a NERD?"

"Yes," I chuckled.

"So much so," he said, "that we never recognized the change. We knew he was under a lot of emotional stress: his wife in a mental hospital and his daughter hitting her stride as a free spirit, but we never caught on to the real transformation."

He paused and gave his head a little shake as if annoyed by its very thought. "You see, most of the things Harmon did were laced with a bit of oddness. And when his eccentricities began to intensify, we figured it was just because he was going through so much, and that he just needed time to sort things out. And based on his years of service to The Church and the college, we found ourselves being as generous and as lenient as we were sympathetic. It was our undoing. The next thing we knew, he was gone."

"Gone?"

"Gone! … and with the money." A faint smile trailed across his lips. "He took it all," he said, his voice dipping with a tone of finality.

"Are we talking about the college's money?"

"And The Church's. And not just some of it, but ALL of it."

We sat staring at each other, our eyes locked. "Where did he go?" I asked.

"Only his shadow knows," he said, "And God of course."

"You mean he actually managed to…"

"Yes!" he said. "We knew he was smart, even cagey, but we never figured him for a crook. It was simply a narrative that didn't fit."

"And he's never been found?"

"No. And that's the third most disturbing thing," he said half laughing. "The first, of course, was his committing the crime. The second was his taking Etta Pritchett with him." The look on his face was suddenly twisted, like he was fighting off a bad smell. "But I guess I can't blame either one of them. I mean if ever there was a match made in heaven, it would have to be those two. I mean I simply can't imagine another human being wanting either one of them."

I sat galvanized by the thought of Etta and Harmon together. I didn't know where to go with it. It was even hard to form words, and, for a second, I even thought to laugh. The thought of Harmon Little committing the perfect crime, and then having to wake up next to Etta Pritchett was a strain to my imagination, out there where dots failed to connect. The image of them embroiled in the heat of passion added a new dimension to obscenity.

"How much?" I asked. The money interested me far more than Etta, even though there was an alien fascination about her.

Dr. Cannon sucked gangster-like at his front teeth, then said, "Four hundred and ninety thousand…give or take."

The sun was now a glaring red ball in the tops of the trees, and I was beginning to feel a slight chill.

"You know," he said, "I often wonder if Harmon ever feels any remorse." His eyes were fixed on the woods across the way. "My guess, though, and this is just my personal take, is that he doesn't."

He rolled his head in my direction and gave me a wry little smile. "I never pretended to know the meat of Harmon's mind," he said, "except when it came to money." His voice took on a tinge of exactness like some country courthouse lawyer giving an off-the-record summation to his closest friends. "Money for him was Holy Writ. He was convinced that money, and the shapes it assumed, was infinitely more complex than the rest of us could ever comprehend. So, as the self-proclaimed guru of money management, and thinking he was the only one savvy enough to give it its due—his ego never allowing him to think otherwise—he was guaranteed the one thing he could never get enough of: *power.*"

He hesitated, examined his glass and the last of its lemonade, then said, "Harmon spoke of money like it was endowed with spirituality. As if it was capable of human experience. He and money were entities unto themselves, guardians one to another. Theirs was a union that worked to establish authority: money as the master, and Harmon as the agent to act on its behalf. Money has its power, alright, but the one thing Harmon failed to see was its power over *him.*"

I sat a little dumbfounded, trying to absorb the magnitude of what he'd said. "Sounds a whole lot like money was his god," I said.

He shifted his eyes in my direction. They were fixed with an undeniable affirmation. "Money had claimed him, Mr. Thatcher. Set him apart. Elevated him, at least in his own mind, to a place of rank, to a place he needed to be. And after a time, he understood this elevation to be what he deserved. I suspect this was when he felt the money belonged to him. It was, after all, his handling of it that caused it to grow."

A look of contemplation burrowed in on him and settled in the wrinkles of his brow. "So now," he said, "the four-hundred-and-ninety-thousand-dollar question is, how can Harmon possibly feel remorse for taking something he believed was rightfully his in the first place?" He locked me into a quiet stare. "I don't think he can," he said. "I don't think he can."

He sat staring out across his yard and the garden across the road, at the trees beyond and into the last of the sun's softening fires with a look that bore the scars of Harmon's betrayal, a look that had grown weary with the hope of ever making sense of it. "You know, Mr. Thatcher, the prophet Jeremiah tells us that the heart is deceitful above all things, and desperately wicked; who can know it?" This is where we left it. It was a point he wanted to make, and one I fully understood. And one we were content to leave as it was.

Chapter Forty-Five
Do Tell

We sat comforted by the quiet that had settled around us, like two old friends content with the mere company of being together. Finally, and with a knot of apprehension, I asked about Harmony.

"Oh, she's still around," he said. "Lives in some trailer park between here and Castle City. She was a wild one. More than Harmon could handle, that's for sure. Dropped out of school soon after Harmon left. She was nineteen, maybe twenty, a legal adult except for drinking. Course the drinking part never stopped her. But as far as any of us know, she never shed tear one after Harmon left. I personally think she was happy to see him go. Truth is, I think they were both happy to be rid of each other. Anyway, she stayed in the house right up until the time the bank foreclosed, then moved in with her boyfriend's family. Had to. She was pregnant and neither one of them had a job. But then her getting pregnant was no big surprise. I could have predicted that one in my sleep. Wouldn't have made a difference if Harmon had been here or not." He went on in a monotone.

"The rest is just as predictable. They stayed with his parents until she had the baby then moved to the trailer park. They never did get married, but she did get pregnant a second time. Then he up and left just like Harmon. Don't know that she ever heard from him again. After that it was welfare cheese and peanut butter, but somehow she managed to get through. Got two strapping boys to show for it; two grown men, actually. Neither one of them look or act anything like Harmon. And that's a good thing." He chuckled. "But last I heard, she was working as a desk clerk for the Castle City Police Department, and, if I can believe everything I hear, working as a barmaid at night and on the weekends. Probably why we don't see much of her, at least I don't. Oh, she'll come back for church now and again, Christmas and Easter, times like that. Even took a night class here at the college once. Other than that, the only things I hear about her are rumors. The biggest one is that Duncan's truck is a whole lot more familiar around her trailer than it ought to be. Of course, it's only a rumor."

He paused to stretch and give himself a pull of fresh air then added, "Harmon did leave her a note, though, before he left. But to this very day I don't know why she chose to show it to me. I guess she just didn't know who else to turn to. But in the note, he told her he was sorry and that he was certain he'd never be back. He said he hoped she might grow to understand that his leaving was the only way to finally realize the happiness that had forever eluded him. Everyone deserved to be happy he said. And as best as I can recall, I believe there was something in there about how he knew she'd have to struggle to keep it together, but he knew that the hard times would make her stronger. And, oh yeah, he told her that he loved her."

Our glasses of lemonade, now reduced to ice, sat sweating on the table between us. I was beginning to feel like I needed to be on my way but couldn't quite break the tie. I found myself wanting to know more but was too embarrassed to ask. Finally, I said, "I appreciate your sharing these things with me. There's a feeling of completion in linking up with the past."

"I'm happy I could make that happen for you," he said. "But I really didn't tell you anything except what's common knowledge. Nothing that the whole town doesn't already know."

"Still, I'm grateful," I said, remaining hesitant to rise.

He was watching me with a slight look of curiosity, waiting for me to leave, I suppose. When I didn't, he finally asked, "You seem a little pensive, Mr. Thatcher."

After another short pause, I asked what I had for thirty years longed to know. "Before I go…" The words were stuck, caught somewhere between the thinking and the voicing. "I was wondering…"

"Yes?" he coaxed.

"Well, I was wondering if you remember a girl by the name of Bea Ardor?"

"Remember her?" he said. "How could anyone who ever knew her forget her?"

That same sensation I felt thirty years ago when I first met her, when I first shook her hand, coursed through me again. "Well then, do you know anything about her?" I asked, trying for mere curiosity.

"Well, yes! She lives right here in town. What do you need to know?"

My brain went soft. I felt like I was suddenly trapped in the dark act of thinking, like I had led myself into some thought cave and forgot the way out. I fumbled, but the right words eluded me.

"Is everything all right?" he asked.

My fogginess was slow in dissolving, but finally, and with my words measured, I said, "It's just that I lost track of her years ago… after Kellen Manly died."

He chewed on the last of his ice, then swallowed hard. "Funny that you would mention it," he said. "Funny because no one knew of her whereabouts for years. Not until Kellen's ashes were sent back here for me to bury." He looked a little surprised at my stunned expression. "You knew Kellen had been cremated, didn't you?" he asked.

"Yes. In fact, I went to Texas to visit his adopted parents: Stone and Judi Remington. It was Christmas. Right after I left Edenfield."

"Yes, I know," he said.

I looked at him a little disbelieving. "How could you have known something like that?" I asked.

"I know," he said, "because Judi Remington is my sister."

We stared as if we had just seen each other for the first time. At length, I tried shaking the cobwebs from my head, tried to understand the inter-connectedness, the relationships, the things I didn't know. But the maze was too thick. At last, I let him know with a look and a shrug that I was more than just a little confused.

"How do you think Kellen happened to come to Edenfield in the first place?" he asked, not really expecting a reply. "How do you suppose a boy from the dust bowl of Texas found his way to the wintery cold of Minnesota?" His speech was concise. "Judi called me a number of times about him," he said. "Told me about his background, how she and Stone had taken him in and how they both thought that Edenfield would be an answer to prayer for him. At first, I was a little leery. She seemed to be trying too hard to convince me that this was where he belonged. Of course, I had no intention of refusing her. She's an impeccable judge of character and I trust her with my whole heart. I just didn't want her to think she could have her way simply because I was her brother. But it was pretty much a done deal from the start. All Kellen had to do was get here and prove himself. He didn't have a problem with either."

"That's not exactly how Kellen explained it to me," I said.

"I'm not surprised," he said. "There are, after all, times when things are better left unsaid. Things have a way of getting distorted when passed around. So, we agreed the less said, the better. Can you imagine the backlash of having everyone know that the president was your unofficial guardian? —and the implications of favoritism? His life could have gone from one bad turn to another overnight. And that was something I couldn't allow, especially to someone who had already suffered enough hurt for a lifetime. It was something that simply couldn't be told. It just wouldn't have fit the scheme of things."

I studied him. "So…were the two of you close?"

"He kept me up many a night," he said, "right here on this very porch. I saw less of him after you came, though. I suppose he'd grown some, needed less of me. But he still came around, just not so often. He sure thought a lot of you. Called you his best friend." He was smiling now, candid. "He was a brave heart, Kellen was. So determined, but so enslaved by a thing…a thing he allowed to bridle him to the very end."

I sat very still, not daring to speak, afraid that I might interrupt the flushing of his memory. "He was very private, you know," his tone now confidential, "and it paralyzed him to think that others might come to know what haunted him." I heard myself silently coaxing him to go on. "He was always trying to pump himself up, make himself bigger than life. Always trying to prove he was more of a man than most. Go to extremes, he would. Go against his very nature, force himself into situations he thought might help him overcome what he called his *affliction*." And he never stopped trying. Never gave in to who he really was." I waited while he rocked. "Maybe I've overstepped my bounds here, Mr. Thatcher. Overstated myself."

I said nothing, just focused on the sun now bathing him in a faint but orange glow. "Kellen was never good about forgiving himself," he said, rocking, reliving, continuing without my prodding. "That alone made him doubly hard to console. There were times when I actually ran out of things to say. Then after a while I began to understand that it really didn't matter. He just needed me to be there…to listen. As a result, we spent many a time just sitting and gazing at the stars, talking about God and eternity and the like. That seemed to bring him peace, despite his perceived sin. But he never quite let himself be comforted by the notion that God could hate the sin and love the sinner. He certainly had his own ideas about things." He smiled, tight lipped; told me with his expression that enough had been said. I accepted his gesture, bothered but grateful for what little he had shared.

"So, what prompted Stone and Judi to send you his ashes?" I wasn't quite as done with Kellen as he was.

"Stone had accepted an offer to teach in Alaska," he said, "and he and Judi felt that Kellen's remains needed a final resting place. They felt he needed to be remembered, and scattering his ashes or burying them in a little Texas town where nobody remembered him or even cared about him would be the worst kind of goodbye. Besides that, every known relative he ever had was either lost, dead, drunk, or plain not interested in remains of any kind. So this being the only other place he ever thought of as home, it was the most likely choice."

"So, what did you do with them?"

"I bought a plot right here in Edenfield. Right next to where I'll be buried. It's kind of comforting knowing he'll be there next to me. My wife on one side, him on the other. Kind of like the son I never had."

The sun was going fast, slipping behind the roll of the horizon. "And Bea Ardor?" I asked.

"Oh, yes, Bea Ardor. I was saying how funny it was that she just showed up after so many years—right here on my doorstep. She and her daughter. Daughter couldn't have been more than five or six at the time. Started right in with barely more than a hello. Said she understood that Kellen's ashes had been brought back to Edenfield for burial, and could I please tell her where exactly. Just like that. Said she'd seen the newspaper article with my name in it." He paused just long enough for his face to take on a ruptured look. "The paper made it into a human-interest story," he said. "What they'll do to sell a paper. Anyway, it created quite a stir the day his ashes were buried. People get bored here in Edenfield, Weldon. Doesn't take much to get them up and out of their La-Z-Boys, especially when there's digging going on in the graveyard. Kept them chattering for weeks on end." He sat staring into the last of the sun, thinking, then added, "Looked to me like she'd had a rough time. Bea, I mean. Pale. Puffy. Turned-down wrinkles in her face. Had a real tired look for such a young woman. But I found out later she'd been taking care of her mother ever since her father died; that and working and raising a child can make a whole lot of difference in the way you feel. And how you feel can make a whole lot of difference in how you look. Bea was an only child, so her mother's care fell entirely to her." He paused again. "She didn't stay long. Just long enough to visit his grave, I suspect."

I was about to ask where she lived when he added, "Then it was about six months later that she and her daughter up and moved here. That was right after her mother died. Mother and dad both died within a year of each other. Left her everything. About a two-hundred-acre farm and some little old motel on the other side of Castle City. The motel wasn't worth anything, just an old abandoned ramshackle of a thing, but the land it was sitting on turned out to be worth a good deal: one of those tracks of land smack in the middle of some developer's dream. Developers are turning dirt farmers into millionaires these days, turning everything from here to heaven into high rise this and industrial that." He said it as though the old ways, his ways, were being pushed aside and trampled under for the sake of greed.

"Bea surprised me though," he said. "I thought she'd be off to the bright lights. She always had a touch of *big city* in her. But she ended up right back here in Edenfield. Lives beyond that big old house where Elizabeth DeForte' used to live. You remember Dr. DeForte', don't you?" I nodded cautiously. "Well then you must know where I'm talking about." I gave him a blank stare. "Over there where the dirt road used to dead end."

"Oh, THERE!" I said.

"Yes," he said, happy that I remembered. "The town opened it up after folks started building more houses. Anyway, Bea told me she came back to Edenfield because it made her feel safe … and because of the memories…memories too fragile to be just tossed aside. I couldn't quite figure that one out. She was always in such a hurry to get out of here. Said she didn't like how most everybody in Edenfield was always wanting to mind her business for her, but in the end figured her life was pretty much an open book, and if she had to live with it there was no reason why everybody else couldn't." He stopped to wait for my thoughts. I had been quiet, only nodding now and again to let him know I was still listening. "Stays to herself a lot," he said. "Has a big greenhouse, grows roses and manages a whole slew of beehives." He laughed. "She's quite a character. Filled out a bit. Kind of chuffy you might say. But she looks good."

"You mentioned a daughter," I said. He raised his eyebrows and gave a big nod. "Is there a husband?"

"There was never a sign or even a mention of a husband," he said. "Matter of fact, her daughter goes by Ardor. Went to college right here in Edenfield. Bright girl. Pretty. Not in the manner of Bea, but lovely in her own right. Name's Rachel. Finished up near the top of her class, then headed for the neon lights – some place with jobs and the prospects of a future, I suspect. Not many graduates stay around as you know. There's just nothing for them here. Even the mill is gone now. We shut it down shortly after Harmon ran away with the money. Had to. Couldn't settle accounts, couldn't even meet the payroll. And Fulton Highlander dying right in the middle of it didn't help any.

"Oh, I didn't know about Fulton," I said.

He gave me a quick glance like he was angry at himself for even mentioning it. I waited while he snorted a couple of times like he was trying to dislodge a gnat from his nose. Then, with a discernible distaste on his face, mumbled something about Orlo Kirkum finding him dead down by the Sands River, slumped over in the front seat of his Cadillac. He paused in mid-sentence with a look on his face as if he were having trouble keeping his lemonade down. "And with his pants and underwear down around his ankles."

I felt my eyebrows rise. "Sara Bennett," he said, "ran the mile back to Orlo's to tell him that Mr. Highlander was in an awful way. Orlo made her stay around until after the autopsy confirmed he died from a heart attack. That was the last we ever saw of Sara Bennett. I'm just glad Fulton's wife wasn't alive to know it."

He left me not knowing what to say. For the first time I had the distinct feeling I had overstayed my visit. The picture of Fulton Highlander and Sara Bennett on the front seat of his Cadillac was the closest thing to grotesque I could think of outside of Harmon Little and Etta Pritchett.

"Well, life happens," I said without knowing what else to say.

"As does its surprises," he added.

Twilight had now replaced the long shadows. I was anxious to leave but didn't want to leave on such a low note. "So, I take it you didn't attend the festivities today," I said, wanting to discard the subject of

Fulton Highlander and Sara Bennett altogether.

"Oh, I've been to enough of those things to last me a lifetime," he said. "Didn't think I'd ever get tired of the pomp, but I did some years back. These days I'd just as soon be in my garden or in my study. I'm old school, you know, and the older I get, the more grateful I am of it." He looked at me as if he truly meant what he said. "Fact of the matter is, the college board brought me out of retirement several years back to chair the student selection committee. It was out of token respect I suspect, but I accepted. And I've discovered that that's about all I care to take on. It allows me to know the prospective students first-hand, and I like that. Matter of fact, I recognized the name Thatcher when I first laid eyes on it. It's interesting how often names repeat here at Edenfield from one generation to the next. Since the day I saw Harris' name, his coming to Edenfield has become of particular interest to me."

"Oh? Why so?" I asked.

"Purely a selfish interest. I had always felt the need to talk with you about Kellen while you were still a student, but I could never seem to coordinate my time with my mood. Unbeknown to all but a few, Kellen's death left me devastated, heart and soul. I felt that maybe talking to the person he referred to as his best friend would somehow be cathartic for me, maybe even for both of us. Your son coming on the scene seemed to bring new hope that I might finally connect with you. But it's only been lately that I've become satisfied with leaving Kellen's memory alone, letting it rest, letting him rest."

I felt like I'd been injured. Like I'd been denied access to what was really at Kellen's core. But my hand was staid. I would have to be satisfied with what I had; would have to hold fast to the few things Dr. Cannon had felt comfortable sharing. And though I now understood that much of what Kellen shared with me had only been the tip of the iceberg, it was possessed of enough life to sustain his memory, even to this day.

"So, tell me," he said, "before your family sends the constable out to look for you, what you meant when you said our meeting was not by coincidence." He had not missed a note.

"Oh," I said, adjusting my back so that I sat a little straighter, "I simply believe that everything has a purpose and a reason. Even meeting like we did here today." I waited with a smile, not knowing if he was so inclined. "I think, in a very real sense, they're God's blessings. Not accidents or coincidences." His steely gaze let me know I was not being taken lightly. "Please don't misunderstand," I said. "I don't think God choreographs every little move we make. I don't think that's His intention. That's why we're endowed with things like reason and logic, and the agency to make choices. But I am convinced there is a higher order and a plan, an intention, for each of us. And what most of us have become comfortable calling coincidence, I see as being His blessing."

"So you believe that everything is ordained of God?"

"Yes."

"Regardless of the outcome?"

"Yes."

"But how can that be?"

"Regardless of the outcome, there will always be something learned. Today, for example, something will pass between us that will make a difference in one or both of us; something that will add to our knowledge, or at least alter it in some way, but certainly change us enough to make us more than we were before we met. That's growth. And that's of God."

"What about the outcomes that result in suffering? Are they of God?"

"I think God's heart is the first one to break at any kind of suffering," I said. "But I also think He intervenes to turn even the worst of things to His advantage. And if that means that some will suffer, then, yes, I believe God will allow it."

We both waited as if to see who could be the quietest, the porch's lengthening shadows adding to the dead calm between us. "It's odd," I said at last, "how Christianity often embraces the notion of suffering as a necessary step for getting right with God; where man lays aside his old nature for a new one, where he allows the cutting away of sin. It's the revelation of past doings and the associate shame that is so encrypted with sorrow. It's a profound kind of suffering, something we need to endure before we can progress, before we can be perfected, before we can begin to share in the fullness of what God has intended for us. So, to these ends, I say, yes, suffering is of God." A sudden breeze came warning us of the night, stirring and cooling, putting an end to one thought and opening another.

He studied me with a wry smile. "You speak in terms of absolutes,

Mr. Thatcher, as though what you say is undeniable." I shrugged, feeling as though I may have come across as too dogmatic. His expression softened somewhat, even bore a touch of compassion.

"I'm sympathetic with your assuredness," he said. "With your passion. It reminds me, in part, of me. But I must tell you that I learned, by way of trial—or suffering if you prefer—that if I was to be believed, I needed to guard against a harshness of conviction."

"I'm not dead to what lies beyond my personal beliefs," I said. "I simply recognize certain things as truth."

"Truth," he said, contemplating its possibilities. "Is there a secret to it? —to recognizing it and distinguishing it from all else?"

All at once, front-porch gossip and lemonade had taken a turn toward the weightiness of argument. My inclination was to tread softly.

"From a very narrow perspective," I said, "I know only what truth is to me. If you need absolutes, I do know absolutely that truth is anything, from any source, that brings light to darkness."

He sat with a thin smile, one that signaled that there were thoughts going on behind it. "But what may be light for some may not be light for others."

"Then ultimately it comes to this," I said, "does the light do honor to God? If so, then it would be difficult, for me at least, to dismiss it as being anything other than truth. God, by whatever name, simply by the virtue of being God, is good, righteous. Love if you will. The light that we shed need only be to that end."

He studied me at some length as if we had reached a level where ideas could be exchanged without words. "Everything you've said seems to be predicated on an abiding faith," he said.

"Yes," I said, "but it has taken me many years to discover what faith truly is."

"And what is it you've discovered?" he said.

I could feel my enthusiasm begin to taper. I didn't like opening myself up to such scrutiny. But before I could answer, he rose and disappeared inside the screen door just long enough to turn on the porch light. "Now then," he said, setting deeper into his rocker, "This faith of yours…"

The weight of his question deserved far more than our time would allow. "Well…," I said, anxious to be brief, "I'm of the mind that faith is the ultimate test." He shot me a quick wrinkled brow. "It's not anything that our forebears overlooked, or the Apostle Paul hadn't preached about. And that is: it's not enough to simply believe *in* God. The test is to *believe* God: what He says He can do and what He promises to do. That's faith. Not waiting for signs and visions so that we might acquire faith. But it's *believing,* and then exercising it, that enables us to align ourselves with His intentions. And on the strength of it, fulfill the test."

The landscape had turned as charcoal as the sky. I sat waiting for him to respond to my sudden silence, but there was nothing beyond the creak of his rocking.

"Yet faith is nothing without charity," he said.

"And dead without works," I added.

He slowed his rocking while he picked thoughtfully at the dirt beneath his nails. Finally, and without looking up, he asked, "What is it, if I may ask, you do by way of profession, Mr. Thatcher?"

"I'm a minister," I said. He peeked up at me from under his thick bushy eyebrows. "Small church. Independent," I added almost as an afterthought.

He stopped his rocking just long enough to lean forward and spit over the edge of the porch. "Do tell," he said.

Chapter Forty-Six
After All These Years

By the time I wound my way back to the dorm, it was almost ten o'clock. Holly was cutting cake, chocolate on chocolate.

"Well look who's here," she said. "We nearly gave up on you."

"Yeah," Harris chided, "we figured you'd hooked up with some of your old classmates…" He stopped and swallowed hard—too big a bite. "Then got all nostalgic and tried to sign up for some night classes." He laughed loud, coughing, and coming close to choking. But then with one immense caw, cleared his windpipe and resumed shoveling one huge bite after another.

"You weren't worried, then?" I asked.

"The only real worry I had," Holly said, her voice tinged just ever so with annoyance, "is that you wouldn't get a piece of cake." She motioned toward the box. It was nearly half gone. I had stayed well beyond what I intended and was relieved that I hadn't caused them undue concern, but at the same time felt a little hushed because they hadn't been.

"We figured the worst thing that could have happened to you would have been a painful trip down memory lane," Harris said, sputtering through a mouth full of frosting. "Nothing as worrisome as you falling down a well or being carried off by wolves." His sarcasm grew right along with his laughter. Maybe it was the sugar or the caffeine, or both, or maybe it was just a time to celebrate, to be happy. Whatever it was, I did what I thought was necessary to become a part of it and plunged headlong into what was left of the cake.

We spent the night in the dorm, across the hall from the room Harris had been assigned. The dorms were empty except for incoming freshmen. Most family members had opted for motels in Castle City. Spending the night in the dorm was Holly's idea. She had never slept in a dorm and was altogether gratified by the space it offered us, space—as of late—that we needed, space not attainable in a motel room. We divided up Harris' sheets and blankets, and I stood guard while she showered in the men's bathroom, the only bathroom. It was the first time I ever slept on the first floor.

We slept across the room from one another, and with the window thrown open to the coolness of a night breeze and the gathering din of bullfrogs and crickets.

"By the way," Holly said from her darkened side of the room, "where were you so long?"

I didn't feel much like answering and lay without moving for as long as I dared, enjoying the heaviness of my body and the hypnotic cadence riding on the night air. With reluctance, I turned in her direction and started to recount where I'd been when the steady rake of her breathing told me she was already past hearing anything.

My mind was restless with the things Dr. Cannon had shared. But it was at the end of the evening when he caught me off guard, when he took me behind a veil of secrecy where I felt like I didn't belong. I hadn't been ready for such disclosure, or for such intimacy. If only I had walked away after my revelation of being a minister. But then how could I when he'd asked me to stay, indulge him for just a while longer. "It's about Kellen," he'd said. But it was the way he'd said it, almost pleading for my understanding. I wondered if it had anything to do with my being ordained that triggered it? —obliged him toward disclosure? At first, I wanted to wake Holly, place her between my dissonance and Dr. Cannon's revelations, but then thought better of it. The night had already swayed too far to the left of comfort and tradition, become too full of things that prick at the soul, and I didn't want the complications of Holly added to it. I would get through it alone.

Saturday, and the campus was full and alive by nine a.m., though there was nothing scheduled until a twelve o'clock luncheon, compliments of the alumni association. Still, there was a modicum of visiting, strolling, and picture taking. For most, it was a way of familiarizing, for some it was re-familiarizing and reminiscing.

The luncheon was the last bit of business before Holly and I were to head home, and another full day before Harris was to begin registration and orientation. Harris was already out and about by the time

I was dressed. Holly was luxuriating with vending machine coffee and a book of meditations. I recognized it as one of those mornings where she was markedly more content to be alone. So I once again took to wandering, and in a direction where I believed a greenhouse and beehives to be.

The road was dry and dusty, and my shoes carried the evidence. I had gone about a quarter mile past where the road used to end when I first saw her. She was stooped over, shaping and pruning what looked like seasoned bushes, but stood up straight when she heard me scuffling along the road. She had on a straw hat with a huge broad brim, but still held her hands as if shading her eyes. I could see heat rising from the earth around her. She stayed that way, staring at me as I drew nearer.

"Hello!" I shouted from the road. She cocked her head as if it might give her a better perspective, then gave me a hello back.

"Are you the lady I've heard so much about? —the one who tends to bees?" I asked.

"Well, I don't know what you've heard," she said with a huge smile and a bit of a laugh, "but I think I'm the only one around here with fresh honey to sell—or give away—depending on who you are." Her face was deep within the shadow of her hat.

"I'd also be interested in some fresh cut roses if you have any." I was pushing for an invite.

She was not at all hesitant and directed me to a cart path that led in the direction of the greenhouse, then headed on a diagonal to meet me.

As we drew nearer to one another, the shadow under her hat began to lighten, and I could see her eyes dead on mine. Another couple of steps and her pace slowed almost to a stop. Her expression said something was too familiar. Suddenly, my being there became frightening. I could feel my pulse quicken, throb in my temples. I waited while she inched her way through the weeds that lined the cart path until she stopped a few feet short of where I was standing. A look of disbelief seemed to hold her in place. The years had been kind to her, gracious. She was radiant, more alive than the sun. A tad fuller in the face, perhaps, but softer—a flower unfaded.

We stood staring without a word, her eyes drifting over me, sorting, remembering, the way we had thirty years ago: silent and searching with all our might for the right words.

"Thirty years," I heard myself say, and for once understood the fullness of how our lives are likened to a vapor.

"Should we hug?" she asked, her voice as tentative as the tears she held in check.

I stood leaden, restrained by awkwardness. The urge to embrace her was almost too great to resist, and I reasoned that there was no reason I shouldn't. The urge was mutual and simultaneous, as natural as if God Himself had orchestrated it. We stayed there, fastened to one another, held by memories good and bad, until she pushed herself away.

"You know, you could have called first," she said, wiping at her eyes.

"So you could have baked a cake?" I said.

We both laughed with a sense of relief. "I've never seen you look more beautiful," I said.

"You obviously have a poor memory," she said, trying not to sound embarrassed, then stepped back to examine me. "You're still the same," she said.

"Of course I am," I said. "It's only been thirty years." She was quick to laugh.

"So, this is your home now," I said, "Edenfield!" I wanted to open the door. I wanted to know everything.

"Yes," she said, "I decided this was as good a place as any to raise a child." She stopped, pulled up short as if all at once remembering. She waited as if having trouble formulating her next thought, her next word. "Actually," she went on after giving her head a shake, "I discovered it was better than most places. Quiet. Safe. Fresh air. Nosey neighbors. A real piece of America." She took off her hat. And as much as I wanted to know the details, I became lost in the brilliance of her hair, its variegations of maize and gold reflecting the sun. But she was too busy talking to notice that I was only half listening. Before long, the roses were forgotten, and we sauntered off toward her house, arm in arm.

The patio lay shaded by two giant oaks. It was configured with black flagstone and bathed in such shadow that it gave the illusion of a pond. I felt its serenity despite bright, candy-colored furniture, gardening tools, bags of potting soil, and empty flowerpots scattered about. "It's my sanctuary," she said, motioning me into a large aqua-striped chair. Its overstuffed cushions gave way to my weight like they were being deflated. For several long minutes I allowed myself to be swallowed by their airy softness, allowed my senses to feel what it must be like on a higher plane. Calm eased its way through me, rested the tension in and about my eyes. It was a calm where the mundane was treasured and where nothing needed to be said or thought for that matter. "I feel like I'm finally home," I said, surprised by my own candidness.

She stood smiling, seeming to understand my sense of peace. "It's the place I come when I feel the need to tap into a little spiritual energy," she said, "or when I want to stop scaring myself with impetuous thoughts ... or when I want to be thankful ... or rejoice and dream ... or offer up the occasional prayer."

"Kind of like a bubble bath for your soul?" I asked. She said nothing. It was so typical of me to joke in order to avoid the things that might turn serious, or *personal.* It had become more than habit of late, ever since my marriage began to roll downhill, ever since the *talks* Holly insisted on having became weighted with severity; *talks* ramped with admonitions I was ill-equipped to handle with any degree of decorum. Soul-harkening homilies, they were (she airing, me relegated to listening); discourses charged with hurt and the fires of discontent ... things I was loathe to see as anything beyond pardon. It was her dark side mingling with my own, and her probing for solutions to what she clearly saw as festering sores, that made me so want to turn away ... our discord simply being too gray-upon-gray a thing for me to confront. It was all so clouded, and I was altogether averse to seeing myself in the light of her accusations; too inwardly focused, perhaps, to muster the stuff for resolutions, to do what was needed to dig out from under it all ... to vanquish the elephants in the room. So, for the most part, I lived with my guard up, parrying what might expose too much of an ever-burgeoning restiveness. But being here today with Bea was different. I knew I hadn't found her to avoid being personal. Still, the thought of opening-up left me feeling unsteady, like it was my first day on a new job.

For a moment we locked stares, then turned away. It was a second's worth of rapture, about as fleeting as one of the breezes in the tops of the oaks. "So, help me understand," I said, clearing my throat, "the part about you praying."

"What's to understand?" she asked.

"I guess I just want to know if it's an integral part of who you are?"

"More now than ever," she said.

"Oh?" I said, my voice rising.

"I guess it took me this long to know that it really works. Why do you ask?"

"I was just wondering about what similarities there might be in our lives."

She gave me a flat, somber stare. "And you think prayer is one of them?"

"It seems so, yes."

A smile played at the corners of her mouth. "Are you saying that prayer, and all that it foretells, has now become a working tool for you? —indispensable and even necessary?"

Things were off to an engaging start, I thought. But why was it that I so often found it necessary to jump headlong into my personal convictions, drag my own altar around so I could, whenever the mood struck, throw myself on it? God and religion, God and spirituality; they were my strengths, but my contentions as well.

"It has become so," I said. Her expression seemed to ask what I meant. "I've taken on the order of the cloth." Her eyes flashed the surprise I expected. After a few halting seconds of feeling like I was on display, I said, "It's quite complicated."

She stood very still. "Hold that thought," she said. "I'll get us something to drink." She moved off toward the house in a manner as crafted and mellow as the big orange cat that had appeared out of nowhere, and without a sound, to pass judgment on my morning intrusion. A field marshal inspecting ground troops from an airplane couldn't have been more detached. Without the slightest regard for his privacy or my presence, he licked and washed and brushed, then sprawled his barnyard-sized frame across one of the chairs' Hawaiian-print cushions.

"There," Bea said, emerging from the back door with two tall glasses of iced tea, "a real man's drink."

"And not a moment too soon," I said, snubbing the cat.

"Well, here's to homecomings," she said, handing me a glass. Our fingers brushed, and for an instant a tingling flashed its way up my arm. It was enough to convince me I wasn't all saint.

"Yes," I said, "and to a more innocent time." We stopped with our glasses suspended. Only now our stares did not turn away.

She watched as I sipped, watched with her glass still half suspended. "What's brought you here, Weldon?" Her voice now with a slight huskiness. "Here to my very door?"

I swallowed hard, laboring for composure. "How could I not?" I said at last. "The truth is I've thought about you for the past thirty years. And when I found out you were here in Edenfield, your memory was, suddenly, no longer enough."

She walked past me to the edge of the patio. I could almost taste her fragrance: jasmine bathed in sweat. For a second, I wanted to reach for her, pull the plug on everything I knew and trusted. Instead, I closed my eyes and fought to hold back the memories. Still, I was glad she had asked me why I was here, and glad I hadn't shied from what I said.

The breeze through the oaks was a sudden comfort yet added an oddness to our silence. The back yard was thick and mossy, and lay dappled in sunlight, but our gazes were fixed on the fields beyond the yard. We stayed that way for several long minutes before she turned and fixed herself into a big coral-colored chair trimmed in brindle. She said nothing, but her eyes were anxious and curious, and fastened on me.

"Is this too much for you?" I asked. "My being here?"

She shook her head then placed her glass against her temple. "Just more than I was ready for," she said, then for a moment disappeared behind the lids of her eyes. "I've often thought about this day," she said. "If I'd ever see you again. What I would say." Her voice trailed without inflection. "But first you," she said. "I want to know about Pastor Thatcher."

I had come piqued with curiosity and seeking to connect with the past thirty years, but all at once she was the one piqued and seeking. I wanted to tell her that I, too, wanted to know about Pastor Thatcher, but I couldn't quite get past her remark about how she'd often thought about this day.

"I'm afraid there's not a lot to tell," I said, feeling a whole lot like I'd been put on the defensive. "I'm married. Have a son. Harris. That's why we're here, my wife and I. Harris will be attending Edenfield." I didn't want to be talking about this but continued for the sake of courtesy. "Our lives are rather uneventful," I said. "We live in a little town upstate. My wife's the local bank manager and helps out whenever she can with Sunday school. We bowl and belong to the Rotary Club, which pretty much takes care of our Saturday nights. And I fish whenever I can, coach little league baseball, and try to have something meaningful to say on Sundays."

She was unmoved, steady; the look on her face dissatisfied with my short answer. I was tentative, not at all comfortable with wanting to turn back the clock. Yet, I began again.

"It wasn't long after I left Edenfield," I said, "that I joined the Army. I always thought I wanted to be a part of it until I got there. Then spent most of my time thinking about how much I wanted to be out. After the Army, I went back to school. That's where I met Holly. We married just a month after graduation.

"I started out working in advertising. Holly went to work for a bank. For years, all we ever knew was work, long hours and being tied to our desks. There was very little time for each other, but the money was good so we stuck with it. We were both products of the old blue-collar work ethic: feeling obligated to our employers, going the extra mile every second of every day, and leaving a pint of blood by our desks before we clocked out each night. It took its toll. We were childless – three miscarriages in five years. Then Harris came along. He turned out to be our one and only. Medical complications prevented us from having more. But it didn't matter. We were just so thankful to have him and each other." I was all at once more comfortable standing than sitting. "After Harris was born, Holly quit her job to stay home. It seemed like the right thing to do since my career had begun to take off. The hard work had finally begun to pay dividends."

"So things were looking up."

"Yes, well ... sort of," I said, trying not to be too vague. "On the surface, things were fine. On the inside, things weren't so simple. At a time when my career was starting to go places, my inner contentment seemed to be missing a component. I thought maybe it was the sudden good fortune – too much too soon. I was only thirty-three at the time and in the throes of evolving without yet fully understanding the rules of engagement. My roles as husband, father, breadwinner, corporate pawn, all at once seemed to converge and erupt and separate me from the very essence of joy. It was the sort of internal strife that stayed with me night and day. Holly couldn't understand what I was going through. All she could see was my discontent, my mood swings. She acted like I had chosen to be that way, and even went as far as to say I wasn't happy unless I was unhappy."

Bea leaned forward in her chair, signaling me her full attention. Behind her and beyond the shadow of the oaks, the yard's mossy grass lightened to the color of chartreuse, then turned to tall spiny weeds, dry and brittle against the greenhouse. "I think when things in our lives start gathering momentum," I said, "there is an innate mechanism that begins to adjust itself so we can stay centered and upright. But as far as I could tell, my innate mechanism was malfunctioning, unable to identify what it was within me that needed adjusting. That left me feeling alone, longing for definition, weighted with this ponderous responsibility to reinvent myself."

"Did you ever seek help?" she asked. Her tone suggested she recognized trouble signs, knew when it was that a person should seek assistance.

"Well, not exactly," I said. "I got a checkup but thought I could handle the rest of it myself, be my own doctor, my own shrink. Which, of course, meant nothing changed. Besides, I figured it was a temporary thing. Just a little stress. Nothing that a little time away from work and some R and R wouldn't take care of. The thing is, I never followed my own advice. There just never seemed to be the time for R and R. I mean no one else at work took it. No one else seemed to need it. I felt like I'd be letting the team down if I gave into it. It was a pride thing. I wasn't about to let myself be seen as a weakling, someone needing an emotional respite. Besides, what was a little stress?"

She sat poised, ready to receive who I was and what I had become. "So, how long," she asked, "did your innate mechanism continue to malfunction?"

I hesitated, wondering how much of me I was willing to reveal. "Long enough," I said, "for me to develop an encroaching feeling of fear. Imminent fear. Dying-in-my-sins fear. I simply didn't know what I was confronting, and after a while, I found myself always wanting to run away, move beyond my ever-expanding hopelessness, my own personal black hole." A look of concern blanched her face. "At this point I realized my innate mechanism wasn't just malfunctioning. It was broken. Altogether *non*-functioning. I was convinced I was the quintessential counterbalance to perfection, without the slightest control over myself or my destiny. It was a time marked with as much depression as anxiety. And after a time, R and R was no longer an option. It was a necessity." Her look of concern shifted to pain. "But that's in the past," I said, not wanting the peculiarities of sympathy.

After she had sipped at her tea and adjusted herself in her chair, she asked in a tone much like the pained look on her face, "Then how did you go from that to standing in a pulpit on Sundays?"

I paused, needing clarity, wanting to be understood. "I was aware of the disconnect in my life," I said, "mostly from the people closest to me. But I had to wonder if there was something in particular that had triggered it, left me feeling so incomplete." Bea settled deeper into her chair. "I didn't have an answer for it, so I just pushed through it as best I could, doubting myself, being afraid. But the R and R had given me a lot of time to think, and it wasn't until I had a real Damascus Road experience, that I realized the hunger and the emptiness that comes from neglecting the spirit, from disassociating myself from God." She sat without stirring. "Not the God I knew as a young man," I said. "The God with the list of prohibitions that left me forever wallowing in guilt, or the God who had me living under the threat of consequences for behaviors He knew I was condemned to commit from the beginning. But the God who made it possible for me to understand the plain and precious gift of His grace." I waited, remembering that sliver of revelation. "I was thirty-five at the time."

I had invited her in, allowed her behind the veil of my privacy curtain. "It was one of those life-transforming moments," I said. "My own personal revival." I stopped short. "My awakening."

"Spiritual awakening," she interjected.

"Rebirth," I affirmed.

"Spiritual birth," she countered.

"Born again," I said.

I felt my tension give way to laughter…our laughter. It felt good. We waited while our smiles relaxed and our eyes pretended to take interest in things besides each other. "The rest," I said, "is pretty much rooted in Edenfield."

She gave me a quizzical look. "Edenfield?"

"Yes," I said, "the good and the inexact, the unarguable and the ambiguous. Oh, there were things that had more impact than others, but over time it all just sort of wormed its way into my soul."

She waited, trying to absorb the fullness of what I'd said. At the end of a long pause she asked, "Like what?"

"Like what God was able to do in spite of all the religion, and in spite of all my indifference to it.

"The Apostle Paul tells us," I said, "that God causes all things to work together for the good of those who love Him. Not just *some* things or just *good* things, but *all* things: mistakes and failings alike. It was when I began to grasp this simple premise, that my time at Edenfield took on a whole new dimension, became the place that held the culmination of *all* things ... good deeds and misdeeds alike. It was that entire Edenfield experience, the culminations of loss and love, pain and disillusionment, and all within the context of emerging autonomy and irrepressible urges...all the stuff that was so overwhelming at the time...that gave me the understanding of *all* things. They were the experiences I least expected to teach me something. But they just seemed to hang on long after I disregarded them. It wasn't until years later, when I had all but given in to the stranglehold of stress and anxiety that I understood that my life at Edenfield hadn't been so much about the stuff of church culture as it had been about what took place because of it, and even in spite of it. It wasn't just about religion, but what went on in conjunction with it. It was the culmination of ALL things and how it played out for those who professed a love for God...and I did, in my own inimitable fashion."

The silence between us stretched long after it should have. There was only the tinkling of ice. "And, so," she said at last, "it was this epiphany that aligned you with God?"

"It was what helped bring me closer," I said. "What made me know that all I'd done, all that God had allowed me to experience, was part of my refinement...what He intended to use for His fulfillment. It's what I've come to embrace as certainty, what's helped me to know that it was Him who chose me, not the other way around."

CHAPTER FORTY-SEVEN
Reaching in Our Own Way for What We Longed For

Bea's smile was slow in coming but worked to let me know she was not a stranger to personal trials, even though her countenance seemed to suggest otherwise—as if there was something about what I'd said that wasn't taking root.

"You look like you've got a million questions," I said.

"I do believe you've left me in a *state,*" she said, her words unvarnished, awed. "I mean that was certainly the last thing I could have imagined for you." Her eyes were wide, surprised, as if needing answers. "But let's for the sake of argument assume you're right: that God chose you." She raised her eyebrows as if to ask if I was with her. I was. "How, then, does that translate into you preaching the gospel?"

All at once there was an awareness, nascent and penitent, of the years that lay between us, between then and now, of what we'd allowed to fade away, cloying reminders of what we once were and what we still hoped to become, what we'd left to fate.

"It's like I never really had a choice," I said after a postured breath. "Preaching was just something I'd never even remotely considered, but then, over time, its very idea just seemed to worm its way into me, past my most guarded gates, and, to the best of my knowledge, without ever being invited. But once seeded, it began to take on the properties of life, hold me in the grip of newness, but then oftentimes with an affecting disquiet. Confounded me if truth be known. Robbed me of what little peace I knew. It was something that stayed with me night and day till I was left with little choice but to confront it head-on, wrestle it like it was something wild. But no matter how hard I pushed back, it kept getting the best of me, kept bearing down till I was made to see it for what it was: something native to God, and that my pushing back was no less tantamount to trying to reverse the course of a river; until I was brought to the understanding that God had intentions far greater than my own, and that I could come to know them if I but took the time to listen to that still quiet voice within. That's when I was brought to know—with wide-eyed surety—that the scrutiny I was under had everything to do with the path He meant for me to take. That was the beginning: *acceptance*…yielding to His will. It was a hurdle to be sure, transcendent in both scope and magnitude, and one not readily adaptable to the faint of heart. But then, slowly, the layers of resistance began to peel away, and the ever-encroaching possibility of me sermonizing began to loom with ever-increasing clarity. It was, in the main, loftier than anything I'd ever imagined. So, even with my pangs of hesitancy, I took hold of it. It was a leap of faith on a profound level, but I did it…rather *we* did it…Holly and I…although she was cooked through with apprehension." I paused just long enough to recall her derision. "Held fast to her job at the bank, she did, and never missed the opportunity to remind me how precarious she thought our financial situation was—and would forever be—because of my want to dispense sacraments. Still I was undeterred. We sold most everything we owned and moved in with her parents while I attended seminary. Looking back, on my yielding to that still quiet voice—what I'd come to know as the voice of God—was like reaching out and claiming something for my very own, something so commending that I couldn't understand why it had always been so elusive. I suppose it was that oneness of mind that kept me blind to things beyond the secular: self-disposed but to my own desires. The rest, as you might imagine, is a lesson in fortitude. In the end, I guess you might say we're all ministers in one way or another, but it was the first time I ever really understood what it meant to have a calling…and over time it was where I found the greatest peace." I stopped here and let the rustling of the leaves high up in the oaks offer their naturalness, hoping I hadn't put her off by sounding too ethereal.

Bea was quiet, a side I didn't know very well. "Any regrets?" she asked, almost as if she knew there had to be.

"Oh, there are moments," I said, "when prayer doesn't seem to reach any higher than the ceiling, when inspiration is flatter than a Kansas corn field, when the bills are heavier than the paychecks, and when I think I just can't look at another macaroni and cheese dinner or handle another look of disappointment from Holly. It's not always what I hoped it would be. But, for the most part, those times pass quick enough, and somehow I gather the strength to carry on."

She rose and pretended to fix her gaze on the huge oak branches above us. "I appreciate everything you've been through," she said, "your journey, your self-discovery, and all those things that have brought you to where you are, but I have to ask what's so unresolved that you think of *me* so often?"

"Closure," I said without hesitating, "or the lack of it, I should say. I needed closure with you, Bea. It's something I never had with Kellen, and I'd made up my mind years ago that somehow, some way, I'd have it with you. The load was becoming too heavy without it."

"How ironic," she said.

"How so?" I asked.

"That the load was so heavy, and yet you carried it for thirty years. Was it necessary to bear up under it all that time?"

"I tried many times to come back," I said, my voice taking on a tone that asked for understanding. "I knew Edenfield would be the logical place to start if I was to ever find you, but somehow I just couldn't bring myself to it. The time just never seemed right. Even this time was a struggle. I guess a part of it was being afraid of what I might discover…about you *and* about me."

I stopped, hoping she would have something to say. Anything. But after an awkward moment, I continued, coaxed by her silence. "But it was more than that," I said. "I'd come to realize over the years that your memories were a source of joy. I'd come to count on them, and I just couldn't risk stacking them up against reality. So I kept you just as you were: a memory. It was my way of preserving you. But the years have a way of changing all that. In my case, it was the weight of not knowing, wondering where you were and what went awry all those years ago. It was enough to make me want more than just your memory. And though I came here this weekend as a caring parent, I knew full well that I was making the trip for me as much as for Harris. I'd simply come to the point of needing closure more than I needed a lifetime of memories. I was determined to find you one way or the other."

I paused in the echo of my own voice. Bea was fixed and still, her eyes unblinking. She stayed that way for some time: pondering…or so it seemed. Finally, she said, "We were necessary, Weldon. Because we gave to each other things that made us more complete than what we could have been alone. I like to think it was love. I don't know if it was something I was too ashamed to admit, or if I was too naive to recognize it. Still, it was there. Mine and Kellen's. Yours and Kellen's. Yours and mine."

The patio was as still as the mantle that had settled between us. She reached and took me by the hand. "I'm glad you've come, Weldon," she said.

Her words had not been what I expected. I hadn't been prepared for her inferences of love, especially regarding the two of us.

We sat staring, reaching in our own way for whatever it was we longed for, hoping it would reach back, somehow connect us to a place with possibilities, even dreams. Though I knew we sat with thirty years of unanswered questions and remnants of unrequited love, I couldn't help but feel as though something was beginning to evolve. And though that something was imperfect, it was evidence of what lay hidden, what had walled us for so many years in the rue of coming to grips. "Now you," I said. "I need to know about you."

She hesitated, contemplating, the air space between us growing thicker. "With the exception of your becoming a preacher," she said, "our paths aren't too dissimilar. I certainly had my share of tough times. And there was always a fair amount of trial, confusion, and doubt, questions about where I was headed and the inevitable fatigue that goes with it." Her eyes shifted to her hands. There was no ring. "And pain," she added as if it were integral, "...a good amount of pain."

Our conversation had taken on an air of heaviness. More than I intended. "So, how about marriage?" I asked, hoping to fend off any chance of her elaborating on her pain. "Did you ever marry?"

"No," she said, shaking her head, wasting no time in answering. "Didn't figure it would be worth much without love. And, for me, love—or whatever you chose to call it – has proved to be a disappointment. Don't get me wrong. I've taken a few stabs at it. Relationships, that is, not marriage. But each time, its gifts seem to fall short. I think I was always looking for what love could do for me. And after a couple of tries at it, when I saw what it *couldn't* do for me, I just gave up. Just lost the will to try anymore." She pulled back, sipped at her tea. "Do I sound jaded?" she asked, smiling. I gave her a maybe-yes, may-no shrug. "But after a while, after I'd lived through enough hurt,

I suppose, I discovered that the most satisfying expression of love was in the giving. So I gave what I had to Rachel. My daughter. It was then that I finally received what love had to give."

It was burdensome to know that Bea had spent her days alone. I thought back to our times together, but more of our one infamous night alone and how she left without a word. I seemed to understand how Kellen's death could have made her leave, made her put distance between herself and all the things that were reminders of him. What I couldn't understand is why she never came back. It frustrated me to think that maybe we could have been something other than memories, or friends; that maybe together we could have discovered what love had to give.

"So, you have a daughter," I said.

"Yes. Rachel. She's grown and gone and off on her own for the most part. I have lots of pictures. I'll show you." When she made no move toward the house; I assumed she meant later.

"So, then, Rachel became the focus of your love."

"The lion's share of it anyway. You know my grandfather once told me that you just can't give love away, because the more you give, the more you receive. It just keeps coming back. And he was right. All I had to do was give in order to get. I learned that love, by its very nature, is the reason why we love. It is its own reward." She rolled her head in my direction. "Now if I could only convince everybody else."

I had the feeling she was nudging me, edging me closer to the core of our anomaly.

"You know," I said, "it sounds like you've tapped into your own truth: loving in a way God would have us love."

"Well, maybe," she said. "But I have to think that loving in the manner that God intends is a love that only God is capable of. Oh, I'm sure we're all capable of it from time to time, but only from time to time. We're just too vulnerable to pleasures for any consistency." Her eyes seemed to dance just for a second. "We're human, Weldon. Programmed to error. Remember?"

Yes, I remember, I thought. All those summer nights. All the times we were human. Our one night together. They were only memories now, but vivid accounts of what once was real, what once was love; what influenced me most, what helped shape my thinking. *Yes, Bea, I remember.*

"More tea?" she asked, catching me by surprise.

"Please," I said, my voice sounding as parched as my remembering.

She eyed me for a long curious moment before turning toward the house. "Weldon," she said, turning back around to face me. "I don't have all the answers, you know. Still, after all these years."

I smiled one of those smiles that said, yes, I know. "None of us do," I said, "Not even those who think they do."

Her smile was warm and approving, as if she couldn't help herself. I returned it like it was my own. "You're not going to get a nosebleed, are you?" she said. Our laughter was simultaneous and infectious, ardent and open-throttled. We stayed there, lost in each other's giddiness until she turned again toward the house and the promise of tea. I watched after her until she disappeared behind the screen door. How beautiful she was, how inviting. Thoughts of Holly and our marriage flashed with stark reality, what it once was and what it had become. I tried to imagine what life would have been like with Bea, what it would have become. Then wondered, too, if it would have become like it was with Holly: distant and full of silences.

What was it about me, anyway, that I couldn't leave the past in the past? —couldn't stop wallowing in its loss? I knew that my memories, for the most part, had become my demons. But for reasons I couldn't understand, I couldn't let them go. Or maybe it was them clinging to me, haranguing me because I was too afraid to confront them. But even with confronting, there was no certainty that contentment would follow. The only certainty was the uncertainty of discovery. So I stayed unresolved, remained my own victim. No wonder Holly had grown so tired and weary of my detachment, my inability to forgo the past. I had grown tired of it myself.

CHAPTER FORTY-EIGHT
Thrown Open to the Wind

Bea placed a pitcher of tea on the apple-green table in front of me, then pulled her chair up close. She poured for both of us then readied herself, I thought, for some profound proclamation. Instead, I got a long somber stare that gathered itself into wrinkles above her eyes. It was a curious look, studious. She was studying my face. I wondered if she could see the aura of resentment I harbored, and how, even to this day, I hadn't been able to forgive her, not so much for leaving the way she did, but for staying gone. And I wondered if she could see how angry I was with myself for hiding all these years.

"I came back looking for you, you know," she said all at once, her somberness clouding her tone. I could feel myself tense. "It was February. I remember because it was my birthday. I thought I'd surprise you." I sat within my mind's own hush, not quite believing what I was hearing. "It wasn't easy for me," she said, remembering with a hint of weariness. "When I asked about you, I was told you never came back from Christmas break." She stopped; her fingers busy on the rim of her glass. "It was an awkward time for me, Weldon. My life had taken some surprising turns, nothing like I wanted. I thought about writing you, but I didn't want you to think I was crying out for help. And the last thing I wanted was your sympathy. So I just forgot about you, put you out of my mind. I'd been through enough, and I wasn't about to add rejection."

The silence between us fell hard and straightaway, a silence that left me finger-painting in the condensation on my glass. From the corner of my eye, I could see the cat beginning to unfold. First stretching this, then that – as fluid as he was precise – then hesitating just long enough to give me a cold uncompromising stare. I was no match for his eyes, luminescent daggers of profanity that they were. After a joust of wills, I let him win, acquiesced to his untiring glare, his breed and breeding. He celebrated by pretending to wash, licking himself without inhibition, no doubt adding to the hairball that already defiled him. I envied the furtiveness of his guile, and wished, just for an instant, it could be mine.

"I had no idea where you went," I said. "But I waited for you from that first winter to the next. It was an ongoing battle I had with myself, but I stayed. A lot of crazy things happened during that time, but all the while I never let go of the thought that I'd see you again. We had such…unfinished business." I wanted to say unfinished love but knew it would come across as self-seeking. "You have to know that you were the reason I stayed as long as I did. But finally, when I felt like I had lost everybody who had ever meant anything to me, especially you, I left. And like you, or at least I thought so at the time, with the intention of never coming back."

She waited with her eyes closed, teetering, I was sure, between her thoughts and mine. I was now feeling guilty without knowing why. I reckoned it was maybe her having suffered because I hadn't been there when she finally did come back, or because I had turned my back on Edenfield and its incessant rightness. I hadn't belonged, but, like Bea, it wasn't so much my leaving that proved to be my offense, but my staying gone. And like Bea, isolating myself from the things I needed most to face.

"It's true," she said, "I never intended to come back." Her eyes were a thousand miles away. "You have to understand. That night. You and me. It was the wrong thing, for all the wrong reasons. And it hit me when I least expected it: lying there next to you. We were, suddenly, two people I couldn't stand the sight of, even after all we had been through, after all we meant to each other."

I almost wanted to stop her but could see she needed to say these things more than she needed my protection. "I couldn't face you afterwards," she said. "I couldn't be sure what was going through your mind. I wasn't even sure what was going through mine. There were the thoughts of Kellen pushing down on me. You had to know that. And I was having trouble getting past hating myself ... and us ... for what we'd done." She rolled her head, ran her hands through her hair.

My shame resurfaced brand new. Only now it was more painful knowing she suffered along with me. "Don't you think I suffered too?" I said. "That night wasn't anything we planned." I tried to be reassuring, loving, forgiving. "It just happened, a moment in time, nothing that should fault us eternally. Accepting responsibility for it is our due, but not to where we're trapped in a procession of guilt for the rest of our lives." I was trying to convince us both, trying to find a way for us to forgive ourselves.

She sat waiting, knowing there was more. I waited with her. Just sat there with a sense of aloneness, reminding myself of Kellen and his silences, his brief journeys to his secret place.

"What happened between us that night," I said, "had been coming on for months." I was all at once desperate to be bold. "I'm sure you know what I'm talking about." I could feel my heart pounding. "It was a culmination of all the signals and silent messages we had allowed to pass between us." My breath was shallow, but I was determined to release what had been locked up for too long. "It was bound to happen, whether Kellen had still been with us or not."

A cold expressionless glare attended her. I hadn't meant to be so severe. There was no way of knowing what would have happened had Kellen still been with us. I only knew that I'd wanted her from the beginning, wanted our night together long before it happened.

"You're right," she said.

Right? I was right? Had the past thirty years washed away the game we played, exposed what sought to free itself from the tangle of lust and friendship and love? Or had she known all along? —felt what I felt even back then? Right then, the cat stretched and rolled and walked off without as much as a sound, his tail at high mast and with annoyance in his swagger. Off, I imagined, to wreak his own brand of havoc.

"And do you know how I know?" she asked. I said nothing, only waited for her to tell me. "Because there is a certain something that lives within each of us that can only abide the truth; the same thing that lets us know what is real and what is not. It was that certain something that let me know about you long before that night; that let me know we were more than just friends. I knew it long before you did. Long before anything happened to Kellen."

She leaned forward in her chair and reached across the table for my hand. Right away, her touch was like a warning, something forbidding. Yet, I yielded like a dog to its master's touch, and one after another, our fingers intertwined like they had minds of their own. I was no match for the pull or the hold she had on me, no match for the touch and feel of her skin. How I wished things could have been different, and how I wished they were different now. I wanted with every fiber to hold her, tell her how much I had missed her and how often I thought of her. I could have guessed she was thinking the same, but I was beyond taking the chance on being wrong. "You know," I said, wanting to bring comfort, "in the same way that I think theology is the only thing confusing about the gospel, I think that we are the only things confusing about that night thirty years ago."

We watched each other through watery eyes, like we had completed the equation; had, together, lifted a veil and allowed ourselves to finally step beyond it. And I knew, at that very moment, that we loved each other more than we loved ourselves.

"You're a disquieted soul, Weldon Thatcher," she said. "As if maybe you've let things go on much too long; as if there are things in your life still festering, still unresolved." She dug a crumpled tissue from her shirt pocket. "I recognize the look," she said, daubing at the corners of her eyes, "because I see it every day in the mirror."

Was I that obvious? That transparent? "You're not wrong," I said. "My soul is at odds. I figure it's because I'm all the time searching it. Figure I owe it that, given the times I seesaw between faith and the lack of it. But I don't see any of that in you."

She looked at me as though she knew I was being kind. "You don't need to lie to protect my feelings," she said. "I've had enough of that. I just want to be recognized for what I am."

"And what is that?" I said.

"*Thrown open to the wind* is probably the best depiction." It came out sounding like she had given it considerable thought. But the look on my face must have said I didn't quite get it. "The times when I am void of understanding," she said. "Times when I can't, even to this very day, grasp why Kellen had to die, or why you left precisely when you did. Times when pieces of my life still fight to go in different directions; times when I feel abandoned, not knowing what life or God expects of me; times when I labor to trust what I claim to know as truth, and times when I labor to continue with the lie that I live." She stopped all at once and shook her head, then daubed at her tears, first with the tissue, then with the sleeve of her shirt.

"Why did you stay away so long, Bea?" It was the one question that had festered for thirty years but still remained brand new; the only one that hurt me to ask, but one that I had no intention of carrying to my grave without an answer. "Why did you take so long to come back?"

We sat without a word passing between us. After a time, she rose from her chair and walked to the edge of the patio. The sky above us swept along with barely a trace of a cloud. Beyond the shade of the oaks, the sun beamed with fiery radiance, its heat penetrating the field beyond, then rising in steamy haziness, making the greenhouse appear like a mirage. For the first time, I became aware of the grasshoppers and their unbroken chirr settling me with an indolence that only comes with the warmth and dust of dog days. Today it came as a comfort, and I was all too happy to yield to its tranquility. We stayed that way for a time, neither of us needing to say a thing, feeling everything we needed to feel. I could only begin to imagine what was going through her mind, but I was able, somehow, to convince myself that it no longer mattered. It was important enough to know that we were both in a secret place shedding old skin.

"Remember I told you how I'd often thought about this day?" she said, her voice in harmony with the fields and their golden colors. "If it would ever come? What I would say?" I waited, awakened by her posture, her tone. I nodded as she turned to face me. "Well, the truth is, I didn't know," she said, "but I do now."

I missed the Alumni Association's luncheon but called and left a message for Holly that I was visiting with an old friend, and that I'd be back by two o'clock. It was four-thirty before I called again.

Chapter Forty-Nine
Whose Hands We Would Hold

Except for the drone of the Volvo, the ride home was as close to silent as Holly could make it. Nonverbal psychic-bashing silence was her way of hitting back. But I reasoned that I deserved it. Being more than five hours late had even gone beyond my capacity to forgive. At first, her remarks had been quick and stinging, with words like *inappropriate* and *impropriety* tearing through the air and landing on my face in sprinklings of spittle. I said nothing in my defense, just gave in without a word. I had long ago adopted the adage that sometimes the best thing to say is nothing at all, and this seemed to be one of those occasions. Still her recriminations came unchecked. And it was only after realizing that I was no longer listening, that she withdrew into irretrievable silence…her place of rage.

My time with Bea had given me enough to think about for a lifetime and had left me room for little else, much less a confrontation with Holly. My staying gone for so long, however, had been wrong, so I took my whipping like a man. And when she was finished, and her silence unalterably in place, I said I was sorry. But my words proved to be just that, only words. My apology wasn't enough, as somehow I knew it wouldn't be. Penance would be the only thing weighty enough to satisfy her.

Her stare was fixed out the windshield toward the road ahead. Now and again she would turn the other away and for very long periods stare out the window, never uttering a word. At last, when the view out her window became nothing but the dead of night, and the view straight ahead became nothing but lights on the highway, she curled up with her back to me and pretended to sleep.

The pain that prompts the games people play was no different for me. I did my own sulking, something my mother and father did, something

I learned while still very young. It was anything but nurturing, and nothing I should have been advocating, much less succumbing to. It was the negative way of making a point, but more than that, it was the attempt to control: the uncompromising mindset of *I'll show you.* For Holly and me, it was emotional arm wrestling, a battle of wills, the loser being the first one to speak. Often it came down to convincing ourselves that it was a test of mettle, that somehow it was a question of pride, even dignity. The only thing I could be certain of was that it drove us inward, focused us only on our own pain. Today was more of the same. Holly had had her say. What I had to say would have to wait. It was just the way the game was played. Much to my dismay.

As soon as I turned into the driveway, Holly shot upright. As soon as I turned off the engine, she was out the door and into the house. She said nothing, just went to the bedroom and closed the door behind her, a gesture that said I needed to find other accommodations.

I went to the basement. The one place where I was assured of solitude, even if Holly had a change of heart. I sat surrounded by the smell of my woodshop and the glare from the overhead light. It was austere, but it comforted with its familiarity. I tried sorting through the last two days and all that had come at me: Harris' leaving, the contrast of the old and the new, the thirty years of memories, and the lives that had touched me. I couldn't pretend to make sense of it, though I knew I had come face to face with the likes of frailty and the obscurity of failings, discovering people I never knew. Had any of it been from God? It was the question I always needed to ask, even back when the carnal part of me was my habit, though I knew without exception that the answer was yes. I had long ago accepted that God often spoke to us through others, through word and deed, if only we'd allow ourselves the sensitivity to hear Him: to be still long enough to know that quiet voice within.

I realized I hadn't always been able to unlock the secret of God's presence, to make the connection between heaven and earth, and had no doubt missed much of what He had tried to convey. It had been the natural part of me that kept getting in the way, even after I had become resolute in my calling. It took years to understand that I was as much spiritual as I was physical, if not more so, but it was learning that each part was vital to the life of the other that made the connection possible, that reconciled me to His voice and to His mystery. I like to think that I now have a sight of heaven, a kind of kingdom vision. And though I can't pretend to be without iniquities, I can now at least confess them, give them full disclosure. I had at least come that far.

Harris being gone had left the night seeming hollow and unfamiliar, had robbed me of his footsteps and his music filtering through the floorboards. Holly's quick exit had made it seem all the more unfamiliar, as if it were a night without sound, save the low dull hum of the woodshop's florescent light.

Images of the last two days had a weight of their own: events and people I only thought I knew reminding me that Edenfield was still a place of subtlety and contradiction, more than just a place of refuge for the saint or one of reckoning for the sinner. I wondered about Harris and about the impact it was to have on him, and if his Edenfield would be the same as mine, as timeless as its customs.

I couldn't be sure what remained of that Edenfield I once knew, the one that brandished a God of fear and retribution, that warned us day and night of the consequences of sin. It was an Edenfield I'd known only through the eyes of my youth, at a time when I was untested in the ways of the world or in the sight of God. It had been a bitter root. But it no longer rankled the way it did, back when Kellen and Bea were the miracles of laughter and dreams. Then again, nothing seemed all that momentous anymore, even on nights when memories ran deeper than usual.

I knew all too well it was long past time to turn old memories loose, to let them die. In many ways they had become like Mother: always there, always threatening to wrench from me what they could. I'd like to think I was beyond needing them now, beyond their haunts of remorse and regret, even beyond the hope of anything they might offer in the way of peace.

I prayed, as I often did, for peace, for reconciliation of the past with the present, the natural with the spiritual. Yet I knew that not everything our heart desired could be reconciled to our satisfaction, to our peace. And that there were times when the only reconciliation was the renouncing of our will: when God would reach to us across our own personal battlefield with nothing but the assurance that His grace alone was sufficient.

My own R and R had been such a time, when I had become nothing but a shell. It had been a time when there was just enough of me left to receive what God had to give. But it was His grace alone that had discerned the intents of my heart long before I understood them myself; His grace that had pierced me enough so that my faith was fed and that His life became life in me. Up to that point, I'd failed to understand the connection between the natural and the supernatural, failed to see its reverence, lacked the faith to make it relevant. It was only with sufficient faith, the willingness to believe beyond cultural mindsets, that I came to know it was for God's purposes, not my own, that I was here. It was the beginning of knowing that our physical experience was only part of the whole. By His grace, my life was changed, and by my faith, my sufficient faith, I came to believe that I could make a difference…at least to those few faithful who chose to sit under my authority, who found comfort in calling me their shepherd.

I often wondered if those few faithful could embrace me beyond my clerical function, beyond the mysteries I fed to their spirits. I wondered about what difference it would make if they knew me as the disquieted soul, when God simply didn't make sense to me, when I struggled not to lose sight of His promises, and when I just couldn't seem to touch that kingdom dimension. But moreover, on nights like these, when I'm made to see the conventions I had come to know as truth being *less offering of hope* to those like Kellen.

My time with Dr. Cannon had gone on longer than I intended, but he had encouraged me to stay even after my goodbye. Just a bit longer, he'd said. It's important. He had been almost insistent. It was about Kellen, he'd said. He'd had a pleading countenance, an expression that begged me to linger a while longer. I felt I had little choice.

"I want to be open," he said. *Of course,* I thought. He was hesitant at first, as if maybe questioning his intentions, but then continued after an uncomfortable pause. "I want you to know," he said, "that I knew a different Kellen than you." His stare had been transcendent, a prop for the magnitude of his words. "I knew two Kellens," he said. "The one he presented to you and everyone else, and the one that caused him a life of torment." Torment? "I want to be fair," he said. "Without offense." *Naturally,* I thought. *Why wouldn't you?* "I won't bother telling you about the Kellen you knew," he said, "…only about the one you didn't. It's imperative that you know." *Imperative,* he said…a Kellen I didn't know.

"Kellen was a tortured soul," he said. "Afflicted, unable to reconcile what defined him and what caused him a life of pretense." I was unclear. The expression on my face told him so. Yet I sat without stirring, veering between his stabs at fairness and his attempt not to offend. "Kellen was certain of only one thing," he said, "that the life dictated to him by convention was in direct conflict with his own." He waited with a pained expression. "Do you know what I'm saying, Weldon?" I didn't and offered nothing but a somber look. "I'm talking about personal preferences." His voice was steady. "Preferences that distinguish us, set us apart, and despite outward appearances, determine such things as who we will embrace, whose hands we will hold." His steely gaze and lingering expression began to edge me toward a place of unfamiliarity, even discomfort. We stayed locked in quiet for some time. At last, he said, "Kellen was, in secret, oftentimes caustic, quick to say he simply could not straighten what nature had fixed with a curve." His eyes met mine with a look that captured the essence of everything he was trying to say. For the first time I sensed his direction…along with my lack of willingness to accept it. I wanted all of a sudden to swerve out of the way, dodge, and run. But I didn't. And he continued, fair and tactful and without offense.

I don't know how long he went on, only that he did it with words taunting and reverberating. Punctuated. Corrupt. Words like enslaved and anguished, bridled and discolored; words like unconformed, singular,…*gay.* I waited in their aftermath, in the sting of their conviction, not knowing when I last felt so laid-bare-to-the-bone.

Time passed. How long, I had no idea, only that my thoughts began to spin and hurl me past things fixed and tried and true. "But what about Bea?" I asked. "And the others? I mean Kellen was always so...so…"

"Engaged?" he added.

"Yes. *Engaged.*"

"All I can tell you is that he spent the biggest part of his life concealing who he really was. Then he had the notion he could reverse it, head it in the opposite direction. That's where Bea came in…and the others. But it was an unhinged door that he stood behind, Weldon. Nothing he could walk through."

We both sat staring into the blackness beyond the porch. "And there was the fear," he said. Fear? We needed to slow down. Couldn't we just slow down? "Fear was the worst part," he said. "Not only of being found out, but of God's judgment, that it would be predicated on the dictates of justice alone, that it would not be tempered with mercy." A ghoulishness had settled over his face, come to life in the shadows cast by the porch light. "It was fear that made Kellen hide deep within himself. And what becomes of us when we hide, Weldon, save for us becoming more secretive and fearful?"

I sat there under the glare of the porch light feeling as inconsequential as the breeze stirring at us from across the road. The night seemed to hold me to the fire of Dr. Cannon's revelations, to the ashes of their truth. And though I knew the gravity of what he said, I knew nothing of the Kellen he talked about. Nothing of anguish or fear, or of desperate hope. I knew the pain of his upbringing, of his episodes, of some inner perturbation, but nothing of enslavement. How had I not seen it? It wasn't often that I'd felt so snared, so forced to face something I wasn't ready for. They were revelations that had gone down hard, left me reeling with things contrary to selection.

How imperfect we all are, I thought. How wanting and lacking and undone. Could we know for certain anything beyond our being a work in progress? —beyond our susceptibilities to a changing world and an unchanging God?

Dr. Cannon sat with his eyes glued to the floor. Suddenly, we were strangers, fixed with the same confoundedness, seeking for answers that seemed outside the spectrum of what we embraced as being *of God.* We were in many ways alike, Dr. Cannon and I, students and ministers of an orthodox order that only few come to know so intimately. And though we were a generation apart, we strived for the same understanding. I imagined his being so close to Kellen's suffering had made it possible for him to step outside the lines of tradition, to separate himself from the strains of fundamentalism. And I imagined it, even amid his loss and disillusionment, as being a place balanced and amenable to differing worlds.

As a minister, I'd sat with those with the same struggle as Kellen, prayed with them, even in such a small congregation as ours. But Dr. Cannon had been passionate, as if pleading Kellen's case, as if asking for his redemption, as if I had the power to grant it. And then there had been his denouncement of The Church, its intolerance and bias.

I said nothing, only marked the weight of his words.

What was it that God allowed, anyway? What manner of things? As a minister, I had come to believe He allowed it all, even things suffused with contradiction, things that ripped at the heart of those like Kellen. And what was I to make of it … this departure from what we embraced as the natural order? Was it a thing meant to test our faith, or maybe to even deepen it?

Questions came quicker than answers. Each with its own set of charges. Each prompting another…then another. In the same manner as I believed God allowed all things, I believed He used all things to fulfill His purposes. Kellen was no exception. He was a recipient of the same hope and mercy, the same forgiveness and salvation allotted to each of us. It was not ours to decide who would be redeemed. Christ's ultimate sacrifice was for *all* of mankind. What then of those fixed with aberrations other than to say they were exactly as God made them? Could they will themselves otherwise? No. No more then we could will ourselves to be like them. Was it a distinctness more assaulting than pride or avarice, slothfulness or gluttony, covetousness or enmity?

"He had hoped one day to tell you," Dr. Cannon said, his words interrupting, spattering across my theological canvas. "It was in his heart to tell you. He just didn't know how. Said he wouldn't ask you to try and understand something he didn't understand himself. And then there was the secrecy. The burden of it. It would have been too much to ask of you. The risks were too great of losing you. You were too much like a brother."

I sat reaching into the silence for some modicum of relief, not acknowledging things one way or the other, numbed by the reality. "And…it wasn't a time conducive to such disclosure," he said. "It still isn't in Edenfield."

Our goodbye had been brotherly, reverential, considerate of each other's station. Our handshake had been sorrowful, the way I remembered it with Cleveland Yates, the way two old friends say so long, not knowing if it will be their last time.

I'd walked back to the dorm feeling as though I'd been forced to acknowledge the unexplainable. Had Dr. Cannon's revelations been a check on my faith? —my sufficient faith? What mystery or miracle was there in any of it?

Over the years, I had grown comfortable with the teachings that we were a nation of kings and priests onto God, that we each had an Ecclesiastical function, and that was to pour out to others what God had poured into us. It was a tenet I lived by, and by which I'd come to embrace as God's divine purpose for my life: to do His will and to finish His work, to offer the power of salvation to those who would believe. And I had grown steadfast in accepting certain things as having a natural order. I knew them only as God's order, plain and simple, and as painful as it was at times to adhere to them unconditionally, they were things I dared not compromise. How could I? Yet, as with Kellen, how could I not?

Throughout the house I could hear the hiss of steam escaping from the radiators, adding yet another layer of solace to my musing, prompting me even deeper into the mysteries surrounding God. I'd been here often enough, trying for ballast, each time not knowing if I'd succeeded in satisfying an overcurious mind, or if I'd peeled away even a single layer in which God was shrouded. With all that had transpired over the past two days, I was even more at a loss, floundering against the makeup of a god so soundly ordained of order. But then there was Kellen who lived every waking moment with the notion of being at cross-purposes, with a left foot down when a right would have served him better; when, without choice, found himself oblique to the straight lines of The Church and its literalist ideologies.

It wasn't so much the lack of inquiry, Dr. Cannon had said, but the lack of understanding and the lack of forgiveness that had grown up around it. He spoke of The Church. I was not a stranger to The Church's jaundiced eye but was unaware of any *un*-forgiveness. Forgiveness was, after all, Christ's credo, the very thing he brought to the world, what lay at the core of His sacrifice…a sacrifice that embraced Kellen as much as it had the least of us. What remained seemed simple enough: love one another. It was at the Last Supper when Jesus knew his time was nigh that He said to his disciples, "Brief are these moments before I must leave you…so I am giving you a new commandment: *Love one another as I have loved you.*" Therein lay the forgiveness.

How many times over the years had I preached that love alone was the fulfillment of all the commandments? Enough certainly to seed my congregation with its cogency, its truth. It was a message held forth in The Church, but to what extent it impacted Kellen was anybody's guess. And though he was a light gone out thirty-one years ago, I could never be sure where his struggle began and ended, or whether he ever saw love in the light of what God intended it to be. But then there was the surety of knowing he was not beyond God's order, that he was, in fact, part of God's plan, and that God's strength was made even more perfect by Kellen's uniqueness. He was, after all, exactly how God made him.

I shut off the overhead light and for a time sat gathering my thoughts. Then for an even longer time sat trying to quiet them. Many long minutes later I made my way up the stairs. I knew what it was I needed to do.

My study was off the living room, and from my bank of memorabilia and treasures I kept on the shelves with my books, I removed the Sam Snead straw with the grosgrain band. It was the only thing I had asked of Stone and Judi Remington. I rolled it over and over in my hands as I often did, marveling at the memories it still conjured and the mysteries it still contained. Its texture and its faded colors were the very real reminders of a life that was; of a playfulness and wit once shared; and of the absurdities that often accompany the leap into manhood. The shelves looked empty without it, but I was resolved. I placed it on the car seat beside me. The same place I had once placed Belle, our beloved Labrador, for her final ride to the vet.

It was six a.m. before I arrived back in Edenfield.

CHAPTER FIFTY
A Place I Once Called Home

I drove slowly past the new retirement village east of town. It was where Lizzy lived. Though it was early, there was activity: some ambling about, others alone in wheelchairs…all in the morning sun. Lizzy was close to eighty and the resident spokesperson for the selection of programs and activities, a position, according to Dr. Cannon, no one else wanted, but one that Lizzy seemed to be born to. She was still the brightest and the best.

I drove straight to the cemetery. It was small, and I was only a short time finding Kellen's grave. Dry and withered roses lay in array at the base of his headstone. Bea said she visited less and less these days. About once a month now as opposed to every day in the beginning, just long enough to tell him bits of town news and bring him fresh roses; and just long enough to tell him the latest things about Rachel. Our daughter, Bea's and mine.

The early morning sun was warm and welcoming, its long shadows adding ascendancy to the collective peace. I made myself comfortable in the grass next to his grave, my shadow stretching alongside his headstone … our images together, brothers, for a final time. I needed it to be the final time, needed it as stridently and as assuredly as the dead once needed the weight of copper pennies to weight the lids of their eyes.

"I'm sorry, my brother," I said, "for what happened to you, and for what happened to all of us because of it. And I'm sorry about Bea and me. Though I know now that the two of you could never have been as one. Still, what I did was wrong because I didn't know it then." There was so much I needed to say. "And I've come back after thirty years to ask your forgiveness." I waited, feeling my own heaviness. "I didn't know about Rachel…until yesterday. It was Bea's idea, her

288

choice to keep it from me. She said it had been a decision of love, a matter of keeping a sacred thing sacred and of sparing us both from making a commitment she felt neither of us could keep. I don't know that she was right, but it was her call. It was a time when she was beyond herself, crazy with grief and confusion. But a time she chose to go alone. She was convinced that Rachel was conceived more out of chance than love, more out of infatuation and bad timing than truth. And she was determined not to settle for a commitment predicated on a moment in time. She didn't want it for herself. Didn't want it for me. But then I'm sure she's told you all this."

I rolled the Sam Snead straw over and over in my hands, traced my fingers along its brim. Its finely woven straw felt almost silky, glazed from years of shelf dust and solitude. "I brought your hat," I said. "Been keeping it for you."

Almost against my will, my atonement gave way to thoughts of Rachel and how I would never fully come to know her, the roads she would travel or the places that would greet her, who she was or what she would become. I was without a choice to know her. Bea had made sure of that. She'd made me swear I wouldn't bear witness to the truth, not to Rachel, not to anyone. It was for the best, she said. Rachel had her own life, and my sudden appearance after thirty years would be more than just a little difficult to explain. *She thinks her father is dead.* Bea had been ashamed when she said it but believed the truth at this point would breed as much contempt as confusion, and that Rachel would be left wondering how many more lies there were, and what else she couldn't believe. She believed that my coming clean at this point would only serve to ease my conscience, and that in the end would only serve to diminish her in Rachel's eyes. Uncovering a thirty-year lie would only undermine the root of their love and bring to question such things as trust and integrity. She was certain that any attempt on my part to repent would ultimately destroy them both. And no amount of contrition could ever undo it. *Think of Rachel*, she'd said. *Just leave it be.*

Bea's pleading had left me knowing that Rachel would never be anything but someone I left behind in Edenfield long ago, just like Bea. Just like Kellen. Just like all the others. On the inside, I was glad Bea had sworn me to secrecy; glad I wouldn't have to confront Rachel with the truth. But it made me wonder about my role now that

I knew, made me wonder about my responsibilities to Bea, to Rachel, to my family…even to myself.

I couldn't help but feel censured by my time and tie with Edenfield, couldn't help but decry the influences that kept me yoked to it after all these years. Had it pushed me away? —been the huckleberry to what lay burgeoning within me? Or had I left of my own accord? —knowing that it was too much to confront; too teeming to weather? The only thing that really mattered anymore was how I would now cope with its memory.

I sat cross-legged in the grass and talked in low tones to Kellen's headstone. "There was so much I didn't know," I said. "So much I didn't understand. I didn't know what haunted you, my brother. Didn't know the demon that possessed you. Didn't know anything about your very real and very private life. *I didn't know."* Things needed to be said—for my sake. Out loud—for my sake. "It was Dr. Cannon who told me ... then Bea. They had carried your secret from the beginning." I struggled for the right words—for my sake. "I'm glad I didn't know back then. I don't know what difference it would have made if I had. Things were different then. All of us on the verge of being grownup, trying to be something a little more gracious than what we were." I looked around, making sure I was still alone. "I know you had to tell Bea. Had to stop her from wanting you. But she never did. And she still thinks she could have changed you given enough time."

I couldn't pretend to know what Bea expected from Kellen, or if it was her naivety or faith that made her so willing to take on the impossible. But it was with certainty that she saw things in Kellen beyond what the world saw, had tried to fashion love without expectation—fixed only on the entanglements of hope and what could be wrested from a wanting intimacy, and when need seemed to be the only thing that mattered.

In much the same way, my relationship with God had gone through a similar trial – when my hope centered only on what He could do for me. But it wasn't until expectations became clearer that I realized He needed me as much as I needed Him—needed me as much as He needed apostles and prophets and teachers. I understood as indisputable, eternal, where I could at length know the only real source of strength came by way of our intimacy; where I could realize peace and humility of mind as things which affirmed that neither of us were complete without the other. It was the personal relationship I had coveted yet had failed to understand. We needed each other.

With the clarity that comes from being alone with the morning sun, I realized I had stayed away too long, avoided an Edenfield that had dared to reveal in me a house of cards, yet held me fast to its light. By my absence, I had, without knowing, sacrificed the peace that comes from closure, from reaching across a centuries-old chasm of religious dogma to the rest that waited in saying goodbye.

I placed Kellen's Sam Snead straw with the grosgrain band square against the base of his tombstone and weighted its brim with rocks. Then sat there in the morning's amber light, bathing in the faces and events of that Edenfield I knew so long ago. They were visions that came without prompting, parading through my mind one after the other ... like uninvited guests demanding attention. I knew, somehow, it would not be their last time, that they would come again. And even though I still thought of that Edenfield as a time of unraveling naivety, a place beset by loss and longing and the want of clarity, it would forever be a place I once called home.

ACKNOWLEDGEMENTS

Few things offer as much gratification as what comes from writing a book, the exceptions being those connections we make along the way, those very special and unique souls we come to embrace as family. To my delight, such was the case with *Edenfield*, and to that end I am pleased to extend my very deep appreciation to those who helped turn my visions into realities and helped bring the breath of life to my pages.

First off, I am forever grateful to Charles Brown, my eighth-grade English teacher who, to this very day, remains the eminent master of syntax. In his hands, my manuscript was given an academic cleansing. Thank you, Chuck, for your academic excellence, and for your care and attention.

To Sue Manis/Milini, extraordinary teacher and friend, who embraced *Edenfield* from its inception and was always and forever gracious with accolades. Thank you, Sue, for your unshakable support and absorbing insights—from first page to last. And thank you, too, for all the impromptu dinners, the chilled glasses of Chardonnay, and taking the time to be a friend.

To my son, Eric; to my daughter-in-law, Carla; and to my grand-children, Makena and Nate, I offer up my deepest and most enduring love for all that we've shared…and for the blessings that are still to come. You are my anchors. I could never write kinder, funnier, or smarter characters than you.

To my wife, Peggy, "my happily ever after" for reading every single draft in between giving me neck rubs, cooking delicious meals, and sharing wellsprings of laughter. Your love, support, and encourage-ment makes it all better.

To Ella Reid and Rio Scafone who filled the landscape with their incredible artistry and unmatched detail. Thank you over and again for your gifts and inspiration.

To my publisher, Jodie Toohey, who believed in my work from the very beginning. Thank you, Jodie, for your insight and expertise, for your gentle nudging and extraordinary patience. You are a gift.

And last but never least, a bundle of gratitude to my fiercely loving friends and dedicated manuscript readers, whose rallied support never let me lose sight of the prize. And so to Jay and Jerry Gilroy, Mary Ann and David Cain, Patti and Steve Brinegar, Alice Shooter and Leigh Bangs, and Sue Anne Gilroy, please know that your encouragement keeps me front to the wind and forever buoyed.

ABOUT THE AUTHOR

Author photograph by Rio Scafone

George Justice holds a B.A. in English Literature and Creative Writing. He has been published five times for short stories, three times for poetry, and was a long-time movie critic for Michigan's *Oakland County Daily Tribune*. During his enlistment with the U.S. Army, he wrote numerous articles (from human interest to military) for *Stars and Stripes*. While at the University of Detroit, he was "one-of-twelve" chosen from a field of over 300 for a semester-long advanced creative writing symposium conducted by then writer-in-residence, John Gardner. His first novel *Greezy Creek* was published in September 2019.

www.ingramcontent.com/pod-product-compliance
Lightning Source LLC
Chambersburg PA
CBHW022105310726
48972CB00007B/1895